"Did you he[ar something? Did I] frighten[ed you?]

Booker took a few soundless, barefoot strides toward her.

"No. Nothing like that." Thea's voice sounded as unsteady as her heart. The rough bark dug into her palm.

"What's wrong, then?"

She faced him squarely. The moonlight clearly defined his smooth broad shoulders, muscled arms and the strikingly masculine set of his jaw.

"I want something."

"All right." He moved toward the night table. "Let me light the lanter—"

"No." She stopped him with a hand on his bare arm.

Motionless, he regarded her hand.

Beneath her fingers and his perspiring, heated skin, his muscles tensed. Reluctantly, she pulled her hand back. "Booker," she said, and it came out little more than a hoarse whisper. "I want you to…" Lord, this wasn't going to be easy! "I want us to—" She took a quavering breath. "I want to make love with you…."

Dear Reader,

Although native Nebraskan Cheryl St.John's first book was only published in our 1994 March Madness promotion, with this month's title, *Land of Dreams*, she has earned her third Gold 5 ★★★★★ from *Heartland Critiques* in as many books. It's the story of a marriage of convenience between a hardworking spinster and an ex-army major who are brought together by their mutual feelings for a needy child. Don't miss this heartwarming tale of hope and love.

Also this month we welcome Susan Paul, a newcomer to Harlequin Historicals with her unforgettable medieval tale, *The Bride's Portion*, the story of a knight forced to kidnap and marry the daughter of a neighboring lord who is trying to destroy him.

And don't miss our other two titles this month: *Pearl Beyond Price*, the second book in Claire Delacroix's Unicorn Series about the descendants of the lost kings of France, and *The Heart's Wager*, a sequel to Gayle Wilson's first book, *The Heart's Desire*. We hope you enjoy them all.

Sincerely,

Tracy Farrell
Senior Editor

Please address questions and book requests to:
Harlequin Reader Service
U.S.: 3010 Walden Ave., P.O. Box 1325, Buffalo, NY 14269
Canadian: P.O. Box 609, Fort Erie, Ont. L2A 5X3

CHERYL ST.JOHN

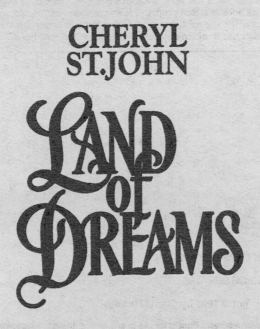

LAND OF DREAMS

Harlequin Books

TORONTO • NEW YORK • LONDON
AMSTERDAM • PARIS • SYDNEY • HAMBURG
STOCKHOLM • ATHENS • TOKYO • MILAN
MADRID • WARSAW • BUDAPEST • AUCKLAND

ISBN 0-373-28865-4

LAND OF DREAMS

Books by Cheryl St.John

Harlequin Historicals

Rain Shadow #212
Heaven Can Wait #240
Land of Dreams #265

CHERYL ST.JOHN

remembers writing and illustrating her own books as a child. She received her first rejection at age fourteen, and at fifteen, wrote her first romance.

She has been program chairman and vice president of her Heartland Romance Writers of America chapter, and is currently proud to serve as president.

A married mother of four, grandmother of three, Cheryl enjoys her family. In her "spare" time, she corresponds with dozens of writer friends from Canada to Texas, and treasures their letters. She would love to hear from you.

To:
Pam Hopkins for her confidence and encouragement;
Pam Crooks, Bernadette Duquette, Pam Hart and
Elizabeth Parker for their critiques;
Sandi Shirah for her invaluable promotion help;
The Friday night gang for the laughs;
and
All the orphans who came west on the rails—
I hope your dreams came true.

Prologue

It would be a safe bet that the iron fence was as tall as his own well-over-six-foot frame. From his vantage point across the street, Booker Hayes contemplated the pale faces peering through the black picket "hedge" enclosing the New York Children's Foundling Home's crowded side yard. Heedless of the other children in the yard, the waifs studied the street, observed puffy white clouds against the blue sky and watched an occasional passerby with undivided interest.

A well-dressed couple strolled past. The woman drew something from the bag she carried and offered it to one of the children. A lightning-fast hand snatched the banana, and the small gray-clad figure spun and ran.

He didn't make it far. The others descended, and the brief skirmish ended with the biggest and strongest boy breaking from the pack, peeling the fruit and sharing it with a smaller boy who had never moved away from the fence.

The woman covered her mouth with a lace hankie, and her escort led her to the far side of the street.

Booker shoved away from the brick building he'd leaned against and crossed the street where a dozen pair of dispassionate eyes examined his approach. His head straight forward, he advanced on the wooden door flanked by two whitewashed pillars.

Raising the knocker and letting it fall, he stared at the brass numbers affixed to the door, attuned to the relative silence of the penned-in youngsters on his right. There were at least sixty of them, he'd guess, and they made less noise than the ten or twelve children he'd seen playing the day he'd been discharged from Fort Scott back in Kansas.

That had been more than a month ago, and it'd taken him this long to track down what remained of his family. *His family*. He shoved the thought away and thrust his chin out.

The door opened, and a pock-faced woman greeted him.

"Ma'am." Booker doffed his flat-crowned felt hat and nodded. "Booker Hayes. I'm looking for my niece. The hospital told me she'd been sent here."

The reed-thin woman ushered him in. "This way."

He followed her past several sets of closed doors, his boots echoing down the cavernous hallway. He resisted wrinkling his nose at the smell of disinfectant. After they reached an enormous set of stairs, she led him to the left and gestured to a long wooden bench that sat against the stairway and faced another pair of doors.

"Have a seat."

Booker folded his length onto the low bench and hung his hat on his knee.

The woman entered the room opposite him and closed the door behind her. A moment later the door opened and she reappeared. "Mrs. Jennings will be right with you."

He nodded.

Her footsteps echoed away in the silence of the building. The shell of a home didn't sound or smell like children. No laughter or high-pitched voices floated down its austere hallways. No fresh-from-the-oven aromas tempted his nostrils. No wagons or dolls littered the highly varnished floors. Booker stared at the gray wall. Not even a small handprint marred its tediousness.

He hated thinking of his niece living under these conditions these past months. He would take her away with him now. He would make it up to her.

Only an occasional distant echo broke the silence. After a good quarter of an hour, lassitude enveloped him. He closed his eyes. If only he'd come to New York sooner. If only Julia had written when she'd first become ill. Perhaps he could have . . . what?

Fresh grief muscled itself into his chest, and he resisted the encroachment on his well-guarded emotions. With his eyes closed and no distractions, his sister's face barged into his memory: winged brows over steady gem blue eyes, a narrow nose and full smiling mouth like their mother's, hair as fair as his was dark. It'd been five years, but he remembered her face as if he'd left her that morning.

They'd parted in Illinois. With her share of the money their mother had left them, Julia and her ambitious husband, Robert, had started an accounting firm in New York. She'd written faithfully for years, even though Booker's appointments made mail delivery difficult to nonexistent. Upon return to his current station, he'd always read her letters with an unaltering sense of loss. Reading the delicately scripted missives, he'd empathized with their fledgling business, rallied with Julia's unflagging determination and spirit and experienced his niece's growth from infancy through toddlerhood, all the while reliving memories of Julia as a girl.

Booker'd only seen Zoe that one time in Chicago before Julia and Robert had headed east. While the rest of the country swarmed westward, the little family had bucked the current and moved to New York.

Above his head, a metallic scrape attracted Booker's attention. Turning, he discovered a bucket resting beside a pair of run-down brown shoes, and snagged black stockings drooping around a pair of bony ankles. Above them hung a faded blue hem that had been let down several times. Booker twisted on the bench and glanced up.

A girl stood on the stairs, one hand on the banister, the other twisting a hank of hair at her ear. Running her palm down the smooth wood, she descended the steps and hung on the post at the bottom. He guessed her to be about thirteen or fourteen. Her limp brown hair hung blunt-cut at chin level. A wide forehead, brown eyes and straight brows dominated her features.

"Hey, mister."

"Hello," he replied.

She swung back and forth. "You looking for a kid?"

He glanced back up at the bucket she'd left on the stairs. Beside it, a rag dripped gray water into the wood. "Yes."

"A girl?"

He nodded.

"Take me home with you. I'll be a good little girl." The coaxing tone that entered her voice, the provocative expression that stole across her high-cheekboned features, would have been seductive had she been a whore. Coming from this girl-child with barely budding breasts beneath her limp apron, the lewd implication twisted something in Booker's gut.

She couldn't have insinuated what he'd imagined. He had to be sick for the obscene thought even to cross his mind! He had to have misinterpreted her meaning!

But she rubbed herself against the banister and met his gaze with eloquent invitation. "What do ya say, mister? I'll be your little girl."

He jerked his gaze away. Embarrassed warmth flooded Booker's neck and cheeks, a wave of disgust on the crest. He still didn't want to believe what he knew had just taken place. Dumbly, he shook his head.

Behind him the door opened, and he jumped, guiltily.

A well-dressed gentleman emerged from the office, settled a bowler on his steel gray hair and nodded to the woman behind him before escorting himself down the hallway toward the front door.

The girl scampered up to retrieve her bucket.

"Claudia! What are you doing down here? You have work to do." The woman's tone and the disdainful expression on her straight-featured face told Booker she had a pretty good idea of Claudia's unchildlike approach. "I'm Mrs. Jennings. I'm sorry to have kept you waiting. Won't you come in?"

Above them, Claudia's footsteps sounded on the stairs.

The square-shouldered matron ushered him into an unimaginative office and closed the solid door behind them.

Uncomfortably warm, Booker resisted the urge to insert a finger inside his stiff collar. He sat across from her and waited while she composed herself behind a desk that held a ledger, an oil lamp and a pen set.

He cleared his throat and began, "Mrs. Jennings, I came to New York to visit my sister and her family. I found that both my sister and her husband died of influenza and their daughter was placed in your orphanage."

She scrutinized his face, his well-tailored white shirt and dark coat. "You've come for her?"

Booker met her level gray gaze. "I'm her family."

"What is her name and age?"

"Zoe Galloway. She was born February 2, 1869."

Mrs. Jennings stepped to a wooden cabinet and opened a drawer. Her thumbnail flicked across the files. She closed the drawer and opened another.

Booker watched her back.

Withdrawing a folder, she returned to the desk.

He waited.

She opened the file and scanned it. "Your niece isn't here."

The meaning of her words didn't register for a full minute. Zoe wasn't here? "Where is she?"

Mrs. Jennings laced her large-knuckled fingers on the open folder and regarded him squarely. "Mr. Hayes. The Foundling Home is overcrowded and lacks funds to care for so many. We try our best to find homes for eligible children before they're—"

"I understand your job is to place children. Where is Zoe?"

At last compassion touched her steely gaze. "You're in the army, aren't you?"

Booker raised a reflective brow. "I've just quit the army. I bought some land a few years back." He stood and walked to the solitary long window with a view of the park across the street. Only a corner of the black iron child enclosure was visible. "I came to the city to visit my sister before I settled in. But now . . . now I'll take Zoe with me." He turned back to her, his hat dangling from his fingers. "Where is my niece?"

"I'm not sure."

He stalked back to her desk. "What do you mean you're not sure? You lost her?"

"Of course not. I'll be able to find her. We keep excellent records."

Booker leaned over her desk. "What the hell are you talking about? Was she adopted?"

"I'm not certain." She unlaced her fingers and spread them on the ledger. "The New York area has been exhausted, Mr. Hayes. It's too crowded here—that's why we have all these children. We have to send them west to find families."

He narrowed his gaze. "You sent her away?"

"Yes."

"How? When?"

"The Pacific Railroad provides cars. Agent Vaughn left for Illinois, Kansas and Nebraska in May with eighteen children, including your niece."

Booker's mind reeled. *Orphaned in the streets of New York. Abandoned in this god-awful place. Zoe shipped out on a train like livestock. Zoe with strangers.* He glanced down and realized he'd crushed his hat brim. *Zoe in a world that turned innocent little girls into Claudias.*

"Mrs. Vaughn is one of our best placement agents." She glanced down at the file. "I made a note of a telegraph message. Mrs. Vaughn still had Zoe with her when she reached Nebraska." Mrs. Jennings sighed, and a genuine look of sympathy crossed her horsey features. "You know, Zoe wouldn't have been that easy to place. There's every possibility your niece will return with Mrs. Vaughn."

Her tone raised his eyes, an uneasiness creeping into his belly. "What do you mean?"

She made a straight line of her lips. "The healthy, capable children are always taken first."

Unenlightened, he leaned a white-knuckled fist on the desk. "What are you saying?"

The woman's brows rose in question. "You're aware of Zoe's afflictions?"

"No."

"She's a cripple."

A crippled six-year-old on a train bound for God knows where.

"And she's mute."

Perfect.

Chapter One

Nebraska—1875

"You're a saint to put this reception together for the children." Odessa Woodridge sliced a cinnamon-scented applesauce cake into thick wedges, wiped the knife with one pudgy finger and licked it appreciatively. "I always say whenever something needs done around here, our Thea's the woman for the job."

Thea Coulson resisted the urge to roll her eyes at her aunt. Instead, she removed the lid from an enormous kettle of savory-smelling beans and plunged a wooden spoon in, scraping the sides and stirring. Certainly, Omaha and the surrounding state of Nebraska considered her the woman for the job. The fact that she was one of the few unmarried women over the age of twenty within a four-day ride automatically secured her the social and civic tasks the married women were too busy for. Never mind that she ran her father's house, caring for as many or more family members as any farm wife.

"It wasn't that difficult, Aunt Odessa. The settlers always bring plenty of food to these festivities. All I did was let everyone know when and where and set the tables up. I think our neighbors were as anxious as I was for spring to arrive. Any excuse would have been sufficient for a get-together." Thea wiped her hands on her cotton apron.

The plump woman surveyed the dessert table with a knowing quirk of her brow; a third of the pies and cakes were obviously Thea's. "You're too modest, my dear. The men in these parts rave about your cooking."

Thea raised a teasing brow. "I'll let you in on a secret about Western men."

Odessa moved closer and raised her face eagerly. "What?"

Her niece's eyes widened, guilelessly. "They're not very picky eaters."

Odessa swatted the air and rolled her eyes.

Thea's gaze wandered across the long row of makeshift tables spread with a hodgepodge of colorful cloths and laden with fried chicken, coleslaws and corn bread, and focused her attention on the children sitting on plank benches under one of the ancient oak trees that dotted the Coulsons' dooryard. Thea had passed the orphans each time she'd traveled to and from her kitchen, and the group had diminished to two boys and three girls, the youngest of whom perched on the end of the bench, her leg jutting out at an awkward angle.

"Things are going splendidly, Miss Coulson," said Mrs. Vaughn, the Children's Foundling Home agent, from beside her.

Turning, Thea glanced down at the slender, dark-haired woman with a fashionable felt hat cocked on her head. The New Yorker's dark eyes glowed with genuine pleasure.

"You did an excellent job of finding families before I even got here. Almost everyone has come for the children they promised to take. Oh, look! Someone's come for John and Chloris, too."

Oskar and Celle Rilke made their acquaintance with one of the older boys and a girl of about ten. The Rilkes from Florence had one child of their own, a girl of seven. As with many of the families who had spoken for the orphans, the homesteaders needed more hands to help around their farm.

From the moment Mrs. Vaughn had written the church about the plight of the New York orphans, Thea's heart had gone out to these homeless, yet faceless, youngsters. Knowing firsthand what it was like to be on the outside looking in, she'd known, too, she wouldn't rest until she'd helped to bring as many of them as possible to good homes and families among her neighbors.

Even the people of Irishtown, usually standoffish and not prone to socializing, had come out for the reception. Thea's gaze scanned her father's property, lighting on couples and families getting to know their new members.

"I do hope the couple from Sheeley Town—the O'Conners—show up for Lucas," Mrs. Vaughn said. "He should have been taken by now, a boy of his age, but he is a problem."

Thea studied the young man. Only three children remained, the one spoken of having moved to lean against the gnarled tree trunk with studied nonchalance. Far too thin for a boy of his height, his freshly pressed shirt and trousers hung on his lanky frame. His hair had recently been cut, but he wore it without a side part or any semblance of care. "How old is he?" she asked.

"Fifteen. He's been in orphanages since he was seven. We've placed him several times, but he always manages to get himself into trouble or runs away and the authorities bring him back."

Odessa stepped to Thea's side. "Shall I ring the dinner bell?"

Thea dragged her gaze from Lucas and nodded. "The children must be hungry. They've had a long, tiring trip." She cast Mrs. Vaughn an apologetic glance. "You, too, of course. All those days and nights in that railcar. You all deserve a rest. I have a room ready for you."

Her aunt rang the bell from the back porch.

"I'm afraid I can stay only until morning," Mrs. Vaughn replied. "I must check on children I placed earlier this year in Lancaster and a few other counties."

Thea marveled at the woman's dedication. She saw her father and stepmother moving toward the tables, and waved them over. "Trudy, will you find Mrs. Vaughn a seat near you and Father?"

Her tiny stepmother smiled benevolently at the agent. "I'd be delighted."

Though not helpful in the kitchen or with chores, Trudy Coulson was a gracious hostess and an excellent seamstress. She and her daughters spent a great deal of time in St. Louis, leaving the running of the house to Thea.

Unfolding a bright red-and-white-checked tablecloth, Thea spread it beneath the towering oak and stood before the remaining children. "Come with me," she said, holding her hand out to the youngest girl and motioning to the freckled one beside her. She included Lucas in her invitation with a pointed glance. "Let's fill our plates and have a picnic right here under the tree."

Without the slightest hesitation, the girls took her hands and stared up at her, trustingly.

"You sure are tall," the freckled child said in awe, and Thea noticed her front teeth were missing.

"Yes, I am, aren't I?" Thea replied. "It sure comes in handy when I pick apples." No one ever mentioned her height anymore. As a child she'd endured merciless teasing from other children. Her stepmother and half sisters used to express their chagrin at her ceaseless growth, but as an adult her size wasn't commented on—rather like ignoring a hideous birthmark or pretending not to notice a disfigurement. The child's innocent observation was refreshing.

"Where do you pick apples from?" Freckles asked.

"Off the trees," she replied, and reached an overhead branch to demonstrate.

Freckles frowned up into the oak branches. "I don't see no apples."

Thea laughed. "If this were an apple tree there would be pink-and-white blossoms this time of year. This is an oak tree. Coming, Lucas?" she asked over her shoulder.

The boy shrugged and remained propped against the tree as though it supplied his sustenance.

Starting across the grass, Thea noticed a growing resistance on her hand and glanced down. At her side, the blond child limped awkwardly, trying to keep up. Thea slowed her pace and helped the girls through the throng around the tables.

"I had a orange once," Freckles announced. "You got any orange trees?"

Thea looked at her with dawning understanding. "No. We don't."

"Look at the food, Zoe," the freckled girl said to the other. "What's them green things?"

"These?" Thea asked. "They're pickles. Do you like them?"

"Dunno," was the reply.

She forked a sweet pickle on each of their plates, then prepared Lucas a plate of chicken, pickles, coleslaw and fresh rolls. Seating the girls on the tablecloth, she carried the plate to the shade tree.

"Hungry?" she asked.

He lifted a shoulder in a churlish shrug.

"I made a plate for you. There's dessert, too, when you've finished this."

He avoided her face, but his eyes slid to the plate in her hand.

"Will you come sit with us?"

He ignored the question and looked away.

"Scared of girls?" she asked with a grin.

His thick-lashed, hazel-gray eyes swept the yard in silence.

"Suit yourself." She placed the full plate on the grass and returned to the other children. Freckles had already finished her pickle and chicken and scraped corn-bread crumbs into her spoon. Zoe, too, ate like there was no tomorrow, saving her pickle for last and savoring it. Thea broke her own pickle in half and gave it to the girls.

She peeked toward the oak tree and discovered Lucas sitting with his back against the bark, barely chewing his food before he swallowed it. Sympathy welled in her throat, and she fought the bubble of emotion in her chest. There'd always been enough to eat in the Coulson home. She'd never been hungry or alone. She'd always had her own bed, and even after her mother had died, she'd had her father and her sister, Maryruth. She'd always known she belonged to a family, that she was loved.

These children had none of those securities. No wonder Lucas was so distrustful. Mrs. Vaughn had explained some of the children's situations. New York City had been besieged with immigrants. Many parents had died in epidemics, either on board the ships that carried them to America, or in the years that followed living in the crowded city. And some parents, because of poverty, lack of work or poor health, simply couldn't afford to keep their children. Hundreds of children had been deserted on the streets or left in the foundling homes, orphanages and hospitals.

"Can we have more?" Freckles asked.

Zoe, still having not spoken, raised hopeful, grave blue eyes to Thea.

"You can have anything you want." She turned to Lucas. "You ready for dessert?"

He swallowed, and his Adam's apple bobbed inside his loose shirt collar. "Yes, ma'am."

"What do you like?"

He shrugged.

She rose to her feet. "I made apple pies this morning," she said with a wink. "All the men love my pie."

Thea returned with a slice for each of them.

"Thank you," Lucas mumbled.

Zoe shifted on the checkered fabric beneath her, peeled back the edge of the tablecloth and picked up an acorn between her thumb and forefinger. She studied it intently, then held it toward Thea, a question on her pert face.

"It's an acorn. It fell from the tree. If the squirrels don't eat the acorns, they turn into trees."

Zoe's eyes, wide with amazement, returned to the nut. She tucked it safely into the pocket of her limp pinafore.

A wagon pulled alongside the barn by the others. A couple climbed down from it and studied the crowd.

Mrs. Vaughn met the new arrivals as they approached the small group under the tree.

Thea and the girls stood.

The plain woman nodded. Her bearded husband offered his hand. "We're the Carstens."

Mrs. Vaughn's expression split into a smile of pure elation. "How wonderful! This is Sarah."

The woman's plain face took on a lovely glow. "Hello, Sarah."

Freckles stood and looked at her prospective parents. "Do you have pickles?"

"Why—" Mrs. Carsten formed a reply, though she was obviously caught off guard. "Yes, we do."

"I like pickles."

The Carstens smiled.

Mrs. Vaughn offered a printed document. "This is the agreement I'd like you to read over before you sign. Sarah is to be treated like any other child of your family, and after a trial period, if you and she agree, you can sign the adoption papers."

Mr. Carsten took the paper. "Will O'Conner and his boy passed our land on their way to Nebraska City," he said. "His wife caught sick and died, so they headed out for Colorado."

"Oh, dear. I'm so sorry." Mrs. Vaughn's dark gaze met Thea's.

"Help yourself to food," Thea offered the Carstens. "It's almost time for the dancing."

The Carstens and Sarah moved into the crowd.

Mrs. Vaughn glanced toward Lucas, then down at Zoe, and sighed. "I'll pass the word and perhaps another family will be willing to have you two."

The child's blue-eyed gaze swam from the agent's to Thea's. She dropped her attention to the toes of her shoes, one of which was incredibly scuffed and worn due to her crippled gait.

A knot lodged in Thea's throat. She knelt and raised Zoe's chin on her knuckle. "I'll bet you'd like to see what's under the edge of the porch over there."

Blue eyes raised.

"Kittens," Thea supplied. "My Tabby had a litter right under the steps, the silly old girl. I made her a bed out of an old blanket at the corner of the porch. You can go look."

The child gave her a feeble smile and limped toward the spot indicated.

Thea turned to the agent. "Do you think someone else will want them? It's such short notice! What will happen to them if no one takes them?"

"I'll do the best I can, Miss Coulson. I've had good luck on short notice before. If no one wants them, they'll leave for Lincoln with me. Of course, I've been there before, so I doubt there will be a willing family. In that case, they'll go back to New York City with me."

"Back to the Home."

"Yes."

"To start all over again." Thea chanced a glance at Lucas. Once again he stood against the tree, as if it were his shield against the unfairness of his young life.

"I'm afraid so. I've had a very good trip, however. I placed sixteen children."

Thea nodded.

Mrs. Vaughn moved away.

Someone had to take these last two pitiful children. A darling little girl and a boy old enough to work. Who wouldn't want them? She didn't allow herself the additional worry that she still hadn't heard Zoe speak and that the child obviously had a crippled leg. Nor did she want to consider that Lucas had an unpleasant attitude and looked like he'd rather run than stay.

Someone had to take them.

* * *

Carrying pots into the kitchen, Thea discovered Maryruth sitting at the wooden table, her two-month-old baby, David, fretting in her arms. Maryruth spotted Thea and gave her a half smile.

"What's the matter with David?" Thea deposited her load and laid her hand on Maryruth's shoulder.

"He's a little fussy."

"Have you eaten?"

"It's too much work to juggle him and a plate, too."

Thea took the snugly wrapped infant from her sister. "Go eat. Dance if you want to. But don't come back for him until you and Denzel are ready to leave."

Maryruth glanced up.

"Indulge me," Thea coaxed. "Time alone with a male?" She raised her eyebrows suggestively.

For a moment Thea thought she meant to object, but then a smile spread across her sister's face and she stood. "Thanks, sis."

Thea kissed her pale cheek. "Sit in the sun for a few minutes. You don't have any color in your face."

"I will." Maryruth turned and scurried from the house, the screen door slamming behind her.

David jumped at the sound. Thea nestled him against her breast and brushed her lips across his downy forehead. "How are you today, my little beau?" After studying his old-man frown and laughing, she snuggled him against her shoulder and rubbed his tiny back. He smelled wonderfully clean, and his blanket and gown were incredibly soft. She inhaled his baby scent, weighed the diminutive bundle against her breast and closed her eyes in pleasure.

Nothing in the world compared to the feelings a baby inspired. She couldn't imagine anything more wonderful than having one of her own to love and cuddle. Except maybe... Thea shook off the idea of a man to provide the baby before the wistful idea had time to take shape. She'd given up on that dream a long time ago.

Did Maryruth know how lucky she was? She ⌐ hardworking husband who loved her. A beautiful son. A home of her own.

Thea's thoughts drifted to the orphans who'd arrived that morning, and she recalled Mrs. Vaughn's tales of life in New York City. How many babies like this one had been abandoned? How many had suffered sickness, inattention or lack of nutrition in the crowded hospitals? How many had died of starvation and exposure in the streets? Tears sprang to her eyes. What horrors had the children she'd met today seen and experienced in their dismal, short lives? Had she done all she could to help?

David slept, his minimal weight a sublime pleasure against her breasts. Kissing his fuzzy head, she reluctantly placed him in the small iron crib in the downstairs bedroom and returned to the festivities.

The dancing was in full swing, with couples following the caller's instructions to the "Texas Star." As always, her two younger half sisters caught and held the admiration of the single men. Madeline do-si-doed with a tall young man, while Lexie, the youngest, smiled prettily at a gangly swain who brought her a jar of lemonade. Elsbeth, the oldest, had married a St. Louis dentist the summer before.

Delicate little creatures like their mother, all three of her half sisters were blessed with lustrous dark hair in shades from russet to mahogany, flawless complexions and dainty hourglass figures. Thea felt like a giant among fairies in comparison to her half sisters, who were dressed in pastels and ruffles, their hair curled and coiffed.

Her gaze drifted and encountered Irving Jackson talking to Lorraine Edwards, the town's new seamstress. Irving was Omaha's hotel owner now, but she'd known him since her family had moved here when she was a girl. They'd attended school simultaneously. He'd made her childhood miserable.

Thea couldn't help studying the attractive woman he was speaking to. Lorraine had hair as black and shiny as a raven's wing, coiled into a perfect coronet with ebony wisps

...orehead. Her petite figure boasted a tiny
...ie kid boots encased her feet.

...gaze slid back to Irving. He'd been the first. The
...o call her "Too-Tall Thea." Those childhood mem-
...es hit the pit of her stomach and curdled.

James Coulson led Trudy from the wooden floor, which
he kept stored in their barn for just such occasions, and
stopped before Thea. "I expect folks'll be breaking up
soon," he said. "Everybody has chores to do before night-
fall."

Thea nodded, shook herself from her unpleasant reverie
and felt sorry to see the festivities come to an end. She had
enjoyed the chance to visit and watch the dancing.

Mrs. Vaughn appeared at their sides. "There you are.
Mr. Bard signed an indenture for Lucas!"

"Bard?" Thea scoured her mind for the name. "I don't
know a Bard. Papa?"

Her father dabbed perspiration from his forehead with
a red kerchief. "Ronan Bard. He's one of the squatters
from Irishtown. Has a dugout, I hear."

"A wife?" Thea asked. "Does he have a wife?"

"He said his wife was at home ill," Mrs. Vaughn supplied.

Apprehensively, Thea scanned the crowd. "Where are
they?"

"Oh, they left. Mr. Bard said they had chores to do.
Don't worry, I'll come back and check on him."

"Oh." A lone figure sitting in the grass beside the dance
floor caught her eye. "Zoe?" she asked.

Mrs. Vaughn sighed. "I'm afraid not. She'll be leaving
on the stage with me tomorrow."

A heavy-hearted ache seized Thea's chest and con-
stricted her breath. Back to New York City. Unwanted.
Knowing no family wanted her. Back to start all over again.
The image injected misery into her heart.

"She can stay with us," Thea blurted out.

Her father stopped in the process of stuffing his kerchief into his hip pocket and gaped at her as though her hair was on fire.

"I'll take care of her," Thea promised matter-of-factly. "She won't be any trouble."

"Thea-girl, this isn't a pup or a lamb you're talking about here," her father reminded her when he found his voice. "This here's a youngin'! We've got enough of our own."

"Yes, we do. We have a great big family, but Zoe doesn't have anyone. No one in this whole world cares whether she eats or sleeps or laughs or cries." She didn't need to mention that she knew firsthand what it was like to be without a mother. "Think of it, Papa. What harm could one more be?"

James's eyes softened as though he read her silent plea, as well. He cast a glance at the agent.

"You couldn't keep her," Mrs. Vaughn hurried to say. "You're an unmarried woman."

"Just until you return next time, then," Thea argued. "You can keep looking for a family for her, and I'll take care of her until you find someone."

The woman raised her brows and nodded. "I could do that."

All eyes focused on James Coulson. He rubbed his mustache. "I hope you know what you're doin'." He shrugged. "Do what you have to."

Jubilant, she hugged him and kissed his cheek. He was the only person she didn't have to bend over to embrace, a special pleasure. "Thank you," she whispered.

Her father hugged her soundly.

"Jim! Jim!" Maryruth's lean husband, Denzel, came running up out of breath. "Jim, there were surveyors down by the river this afternoon!"

Denzel had the attention of more than their small group. Bystanders turned to catch his news.

"You sure?" James gave his fair-haired son-in-law the once-over. "Railroad people?"

"Nah," Burnet Hyatt, the squat-figured postmaster, denied, elbowing his way into the conversation. "Years back the railroad surveyors came in teams. Tents and all. These here fellas got a rented buggy."

"It's got to be the one who bought the Hazel Creek section," Denzel said with a furtive glance at his father-in-law. "Took his sweet time, didn't he?"

A scowl crossed her father's suntanned face.

Around them, the crowd quieted. It was common knowledge that Jim Coulson'd had his eye on that piece of government land ever since he'd paid off his and his late wife's two sections. It was a prime strip of bottom land with access to the train and the city, and it abutted his property on the north.

Alternate sections along the railroad's path had been given to Union Pacific, and as the tracks were laid the sections went up for sale. Jim had bided his time. He had the cash in the bank waiting to pay for that land, his homesteading days long past.

Four years ago the railroad sold the hundred-and-sixty-acre Hazel Creek section to someone with first option—no doubt a war veteran.

No one knew who. The land had been leased to a farming family by the name of Wynn on a year-to-year basis, and the owner had never shown up to work it himself.

Until now.

Chapter Two

Lucas piled the dilapidated cart with corn and pulled it to the reeking pit, his tired muscles screaming at the effort. The stench from the pit below twisted his empty belly painfully. Wary of the enormous hogs crowding toward the side in the slimy mud, Lucas groped for solid footing on the edge and dumped the feed into the hole. He backed away quickly as the hungry animals squealed for a front position.

Behind him, Ronan Bard's scrawny dogs yipped, and Lucas turned. The mongrels chased a squirrel into the brush.

"You got supper on, boy?" hollered Lucas's keeper from fifty yards away. He was carrying two dented buckets dripping with water from the stream.

Lucas watched the man's approach with contempt. "I ain't had time yet," he replied when Bard got closer.

"Ain't had time, my eye, ya good for nothin' slum boy. Git yer skinny ass in there an' fix somethin' t' eat afore I take the razor strap to ya." Bard spat at Lucas's feet and carried the buckets into the cave.

Reluctantly, Lucas followed. The wooden door was the dugout's only opening, so in fair weather it stood open, allowing a meager panel of light into the dwelling. The dank, dark interior smelled of dirt and smoke and stale cooking odors. Dry weeds dangled from the hay-twist ceiling, an occasional wind dislodging a shower of dust.

Lucas swallowed his disgust and emptied a can into a blackened pan. Shoving a few corn husks into the stove, he lit a fire and heated the beans.

Bard sat at the rickety table, broke a dried biscuit and spread lard on it. He grunted at the tin plate of beans Lucas sat in front of him, dunked the biscuit and tore off a chunk with his stained front teeth. "Sit," he ordered around the mouthful.

Lucas perched his narrow buttocks on an upended crate and took a hard biscuit. He ignored Bard's smacking noises and ate, thinking of nothing. Lately, he spent most of his time focused on not thinking, not feeling, not caring. There wasn't much in life to care about when he really thought about it.

Food. Now, food was important.

Bard's belch punctuated Lucas's thoughts.

A glass of milk would sure taste mighty good. Sometimes Lucas let himself remember the day he'd been at the church lady's picnic. He saved that memory for the really bad days, though; the days a good memory was all that kept him alive.

She'd sure been tall. Closer to heaven than most people, he guessed. She'd smiled like an angel must smile. He'd warmed himself in New York City's big churches many winter nights. He'd studied the angels on the lofty stained glass windows, and he was almost certain that when an angel smiled, she couldn't be no prettier than the church lady. All gold and warm, a pretty that turned into a feeling and slid right to your stomach.

She'd been right about her apple pie, too. Lucas had never tasted anything straight from heaven before, but that pie was it. If he was hers, he'd eat apple pie for breakfast, dinner and supper. And a piece before bed, too. Wonder what that'd feel like on a belly.

A cup landed in his plate, splattering his last few beans on his already stained shirtfront. "Wake up, slum boy! Clean them dishes. There's cows to milk."

Lucas glared hatred at the man. "I was still eatin'."

"Don't back talk me, boy! You was dreamin'. Like yer always dreamin' 'stead o' workin'. I feed you, and you try to get out o' workin'."

Lucas stared back, wishing the hateful man dead.

Bard yanked an ax from a makeshift cupboard and disappeared through the open door.

The scarred tabletop blurred. Lucas concentrated on the aged ring burned into the wood until his vision cleared. This wasn't the worst place he'd ever lived, but it was close. The man had lied about having a wife at home. And heaven only knew where he'd found references for the agent. Lucas could tolerate the bedbugs that chewed him alive at night. He could endure the endless meals of beans and salt pork and dry biscuits. He could even tell himself this snake-infested hole was better than the garbage-filled alleys of New York.

What he couldn't abide was that crude, smelly man. Gophertown, he'd heard some of the townspeople call this section; Gophertown, because the occupants lived in holes dug into the side of a hill. Bard belonged in a hole, Lucas was convinced. However, the hole should have been six feet deep and covered with dirt while he was in it.

"You lazy, good for nothin' alley rat!" Bard shouted from the doorway, and Lucas jumped, falling backward off the crate.

Buttocks stinging, he leapt to his feet.

"I knew you wasn't doin' them dishes. You got to be watched ever' minute!" Bard flexed the leather razor strap between both fists, leveled his rheumy gaze and stalked him.

Lucas was lighter and faster, and he escaped Bard's first clumsy attempts. Dodging and darting in the darkness, he tripped over a stool and fell to the hard-packed dirt floor with a grunt.

Bard was on him like a fly on dung.

Lucas closed his eyes, buried his face in his elbows and rolled into a ball beside the stove. The first blow struck, and he almost cried out. With the next, he gritted his teeth and cringed until his eyes rolled back into his head.

The lashes stung like jets of fire across his spine. Rage festered in his agonized young mind. With a strength born of gripping hatred, he jackknifed sideways, grabbed the nearest table leg, yanked himself away from his tormentor and scrambled beneath the table.

Panting, Bard leaned back against a rickety makeshift cupboard. Cans fell and rolled across the dirt floor. Lucas's eyes never left Bard's worn boots. They moved toward the door.

"Do them dishes, ya skinny bastard."

As soon as the man was gone, Lucas closed his eyes and allowed himself a grimace of pain and festering hatred. Nausea rose in his constricted throat.

He crawled from beneath the table. His back and shoulders stung. His face was wet, but he didn't know how that had happened, because he never cried. With sharp movements, he shoved his extra shirt and socks into the drawstring bag he'd brought from the Home. Deliberating for mere seconds, he opened the potato bin and removed the slim .36 caliber he'd discovered earlier.

After a quick glance, he darted across the yard through the tall weeds, ran as fast and as far as his aching legs would carry him, and finally found a wooded area for cover.

Without a backward glance, he caught his breath and limped alongside the stream.

After knocking on the back door, Booker wondered if he should have gone to the front. But the drive led to the back porch, and judging by the hard-packed dirt path and scuffed stairs, this was where the family entered. The door opened.

The statuesque woman who greeted him wore her strawberry blond hair caught up on the back of her head, one loose strand dangling over her ear to her shoulder. Catching the wayward tress with long fingers, she tucked it into the shiny mass. Her pale pink skin was flushed, and her blue-green eyes assessed him curiously. His attention was called to her unadorned loveliness. Booker self-consciously realized his clothing was wrinkled from the train ride, and he hadn't shaved in days. He hadn't wanted to waste the time.

"Sir?" she asked, wiping one long-fingered hand on the white cotton apron she wore over a drab brown house-dress.

"I'm looking for Thea Coulson."

Her gaze drifted over his shoulder to where he'd tethered Gideon to a stump, then returned. "That's me."

"I expected someone older."

She smiled with charming, open friendliness, crinkling her red-gold lashes. "Time seems to be hurrying that right along, Mr...."

"Hayes, ma'am. Booker Hayes."

She stepped back without hesitation. "Come in. What can I do for you?"

He moved past her into the bright, cinnamon-smelling kitchen. She gestured to the table covered with a sunny yellow gingham-check cloth that matched the curtains on the two enormous windows. The sights and scents reminded Booker of times long past, of childhood mornings shared with his mother and sister. At her invitation, he slid out a chair and sat.

She placed a mug of steaming black coffee in front of him, and he noticed the sprinkling of freckles across the back of her hand.

"Mrs. Jennings gave me your name."

"Jennings." She sat across the table and tapped a forefinger on the checked cloth. "I'm trying to remember who that might be."

From another room, a baby cried. Immediately, she rose. "Excuse me a minute."

He watched her hurry toward the sound. The plain brown dress did little to flatter her well-molded figure, but Booker couldn't help noticing the way the apron's sash rode her arresting backside.

She returned a few minutes later, a baby on her hip, and paused at the stove to spoon something gray and unappetizing into a dish.

"Sorry," she said, returning to her seat and settling the infant on her lap. "This is David."

Booker regarded the child's wide blue eyes and fuzzy golden head. "How do you do, David?"

Mrs. Coulson tied a white cotton towel around the boy's neck and reached for the dish. "Now, where were we?"

Carrying half a spoonful to her lips, she blew on the contents and touched it to her upper lip before feeding it to the baby.

Booker observed the procedure with interest.

"Good boy, David." The spoon dipped back into the shallow dish, hovered before her pursed lips, and she blew. Gently. "Mr. Hayes?"

Enraptured, his gaze collided with her aquamarine eyes. Booker cleared his throat. "Mrs. Jennings," he reminded her. "She runs the New York Children's Foundling Home."

"Oh, of course." The corners of her full mouth started to turn up, but the smile faded. "You're from the Foundling Home, then?"

"No. No, I'm not from New York. My sister died there, and I'm looking for her child. Mrs. Jennings told me you'd organized homes for the orphans, so I'm hoping you'll know where I can find her."

Her features took on an expression of concentrated detachment. "I'll do what I can." The baby grunted, and she spooned another mouthful between his lips, scraping his chin with the edge of the spoon. "Who are you looking for?"

"Zoe Galloway."

David's mouth hung open birdlike, anticipating the next bite. Thea's heart sank to somewhere around her suddenly trembling knees.

This man had come for Zoe.

Cautiously, she met his penetrating dark gaze. His thick short hair was black, the growth of whiskers on his chiseled cheeks blacker yet. Fine white lines at the corners of his mahogany eyes testified to hours in the sun. His square chin, straight nose and hard mouth didn't relieve his severe appearance. She had the uncomfortable feeling that he already knew she had Zoe, that he knew everything about her and was just waiting for her to try to deny it.

David whimpered.

"Have you seen Zoe, Mrs. Coulson?"

Thea shoveled a spoonful of oatmeal into the baby's mouth. "Yes," she replied when she found her voice. "I know Zoe."

Mrs. Vaughn had told her she wouldn't be able to keep Zoe. Thea'd told herself for the last two months that, eventually, suitable parents would show up to adopt the little girl. From the first day, she'd reminded herself not to grow too attached, not to consider Zoe hers. But instructing herself to stay detached and actually doing it were two different things.

Zoe had eaten an excessive amount of dinner the first day, and supper again that night, then lost everything. For a week everything she'd eaten had come back up. For days she'd been pitifully sick—so sick that Thea had summoned Dr. Gilbert all the way from Fremont. He hadn't arrived until near morning, and, after a brief examination, he'd explained that Zoe's stomach wasn't used to so much food. Thea had fed her small, bland amounts to adjust her stomach, and eventually she'd been able to eat normally.

Through all that the child had never cried, never spoken, never moved farther than a few feet from Thea while she was awake. She'd become Thea's tiny shadow. Thea knew she should check on Zoe now to see if she'd awakened from her nap.

"Where is she?"

Mr. Hayes's question cut through her thoughts. She fed David the last bite of cereal and met the man's examining gaze. She had to tell him. She didn't want to, but she had to. "She's upstairs."

His clear-cut features didn't register emotion. His black brows rose fractionally.

"Mrs. Vaughn left her with me. Until..." God, she didn't want to do this! "Until she found a family."

"Is she all right?"

"Yes. She's healthy. She had some problems eating at first, but she's better."

"Mrs. Jennings said she's a cripple."

Thea's spoon dropped into the empty bowl with a clatter. "Zoe is not a cripple!"

She wiped David's chin with the towel and threw the cloth down on the tabletop.

"Can she talk?"

Calming herself, Thea loosened her grip on her nephew and smoothed his hair. "I don't know."

"Either she talks or she doesn't," he said matter-of-factly.

Evading the stranger's eyes, she rose, placed David on a quilt in the corner and arranged his toys within reach. "She hasn't said anything," she finally admitted, straightening. "But that doesn't mean she can't."

He seemed to think that over. "All right," he said at last. "Thank you for looking after her. I'll take her now."

Beneath her apron front, Thea's heart thudded. "Mr. Hayes—" she struggled for words "—you can't just take her away. Where will you take her? Do you have a wife to look after her?"

He allowed a wry grin to turn up one side of his mouth. "I'm perfectly capable of taking care of her, Mrs. Coulson."

Panic rose in her chest.

"I have some land nearby," he assured her, and his deep voice had taken on an almost soothing quality. "I'm going to build us a house."

Confusion and worry blotted out the information. "She's so little," she almost whispered. "And she's frightened." Thea fought to control the tremor in her voice. "Can you imagine what she's been through?"

A look of pain crossed his hard-set expression. "Yes. I can."

"She's just begun adjusting to living here. I—I can't bear to think of her being uprooted again so soon."

Mr. Hayes stood, pushing the chair behind him with the backs of his legs. "What are you suggesting? What? Do you want Zoe yourself? Do you plan to fight me for her?" He took a few steps toward her. "If you do, lady, you'll have a hell of a battle on your hands, and you don't stand a chance of victory. She's my sister's child! My blood relative!"

Thea raised her eyes to meet his furious, dark scowl. He was right, of course; she didn't stand a chance. Just because she'd foolishly allowed herself to grow attached to Zoe didn't give her any rights. The little girl rightfully belonged with him if—she examined his sharp features, the black growth of whiskers lending him an even more menacing countenance, and her heart broke imagining Zoe with this uncompromising, rock-faced stranger—if he was who he said he was.

For once, as she pulled herself up and stared back at him, her height gave her a definite advantage. A normal-sized woman would have been dwarfed by this man's massive stature. "You can't take her. Not like this. Not without Mrs. Vaughn's consent. I don't know you, Mr. Hayes." She paused and another thought struck her. "Does Zoe know you?"

She'd hit a nerve. His granite expression cracked. He cleared his throat. "I haven't seen Zoe since she was a baby. But that makes no difference. She belongs with me."

"Maybe she does," Thea conceded. "But Mrs. Vaughn and the Foundling Home will have to decide. Understand," she pleaded, her voice softening, "I can't just send Zoe out the door with a man I've never laid eyes on before. I feel . . . responsible for her."

Thea wasn't certain how he'd accept that admission. For several tense minutes he said nothing.

"I want to see her," he said at last.

Apprehension tightened every nerve in her body. Thea glanced at his hip. No weapon rode there, but that didn't mean he didn't have one concealed beneath the dark jacket. He was a powerful-looking man...a stranger. Trudy and Thea's half sisters had gone visiting. Her father and Denzel wouldn't be back until noon. How would she defend herself and the children if Mr. Hayes threatened them? She glanced at David, content with his playthings. Then she thought of the revolver she kept in her bureau upstairs.

Reconciled, she led him up to her bedroom. In the center of the four-poster, Zoe slept. Thea's wedding ring quilt was tucked around the little girl's legs and feet. Aunt Odessa had sewn the quilt thirteen years ago for Thea's hope chest, and a few winters past Thea had resignedly decided to enjoy it before the moths did.

She breathed an inward sigh of relief at Zoe's sound sleep and stepped to her bureau.

Mr. Hayes stood beside the bed and studied the child. Stealthily, Thea opened her top drawer and found the gun beneath her handkerchiefs. Gripping it, she buried her hand in the folds of her skirt.

After several long minutes spent watching his niece sleep, he glanced around, took stock of the hand-crocheted white bedspread and curtains, the rose-patterned wallpaper and the silver-backed brush and comb set on Thea's bureau. When he turned, she wondered at the glitter she thought she'd seen in his eyes.

He strode from the room, and she followed him briskly down the hall, the stairs, through the house to the back door. He jerked the door open and marched into the yard.

Thea felt foolish holding the gun at her side. What would she have done with it? "Mr. Hayes..."

He stopped and cast her a dark glare.

She couldn't think of anything to say. If he was who he said he was, he would get Zoe next time. "Where will you take her?"

The man didn't waste time with careless gestures. "There's a soddy on my land. I'll stay there until I get my house finished."

A soddy? She'd lived in one twenty years ago before her father'd built their home. There'd been snakes, and the roof had leaked.

The black stallion with white-stockinged forelegs snorted from the yard's edge and shook his massive head impatiently, his snaffle ring jingling across the open yard. Mr. Hayes calmed him with a quiet word and the touch of his palm over the beast's nose.

Thunder rumbled in the distance, matching Thea's turbulent emotions. The self-assured man settled a flat-brimmed hat on his head and swung into the saddle in one graceful movement. A rifle hung in a leather holster from the military-issue saddle.

With two fingers, he touched the hat's brim in a parting salute. "If you mean to use that gun, make sure it's loaded. I'll be back."

A jagged streak of lightning punctuated his vow. He wheeled the horse and galloped in a northeasterly direction. From the west, Thea heard her father bringing the team in before the storm broke. Behind her, David fussed. Maryruth would be coming for him soon. The men would be ready for dinner in an hour, and she hadn't started it yet.

Thea closed the door and leaned her forehead against the wood. *He'll be back.*

Booker cast a glance at the threatening sky and tugged his slicker from the roll behind him. How ironic that instead of finding Zoe in some hovel or a state of near starvation, he'd found her safe and warm on a beautiful woman's bed in a dress, obviously new and of good-quality fabric. Why did that fact cut him almost as deeply as if she'd been mistreated or hungry?

He was grateful that the Coulson woman had taken her in and cared for her. Even though the woman had at least one child of her own, she'd made time and a place for Zoe.

Damn! Mentally, Booker cursed himself. If only he'd been able to get to New York sooner! He should have been there for Julia when Robert died. And he should have been there for Zoe when Julia died. He would make it up to her. Zoe needed him, and he would take care of her.

He'd been in the army too long. He'd been without a home too long, sleeping in a bedroll on the hard ground listening to snores and grunts, eating army grub and living day after day in the saddle, a Winchester and Red Horse, an Arapaho scout, his only companions. He'd spent too much time guarding other men's lives, other men's wives and families. It was long past time to make a place for himself. For Zoe.

Pulling the slicker over his head, he readjusted his hat as fat, spattering drops began to fall. Not relishing the long ride back to Omaha where he'd taken a room in a boardinghouse, Booker urged Gideon toward where his property abutted the Coulsons' on their northern border. He'd weather out this storm in the sod house.

Thunder rolled across the heavens, and he kicked the horse into a gallop. In less than half an hour he'd located the stream and followed it to the old buffalo wallow shown on the map Augie Wynn had given him. Augie had farmed this hundred-and-sixty acres for the past four years. He and his family had moved on to the Dakotas when Booker decided it was time to use the land himself.

He topped a shallow rise, and lightning illuminated the soddy. Booker smiled. It was in as good a shape as Augie had promised. A lean-to jutted from the north side, a sound haven for Gideon to rest. Booker unsaddled the animal, wiped him down with a gunnysack and gathered his rifle, saddlebags and bedroll.

He dashed through the pelting rain. The door swung open on silent leather hinges. Booker fumbled in his gear for matches and lit one, holding it aloft to orient himself in the darkness. A lantern stood directly in the center of a sturdy table. Striking another match, Booker turned up the wick, held the match to it and replaced the lamp, noticing the clean glass.

He glanced around, his eyes adjusting to the lantern's glow. Everything was clean and tidy. The Wynns had been gone for at least a month, yet there wasn't even a coat of dust on the tabletop.

Booker removed his hat, and his sixth sense kicked in. He ducked out of his poncho, slowly, shifting the Winchester from one hand back to the other. He pulled back the lever, feeding a bullet into the chamber, and turned.

A cot hugged the limed wall, and beneath a cozy pile of furs, a bulge indicated its occupancy. Booker knew he'd made enough noise to wake the dead, but the sleeper didn't seem disturbed. He stepped closer. "Hello?"

A slight movement rustled beneath the animal skins.

"Hello," he called louder.

The form rolled but remained buried.

Booker took the last remaining step, rifle ready in his right hand, and jerked the fur back with his left. "Well— what the hell—?"

A youth with tousled hair and sleepy hazel-gray eyes was pointing a Colt Navy .36 at his heart.

Chapter Three

Thunder rumbled in the background. Cushioned from the weather in the roomy, wood-paneled dining room of the sturdy, two-story house, the Coulson family gathered around the enormous table.

"We had a lovely morning," Trudy cooed, and helped herself to a tiny portion of the creamy mashed potatoes as they passed. "Didn't we, dears?"

Madeline responded with an enthusiastic nod. "Mrs. Creighton decorated her parlor in the most stunning shade of emerald green."

Almost a carbon copy of her married sister, Elsbeth, Madeline was an accomplished seamstress. Her stitchery surpassed even the older ladies' of the Mission Circle. Throughout the Coulson home, her needlepoint screamed for attention—the exquisite marigold clusters on the dining chairs, assorted cushions and even a lampshade in the parlor. Nearly every wall displayed her needlepoint.

Even though there'd been no decision made on the groom, Madeline's energies had been directed to her wedding dress for the past eight months. The project was a masterpiece of tiny seed pearls and delicately embroidered ribbon-bearing doves on pristine white satin. With her minute figure and dark, shiny hair, Madeline would be a stunning bride.

"Perhaps when we're in St. Louis we can shop for new drapes and a carpet for the parlor," Trudy suggested, a familiar enthusiastic twinkle in her eye.

Thea's father smiled benevolently and stabbed a thick slice of beef from the platter.

Thea took her seat on her father's left and smiled across the table at her stepmother. "We could use some new kitchen towels while you're shopping."

Trudy offered a distracted half nod. "Lexie, dear, will you remember toweling when Madeline is shopping for fabric?"

Lexie gave a delicate shrug and buttered half a slice of Thea's bread. It grew more and more obvious to Thea that Lexie didn't share her mother's and sisters' enthusiasm for shopping, nor did she share their zeal for the society customs they'd brought from St. Louis. She seemed to much prefer riding horseback over sitting in the shaded buggy, and she'd read all of Thea's books at least once. Whenever possible, Lexie enjoyed time to herself.

From the other end of the table, Denzel spoke up. "Did you have company, Thea? Someone was riding out when I brought the team in."

Denzel waited for a reply. Maryruth cast a questioning glance. Thea snuck a peek at Zoe, who sat at her elbow. Silent as always, the pale-haired little girl calmly ate her meal.

"Yes, I did," she began carefully. She'd planned to talk to her father alone, but she had been so busy preparing the meal and mopping up the muddy floor, the occasion hadn't presented itself. "A gentleman claiming to be a certain person's uncle came to see me."

Maryruth's gaze slid knowingly to Zoe. "Did he have any proof? Did the certain person recognize him?"

"He didn't show me anything," Thea replied. "The little person was n-a-p-p-i-n-g, and it had been years since he'd seen—h-e-r."

"What did you do, Thea?" her father asked. Rain drizzled down the floor-length window behind him.

"I told him he'd have to bring Mrs.—the agent back with him."

"Good." Jim chewed thoughtfully. "Where's he from?"

"I'm not sure," she replied with a quick glance to make sure the conversation had gone over Zoe's head. "He had army-issue boots and saddle. Said he had some land nearby and was going to build a house."

"Did he tell you his name?" her father asked.

Thea spelled out Hayes.

Jim Coulson regarded his son-in-law. Denzel stared back at Thea, an odd expression flaring in his gray-green eyes.

"What?" she asked softly.

"He's the son of a—"

"Denzel," Maryruth cut in gently.

Denzel laid his fork down. "He's the bluecoat who owns the Hazel Creek section your pa wanted. Augie Wynn told 'em at the mercantile that he'd be comin'. He leased the property to Wynn till he was damned good and ready to get here himself."

Thea rolled the information over in her mind. Mr. Hayes . . . Zoe's uncle . . . was the man her father'd lost the creek land to? She cast a tentative glance at her father.

He avoided her eyes and peppered his steak.

The subject had been an unpleasant one in the Coulson family for the last four years. Mr. Hayes's integrity and parentage had been questioned more than once. Thea had imagined him a land baron ogre, not a disturbingly handsome man. His stern expression and clipped manner characterized a soldier unaccustomed to having his wishes denied.

Mr. Hayes had the land her father wanted, and now he wanted Zoe. A cold disappointment settled in Thea's heart. If a wealthy, respected man like her father couldn't do anything about Booker Hayes, what could she hope to do?

Thunder volleyed above the soddy. Rain pelted the bark roof. The noise registered, but Booker's attention focused on the old weapon the youth pointed without the slightest tremble in his long, knobby-knuckled fingers. His gaze locked with the boy's, he backed up and slowly leaned to lay the Winchester on the table. "I don't mean you any harm, son. I just need a place out of the storm."

The lad's wary hazel eyes inspected him from head to toe and back. "Who are you?"

"Name's Hayes. Got caught in this downpour on my way to Omaha. I knew the Wynns had moved on, so I thought I'd stay the night in here out of the weather."

"You a lawman?"

"No."

The boy's distrust wasn't appeased; he kept the gun in his hand and Booker under observation as he slid from the narrow cot and gestured with the barrel. "There's a bed over there."

Booker nodded. "Want a fire in the fireplace?"

"Suit yourself." Lightweight summer drawers hung on the boy's lanky frame. Cautiously, the youth perched on a chair at the table.

Gathering small pieces of wood from a pile near the door, Booker soon had a fire burning in the fieldstone fireplace. Some of the dampness seeped from the room. He hung his slicker and suit jacket over the backs of chairs and slid his gear under the bed. He tossed his bedroll on top. Finally, he returned and reached for his rifle.

"I'm going to take the bullet out of the chamber. If the rifle gets bumped or falls, it'll go off."

The boy's gray gaze jumped apprehensively to the Winchester and Booker ejected the bullet.

Using the opportunity, Booker grabbed the Colt from the kid's lax grip. The youth lunged from the chair and attempted to retrieve the gun.

Booker merely turned sideways, checked the empty chamber and tossed both guns beside his bedroll. Immediately, the boy dropped his hands from Booker's forearm.

The kid was hiding. A runaway, probably; he didn't have the look of an outlaw. Booker'd seen his share of outlaws.

He'd seen men living on the edge of civilization, seeking escape in one form or another. He'd seen what this hard country could do, and he hated to see it in one so young. But this kid's wariness wasn't hard-edged—his caution was simply self-preservation. His story could take any form.

The boy backed away from Booker, edging toward the door.

"Look, kid. I'm not going to hurt you. What are you going to do? Go running out into the rain in your drawers?"

Shamefaced, the lad studied a spot beyond Booker's shoulder.

"What's your name, son?"

"I ain't your son!" A belligerent tone covered his embarrassment.

Booker nodded. "No. You're not. Do you have a name?"

He raised his chin. "I got one."

A minute passed.

"Okay," Booker conceded, and turned. "A man doesn't have to tell anything he doesn't want to in these parts." He opened his bedroll and smoothed it out over the mattress. "I just figured since we're spending the night together, we could exchange a few pleasantries, but consider your business your own." He unbuttoned his shirt, shrugged out of it, loosened his trousers and glanced up.

The boy jerked his gaze away.

Booker sat on the bed's edge and worked his boots off.

"Lucas."

Booker raised his head.

Lucas met the stranger's dark eyes. He was intimidating, no doubt about it. Tall as a tree, dark as midnight and flint-hard as the devil himself. But his calm manner and matter-of-fact speech balanced out his stern appearance. The man exposed his muscled upper body, tanned skin smoothed over rock-hard muscles, and his broad chest covered with a pelt of black, curly hair. Lucas couldn't help but admire the man's physique and strength, a far cry from his own knobby, undeveloped body; nonetheless, a common thread wove itself into the crackling warm air.

They were two men needing a place for the night. The stranger's preparations for bed made him more human, somehow. He took off his boots just like everyone else.

"Pleased to meet you, Lucas. If you had ammunition for that relic, would you know how to shoot it?" The black-haired Hayes stepped out of his trousers.

Lucas hadn't a clue what to do with a gun, but he didn't want to tell the man that. He shrugged.

"Thought not," the unsparing man replied. "I'll bet you're a quick learner, though. If we're both still around tomorrow, I'll give you a lesson." He slid the guns under his bed, opened his bedroll and crawled inside. "Blow out the lantern, would you?"

Lucas stared at the long form beneath the covers. The man had exposed Lucas's helplessness, but didn't seem inclined to take advantage of it. For whatever reason of his own, he appeared content to take shelter in the sturdy little sod house and leave Lucas to himself. No one had ever left him to his own means before. Adults always wanted to herd him about, put him to work, decide what was best....

He blew out the lantern and slipped back beneath the furs. It looked like Hayes would let him go his own way, and though he couldn't trust the man, he could abide him— for the time bein'.

Thea smoothed Zoe's corn-silk hair back from her forehead and inhaled her fresh, clean scent. They lounged against the headboard of Thea's bed, a book in Thea's lap. Zoe yawned and pointed to the page. In her white nightgown with eyelet at the neck and hem, she painted a picture of childlike innocence and trust.

Thea blinked against the sudden sting behind her eyes and focused on the illustration Zoe's tiny finger pointed out. "It's a colt, sweetheart, a baby horse. Isn't it pretty?"

Zoe trusted her. She counted on her to care for her and keep her safe. Heaven only knew what she'd witnessed and lived through since the deaths of her parents. Certainly, life had not given her the sense of security and love she needed to thrive. Thea knew she could give her those things. She knew beyond a shadow of a doubt that she'd be a wonderful mother.

The child cast her a blue-eyed plea. Thea drew her body close enough to snuggle and read until Zoe slept. She eased her down into the bed and covered her with the sheet and quilt. Kneeling beside the bed, she ran her fingers across Zoe's silken cheek, fanned them through her golden hair and leaned to kiss her brow. Such a beautiful child—fair and lovely and just the right size.

Of their own volition, her eyes slid to Zoe's legs beneath the light cover. She knew the humiliation Zoe would suffer. She'd learned just how cruel children could be. They would taunt and ridicule her because of her leg. The world was full of Irving Jacksons.

Bathing her, Thea had been unable to discover any reason for her limp. She had no scars or deformities. But Thea was no doctor.

Standing, she pulled the pins from her hair, uncoiled the length and methodically worked her brush through. After plaiting a loose braid, she undressed and slipped her cotton nightdress over her head. The sheets were cool and crisp, but the pleasure was lost on her.

When that Hayes fellow came back with Mrs. Vaughn, she would have to give Zoe up to him. He wouldn't have gone to so much trouble to seek her out if he wasn't telling the truth. Despite his callous demeanor, he must have a soft spot inside for Zoe. She remembered the glimmer in his mahogany eyes when he'd turned away from the sleeping child. Maybe Zoe looked like his sister. Maybe she was the only family he had, and maybe he did plan to build a house for them.

Thea stared at the moonlight reflected on the ceiling and reminded herself of her own family and many blessings. She didn't have a husband or child of her own, but she did have a family to love and who loved her. Until Zoe had come along, that had been enough.

Now... Now Thea was reminded of the dreams she'd buried. Dreams of her own house, her own children, her own...

No. She couldn't do it. Couldn't conjure up all those long-buried fantasies. Couldn't revive the fancifully woven hopes and yearnings she'd managed to cast aside. Couldn't torture herself with bold pipe dreams that would never be.

She squeezed her eyes shut, and tears trickled down her temples into her hair. She was oversize, orange-haired, and well past marrying age. She'd long ago thrown her passion and ardency into caring for others, vicariously enjoying glory and attention through her lovely half sisters.

Zoe belonged with her uncle. *I could be a mother to her.* She'd had no business allowing herself to fall in love with a child who wasn't hers in the first place. *I could give her all the love and attention she needs and that I need to give.* When Mr. Hayes and the agent came for Zoe, she would have to comply with their wishes. *Don't take her; God, don't let him take her!*

The rain dwindled to a light pattering against the roof. Thea ran her palm across the delicately stitched wedding quilt that was to have been on her marriage bed. She listened to Zoe's even breathing and once again struggled to accept the fact that she would not have a child of her own.

Could be the dark man wasn't Zoe's uncle at all... Perhaps he'd see she was the best one to care for Zoe.... Perhaps he'd give up and go away.

Perhaps she'd sleep sometime before morning.

Lucas awoke with a start. Sunlight streamed through the open doorway. From outside came the sounds of footsteps and water splashing. He slid from the cot and dressed.

He could hear Hayes's low voice as the man spoke to his horse. Lucas checked beneath the bed. No guns. Cautiously, he stepped into the sunshine.

"Morning!"

Lucas jumped and turned. Hayes was fully dressed in slim black trousers, a soft flannel shirt, polished knee-high boots and a black, flat-crowned hat. He led a massive night-black stallion by the reins.

"Hungry? You'll find something in my saddlebags under the bed." He checked the cinches beneath the horse's belly and tugged one tighter.

"You leavin' without your gear?"

"I'll be back. I have business in town."

What kind of business? Business like squealing to the authorities? Obviously, Lucas's short stay was over. He'd been lucky to find this place the day before. Too bad he couldn't've stayed awhile. Till he figured out what to do, where to go and how to get there without the authorities or that lowlife Bard finding him.

"You want a ride into town?"

Lucas glanced up in surprise.

Hayes mounted the stallion, leather creaking beneath his considerable weight.

Lucas shook his head.

Hayes settled his hat low over his eyes. "Need a job?"

He contemplated the man and the question. "What kind o' job?"

"I'm building a house here." He nodded across the clearing. "I'm in a hurry, so I'll hire out most of the work that needs doing."

Lucas considered his statement with surprise.

"I'm building a gristmill over south by the rails," Hayes continued. "There's a lot to be done. You can stay here. Food and bed and, say, ten dollars a week till the job's completed."

Ten dollars a week! Why, it wouldn't take him long and he'd have enough to get clear o' this place...maybe to buy passage on a boat somewheres. Get far enough away from the people who wanted to say how he should live his life while they didn't care what he wanted. It sounded too good to be true. Anything lookin' this good *probably* wasn't true.

Nobody ever did something without wanting something in return. Skeptically, he cast Hayes a sidelong look. "What's the catch?"

"Catch is you earn it, kid."

The man hadn't shot him. Hadn't tossed him out into the rain. Hadn't dragged him into town and turned him over to the law. Lucas still couldn't trust him, but he'd take his chances. What did he have to lose? "You live here, then?"

"I'm going to. My things don't come for two more days."

"Anybody else live here?"

"My niece and an Indian friend will be coming soon."

Lucas conjured up a picture of a near-naked brave, wielding a tomahawk. His scalp prickled. "An Injun? Coming he-re?" His voice broke embarrassingly on that word. "How come? How'd ya meet 'im?"

"I met him before the war. I didn't see him while I fought—"

"Did you kill a lot o' rebs?"

"I was an officer. I did what I had to do. Afterward, I was assigned to protect the railroad crews coming this way, and I ran into Red Horse again. We shared a lot of campfires."

"What's he coming for?"

Booker's expression said that answer should be evident. "He's going to help me."

"Build the mill?"

"And run it."

An Injun was gonna help him. The idea of seeing an honest-to-goodness Injun intrigued Lucas. He pretended he didn't care. "What d'you want done while you're gone?"

Booker stroked his freshly shaven jaw with a thumb. "Why don't you cut some firewood and stack it next to the lean-to. Not much to do until I bring back supplies. Do you know how to cook?"

"Some."

"Yeah, me, too." He shrugged. "I'll be back before dark."

Lucas watched him ride away, the eager stallion kicking up dust clouds. He turned back and regarded the sturdy sod house with new eyes. "Well, what d'you know?" he said out loud.

A pretty good place to stay. Food, plus ten dollars a week. And a real live Injun. He'd stay to see that for sure. If Hayes didn't bring the law back with him, he'd see how it went. And if anybody so much as laid a finger on him, he'd be gone.

Thea placed the last stitch in the cloth doll, broke the thread with her teeth and stuck the needle in her basket beneath the rocking chair. "Look, Zoe."

From her position at Thea's feet, Zoe scrambled to her knees.

Thea showed her the finished doll and the tiny dress made from a scrap of the same pastel blue checks Zoe herself wore. Zoe's six-year-old fingers stumbled over the fastenings, and Thea helped. Zoe turned the doll back to face her and traced the delicately embroidered eyes and mouth with a finger. She raised her cherubic face and smiled at Thea.

"You're welcome." Thea ran her palm over the child's silken hair and kissed her forehead.

"I think she likes it," her father said from his chair near the unused fireplace. "It looks like a doll you had when you were a little girl."

"You know I was never a 'little' girl, Papa," Thea said with a twist of irony in her usually teasing tone.

From another room, they could hear Trudy's high-pitched, slightly off-key voice, singing as she and Madeline continued their nightly work on The Dress. Lexie lounged on the sofa with a book.

Her father grinned. "You'll always be my little girl."

"Yep." Zoe slipped back to her spot on the floor, and Thea reached for the sewing basket. "I'm afraid you're stuck with me." She grinned. "Good thing I'm useful."

From the dooryard, one of the dogs barked. Minutes later, steps sounded on the front porch. Her father stood at the same time the sharp knock sounded on the door. He stepped over to open it.

"Mr. Coulson." The deep baritone sent a shiver down Thea's spine. A dark hand thrust from the night waited for her father. "Booker Hayes, sir. I need to talk to you."

Jim shook the hand and stepped back. "Come in, Mr. Hayes."

His dark presence filled the doorway, black pants and hat blending with the pitch black behind him. A stark white shirt enhanced the width of his chest and shoulders.

Zoe's hand gripped Thea's calf.

"You've already met Thea."

Mr. Hayes doffed his hat. "Ma'am."

"Mr. Hayes."

"My daughter, Alexis."

He raised a curious black brow, his gaze scooting between Thea and Lexie. "Miss."

Lexie nodded and excused herself to her room.

"Sit." Jim Coulson returned to his chair.

Thea's heart pounded in her chest as though her father had just invited Satan himself into their home, rather than this perfectly polite man who seated himself in a chair and hung his hat on his knee. Trembling inside, Thea remembered her manners and stood. "I'm sorry. Let me take your hat."

He handed it to her, but his concentration centered on Zoe, who clung to Thea's skirt when she crossed the room. Keeping the child under observation, his features changed subtly, with an almost imperceptible softening around his mouth and a flicker of pain behind his eyes—there one instant, gone the next.

"What's on your mind, Mr. Hayes?"

The man's attention drew back to his business. "I'd appreciate it if you'd call me Booker. We're going to be neighbors."

"The Hazel Creek section, I hear."

He nodded his dark head.

Thea twisted the hat brim in her hand unthinkingly. Why had he come back? She'd told him he couldn't take Zoe without the Home's orders.

"Fine piece o' land," her father said with regret. "Had my eye on it myself."

"It's the best site I found when the rails were going through."

"You a surveyor, maybe? Railroad man?"

"No, sir, I—"

"I'll call you Booker if you call me Jim."

"All right, Jim. I was in the army. My regiment guarded the surveyors and later the rail crews."

"Met a few Indians, did you?"

"A few."

Thea wanted to scream at their polite exchange. She wanted to throw his damned hat in his face and send him back wherever he'd come from. As if he knew her thoughts, he turned and caught her mangling his Stetson. She hung it on a hook near the door and met his foreboding gaze.

She resented his unyielding expression. She wanted to see it crack. "I'll bring some coffee."

She took Zoe in to Trudy and Madeline and poured two steaming cups.

Mr. Hayes accepted the mug, carefully avoiding her fingers. His eyes met hers, though, and a dark undercurrent passed between them. "I wired Mrs. Jennings."

Apprehension tightened her scalp and stiffened her spine. *You knew he'd be back, Thea. Get used to the idea.*

"Should I know her?" Thea's father asked.

"She's the director of the orphanage," Thea supplied softly, and took a seat on the sofa nearer her father. *Just say it, Hayes. Just rip my heart out, and get it over with.*

Jim acknowledged the information with a nod.

"She contacted Mrs. Vaughn in Lincoln," the raven-haired man continued. "Day after tomorrow, Mrs. Vaughn will pick up the papers, meet me, and we'll come for Zoe."

He might as well have pounced, boots first, smack in the middle of her chest. *There. Done.* Funny, she didn't feel like her heart would stop. She didn't even feel like crying. She only felt like telling him to go to hell, and with a little smile, imagined her father's horror if she did.

"You're family?" Jim asked.

"Zoe is my sister's child," Hayes said, nodding. "After I was discharged, I went to visit. I hadn't seen her for five years." His hesitation was almost imperceptible. "She and her husband died in New York last winter. I wasn't aware of their deaths, or of the fact that Zoe was taken to that place from the hospital."

Finally, he had her complete attention. She'd wondered so often. "Did you see it?" Thea whispered.

His mouth tightened. "The Home?"

She nodded, trepidation sucking breath from her lungs.

"I saw it." His fingers tightened on the cup.

"And?" she prompted.

"It's clean. Mrs. Jennings is an efficient woman who does the best she can for the children."

What he didn't say spoke to Thea in a voice louder than his careful words. She didn't want to know any more.

He turned back to her father. "I made arrangements months ago when I first knew I'd be quitting the army. I contacted Ezra Hill and wired money ahead for building supplies. Arrangements have been made for the crews. Today I bought a wagon, horses, food. Everything's ready and waiting. Mr. Hill starts tomorrow."

How could he afford all that? Hands cold as ice, Thea laced her fingers. "Will you take her to that sod house, then?"

"It's not a bad place. The roof didn't let a drop of rain through last night. The inside is clean. The house will be finished in a few weeks."

Who will be her mother? Have you thought of that? Did you consider Zoe's feelings in all your carefully structured plans?

"You know, we've used that creek to water our east herd for as long as I can remember," Jim said with an odd tinge to his voice. "I'll have to dig a new well."

"Feel free to use the creek until the well's done," Mr. Hayes offered. "As long as you like, for that matter."

"What about your cattle?" her father asked in surprise.

"I'm going to breed a few horses," he replied. "And plant trees. But I'm not going to farm. I'm building a mill."

"There's a mill in Florence. Not enough timber around here yet to call for another one."

"A grain mill. Not steam-powered. Like you said, there's not enough wood."

Jim Coulson nodded.

"The steam-powered grist and sawmills in these parts will be converting to water power before long," Hayes continued. "More horsepower, faster production time. I'll be one step ahead." That information hung in the air for a few jarring seconds.

A grin spread across her father's face. "Damn! That's a smart move, boy. Why the hell didn't I think of it?" He slapped his leg. "Wheat fields as far as the eye can see. The railroad right there. You'll do one hell of a business."

"That's the way I see it."

"Anybody can build a mill," Jim added. "You'll need a millwright to make it work."

"Man by the name of Gunderson came by earlier this spring to confirm the site I picked. He's working over in Nebraska City right now. Has a job in Jefferson County and should arrive here about the time I have my house done."

"Why here?"

"I scouted waterways all along the railroad. Hazel Creek is a constant water source. The banks are high and sound, and it has a rock bottom. Add to that the local demand, and I have a perfect spot."

Jim picked up his pipe from a side table and tamped tobacco into the bowl. He clamped it between his teeth and struck a match, one thick gray brow rising inquisitively.

"You an' this Gunderson fella gonna use an overshot wheel?"

"No, sir. Wooden wheels take constant maintenance. They freeze up in the winter. I've ordered a Leffel turbine. It's a horizontal iron wheel completely submerged."

"Build a dam? Do you have water rights?"

Listening to their camaraderie blossom, helplessness and frustration swiftly glided into anger. Thea stood in an indignant rustle of skirts. "I don't believe this," she huffed in irritation. "You're discussing wheat and dams while there's a child's welfare at stake."

"Thea-girl," her father said. "Mr. Hayes is our neighbor."

"Don't 'Thea-girl' me," she said, knowing she'd regret the words as soon as they were out of her mouth. "He came here to take Zoe away, and you're carrying on with him like he's an old friend! 'Here, use my creek.' 'Well, gee thanks, I'll bring your mill my business.'" Heart hammering, she turned away.

"Thea!" her father said in the sternest tone he'd ever used with her. "Mr. Hayes didn't have to come tonight. It was kind of him to give you time to prepare. To get Zoe used to the idea."

Kind? Something in her chest stretched tight, pushing an unbearable ache into her throat. Her chin quivered uncontrollably, pulling her lower lip down. Thea caught it between her teeth. Kind would be putting a bullet between her eyes right about now.

"Thea," her father said.

She bit her lip, garnered her self-control and turned back. "I'm sorry, Mr. Hayes. It was 'kind' of you to come tonight. I'll have her ready when you return."

Her sarcasm pierced Booker. Tension crackled between them, and he had the impression she was a volcano ready to explode. He watched her compose herself and perch stiffly on the sofa. Her softly curling strawberry blond hair and porcelain complexion combined with her shimmering blue-green eyes and vulnerable mouth to convey an indelible impression of delicacy. Her gaze slid to his boots. He felt like the villain in a dime novel. What he was doing hurt her. He couldn't help that. Uncomfortable, he turned back to Jim Coulson.

"I'm sorry," Jim said. "She's not behaving like herself. It's just that she's grown so fond of the child. I was afraid of this."

"It's all right. I can see that your wife cares for Zoe. I wish it didn't have to be this way. It's unfortunate that—"

"My wife! Ye gods, man, you think an old coot like me'd have a wife that age?" Jim half snorted, half laughed. "Thea's my daughter!"

Thea stared at her lap.

With that revelation, Booker recognized the resemblance between them. Why hadn't she corrected him the day before when he'd addressed her? She wasn't Coulson's wife? Booker wondered at the immediate sensation of relief that burst within his chest. What did he care?

Coulson called his wife from another room and introduced a tiny dark-haired woman of his own age. "This is my wife, Trudy." Coulson still grinned. "More like it, huh?"

Booker returned the grin. "Pleased to meet you, ma'am." Her appearance only confounded Booker's thoughts. Thea looked nothing like this woman or the young girl Coulson had introduced as his daughter.

The flighty little woman smiled and tittered. "Would you care for a cup of tea, Mr. Hayes?"

"I have coffee, thanks."

"Where are you living?" she asked.

Booker explained the situation once again.

She clapped her small hands in delight. "How wonderful! New neighbors are a grand social event around here, you know."

He nodded as if he knew indeed.

"Of course, we must have a housewarming when your home is finished. But I'm sure Thea's already thought of that. Thea organizes everything in these parts, don't you, dear? She'll have a lovely party cooked up before you know it."

Thea shot the woman a look that could have curdled milk.

"That's thoughtful of you, Mrs. Coulson, but it's not necessary." Booker took a sip from his mug.

"Don't give it another thought. Do you have a wife, Mr. Hayes?"

He nearly choked on a swallow of coffee. He pulled the mug away with a jerk and wiped his lip with a knuckle. "No, ma'am."

"Someone special?"

Jim Coulson rebuked her gently. "Trudy, give the man some air."

She folded her hands in her lap, innocently.

Someone special? Involuntarily, his gaze slid to Thea. He studied the top of her head, the appealing curve of her neck, the slender twist of hair that lay against her skin. He'd never given the wife idea much thought. Booker cleared his throat. "No. There was no place for a wife in my line of work."

"Well, now you're settling down. You might even meet someone at the housewarming." Trudy smiled as though immensely pleased with herself.

Thea raised her head and met his gaze levelly. He expected bitterness or condemnation, but the look in her blue-green eyes caught him unexpectedly. Disappointment and a hint of irritation, yes, but resignation had smoothed away the anger.

"You'll need help preparing rooms, Mr. Hayes. I'm an adequate housekeeper. I'd be pleased to see that the house is ready for Zoe."

Booker studied her sincere expression.

Jim Coulson nodded approvingly.

Something had happened here, Booker realized. Something that bothered him more than he understood. Resentment was normal. Anger was normal. Denying those emotions wasn't.

Beautiful, gentle Thea Coulson had a fire storm raging on the inside. He'd seen it as clear as day only minutes ago, and now it was gone. With that realization came a disturbing inclination to discover how deep those emotions were buried—and just what it took to unleash them. It would take a better man than he. Even if he was up to the challenge, it couldn't be him. He found himself offering her an apologetic smile.

He would be the one to hurt her by taking the child they both wanted away from her.

Chapter Four

Midmorning two days later, a wagon pulled into the dooryard. Thea turned to Maryruth. Her sister had appeared shortly after breakfast, claiming she needed help with a dress pattern. Thea had seen through her excuse and welcomed the emotional support and physical company. Maryruth raised her head from the fabric she'd been cutting on the kitchen table and stared back. Together, they moved to the window.

Mr. Hayes lifted Mrs. Vaughn from the wagon and set her on the ground as though she were a doll. The dark-haired woman adjusted her fashionable hat and led Hayes toward the house. Heart pounding, Thea pulled back. Maryruth gripped her hand.

"I'm all right." Thea squeezed her sister's fingers, took a deep breath and observed herself in the mirror just inside the pantry. She recognized the despair in her reflection, drew a thin disguise over it and ran a nervous hand over the skirt of her somber dark blue dress. Even in the shadowy storage room, her lack of sleep was obvious. Slowly, distractedly, Thea fingered the dark circle under one eye.

"Thea," Maryruth prompted gently from the doorway.

Thea returned to Zoe, who was playing with scraps of material on the table. "Your uncle is here, Zoe."

Color drained from the child's face. Her eyes widened into two enormous pools of liquid blue, and her pale lips formed an anguished O. She wadded a piece of fabric in her fist and shook her head, vehemently.

"He's a very nice man, and he loves you," Thea coaxed, praying for strength. She knelt beside Zoe's chair and gazed into her anxious eyes. Zoe bolted from the chair and wrapped her arms around Thea's neck in a viselike death grip. Numbly, Thea murmured something soothing and heard Maryruth open the door behind her. Her heart pounded in her chest until she thought it would explode. Against her breast, she felt Zoe's heart hammering even faster than her own. The child's distress shot pain more devastating than anything she had imagined knifing through her chest.

The terrified child clung to her, and Thea knew she was staring at the familial intruder over her shoulder. Thea stood. She turned and forced herself to look at Mr. Hayes and the agent. Zoe burrowed her face against Thea's collarbone.

"Hello, Miss Coulson." Mrs. Vaughn drew a paper from her handbag and unfolded it. "I have papers here to prove Mr. Hayes's credibility and right to Zoe. Would you like to see them?"

Thea shook her head as best she could with Zoe's head lodged beneath her chin. "No," she whispered. She trusted the agent.

Mrs. Vaughn gave her a sympathetic shrug and a half smile. "Zoe looks wonderful. You've taken good care of her."

Thea's gaze inched from the agent to Zoe's formidable uncle. Dressed in black trousers, a white shirt and string tie, he presented a challenging picture of strength and confidence. His hard-boned face bore an unreadable flush. Neither his expression nor his voice bore an apology. "Let's get this over with," he said roughly.

Thea forced her wooden legs to carry her across the room. Maryruth gathered the drawstring bags made from flour sacks that contained clothing and toys Thea'd made and led the way outside. Mrs. Vaughn followed. Thea fell into step behind her, and Hayes took up the rear. The July sun beat down on her hair, but Thea's insides trembled with a cold, hopeless ache.

Dazedly, she watched Maryruth place the bags in the back of the springboard and recognized Mrs. Vaughn's distress in the nervous twisting of her handbag.

Hayes stepped in front of her, filling her line of view. His attention centered on the blond head beneath Thea's chin, his eyes never rising. "Come, Zoe," he said softly. "It's time to go."

Zoe's arms tightened to a stranglehold around Thea's neck. He reached for her, securing his hold at Zoe's armpit, his other hand cupping her chin. Her surprising strength cut off Thea's breath. "It's all right, darlin'," Thea coaxed. "You'll be safe. I promise."

Saying the words she prayed were true, she raised her questioning gaze to the man who held Zoe's future in his hands.

His dark eyes rose to hers, finally, and he answered with a reassuring nod.

Thea reached behind her neck and pried one of Zoe's hands loose. Hayes struggled with the other hand, a long strand of Thea's hair catching painfully. It took Maryruth to loosen the tress and unwrap Zoe's legs from Thea's waist. In a moment of vivid clarity amid the chaos, Thea met Zoe's eyes as her uncle wrenched her away, and the little girl's silent, fear-contorted face twisted her heart and took her breath away.

At first Thea thought she'd made the sound herself, a high, keening wail of grief and misery that started as a mewl and grew in alarming intensity. She folded her empty arms against her ribs and saw Zoe held against the man's body, her back to his massive chest, her mouth open. Stabbing realization slowed her pulse to a near stop and then chugged it like a freight train, her ears roaring with shock. *Zoe.* The mournful sound came from Zoe.

Thea clapped her hand over her mouth to keep from echoing the pain-induced cry. Her heart lurched up into her throat. Her sister wound her arm around Thea's waist and urged her to turn toward the house.

Zoe's cry bled into a howl, a lamentable, plaintive cry that reverberated off the buildings and shattered Thea's last shred of composure. She stumbled on the stairs. Maryruth steadied her, led her into the house and slammed the door against the shrill sound of Zoe's distress.

Thea accepted her sister's embrace, sobbed against the top of her head for several minutes, and slowly realized Maryruth was crying almost as hard as she was. She rubbed her sister's shoulders soothingly.

From the back bedroom, David's cry alerted them that his nap was over. Maryruth wiped her eyes on her apron and hurried to tend him. Thea ran up the stairs to her room. Closing the door behind her, she slumped against the cool wood. She'd known better. She ran to the window and parted the lace curtain.

The wagon was gone.

She'd known better, but she'd barged ahead anyhow. What else could she have done? Nothing. Though these precious weeks with Zoe had keenly pointed out the void in her life, she wouldn't have missed them for anything. She would tuck away the hurt and cherish the memory like a heartwrenchingly beautiful sunset or a spring flower—an exquisite but fleeting joy. She turned back to the silent room, the pristine spread, the neatly folded quilt, the hope chest at the foot of her four-poster.

Hope.

Thea's disconsolate gaze fixed on the wooden chest. Fruitless, broken, withered hope. *Hopeless* was more like it.

Anguish as deep and volatile as raging floodwaters engulfed her soul. Thea kicked the chest with all her pent-up hurt and frustration, kicked it again for good measure, and sank to the bed's edge, her toe throbbing. Zoe had never been hers. The knowledge didn't make her loss hurt any less.

Resolutely, Thea swiped at her tears with an impatient hand. She would get over it and go on. Like she always had. Like she always would.

The firelight at his back, Booker towered above the cot, casting a dark shadow over Zoe. She lay curled in a ball, the cloth doll clutched to her chest.

She'd stopped screaming a few miles from the Coulsons', thank God. Her frantic desperation had unhinged his resolve. That pathetic wail had lacerated his heart, and the screams... Lord, those screams.

Poor Mrs. Vaughn had been as much at a loss for a means to comfort the child as he. She had carried Zoe's belongings into the soddy behind Booker. Once the agent was gone, Booker attempted to prepare a pot of stew. His biscuits didn't turn out as well as Lucas's, but he'd done his best.

Lucas had appeared miraculously as Booker placed the food on the table. He glanced at Zoe where she lay facing the wall, showed Booker that he'd washed his hands outside, and sat. Booker had coaxed Zoe, had even gone so far as to carry her to the table, but she'd scurried back to the cot, gathered her things around her and acted like the rest of the world didn't exist. He'd expected it to feel good having Zoe with him, but already he doubted his decision. Booker and Lucas had eaten in silence, each occasionally casting a glance across the room.

Booker studied her now, her once perfectly braided hair loose and tangled from her earlier struggles. Each time he'd tried to stow her clothing away, she'd grown agitated and wrestled him for possession. Finally, he'd given up, allowed her to arrange the toys made from wooden spools and clothespins beside her, and ignored the flour-sack bags at her feet.

"It's time we got ready for bed, Zoe."

The fingers of one hand moved against the doll's bluechecked dress. She held her other fist tightly clenched.

"Can you help me find your nightclothes?"

No response.

"We'll get you changed, and then I'll fix you some hot cocoa. Maybe you'd like a biscuit. You have to be getting hungry."

No response.

He took that as a good sign and stealthily worked open the drawstring on the first bag. His search revealed brightly colored dresses and ruffled aprons, all new, all painstakingly sewn and perfectly pressed. The second bag held tiny underclothing trimmed with delicate lace and embroidery. Pink ribbons adorned drawers, chemises and a petticoat. Nightgowns, stockings and extra shoes lay at the bottom. Shaking a lightweight gown out, Booker imagined Thea stitching each seam and hem. In his mind, he painted a domestic picture of her long fingers touching the material, heard her speak softly to the platinum-haired child at her side and saw her lips curve into an indulgent smile.

He held the fabric in his palm and studied Zoe. Grief, deep sorrow and confusion engulfed his senses. A stranger had cared for Zoe with as much love and care as her own mother would have. Julia would be comforted to know that Thea Coulson had taken such an avid interest in her daughter. She would be delighted to see the clothing and toys lovingly made by hand just for Zoe. A dark thread of concern wove its way through his conscience. Would Julia be as pleased to see his intervention?

He had loved his sister deeply. Zoe was his only link to Julia. He was Zoe's only family now, and Julia would want him to care for her, he assured himself.

The child's lack of response dredged up other emotions as well. Uncertainty. How long would it take her to come around? Indignation. The Coulson woman had gained his niece's affections. Jealousy. Zoe had clung to her in terror and wanted no part of him. Rankling determination. He would make this work.

"Come on. Why don't you sit up for me?" Booker brushed her tangled hair back from her face with his fingers. Her thick lashes blinked with each stroke. Her coloring was so like his sister's, looking at her anchored a sorrowful joy in his chest. At his gentle urging, Booker's fingers met resistance in her diminutive shoulder. He pulled her to face him.

Zoe crumpled her face against the doll, and silent sobs racked her small body.

"Hush, don't cry, now. I just want to take care of you. Won't you give me a chance?" Booker recognized the odor at the same time he spotted her wet clothing and the soaked bedding beneath her. A tremendous rush of guilt and incompetence shook him to the core.

"Zoe," he whispered hoarsely, and touched her forehead with his lips. "I'm sorry." Tears welled behind his own lids. "It's my fault," he said against her temple. "I didn't show you where to go. I didn't even ask if you had to. Don't feel bad. We'll just change you and get you comfortable again."

What the hell was he doing? What in heaven's name did he know about taking care of a little girl? Another rung on his ladder of confidence splintered, and he had to catch himself. He would learn. This was all new to him, but he could learn.

Eventually, he coaxed her from the wet cot, leaving the doll within her sight. One fist remained curled solidly around something he'd begun to wonder about. He undressed her awkwardly, sponged her sturdy little body with water Lucas had warmed on the stove and showed her the chipped chamber pot under a rough-hewn washstand. He and Lucas used the outhouse, but since she didn't seem inclined to inform him of her needs, he deemed this arrangement best for her.

She didn't touch the mug of cocoa until Lucas held it to her lips and gave her a nod. Slowly, she raised her gaze to Lucas's face. Blue eyes, agonizingly like Julia's, flickered across the youth's face, and with something like cautious cooperation, she took a sip. Booker almost groaned with frustration. Instead, he turned his back on them and remade Zoe's cot with clean bedding.

When he turned back, she still hadn't touched the biscuit, but half the milk was gone. Booker nodded his appreciation to Lucas and tucked Zoe into her bed. "Tomorrow we'll put up more hooks for your clothes," he promised. "You can sleep with your doll and toys if you want to." One hand remained tightly fisted.

Zoe snuggled into the fresh bedding, the doll beneath her chin. Within minutes, she slept. Long lashes fanned across her pink cheeks, her bow-shaped lips parted slightly. He watched her even breathing. Cautiously, he opened her relaxed hand with one long finger, and frowned in perplexity at the treasure she'd held clenched in her fist since that morning.

An acorn?

The night before, Lucas, pretending not the least concern, had watched Hayes wheedle and cajole Zoe. He'd stifled his amazement when the hard-faced man had knelt and kissed her head. And he'd gained insight into the big man's character when Booker had changed her bedding and bathed her as gently as anything he'd ever seen. Lucas had taken his share o' lickin's for bed wettin', so he had no point of reference for the man's casual acceptance.

Lucas had hidden out long enough for the Home agent to come and go. He'd certainly been surprised to see Hayes's niece turn out to be the quiet little girl who'd come west on the train with him. Zoe had recognized him, but there was no harm in that. She couldn't talk. Lucas felt reasonably safe here.

He'd made tolerable flapjacks this morning while Hayes shaved and tended the stock. The man had eaten them without complaint. Zoe hadn't touched hers. Hayes watched her whenever she wasn't looking at him. He frowned and scowled a lot, too.

After breakfast, Hayes had strung lines from the lean-to to a slim tree, filled a tub with water and set about laundering their bedding and clothes.

Now, his dungarees and boots still damp, Hayes led Gideon from the lean-to and adjusted the saddle. "I'm late for the work crew, Lucas. You coming?"

For the last two days he'd helped Hayes dig and haul fieldstones, and he'd managed to stay far enough from the crew that no one from town would recognize him. "What about her?"

Booker glanced into the soddy. "We should have enough stones to start building the fireplace today. We'll rig her a tent out of the sun."

Lucas fetched Zoe, and Booker harnessed the team to the wagon. Booker had given the house and mill sites a lot of consideration, mapping out on paper where each field, creek, stream, ditch and natural object was located. He'd selected a spot for the house with a south and southeast slope to check cold winds and snow in winter. The house and barn would act as windbreaks to the yards, at the same time being open to the sun. To use the railroad and stream to the best advantage, the mill would be built to the far east.

Zoe sat in the shade beside the wagon while they dug the last of the stones. Because of the heat, Booker forced her to drink water, but she stubbornly refused to eat. Back at the house site, he stretched a tarpaulin between two wagons, and Zoe napped into the afternoon.

Ezra Hill had the foundation ready. He and his crew, John Starnes and Wren McPeters, helped Booker construct the fireplace. Finished, it was a masterpiece of workmanship, eight feet wide with a low, flat hearth. Flat stones to serve as shelves jutted from the chimney in staggered succession. Ezra whistled through his gray-shot beard and swore he'd never seen the likes.

Hot, tired and filthy, but satisfied with the day's work, Booker led the children and animals back to the soddy. He stared at the bedding and clothing still flapping on the line, a curse on his tongue. His stomach growled, and he wanted nothing more than to bathe in the cool creek water.

"I'll start supper," Lucas offered, lifting Zoe from the wagon.

Booker nodded in gratitude, pulled the wagon beside the soddy and unhitched the team. He led them into the lean-to and scooped grain into the wooden trough, fatigue further undermining his confidence. How the hell was he going to manage all of this on his own?

He hadn't the vaguest idea.

The next two days passed much the same. On the third night, after a battle of wills over supper, Zoe again went to sleep without eating. This couldn't go on.

Booker didn't know which was worse: her initial fear had been hard to accept, but this—this apathy—shot fear through his heart. A six-year-old who didn't care to eat, play or share the company of others was disturbing to see. Unmindful of thirst or hunger, she lay or sat in neutral listlessness wherever she was placed. She made occasional, perfunctory use of the chamber pot, and sometimes stroked her doll or twisted a rope of wooden spools.

She didn't speak or walk or give any indication of acceptance. Booker worried that her withdrawal would become so complete she'd stop seeing or hearing.

Smoothing her hair from her face, he studied the hopeless tangle he'd attempted to brush and tie back that morning. The ribbon hadn't lasted past the first hot breeze, but Zoe hadn't seemed to notice.

What was he going to do? He couldn't let her waste away before his eyes! He'd been so certain that he could do this. That he could care for her and make a home for them and do the right thing. But the right thing wavered more and more out of focus all the time.

Booker stood, taking stock of Zoe's small form beneath the light cover. He simply wasn't going to be able to do it alone. Work on the house was barely under way. The heavy construction came next, the barn following, and then weeks and weeks on the mill. Lucas's help was invaluable, but still insufficient. Booker needed someone to care for Zoe.

Someone who could get her to eat. Someone to be a mother to the girl. And though it pained him to admit it, just anyone wouldn't do. Zoe needed Thea Coulson.

He turned. Lucas sat at the table, sketching a horse on a piece of bark with a charcoal sliver. "You're good," he said.

Lucas's head shot up. He shrugged his bony shoulders. "Nah."

"You are, Lucas. That looks just like Gideon."

The boy half smiled. "It is."

Booker touched his shoulder, and Lucas flinched. He drew his hand away with a frown. "I'm going to the creek to wash, and then I have some business to tend to. Will you watch after Zoe?"

"Sure."

Booker gathered clean clothes and his hat. "You're earning your pay. I couldn't have done as much without your help."

Lucas flushed at the compliment. "Yeah, well. I need the money."

Lucas was obviously a perfect example of someone who'd grown up without a loving touch. If it was within Booker's power, he'd see that Zoe didn't suffer the same negligence. He took his gun and left.

Thea listened to Madeline and her stepmother coo over the progress of The Dress as they prepared themselves a cup of tea and returned to the sewing room. She sighed and turned back to her task.

If she had to listen to one more word of praise for the nuptial garment, she'd scream. After borrowing a book from Thea, Lexie had wisely escaped to her room for the evening.

Jars stuffed with sliced beets lined the worktable. Thea stirred her boiling vinegar mixture and poured the pungent liquid into each jar, her apron wrapped around the pan's handle.

"Thea-girl?" her father called from the other room. "Someone here to see you."

Thea wiped her beet-stained hands on her apron and removed it. Who would pay an evening visit? She never had any callers. She stepped into the parlor.

Booker Hayes rose from the sofa.

"Miss." His black hair was freshly combed. A clean white shirt accentuated the breadth of his shoulders and the tanned skin at his open collar.

"Mr. Hayes." She tried not to gape at him, and hid her stained hands behind her back. She hadn't prepared herself to see him so soon. She'd imagined various scenarios; running into him in town or facing him and his niece at church, but she surely hadn't expected the man to show up in her parlor! "What can I do for you?" she inquired, and remembered asking the same thing the first time they'd met.

"I'd like to talk to you." He skimmed a palm nervously down his denim-clad thigh. "If you don't mind."

Jim Coulson rose from his chair. "I'll just go—"

"No, Papa. Stay there. Mr. Hayes and I can talk on the porch."

He held the door for her. She sat in the wooden swing, and he sat on the railing. His horse munched grass at the edge of the yard. Moonlight glistened off Booker's ebony hair and outlined his cleanly shaven rigid jaw. A soft summer breeze carried the scent of bay rum to her nostrils.

"I don't quite know how to say this," he said at length.

Fear pierced Thea's chest. "Zoe?" she asked. "Is something wrong with Zoe?"

He turned his face away, silhouetting his strong profile against the moonlit yard. She saw him swallow.

"Mr. Hayes, what is it? Is she sick? Hurt?" She clenched her fists in her lap and leaned forward.

"No." He faced her. "Nothing like that." He cleared his throat. "I have a proposition for you."

He had her interest. "What kind of proposition?"

"I can't take care of her by myself. I have to build a house and a mill. I can't cook and wash and work from morning till night, too."

A thousand questions skittered through Thea's mind. Did he mean to give Zoe back, then? Didn't he want her, after all? Had he changed his mind? "What do you want from me?"

"I'd be willing to pay you to help with those things," he replied.

Anger throbbed to life. She averted her face and set her lips in a firm line. "You want a housekeeper?" she asked, her voice rising on the last syllables. "It's downright cruel of you to ask me." She stood. "You must know how I feel about Zoe, yet you've come to rub salt in the wound. What kind of torture is this?"

"No." He was before her in an instant. "It's not like that at all." He grasped her arms above her elbows and examined her face. "I know I probably acted rashly, but I never set out to hurt you or Zoe. It was just unfortunate that you'd taken to Zoe before I got here."

Thea snorted and tried to pull away. "Unfortunate," she said flatly.

Her strength was no match for his, and he held her in place with a firm grasp. "Listen."

Thea raised her chin, her exasperation unsoothed. "So my unfortunate connection qualifies me to be your maid?"

A long, tense moment passed. His hands loosened on her arms. "No. Zoe's connection to you qualifies you to take care of her like I can't. She won't have anything to do with me." His tone had changed, an almost cool detachment she sensed he needed to project. He released her, but the warmth from his hands remained. He wanted Zoe to love him, and her rejection had to hurt. "I'm asking for your help," he said gently.

Thea remained facing him, close enough to touch, close enough to catch his freshly bathed masculine scent. She hoped he couldn't smell the vinegar she was surely saturated with. His voice sent a strange heat coursing through her veins.

"I think you want to be near her badly enough to agree," he continued. "You can spend as much time with her as you like for as long as you like. I won't interfere with your relationship. Just come help me take care of her."

"Come . . . to your place?"

He nodded in the darkness. "Bringing her here would only delay her adjustment. She'll be living with me. She has to get used to that—and me."

Her vexation waned. His reasoning seemed sound enough. But she was torn. Self-preservation told her to refuse, run back into her comfortable home and resume her safe, spinsterly duties. She had responsibilities that she couldn't duck out of on a whim.

"What about me?" Thea asked. "What will happen to me if you get married?"

"Well . . ." He didn't seem to have an answer. "I don't know. Who can say? By then, Zoe may be old enough to get married herself."

Torn, she dropped her head back and gazed sightlessly at the porch ceiling. "I don't know." Thea weighed the pleasure of being part of Zoe's life against the pain of another separation.

Thea considered her future. One of these days she would own a great deal of land herself. Her Aunt Odessa and Uncle Adler's land would be divided between her and Maryruth. And a share of her father's property was hers, as well. Her half sisters, not wishing to live out here, would sell her their shares. She'd be a landowner in her own right. She had her own life.

A lonely landowner. A lonely life, her heart intoned silently. She was securing her future with property, not people.

"My father depends on me," she said at last. Did he think she had nothing to do all day long?

"Zoe depends on you, too," he said.

She shot her attention back to his face.

"She needs you to be a mother to her."

His words effectively cut through her objections. Mentally, Thea scrambled to reconstruct her defenses. Was he playing fair? Could he see motherhood was something she'd always wanted? Even knowing how much she could be hurt in the process, Thea wanted to jump at the chance to be Zoe's mother.

"She hasn't eaten for three days," Booker said, playing his trump. "I don't know what to do."

Three days! An ache seized her heart for the little girl who was too miserable even to eat. She searched Hayes's eyes, black in the darkness.

He'd seemed so confident, so sure he knew what he was doing the first time she'd met him. This glimpse of vulnerability was almost harder to deal with. In all fairness, it had taken considerable strength of character for him to come to her after all that had gone before.

Her posture relaxed. A cricket chirped from the end of the porch. He deserved credit for his honesty, too. "Give me your word that if you get married, neither you nor your wife will keep me from Zoe."

"You have my word." He stood, the moon a halo behind his head and shoulders. "Just to be fair, I should point out that I'm getting the best end of this deal."

What kind of man was this? What was she letting herself in for now? "Perhaps that's a matter of opinion."

"What will your father say?"

She smiled. "A lot, but it will end with 'Thea-girl, I hope you know what you're getting yourself into. But you do what you have to.'"

"I like your father."

The man *was* a good judge of people. "So do I."

"Can you come in the morning?"

"I'll talk it over with him tonight."

He stepped back. "You won't be sorry."

Oh, yes, I will. I'll be sorrier than you'll ever know. But I'll do it, anyway. She watched him walk to his horse with a broad-shouldered, lean-hipped gait. He took his hat from

the saddle horn and settled it on his head, touching the brim
in a parting salute. "Miss."

The enormous beast carried him into the night.

*Be careful, Thea. There's more at stake here than you can
afford to gamble with.* Oh, no. She wouldn't let him get to
her. She'd learned her lesson well. But she couldn't turn
aside this opportunity to be with Zoe. She'd just have to be
careful.

Chapter Five

"Thca-girl," her father said the next morning, "I hope you know what you're gettin' yourself into. But you do what you have to."

Thea hugged him soundly and gathered her packed basket and hat.

"Madeline will help with dinner today," her father said. "I'll see if Maryruth can come at suppertime. Denzel eats here, anyhow."

Thea faltered at the doorway, imagining Madeline preparing the noon meal. "I left bread for today. Tell Madeline we'll make more tonight."

Her father pushed her onto the sunny porch. "Go."

"This feels so strange, Papa."

He gave her a wry grin. "You have to live your own life, Thea. We'll get by for a while."

The dew had already burned off the grass. She strode across it and waved from atop the rust brown mare he'd saddled for her. He was right. If she'd married when other women did, she'd have been gone ten years ago.

The day was pleasant, a lazy, sun-warmed morning. Grasshoppers sprung out of the dry weeds in front of the mare. Thea enjoyed the ride, something she never took time to do simply for pleasure.

She'd never seen the soddy the Wynns had lived in, but she'd ridden the property line often and immediately recognized the unplanted bean field that signaled the place was just to the west. The primitive homestead struck her with a twinge of nostalgia. While her mother was alive, she, Maryruth and their father had lived similarly.

Mr. Hayes's ebony stallion cropped grass nearby. He nodded and flicked an ear in interest as she passed. "Hello!" she called out to the soddy. "Hello?"

Mr. Hayes ducked beneath the doorframe. "You came," he said, and reached for the bridle.

Thea swung her leg over the horse's rump and alighted, smoothing her riding skirt. She watched his gaze flick over her wide-brimmed hat. "I'm here."

"How long can you stay?"

His top shirt buttons were undone, and her gaze faltered over softly curling black hair. She'd never been distracted by a man's chest before. Startled at herself, she immediately brought her attention back to his face. "All day. Until after supper, anyway. I'll ride back before dark."

Relief passed over his tired features. "I'll unsaddle her, then. Go on." He nodded. "Zoe's inside."

Thea stepped through the open doorway. Her eyes adjusted to the semidarkness, and she scanned the tidy room, finding Zoe on a cot against the wall. Tossing her hat on the table, she flew to the narrow bed. "Hey, darlin'. Look who's come to see you."

Zoe turned her head at the sound of her voice.

Thea sat beside her and touched her face. "Hi."

The expression that washed over her cherubic face caught at Thea's heartstrings. Her tiny chin quivered, and she threw herself into Thea's arms. Thea folded Zoe against her breast and pressed her face into her hair.

They sat that way a long time, Thea rocking her in a soothing rhythm. "I've missed you," she said at last.

Zoe pulled back, and her blue gaze pored over Thea's face and hair.

"Your uncle says I can see you whenever I want from now on." She tried to thread her fingers through the hair at Zoe's temple. "That means I'll be here every day. Would you like that?"

Zoe nodded.

"Me, too. First thing we'd better do is get a brush through your hair. My goodness!"

"She hasn't let me brush it for a couple of days."

They both turned toward the door at the sound of Mr. Hayes's voice. He took a few steps into the room, his face carefully devoid of expression. "Looks like you two will be all right if I leave now."

Thea glanced around the room, almost embarrassed. Zoe's obvious preference could easily become a sore spot with the man. "I think so."

"You'll find the supplies. There's a barrel of salt pork in the corner. Firewood and cobs behind the lean-to."

She stood, and Zoe clung to her skirt. "Will you be here at noon?"

He shifted his weight. "Look, Miss Coulson—"

"You may as well call me Thea."

"All right. Thea. I don't expect you to cater to my needs. Just hers." He indicated his niece with a nod.

"Her needs and yours are quite similar at dinnertime, Mr. Hayes. I'll be cooking. You might as well eat."

He seemed to absorb that thought. "Okay. My hired hand will be here, too." He headed for the door and turned back at the last minute. "And it's Booker."

He stooped under the doorway and was gone.

Booker. She couldn't help herself. She gave the room a curious once-over, studied his jacket on a wall peg, and noticed a dusty pair of boots beside the door. A cot like Zoe's lay along the opposite wall, but her attention focused on the iron bed on the back wall. Booker. A thousand tiny moth wings fluttered in her belly. Increasing intimacy with this man did not reflect her decision to be careful.

She spent the better part of an hour brushing and washing Zoe's hair. They sat in the sun to dry it, perched on stools she brought from the soddy.

She took inventory of the food and decided to bake bread before the day grew any hotter. Inside the soddy it was surprisingly comfortable, even though the Nebraska sun beat down mercilessly. Thea peeled and sliced an apple and sat Zoe at the table. To her immense relief, the little girl nibbled on the fruit as Thea worked.

"I'm going to get some wood for the stove." She headed for the door. Zoe hopped down and followed.

Talking to Zoe while rounding the corner of the lean-to, Thea ran smack into a rock-solid, naked chest. Muscled copper arms reached for her. With a shriek, she threw her hands up and fell back, knocking Zoe to the ground with her. They fell in a tangled heap in the dirt. The stranger leaned over her, a hank of straight black hair falling over his shoulder. The curved yellow tooth dangling from a rawhide thong around his neck swung within an inch of her nose.

Thea's heart hammered wildly in her chest. Shielding Zoe with her body, she gaped up at the craggy-faced Indian.

"Sorry, ma'am. I thought you saw me there," he said in perfect English. "You all right?"

Thea scrambled to her feet, righted Zoe and brushed both their skirts off. "Yes. We're fine. I didn't know anyone was out here."

"The major's been expecting me." He offered his hand for her to shake. "Red Horse."

Considering his good manners, the open vest only partially covering his hairless, bronze chest could have been a business suit. She took his hand. "Pleased to meet you, Mr.—Red Horse. I'm Thea Coulson, and this is Zoe Galloway."

The Indian knelt and peered into Zoe's face. "The major's niece," he clarified.

Zoe plastered herself to Thea's leg, keeping the Indian under close observation.

"I have a gift for you." The stranger opened a drawstring pouch at his waist and removed a handcrafted piece of jewelry.

To Thea's surprise, Zoe leaned forward and allowed him to slip the beaded necklace over her head. She inspected it at close range on her chest, then glanced back up.

He stood. "Where is the major?"

"Mr. Hayes is working on his house. It's about a quarter mile northwest."

Red Horse raised one hand and loped to a pinto waiting behind the lean-to. Thea shook her head and watched him ride off. *Major* Hayes?

The sun was high in the sky when Booker returned with his friend. They washed at the basin outside before stepping into the comparatively cool soddy. His mouth watered at the aroma of freshly baked bread. Moving a pile of clothing from an extra bench, he brought it to the table. "I guess you met Red Horse."

Thea bustled between the stove and table, placing sliced bread and bowls of steaming stew in front of them. "Yes. We met." Her self-conscious gaze skittered to Red Horse's face and away. "Are you the hired hand Mr. Hayes mentioned?"

"No," Booker answered for him and glanced toward the open door. "I don't know what happened to that boy. He was beside us one minute and gone the next." Lucas had been enthralled with Red Horse, dogging his heels all morning. Booker couldn't imagine where he'd suddenly taken off to.

"I was an army scout," Red Horse supplied. "Took my leave same time the major did."

Across the table, Zoe's attention never left Thea. She ignored the food on her plate until Thea sat beside her and placed a napkin in her lap. Following the woman's example, Zoe unfolded her napkin, draped it across her knees and picked up her spoon. With complacency, she scooped up a carrot and chewed.

The sight set Booker's mind at ease in one respect; she was eating. On the other hand, Thea's ability to accomplish in one morning what he'd tried to do for three days nettled him. He chewed a bite of warm, buttered bread and reconciled himself to let well enough alone. She'd done what he'd asked her here to do.

"I'll pack a lunch for the hand," she offered.

He regarded her striking strawberry blond hair and the easygoing smile that curved her generous lips, and glimpsed a streak of flour on her neck when she turned to butter Zoe's bread.

Rest satisfied, Hayes. Winning Zoe over was going to take some time. And after all, he had plenty of it. For the first time he could remember, he wasn't going anywhere.

The hired hand didn't show for supper, either. Thea covered a plate of food with a napkin and left it on the table. She wiped her hands on a dish towel, noted the growing pile of laundry with a sigh and gathered her basket and hat.

Immediately, Zoe grasped her hand. Thea glanced down at her worried face and knelt. "I'll be back in the morning, Zoe," she promised, taking her shoulders gently. "I have to go home to sleep, but I'll come back first thing tomorrow. Honest. Probably as soon as you're awake. You get up and wash and dress, and I'll be here, okay?"

Zoe didn't look appeased. Thea glanced at Mr. Hayes, waiting by the door. "I'll ride with you," he said.

"But, Zoe..." she objected.

"Red Horse will be here."

"She doesn't know the man," Thea said gently, knowing the Indian waited just outside.

"She already likes him better than she does me."

Unfortunately, she couldn't argue with that, though the idea of Zoe being here with a stranger didn't set easily.

"I would trust my own life to Red Horse," Mr. Hayes assured her. "Have, in fact."

She hugged Zoe.

Tears welled in the child's eyes.

Thea hurried out the door.

"Good evening," Red Horse said, handing both horses' reins to Mr. Hayes. "You cooked a fine meal."

She nodded her thanks, and he stepped silently into the soddy.

Zoe still on her mind, Thea's brain didn't register how close Mr. Hayes stood or his intention. Raising her foot to the stirrup, she pulled herself into her saddle in one fluid motion. She glanced down.

Mr. Hayes took a step back, almost seeming embarrassed. Averting his face, he handed her the reins.

She accepted them, a realization dawning. Warmth crept up her neck into her cheeks. He'd been waiting to assist her! He was no doubt accustomed to delicate, feminine ladies who required his aid in mounting. She settled her hat and nudged the mare forward.

He mounted and rode alongside her. "You're angry I came with you?"

"I'm not angry. I just think Zoe needs you more than I do."

"I can't let you ride home alone, Thea. Red Horse will protect her."

"Protection isn't the issue." The mare stepped across a stone, and she rocked with the motion. "She's lost everyone she loved. Don't you understand she's afraid?"

"I understand better than you give me credit for. But I've been in the army too long to minimize the importance of safety."

She looked him square in the eye. "Surely by now, you've noticed I'm no hothouse flower."

"Are you armed?" He studied her from beneath the brim of his black hat. Beyond his shoulders, a streak of tangerine marred the otherwise perfectly blue sky.

She shook her head. "No."

"Even I would be vulnerable without a weapon," he reasoned. "If you want to ride alone, bring that gun you keep in your bureau."

Sheepishly, she turned her attention to the landscape ahead. Several moments of silence passed. "I need to go into Omaha for supplies within the next day or so," she said, hoping to change the subject. "Do you object to me taking Zoe along?"

"I'd feel better if I went along."

"What are you afraid I'll do, run off with her?"

"No." He leaned forward and grasped the mare's bridle, stopping her alongside his stallion. "Your safety concerns me."

Her gaze flicked over his dark features. "Hostile Indians are few and far between these days. But I'll take the gun."

He tilted his chin in thought. "Doesn't have to be a hostile Indian, Thea. You're an attractive woman. Anything could happen."

She widened her eyes in surprise.

"I'll think about it." He released her horse and rode beside her to within eyesight of the Coulson house, then touched his hat brim. "See you in the morning."

An attractive woman? The entire time she helped Maryruth with the supper dishes, Thea couldn't stop thinking about those words. She kissed David, waved her sister and Denzel off, and showed Madeline how to knead bread dough. While the dough rose, she started the ironing. By the time the bread was out of the oven and the last shirt had been pressed, everyone else had long been asleep and the house was dark and silent.

Thea lit the lantern in her room and sponged her body with warm water she'd carried from the stove. Dressed in a fresh gown, she blew out the lantern and slipped between the sheets. Her body ached, and each limb felt as though it weighed more than her horse. She wondered if Booker'd had trouble getting Zoe to sleep.

Booker. It was going to take all her strength and willpower to keep her mind on her tasks when he was around. She noticed things about Booker Hayes that she'd never noticed in a man before. She'd responded immediately to that glimpse of ebony hair at his shirt opening. She almost felt feminine when his dark eyes touched her face, her hair.

She didn't know where to look when confronted with the broad expanse of muscle that flexed just beneath the thin fabric of his shirt. His strong, dark hands elicited images she wasn't prepared to deal with. The fluid manner in which he walked and rode . . . his voice . . .

Tired as she was, Thea's body quickened with poignant sensitivity. She rolled to her stomach and stifled a groan in her pillow. No. She hadn't allowed prurient thoughts to torment her since she'd given up hope for marriage. To indulge herself was to open up to self-pity and frustration, and she wouldn't fall into that destructive pit again.

She was stronger than that, she told herself. Booker Hayes would not make her unhappy with herself or her life. She wouldn't let him.

Her conscious decision an internal battle, Thea drifted into exhausted slumber. But Booker Hayes wasn't easily banned from her dreamworld, either. Phantom images of his body, his mouth, his hands, touched her vulnerable senses. She slept on a threshold of sensation and awoke impatient. It seemed as if the sheets were draped across her raw nerves. Her hair and skin were damp with perspiration.

Thea stared at herself in her pedestal mirror. The carnal dreams she'd tucked away years ago had returned with a vengeance. The details were still hazy—she had only a maiden's idea of the marriage act. The resulting hypersensitivity was sadistically familiar. But something was different—far, far different. In the past, the man she'd dreamed of had been a blur of features and feelings, a faceless, harmless nonentity. This time her fantasy lover had a face—dark-eyed and severely handsome. A body—hardmuscled and tall as an oak. And a name—Major Booker Hayes.

Booker stretched his sore muscles and studied the noon sky overhead. "Miss Coulson left us a cold dinner. What do you say we wash up and eat?"

Beside him, Lucas set down a bucket of nails and nodded.

"You go on," Booker said. "Red Horse and I will set this last beam and be along shortly."

"You want I should take the horse?" Lucas asked.

The boy's question brought an amused slant to Booker's mouth. He didn't know where the kid had been his whole life, but he took to everyday things with a refreshing eagerness. Lucas had been tongue-tied over the horse Booker had bought for his use. He'd looked it up and down, walked around it and finally said to Booker, "I can't ride it."

"Why not?" Booker'd asked.

"I ain't never rode a horse before."

Booker accepted that fact like he did every other curiosity concerning the youth. "Then you'll learn."

He'd taken time from the construction the past few mornings to instruct Lucas on saddling, riding and caring for the animal. "He's yours while you work for me," Booker explained. "Ride him whenever you want. Just as long as you remember everything we went over about caring for him."

"I will!" Lucas ran toward the horses corralled a short distance from the new house. Minutes later, hoofbeats faded into the distance.

Booker and Red Horse finished nailing the last board on the two-story framework, then stood back and admired it. The house was ready for a roof.

He called a parting to Ezra and they headed for the soddy, pausing at the creek for the horses to drink their fill. Red Horse staked the animals in the shade while Booker ducked around the lean-to.

Splashing water led him to Lucas, stripped to the waist, washing in the dented metal basin. The white skin of his upper body was a stark contrast to his tanned arms and neck. His ribs were still visible, even though Booker knew he'd gained considerable weight since he'd been there.

Oblivious to Booker's approach, Lucas splashed water on his chest and dunked his head in the basin.

Booker stopped dead in his tracks. Lucas's scrawny back was a mass of scars, some white with age, many pink and recent. They crisscrossed his spine and extended around his side, a blatant testimony to barbarity.

Anger loomed red in Booker's vision. "Who the hell did that to you?"

Lucas jumped and turned toward him, grabbing his shirt with a ripping sound as it caught on the nail on the side of the lean-to. He pulled it on hastily, without bothering to dry off.

"I asked who did that to you!" Booker nearly shouted, his voice louder and harsher than he'd intended.

Lucas seemed to cringe inwardly. He took the towel and dried his face and hair. "Just forget it."

He tried to move past Booker, but was stopped by the massive body stepping in front of him. "How did you get those marks on your back, Lucas?"

"I thought people out West didn't owe no explanations!" Lucas nearly shouted back. "It ain't none o' your business. I earn my keep like you said."

Fuming with anger, Booker tried to calm himself. If he pushed too hard, Lucas would run. And for some reason he couldn't explain to himself, he wanted the boy to stay. The thought of someone coldheartedly beating him made Booker's blood boil. Many of those scars were so faded— he couldn't have been more than a child!

No wonder Lucas had never taken his shirt off, regardless of the heat. No wonder he'd flinched whenever Booker had touched him. Some of those marks must have been fresh when Booker'd first discovered Lucas in the soddy. He'd run away from someone bloodthirsty, someone cruel. And Booker couldn't blame him one bit.

"All right." He raised his palms. "You don't owe me an explanation." He stepped aside. "But someday... if you ever trust that I'm your friend... I'd like to know."

Unfathomable pain and mistrust were locked behind the gray gaze that bore into his. "I don't have no friends."

Booker forced himself to stand silent and still as Lucas moved past him. "I'm sure you haven't had a friend," he said after Lucas was gone. "Until now."

"Let's not leave her the dishes," Booker suggested as the three of them finished eating. The creaking wagon pulling near the soddy interrupted their hasty cleanup.

At the sound, Lucas's head shot up, and he half rose from his seat like a bird ready for flight. Lucas had been silent throughout the meal, but at least he'd eaten with them, which was more than Booker'd been able to get him to do for the past couple of days. Booker eyed him curiously on his way out the door.

He approached the wagon. "No problems?"

"None." She smiled.

He moved to assist Thea, then, remembering the ease with which she'd mounted the mare the day before, changed his mind and hung back.

She climbed down and moved away, purposefully. In the wagon Zoe stood waiting. Thea merely smiled at him.

He took the hint and held his hands out to Zoe. She started to balk, but Thea stepped to the back of the wagon. The six-year-old gave him a sidelong glance that said she knew she'd been bested, and allowed him to lift her down. "Welcome home," he said in her ear as he placed her on the ground. "I missed you."

She ran to Thea's side. Booker strode back and dropped the wooden gate. Immediately, Thea climbed into the wagon bed and sorted through parcels and crates. "I got everything on your list except the glass. They'll cut it and have it ready in a day or two."

Booker nodded. "What's all that?"

She glanced at the paper-wrapped packages he waved toward. "Fabrics. Sewing supplies. I was wondering..."

He glanced up into her flushed face. "What?"

"What have you planned for the house? You know, for curtains, coverlets, rugs, things like that?"

"I found Julia's—my sister's things and paid storage to get them. Some of them were our mother's. I don't know what all is there, actually."

"Where are they now?"

"Locked in a railcar in Omaha."

She dragged a stack of packages to the back of the wagon. "That must be costing you dearly."

He lowered the pile to the ground. "Actually, Amos McAlistair owed me a favor, so it's not costing me anything."

Straightening, she fixed her blue-green gaze on him. As she stood, her hat fell back, offering her bright red-gold hair to the sun. "Amos McAlistair owed *you* a favor?" she asked, obviously recognizing the name of one of the railroad's major shareholders.

"Yeah, well, my regiment saved a shipment of his gold from being stolen."

A movement in the doorway snagged her attention. Lucas peered from the soddy, made a stumbling attempt to bolt from the house, then stopped paralyzed in his tracks, frozen beneath her gaze like a rabbit trying to blend with the scenery.

Thea's chin dropped. *Lucas!* What on earth was he doing here? The unholy dread on his young face sent a shaft of alarm to her own heart. Apprehensively, she glanced from Lucas to Booker. "Booker?" she asked.

At her use of his name, his black eyebrows rose a fraction. He turned toward the youngster. "Oh, you haven't met Lucas yet. Come meet Miss Coulson."

As though she were a terror-breathing wild animal, Lucas forced one foot in front of the other until he stood behind the wagon.

"Thea, this is my hired hand, Lucas. Lucas, Miss Coulson's the one to thank for the meals."

Thea absorbed the situation. For some reason, Booker didn't know she'd met Lucas before. That's why Lucas was scared stiff of her reaction. Thea recalled Mrs. Vaughn's report of Lucas, his history of being a runaway, and made a quick deduction: he'd run away again.

She bent to one knee in the wagon bed, offering her hand. "Lucas."

He jerked toward her, took her hand and stared into her eyes, his own a steel gray shade of dread. "M-Miss C-Coulson," he stammered. "Thanks for the food."

"You're most welcome." She released his hand. "I must admit I was curious as to why you didn't come into meals with the other men. I thought maybe you didn't like my cooking."

His face flattened. "Oh, no, miss! I ain't never ate such good food. Well—once maybe."

She watched his ears turn pink and his cheeks blotch with embarrassment, and she couldn't hide a grin. "What's your favorite food, Lucas?"

He swallowed and his Adam's apple bobbed on his skinny throat. He shrugged.

She pinned him beneath her relentless gaze.

"Apple pie!" he blurted as though she held him at gunpoint.

She'd teased him enough. Thea laughed out loud. "I know where there are some fine apple trees, Lucas. Can you peel apples?"

"Yes, miss."

Thea turned her smile from Lucas to Booker. "How about you? Are you partial to apple pie?"

Booker glanced down at Zoe. She regarded him with a solemn blue gaze, obviously no help to his confusion. He turned to Thea with a raised brow. "Have I missed something important in this conversation?"

She laughed again. "Well, since you're here, you may as well unload this wagon for me. Zoe and I need a bite to eat."

Booker moved directly beneath her. She had no choice but to consent to his assistance. Hesitantly, she placed her hands on his wide shoulders. Beneath the shirt, he was warm and solid. His hands spanned her waist, and she couldn't help the peek she shot at his long thumbs pointing at the middle of her belly. The image evoked a memory, the vision flashing in her mind like a streak of lightning.

She forced herself to look back at his face. The previous night's dreams came back to her in all their erotic glory. Her dream lover's face blended with the flesh-and-blood man, resurrecting a shameful warmth that slithered through her veins. Warm, dark skin... silky hair... the heat of his lips on her fevered flesh...

Oh, Lord, she had to gain control of these lustful thoughts. If he had any inkling of what she was thinking, she'd die of mortification. She had to behave normally.

She hopped, and he caught her weight, the muscles in his shoulders bunching beneath her fingertips. Gently, he stood her on the ground. If she didn't know better, she'd think her weight hadn't been an effort to maintain. His expression hadn't wavered. He hadn't grunted or popped a blood vessel anywhere she could see.

Her hands remained on his shoulders a little too long; his touch lingered at her waist even longer. She stepped back, and the warm impression of his fingers remained, her pulse throbbing at an exquisite level of susceptibility.

The man was dangerous to her well-being. She hoped she covered her supersensitivity to him as well as he hid the burden of her size and weight.

"I'll bet you're a good poker player," she said softly, then took Zoe's hand and walked toward the sod house. He'd have a good laugh if he knew what she'd been imagining. She had to be more careful. Her sanity depended on it,

Chapter Six

Booker and Red Horse took the wagon to the new house, leaving Lucas with instructions to help Thea with the soddy's share of supplies. From the yard, Lucas watched the wagon rumble away, his stance like that of a deer listening for a fox. Thea pounced on the opportunity to catch him alone.

"Nice to see you again, Lucas," she said, and strolled across the yard.

He pivoted at the sound of her voice, but said nothing, just stared at her with eyes as big and gray as storm clouds.

"I'm mighty curious as to what you're doing here," she admitted.

He looked away and kicked the dirt with the toe of his boot. "You didn't tell him."

"Tell him what?"

His gaze shot back to her face. "You know."

"No, I don't know, but I sure would like to."

He looked away again.

"Did you run away?"

He shrugged.

"You know the agency will find out sooner or later."

"You gonna tell Hayes?"

Her voice softened. "You should do that."

"He don't have t' know."

"Lucas, he's probably breaking some law or another by keeping you here."

"Yeah, well, if you tell 'im, I'll just run off somewheres else."

"I'm not going to tell him."

His stance relaxed. "Thanks," he mumbled.

"You tell him when you think it's right."

He watched her walk back toward the house, her angel's hair shot with rays of the afternoon sun. She'd let him off the hook.

He'd never had it so good. He ate three meals a day, slept in a clean bed, and so far nobody'd lifted a finger to him or the girl.

He'd hidden his pay under the cot's thin mattress. His first money. Just knowing it was there gave him a sense of freedom he'd never known. He could buy something. Something that belonged only to him. Something nobody else had outgrown or cast off or gotten tired of. A few more weeks and he could buy ship's passage to someplace where nobody cared about orphanages or foster homes or indenture papers. Somewhere free.

He could trust the church lady. She'd said she wouldn't tell Hayes. Angels didn't lie.

Thea kept her word. She didn't tell Mr. Hayes. Day after day, she cooked and laundered and cared for Zoe. Night after night, she baked, ironed and kept her father's household running before dropping into fitful, dream-filled slumber. The hard work and long hours took their toll.

Early one afternoon, intending to lie beside Zoe for only a few minutes while the child napped, Thea fell into exhausted sleep. Much later, sensing someone's presence, she opened her eyes.

Booker stood beside the cot. She started to sit up, but he stopped her with a raised palm. "No," he said softly. "Rest."

Her eyes followed his hand as it traveled to Zoe's head, smoothed her glossy curls and drew one finger across the sleeping child's cheek and lips. "She looks so much like Julia," he whispered.

Thea heard his sorrow and knew how much it would hurt to lose a sister. "She must have been beautiful," she replied.

"Yes. Yes, she was. She was fair like Zoe . . . and delicate." He drew his hand away, and his dark gaze came back to her. "The house is almost finished. After everything's moved in, you deserve a few days of rest."

An apprehensive flutter rose in her breast. "That's not necessary."

"I think it is. You're exhausted."

"But—Zoe . . ."

"I can take care of her for a few days. Wouldn't you like to take some time for yourself? Go shopping or something?"

"I can do my shopping in an hour in town."

"How about a trip to St. Louis? Did I hear you say you have a sister there?"

Thea'd taken her share of trips to St. Louis, thank you very much. Originally, Trudy and Thea's half sisters had done their best to try to make her one of them. They'd clucked over her hair and her coloring and tried to teach her feminine wiles to appeal to a man. Most of their advice had begun with "a girl of your size," until Thea had wanted to disappear.

And in a sense, she had. She'd chosen dark colors so as not to draw attention to herself. She rolled her unruly hair back into a love knot. Being inconspicuous was easy when she devoted herself to caring for others. St. Louis held no attraction for an ungainly woman such as herself. "I have no need to go to St. Louis."

"You spend all your energy on Zoe, on this place and your family. What about you?"

"That's my life. I'm satisfied with it."

He shrugged. "All right. But I will see to it that you get some rest."

Thea watched him leave the soddy, another ounce of unease added to the growing weight in her chest. She was happy with things the way they were. Why wasn't he?

* * *

"Oh, Zoe, isn't it beautiful?" Holding Zoe's hand, Thea stepped into the small foyer. The smell of fresh wood and varnish lent an expectant atmosphere. A polished oak banister drew her attention to the stairway, and she ran a hand over the smooth wood. "It looks so different than the last time, doesn't it?"

Their feet echoed on the smooth hardwood floors. Plastered walls and tall windows gave the house an open, airy, solid feel. To the right of the foyer, a carpeted den with a wall of shelves awaited books and furniture. An enormous stone fireplace dominated one entire wall, and immediately, Zoe perched on the low hearth. Winter nights in front of a cozy fire sprang into Thea's imagination.

The room to the left of the foyer could not be called a parlor. It was too big, too comfortable, too—Thea smiled—masculine. Thea circled the spacious, well-lit kitchen, running her palm over the excessive work space, the new wood-burning stove with a reservoir for water, and the smooth varnished cupboards.

Again today, as it had more and more often, the question occurred to Thea: how could he afford all this?

Zoe ran ahead of her up the stairs where five bedrooms boasted walk-in storage closets. A set of eastern windows dominated the largest room, offering a magnificent view. Thea stood before the glass panes. This would be Booker's room. He would watch the sun rise from this spot, and could easily see his mill once it was built. From here he could keep an eye on his property and his investments, and hear the train as it approached the stream trestle.

As if in reply to her thoughts, the train's whistle pierced the afternoon stillness. Below, Booker and Red Horse each led a springboard in the direction of the tracks. "They're going to get the furniture from the railcar, Zoe."

Thea turned back to the room. Zoe sat on the floor, staring at the acorn in her palm. The practice had begun to worry Thea. "Whatever *are* you doing, darling?" she asked, and knelt beside the little girl.

Zoe looked up at her with puzzled blue eyes.

"I wish you could talk to me."

Zoe raised her palm.

Thea nodded with a sigh. "Yes. It's an acorn."

Zoe curled her fingers and tucked the acorn back into her pocket.

Standing, Thea held out her hand. "Let's put the food away. We'll be eating supper here. And you'll be sleeping here tonight."

Alarm crossed Zoe's features. She scrambled to her feet and grabbed Thea's hand.

"Just like always," Thea assured her. "Just like at the soddy. This is just a bigger house. You'll go to bed, and in the morning I'll be back."

Zoe's mute face plainly stated they would have a problem on their hands come evening.

After several trips back and forth from the railcar, the men had what furniture there was moved in. They stacked crates and barrels in the "parlor," to be sorted through as time permitted. Nothing was labeled, and by evening, most parcels had been opened just to find a few needed items, creating a state of havoc. Giving up on finding anything that night, Thea used the dishes and pans from the soddy.

As she'd suspected, Zoe balked at bedtime. Thea had stayed well past her usual time. It was nearly dark when she finished bathing and dressing Zoe.

"Ready for bed, pumpkin?" Booker asked from the kitchen doorway.

Zoe slid off the stool beside Lucas where they'd been sipping hot cocoa, and limped barefoot to Thea's side.

"Come on, love," Thea coaxed. "Let your uncle take you to bed."

Zoe shook her head and clung to Thea's skirt.

Booker tucked his fingers in his back pockets. "How about we take you together?"

Thea set down the skillet she'd been scrubbing and dried her hands on a towel. Giving Lucas a wink, she and Zoe followed Booker up the stairs. He led them down the hall.

"This is the room I offered Red Horse. I've never seen him sleep indoors, so I don't know if he'll use it." The next room he pointed out as Lucas's. With a sweep of his arm, he gestured them through the open doorway closest to his room. Thea stepped in. She'd been so busy preparing and cleaning up supper amid the chaos that she hadn't realized what Booker had spent his time doing.

Inside the room, a single-sized bed with simple mahogany head and footboards stood to the left. Beside it, the toys Thea had made for Zoe lined a small bookshelf. Across the room sat a matching chest of drawers. Above the chest on the wall hung an oval-framed daguerreotype of a young couple.

Thea watched Zoe's face. Zoe studied the bed and toys, then gazed upon the framed likeness Thea knew must be the child's parents. Recognition flared in her expression and, before Thea's eyes, she seemed to relax. She glanced up, and Thea had to blink back tears and force a smile.

Booker sat on the edge of the bed. "There are more things, Zoe. Handkerchiefs, photographs. You can have whatever you'd like. I'll keep the jewelry for you until you're older."

"Is this her own bed?" Thea asked through the thick tears in her throat.

Booker nodded. "I didn't know which spread was hers, so I guessed."

Thea studied the pastel quilt, its fabric pieces of rosebuds and pink checks forming delicate fans. "Looks like a pretty good guess."

Zoe limped to the bed and laid her tiny hand on the quilt. She peered up at her uncle through golden lashes. Then, hesitantly, like she'd bolt if he made the slightest move, she reached up and placed her palm against his cheek, darkened with the evening shadow Thea'd come to expect.

The gaze he cast on the child was nothing short of adoration. The only muscle that moved was one in his jaw.

Thea swallowed tears.

What seemed like an eternity later, Zoe pulled her hand away, selected her doll from the shelf and waited expectantly beside the bed.

Thea came to life and pulled back the quilt. Zoe climbed into the bed and snuggled against the sheets. "Good night, darlin'," Thea whispered, and kissed Zoe's forehead.

Booker blew out the lantern on the wall inside the door, and together they stepped into the hallway.

The temptation to turn and peer back into the room was too great to resist. Visible in the dim light from the lantern on the hallway wall, Zoe's fingers caressed the doll's dress. She snuggled her chin against her chest, and moments later, her fingers stilled.

She was so little, so young and impressionable, and she'd been through so much. Her pleasure over her own possessions had been obvious. Zoe's anxiety had diminished as soon as she'd seen the room. Inspired by his obvious love, Booker had discovered a way to comfort her.

Appreciation glowed inside Thea.

She turned to find Booker's chin inches from her face. His warm gaze fell to her smile. Suddenly, their shared love for the child seemed a rare intimacy. The lantern light clearly defined Booker's straight nose and lean jaw. Thea remembered Zoe's tiny hand against his skin, and her own palm itched to see exactly what that evening stubble felt like.

She remembered, too, how hard and impassive she'd thought his face the first time she'd seen it. But she'd witnessed warmth and obvious love soften those same features. The more she glimpsed of the real man inside the granite facade, the more she had to guard her own emotions.

Self-consciously, he took a step back and cleared his throat. "It's late. I'll get the horses."

Realizing they'd been standing outside Zoe's room like doting parents, Thea turned away. "I'll dry the last pans and get my things."

She met him in front of the house. The moon, a friendly presence, cast dappled shadows. She mounted the mare and nudged her forward. Booker fell in beside her. They rode in silence for several minutes.

"Zoe's a lucky little girl," she said at last.

He adjusted his hat's brim. "To lose her parents and get thrown into that god-awful place?"

"No." She observed hundreds of fireflies turning a bean field into a reflection of the heavens. "To have you to care about her. All of the children in the orphanages lost their parents, but none of them have someone to make their life better—to care what happens to them, and see that they're happy and loved . . . like you do for Zoe."

"And you," he said after a moment.

A soft breeze ruffled the loose hair on her neck.

"Maybe she'll feel safer now that she has her own things," he said, and she felt his hope.

"I'm sure of it," Thea replied. "She thanked you, you know. When she touched you."

He only cleared his throat.

Thea smiled into the darkness. How could she have ever doubted this man's sincerity, his integrity? Everything he did, he did for Zoe. Her smile faded. Her own motivations were unscrupulous compared to his. In the first place, she'd needed Zoe to fill an empty spot in her life. Selfishness led her to agree to care for her. She didn't want to be lonely. She didn't want to be an old maid with no one of her own to care for.

Zoe would learn to love Booker, she could see that plainly now. Who wouldn't? Patiently, lovingly, he would earn her trust, embed himself in her life and in her heart. And then—though the night was sultry, a shiver of dread passed through Thea's heart—where would that leave her?

The following morning, Thea arrived earlier than usual, the familiar basket on her arm. But this time, instead of food, the basket held a gift. She placed it on the kitchen floor.

A rustling sound followed by a faint mewl caught Zoe's interest. She hobbled over and sat, her face mere inches from the basket. The sound came again, louder this time.

"Go ahead. Open it," Thea urged.

Zoe raised the wooden lid. Furry gray ears and green eyes met her amazed discovery.

Thea laughed. "She's for you. Remember the kittens under my back porch? They're big enough to leave their mama. They've been running all over our yard. I thought she'd like it here. Every house needs a mouser."

Zoe scooped the kitten into her arms with a smile. She rubbed the animal's head and touched her whiskers with one finger. She raised the kitten to her face, and a tiny pink tongue flicked out and laved her cheek.

Zoe actually laughed out loud.

Thea stared in surprise.

The little cat continued to stroke Zoe's cheek with its tongue. Zoe's giggles brought more warmth to the room than the morning sunshine. Thea laughed in pleasure at the sound.

Booker paused in the doorway and listened to their combined laughter. It wrapped around his bones and started to thaw his well-seasoned armor. Experience had convinced him he didn't need a woman in his life. His dalliances with army wives had taught him women were unfaithful. The daughters had proven females were unscrupulous. He'd quickly learned to become inured, and he'd grown too cynical to let a woman get to him.

This woman was beyond his experience. The rules she played by followed no game he was aware of. She wasn't looking for anyone to take care of her. Competent, hardworking, honest, Thea possessed qualities he'd never expected to find and admire. She was accepting, even vulnerable. And she loved Zoe.

Without being noticed, Booker basked in the unaccustomed goodness of their laughter, memorized the exact shades of their two bright heads bent together in the mellow morning sunlight—one so blond it was nearly silver like his sister's, the other, warm marmalade, like nothing he'd ever seen before—and he allowed a smile to touch his lips and his heart's core. A man could do a lot worse than a woman like Thea Coulson. Why hadn't she ever married?

Soundlessly, he turned and left through the front door.

At her father's suggestion, Thea invited Booker and Zoe for Sunday dinner. Jim thought a meal together would cut Thea's Sunday chores in half. Though she agreed, she'd hesitated to ask until Red Horse offered to take Lucas fishing for the day. She couldn't have asked Lucas, knowing he wouldn't come for fear of being recognized.

Booker accepted readily. He and Zoe met the family at church. After the service, Thea stood on the lawn, greeting friends. Agnes Birch approached, the ample bosom beneath her azure dress like that of a puffed-up hen. "Did you know Zeb Barnett is sickly, Thea? Do you think we should organize meals?"

"I think that would be nice," Thea replied, knowing what Agnes really meant was "aren't you going to do it?"

Her husband, Edgar, a thin, friendly faced gentleman, joined them and greeted Thea. "Morning, Thea. That sure is a pretty little girl you have with you."

Thea smiled and glanced down at Zoe, her pigtails only slightly off kilter. "Thank you, Mr. Birch. I think so, too."

Malvina Beck, another of the members of the mission circle, stepped beside Agnes. "Did you see that Edwards woman came to church again. Look how the menfolk crowd around her!"

"It's disgraceful," Penelope Dodd said, maneuvering herself into the group.

Thea glanced over at Lorraine Edwards, her dark hair hidden beneath a wide-brimmed straw hat. A fashionable green satin dress hugged her slender curves, the hem daintily brushing the stops of her tiny black shoes.

"Calls herself a seamstress," Agnes said with a disgusted harrumph. "But everyone knows she has men callers of an evening."

Thea turned and glanced between Agnes and her husband. Edgar gave her a shrug, like he knew enough to stay well out of the conversation.

"Thea, we're leaving," Maryruth called.

Zoe clung to Thea's skirt when Booker came for her, so her uncle acquiesced and followed the Coulsons home on his own.

Immediately, Jim, Denzel and Uncle Adler—Jim always called him "Snake"—took Booker away. From the kitchen, Thea could hear the clank of horseshoes across the dooryard. Maryruth, her aunt and Lexie helped with the food while Trudy and Madeline set an elegant dining table.

"It would have been easier—and a lot more fun—to simply set up the tables in the yard," Maryruth said in an aside.

"At least we'd get a breeze to cool us off," Odessa agreed.

Thea shrugged and cast them a "you know Trudy" look. Thea had awakened at dawn to bake pies and bread before church and to give the kitchen time to cool down. Now, with potatoes boiling on the stove, the kitchen once again filled with unbearable humidity.

Maryruth looked as hot and tired as Thea herself felt. David had begun to creep on his hands and knees, so she couldn't let him out of her sight for a second. He sat in the wooden high chair banging a spoon against the tray with an earsplitting racket. Thea caught his attention with a wide smile and traded the spoon for a pot holder.

Making one last check on the food, Thea stepped onto the back porch and rang the dinner bell. The men appeared around the corner of the barn. She waved.

"I've been lookin' forward to this," Snake Woodridge said, and slapped his brother-in-law on the back.

Jim Coulson grinned. "Nobody puts on a spread like my Thea-girl."

Bringing up the rear, Denzel agreed. In turn, Booker washed at a basin near the back door and followed the men into the house. They still wore shirts and ties from church that morning, but their sleeves were rolled to their elbows in deference to the heat. They trooped into the dining room and seated themselves.

Thea stood behind a chair next to her father's place at the head of the table. She gave Booker an encouraging smile and gestured for him to take the seat. He slid into the chair, feeling her behind him. The chair beside him remained empty. Jim Coulson said a brief prayer, and the bowls and platters were passed.

Thea sat beside him long enough to place a few things on her plate. David splattered mashed potatoes on Snake's sleeve, and she hurried to wipe it clean with a damp towel. She refilled water glasses, brought a second platter of chicken from the kitchen and filled the gravy boats.

Booker ate slowly, listening to the flurry of conversation and watching Thea inconspicuously see to everyone's needs. She hadn't taken a bite of her food. He glanced at her father.

"William Bowen has a pretty fair chance at that first-place ribbon," Jim told Denzel, and gestured with his fork. "That's the biggest sow I've ever laid eyes on."

Madeline and Odessa chattered about who they'd seen at that morning's service. Madeline cast Booker furtive glances under her dark lashes. He couldn't help wondering why she didn't get up and help Thea.

Thea's younger half sisters were classically beautiful. Madeline wore her lustrous dark hair fashioned in an up-swept coiffure and drew attention to her striking coloring with an emerald green dress. She and Lexie both had petite figures, high cheekbones, full, rose-hued lips and high foreheads.

Lexie, dressed appropriately for a young girl in a corn-flower blue dress with a demure white collar, spoon-fed the baby.

Maryruth had the same red-gold hair and fair skin as Thea, but it was hard to tell if she was younger or older than her sister.

Booker snuck a glance at Zoe seated on the other side of the empty chair. She bit off a piece of her chicken leg and glanced over at him. He winked.

She actually grinned.

Breathless, Thea slid onto the seat and picked up her fork. "Can I get you anything?"

How about a hammer so I can nail your butt to this chair? He shook his head.

"I've smelled those pies since I woke up this mornin'." Jim Coulson grinned at his daughter and pushed his plate back. "Is the coffee ready?"

Thea slid her chair out with the backs of her legs as she stood. "Apple or peach, Papa?"

Booker watched in amazement as she gathered dirty plates and headed for the kitchen. He glanced down at her plate. She'd taken one bite.

Throughout the rest of the afternoon's activities, he wondered if she had eaten after the others were through. He hoped she had. She couldn't keep up the pace she traveled at without nourishment.

They crossed paths from time to time. Glancing up from the men's banter, he spotted her walking Zoe and David toward the orchard.

Denzel plucked a long blade of grass and bit the stem. "You know, Hayes, none of us think anything of Thea's bein' at your place all the time because we know her. But there's some talk in town."

He'd arrested Booker's attention. "What kind of talk?"

"You know. It's not exactly proper for a maiden woman to be alone with a man."

"We're not alone! Zoe lives with me. So does Red Horse and another hired hand."

"An Indian, another man and a little girl aren't really chaperons." Denzel shrugged. "I'm not criticizing, I just thought maybe you should know."

Booker cut his glance to Thea's father. "Sir—"

"No need to say anything, Hayes. Like Denzel said, we're not the ones thinkin' ill of you two." Jim Coulson drew on his pipe, and a smoke wreath formed around his head, then drifted away.

"I can't let people think wrong of Thea," Booker declared. "I never realized the harm."

They fell silent as she strode across the grass with tall glasses of cold lemonade on a tray. The subject wouldn't leave Booker alone. Even though he enjoyed the friendly camaraderie and the day away from work, Denzel's revelation disturbed him.

Before the sun set, the bell rang again, and he followed the family to discover sandwich makings, pies and a pitcher of milk on the kitchen table.

After everyone had eaten again, Maryruth and Denzel took their sleeping baby and left. Odessa and Snake followed. Jim and Trudy disappeared into the house.

Perched comfortably in a chair on the wide back porch, Booker listened to Thea and her younger half sisters finish the dishes. Zoe sat on the wooden steps, two kittens, obviously siblings of her kitten's, trapped in her skirt. A calf bawled in the distance.

The screen door opened. "Want a cold drink?"

Booker frowned up at her. "If I do, I'll get one."

A line of confusion furrowed her brow.

"Sit, Thea."

"I will in a minute, but I—"

"Please, Thea. Sit here with me."

Untying her apron, she slid it off and hung it on the door handle. She sat in a chair beside him. They listened to the night sounds as darkness fell. Zoe moved to sit in the shaft of light from the doorway. One of the kittens escaped, and she let it go. Booker caught her yawn.

"Want to come sit with me, pumpkin?" he asked.

She crawled across the floor and sat between them. Occasionally, her arm brushed his pant leg. It was enough for now.

"Suppose Red Horse and Lucas ate fish tonight?" Thea asked.

"I'm sure they did," he replied.

"He probably made Lucas a pole." She smiled.

"No," he corrected her. "A spear."

She glanced toward him in surprise. "Really?"

He nodded. "Only way I've ever seen him fish. His patience is the envy of any saint. Stands like a statue in the water until the fish don't notice him. Waits for a big one, then *wham!*"

"My goodness!" Zoe's head lay in Thea's lap, and she caressed her absently.

"Is she asleep?"

"Sound."

"I should have taken her home earlier, but I wanted to talk to you."

"All right."

Booker stood. "Do you think we could lay her down and take a walk?"

She nodded in the darkness. Bending, he lifted Zoe's weight effortlessly, and followed Thea into the house. She led him into a tiny bedroom behind the kitchen, and he placed Zoe on a narrow bed.

"Let me tell Papa and Trudy she's in here."

He waited on the back steps, and minutes later the door creaked open. Two steps above, she towered over him, and he realized for the first time how tall she actually was. She descended quickly, as though she'd noticed, too.

He set a slow pace along the drive. The house and barn fell behind them. One of the dogs followed at their heels until something in the weeds caught his attention, and he ran off.

"Did you ever eat today?" he asked.

"What?"

"Did you eat today, I asked," he clarified.

"Well, sure I ate today. That's what today was all about, wasn't it?"

"I don't know. I never actually saw you take more than a bite between jumping up and waiting on everyone."

They walked on in silence for several minutes.

"This is all too much for you, Thea," he said, referring to the way her family took her for granted. The way she worked at both homes, catered to two households. He couldn't forget the sight of her napping beside Zoe days earlier.

"It's not too much for me," she denied.

"It is."

"It's not."

Lord, but she was a bullheaded woman! In frustration, he stopped and faced her. Her hair caught highlights in the moonlight the same way it did in the sun. He wondered what it would look like loosened and spread across her shoulders. What it would feel like in his hands.

Booker sighed and rubbed the back of his neck. "Well, that's not all."

"What else?"

"People are talking."

"About what?"

"About you and me."

"What about us?"

"About us—together—alone. At my house. You know, *talking* about us!"

He could have sworn a smile passed her lips.

"Let them talk." She walked on.

"Whoa, just a minute, lady," he said, catching up with her. "Let them talk! What kind of logic is that? I don't intend to 'let them talk.'"

"What harm is there?" she asked innocently.

"Thea." He stopped her with a hand on her arm. She halted, and he let go. "Think about your reputation."

To his indignant surprise, she threw her head back and laughed out loud.

"What the hell's so funny?"

Thea choked on another gale of laughter, finally drawing her face into a mask of seriousness. "Mr. Hayes, I don't have a reputation. You don't get it, do you? I'm on the shelf. Over the hill. Out to pasture. An old maid. Nobody'd think twice about Too-Tall Thea keeping time with a man!"

She shook a finger toward the town as though pointing the citizens out. "They know you wouldn't want me any more than any of those other single men ever did."

With a sigh, she cocked her head. "If anybody's reputation is in danger here, Mr. Hayes, you'd better consider that it's yours." Her wry words contrasted with the girlish tilt of her head. "If the town thinks you're involved with me, you're the one who needs vindication."

He absorbed that rush of information. He'd known all along, he guessed. An unmarried woman living with her parents was highly unusual, especially in these parts. But he couldn't imagine others not seeing her sensuality, her beauty and charm. What was wrong with them?

"Then they're fools," he replied.

"That may be, but—what did you say?"

"I said they're fools. Blind fools."

She turned her face up to his in the moonlight, and he saw her disbelief. He'd watched her with Zoe, with her family, had observed the way others took her sacrificial good nature for granted, and was astonished that anyone could overlook her femininity. Army days behind him, Booker had a great need for gentleness in his life. Thea was the embodiment of that gentleness.

He did what he'd wanted to do since he'd first met her: he pulled her into his arms and kissed her.

Chapter Seven

Booker Hayes hauled her against his solid chest and his lips closed over hers before Thea had time to register his intent. He angled his nose alongside hers, his lips surprisingly warm and insistent, and at first all she could do was wonder what in the world he was doing!

Kissing her! Was this some joke to prove the point he'd been trying to make? His hands on her upper arms radiated warmth through the thin fabric of her shirtwaist. Her breasts crushed against a chest as hard as oak. And his mouth…oh, his mouth. A kiss, she discovered, wasn't just pressing lips to lips. A kiss was molding one mouth to the shape of another's, testing its pliancy with infinite nerve endings, and experiencing an allover fusion of intent that merely centered where lips met. Thea realized she'd closed her eyes, but couldn't recall when.

His chin scraped delightfully against hers, and without conscious thought, she raised her right hand and indulged herself in the sensation she'd wondered about, placing her fingertips against his jaw and skimming them over the foreign texture.

Booker's hands released her arms, his right arm banding her waist and drawing her flush against him. His other hand splayed in the hollow of her spine.

He angled his head the opposite way, and Thea learned how natural it was to follow him, to tilt her face and meld her lips against his in an unsynchronized play of sliding, probing, increasing pressure.

Like a newborn sucking air into its lungs for the first time, Thea kissed him until her chest hurt and her eyes welled with tears. All the wonder, all the forbidden, midnight fantasies, all the questions and longings and needs she'd buried, clawed their way into the kiss and revealed with vivid, soul-torturing clarity the incredible pleasure she'd missed out on.

Booker's hand kneaded her back, slid to her waist and spanned her ribs. With heart-stopping slowness, he dragged his palm across her cotton blouse and paused with his thumb beneath her breast. Thea's pulse pounded in her ears. She delved her fingers into his hair, her other hand rising to his shoulder, and waited, realizing she wanted him to touch her.

Instead, he removed his hand, leaving an ache where heat had been, and circled her wrist with his fingers. He disengaged her other hand from his hair, too, and he took his mouth from hers, stepping back.

They stood connected only by his fingers around her wrists, staring into each other's faces, their awkward breathing audible.

"Still think there's nothing to worry about?" His breath grazed her cheek.

The inches between them seemed an embarrassing chasm. Thea noticed her breasts, abdomen and thighs, which had been pressed against him, pulsed with the heat and dampness of the humid night. "Why did you do that?" she asked.

"Why did you?"

Because I wanted to know. Because somehow I knew it would be like that with you. Because you slashed through every barrier of denial I'd constructed for myself and made me unsatisfied again. She pulled away from his easy grasp, and he let her go. She gripped both elbows and hugged her forearms against her quaking midriff, her profile turned to him. "It wasn't very funny, if that's what you intended."

"Am I laughing?"

She shot her gaze back to his face. "You never laugh."

Moonlight glinted off his blue-black hair, hair she now knew felt thick and silky-cool against her fevered palm. In the darkness, she saw the grim set to his stern jaw and knew again the distinctive rasp of his evening shadow beneath her fingertips. Intimate knowledge. Intoxicating knowledge. Knowledge that to her was definitely no joke.

"Well." Booker's shoulder rose and lowered in a slow-motion shrug. "I guess now that my reputation is ruined, you'll have to marry me."

Thea's chin dropped. Seconds passed. She closed her mouth and stared hard at the black ground. "Why are you doing this?" she whispered through her constricted throat.

"Zoe needs a mother," he replied. "You made me promise I wouldn't keep her from you if I married. What better solution than to marry me?"

Speechless, she dared slant a glance at him.

"Zoe will be happy. The townspeople won't talk. Your father won't have to come after me with a shotgun. And you'll have Zoe."

Thea couldn't sort her jumbled thoughts. He was suggesting she marry him! "Are you proposing?"

"I am. Will you marry me?"

"And what do you get out of all this?"

"I told you I was getting the best end of the deal last time. I still think so. You have to make up your mind what you want."

She placed both hands against her scorching cheeks and attempted to commandeer her senses. She'd been kissed and proposed to. *Her*. Thea Coulson! What a liberating, overwhelming night! She teetered precariously between hysterical laughter and ungovernable tears, knowing exactly what she wanted to answer.

A husband and a child of my own.

Her heart pounded erratically in her aching breast. She glanced back at the house in the distance, yellow light spilling from the parlor windows. "I'm twenty-nine years old," she said at last.

"I'm seven years older than that," he replied.

"I have a respectable dowry."

"You don't have to point your assets out to me," Booker said. "I know everything I need to know."

Everything he needed to know. How old she was. How big. The unbecoming combination of her brassy hair and pale, freckled skin. Her inexperience with courting and her lack of feminine frailties. And he would marry her, anyway.

Booker Hayes was a severely handsome man. His strong, muscled body and intense dark eyes equaled his gentlemanly manners and ambition. He was clean, hardworking, and would soon operate a profitable business.

Marrying him would mean being with Zoe permanently. She would never have a better offer.

As good as it sounded, a niggle of doubt germinated in the back of her mind. What would she really be getting herself into if she agreed? If she was honest with herself for a heartbeat, she didn't know this man from Adam.

Before her apprehension sprouted into an actual deterrent, she shriveled it with the thought of her life continuing the way it had and dropped her hands to her sides. "Mr. Hayes," she said before caution could change her mind, "I accept."

"Thea-girl, do you know what you're doin'?" Jim Coulson asked a few minutes later around the pipe between his teeth. The three of them sat in the Coulsons' parlor.

Her eyes slid to Booker's, and her fiancé had to study his thumbnail. "I do, Papa. I'm going to be Mr. Hay—Booker's wife." The words sent a little shiver of excitement through her stomach. "He needs a wife and a mother for Zoe. No one could do that as well as I."

"I know that, lamb," her father intoned. "And I know how you feel about the girl. She'd be lucky to get you for a ma." He didn't ask her how she felt about Booker Hayes. Nor did he mention that the joining of their two properties would eventually be one of the most vast holdings in the state. What he did was look Booker straight in the eye and say, "You're a damned lucky man to have Thea willin' to marry you."

Her father studied her with an unsettling mixture of sadness and acceptance. "Thea's a good companion. Never wastes herself on nerves or gettin' mad. She looks life square in the eye and accepts the hand she's dealt."

Thea realized he would miss her. Love for him welled in her heart. He was the only man she'd ever known, ever loved, ever spent time with. He'd always been proud of her and treated her with love. She reached across the space separating them and squeezed his hand.

"She takes her obligations seriously, Hayes," he continued. "There isn't a finer woman this side of the Missouri."

"I agree with you, sir. I have every intention of making a home and providing for her the best I can."

"See to it," Jim said. "And see to it she don't want for anything. *Any*thing," he punctuated by jabbing the air with his pipe stem.

"I will, sir."

"When will this wedding happen?"

Booker glanced at Thea.

She raised her brows as if to say "Me?"

"We could announce it at the housewarming," Booker suggested.

"Grand idea." Thea's father released her hand and leaned back in his chair. "Are you ready to tell the womenfolk?"

Thea imagined the fussing and squealing, and instantly thought of The Dress and all it entailed. "Let's wait, shall we, Papa? I'd rather surprise them at the housewarming."

"Won't give 'em much time to plan your wedding," he said with a raised brow.

Thea couldn't suppress a grin. "That's what I'm hoping. I can't let Trudy try to stuff me into a dress like Madeline's. I don't think there are enough seed pearls in the Western Hemisphere."

Beside her, Booker chuckled. A deep, resonant sound that struck a vulnerable chord inside Thea. She'd seen his anger and frustration, been the object of his concern a time or two, but his laughter revealed a side she wasn't prepared to deal with, the side that loved Zoe with single-minded determination. The side that she feared she could succumb to with little encouragement.

She turned and discovered the deep furrow that formed in his cheek. His smile revealed even, white teeth and did something peculiar to her stomach. "Why, Mr. Hayes, I do believe that's a smile I see on your face."

His gaze flickered over her hair, her eyes, and faltered at her mouth. "And I believe I'd better get Zoe home to her own bed."

Thea stood. "Bring your horse around. I'll carry Zoe out and lift her up to you."

He nodded at Thea, stood and shook Jim's hand.

Minutes later, he waited near the back door. Thea carried Zoe, sound asleep, to the top of the porch stairs. "Think she'll sleep through the ride home?" she asked.

"I imagine."

He made no move to mount the stallion, but stood, hat in hand. Thea waited.

"What I said in there—to your father—is the truth. I'll see to it you're taken care of."

"I have no need to be taken care of."

"Everyone needs something. What can I promise you?"

She shifted Zoe's weight against her breast and remembered being held against his hard chest. What could he promise her? That he'd kiss her again and again like he had tonight. That she'd feel the same way she did when he touched her for the rest of her life. "Just that..." She paused. "You'll smile more often."

In the moonlight, she saw his cheek crinkle.

He climbed the steps, leaned across Zoe and brushed his lips against Thea's. Lightly. Unsatisfactorily. A mere hint of the real thing he'd shown her tonight. Turning, he jumped to the ground, mounted the horse and sidled him as close to the porch as possible. Thea handed the sleeping child up into his arms.

"See you in the morning?" he asked.

"I'll be there."

She watched long after the stallion disappeared into the darkness, long after her heart refused to resume its normal cadence. It beat differently. The irises by the back porch smelled more fragrant. The stars were nearer, brighter. The night didn't seem as humid, as dark. Nothing was the same.

She was going to marry Booker Hayes.

Nothing would ever be the same again.

In the still, dark night with a warm, gentle breeze stirring the lace curtains at her window, Thea's dream lover slipped in and stole her from the room. Tall and broad-chested, with hair as black as a moonless midnight, he coaxed her from exhausted slumber into a dreamworld of heightened perception. Without words, without the least effort or suggestion from her, he knew exactly what she waited for. Though she'd never seen the darkened place he carried her to before, the surroundings were familiar and comforting.

Thea's body tingled with anticipation. The dark-haired figure placed her gently on a moss-soft bed, knelt over her and covered her lips with his, instinctively melding his overpowering heat to hers. He surrounded her with sensation, promised untold pleasure with his ravaging lips and hands. Thea returned his kisses, buried herself in his scent and his heat, and knew he was hers forever, that he loved her beyond measure.

She hadn't noticed until now that neither of them wore clothing. His heated skin conducted agony and delight through her arms and legs and breasts and she remembered how beautiful he made her feel. He'd always made her feel good. Even about herself.

His inflaming kisses spread from her lips across her shoulders to her breasts. A fine sheen of perspiration broke out on her fevered skin. He covered her with his body and she knew this was the pleasure he meant for her, pleasure only he could give. His hands and mouth branded her with his heat. Surely she'd burst into a ball of flame if he . . .

Thea opened her gritty eyelids and stared at the ceiling. Drenched with perspiration, her nightgown lay plastered to her body, the hem bunched between her legs. She turned her head toward the window, her damp hair sticking to her neck. She licked dry lips.

The dream had been more vivid, more disturbing, than ever before. She knew what it was like to be kissed now. She knew the urgency of a man's hard body pressed to hers. She knew what she'd missed out on.

Pushing away from the damp bedclothes, she stood in the darkness, drew her nightgown off over her head and tossed the clammy fabric down. At the washstand, she brushed her hair back and splashed tepid water on her neck and face.

Groping until she found a fresh cotton gown, she pulled it on and perched on the wooden rocker near the window, drawing the curtains back and allowing the breeze to caress her hair and skin. Booker Hayes had asked her to marry him.

She had accepted.

The concept was so unreal it could have been part of the dream. But, no, it had happened. Her mind rolled back over the disturbing fantasy. She would marry Booker Hayes. A severe, dark man who'd shown up on her doorstep only weeks ago and turned her life upside down. She would move into his house.

She pictured the enormous airy room with the eastern view. *She would share his bedroom.* A pulse throbbed insatiably in the most disconcerting spot. *His bed.*

They would most likely have children together.

Dear, God... She spread her hand open over her rapidly beating heart. Once married, she would be intimate with Booker Hayes, former army major, fighter of wars and Indians, landowner and mill builder. Guardian of the child she wanted. *Father of her own children?*

Thea didn't know whether to be ecstatic or terrified. In a few short weeks she would be his wife. She drew a ragged breath. This was either the best thing that had ever happened to her or she was the biggest fool who'd ever stared into the far-reaching Nebraska night sky and wished upon a bright-burning star.

"Morning, Lucas." A rap sounded on the door, and it took a minute for him to orient himself to the room. Hayes's boots sounded on down the hallway.

The smells of coffee, cinnamon and bacon drifted on the fresh morning air. The back door opened and closed, footsteps sounded on the porch, and water sloshed on the ground, followed by softly spoken words. The Angel.

She could be talking to the cat, to Zoe—to anyone. She had a kind word for everyone. He heard her enter the kitchen again, and he rolled over on the crisp, cool sheets. His stomach growled, but it was a pleasant feeling of being alive, a response to the savory smells from below, not a bone-deep, gnawing hunger that never went away, not a way of life.

He hadn't been bitten by a bedbug, eaten salt pork, beans or biscuits, or been clobbered black and blue for weeks. It was almost too good to be true. The church lady offered him milk and pie every time he turned around. How long could a good thing last? He had no idea since he couldn't remember ever having had a good thing happen to him before.

Lucas's need to use the outhouse got the best of him, and he rolled from the bed. Clean dungarees, shirts and summer union suits lay stacked on a wooden chair, the only other piece of furniture in the room besides the bed. He set the underclothing aside and slid the crisp denims on.

At the returning sound of Hayes's boots in the hallway, Lucas grabbed a shirt and shoved his arms into the sleeves.

"You awake in there?"

Lucas opened the door.

"Well, look at you. You going to be able to walk in those new pants?"

Lucas showed him he could indeed walk while buttoning his shirt at the same time. "I'll pay you back," he said half under his breath.

"Not me," Hayes replied. "Miss Coulson bought those dungarees for you. Made the shirts herself. Come on," he said, turning toward the stairs. "Breakfast is on."

To hide his surprise, Lucas turned back and hastily made up his bed. The Angel had bought him new clothes. Not something outgrown and donated by a self-righteous do-gooder. Not clothing that made him wonder if the former owner had died in them. Gifts ... purchased and sewn just for him. Beneath his new shirtfront, a peculiar feeling flitted in his chest. A warm, suffusing feeling he had no experience with, no name for.

He knew shame and hatred and anger, and could easily identify hunger and disgust and desperation. But this...this feeling was something altogether different. And it frightened him because it felt so good.

For weeks Thea painted and papered, unpacked and sewed, arranged furniture and planned the housewarming. Everything had to be perfect. By late July it nearly was.

Maryruth came to help her one afternoon, and David napped beside Zoe on a quilt they'd spread on the floor of Lucas's room. Thea hung the bright blue pair of curtains she'd finished hemming and stood back to admire the sun shining through the colorful fabric.

"Thea!" Maryruth rasped from the hallway in a loud whisper.

Thea met her in the hall.

"You've got to see this," she said, and took her sister's hand.

"What?" Thea allowed her to tug her toward the master bedroom.

"You won't believe what the men just carried up the stairs."

Thea had heard the commotion on the landing, but she'd grown accustomed to Mr. Hayes's and Red Horse's occasional forays into the house during the day. Deliveries by train and last-minute details to the house constantly interrupted their work on the dam.

Maryruth pulled her into the east bedroom. Thea's attention riveted on the room's focal point. An enormous bed stood, its head several feet from the wall, in the center of the room, the brilliant noonday sun illuminating its uniqueness. The headboard and footboard were enormous slices of tree trunk, the bark still attached but halved with the straight bottom edges resting on the floor. The half circles, the head larger than the bottom, were varnished to a high gloss, hundreds of rings testifying to the tree's unbelievable age. Thea'd never seen anything like it in her life.

Maryruth perched on the lofty, bare mattress, the headboard three feet higher than the top of her head. "What do you make of it?"

Thea reached out and touched the warm-colored slick wood. "I have to admit there's a natural beauty about it that is ... matchless." She touched the outer strip of bark. "Rough on the outside. Aged and beautiful on the inside." She glanced at her sister. "Like him."

Maryruth studied her curiously. "Are you sweet on Booker, Thea?"

Sweet on him? Is that what she'd call it? "I don't know," she answered. "I don't know what I feel for him. I just know that he's the only man besides Papa who's ever paid attention to me." She dared a girlish question. "Do you think he's handsome?"

She hadn't seen her sister smile with such heartfelt warmth for a good long time. "Yes."

"And he's tall." Thea bounced on the mattress and faced her. "It's been hard for me to wait to tell you, Maryruth. I didn't want Trudy and the girls to know because I didn't want them to fuss, but he's asked me to marry him.''

Maryruth's eyes widened in surprise. ''What have you told him?''

''I said yes. We're going to announce it at the house-warming.''

''Oh, Thea,'' Maryruth whispered, tears filling her sad eyes. She laid a hand on Thea's knee. ''I hope...I hope...''

''What, Mare?'' Thea covered her hand with her own.

''I hope you're not disappointed,'' she whispered. ''I hope he's everything you think he is.''

She touched Maryruth's pale cheek. ''Whyever are you so gloomy? How can I be disappointed any more than I have been?'' Maryruth's words struck too close to her own misgivings. ''Be happy for me.''

Maryruth hugged her tearfully. ''Of course. I am happy for you, Thea.''

''Come on. Help me finish Lucas's room before you have to leave.''

Maryruth's doubts so closely paralleled hers that, in the days following, Thea found herself wondering if those doubts were grounded in anything other than misgivings because of the short time they'd known Mr. Hayes. For the first time she wondered if Maryruth had experienced a disappointment of her own. She'd been crazy about Denzel, anxious to marry him and have his children. Now that she thought about it, Maryruth hadn't seemed her own happy self for quite some time.

Maybe marriage wasn't all Maryruth had expected it to be. Maybe marriage was never what a woman expected it to be.

A hundred times in a hundred situations, Thea had wished for a mother. Someone to whom she could ask questions. Never had she needed her mother as badly as she did now. She wouldn't dream of confiding in Trudy. As girls, she and Maryruth had shared so much: fears, the loss of their mother, even their bed. Many a night they'd lain awake spinning tales of the rich, handsome men they would meet and marry. If there was a way to ask Maryruth about her doubts she would find it.

Work on the dam was backbreakingly slow. The July sun beat down unmercifully on Booker's bare, peeling shoulders. He paused in maneuvering a wheelbarrow load of rocks. He straightened, grimacing at the pain that shot up his back and removed his hat. Soaking his kerchief in a pail of sun-warmed water, he wrung the excess on the ground and tied the fabric around his forehead before settling the hat back on his head.

At least the backbreaking work took his mind off Thea for a few hours at a time. And at night he was too exhausted to do anything but fall onto his bedroll.

Booker studied the progress of the men submerging rocks in an attempt to divert the creek until the real dam was constructed, and thought instead about the bed he'd ordered all the way from Colorado. A beautiful piece of craftsmanship and natural beauty. It spoke of unadorned loveliness. Like Thea.

Much as she tried to draw attention away from herself with drab clothing and somber hairstyles, he'd seen through her guise. In each room she touched, every window and wall she treated, bright color appeared like paint behind a brush, her love for color and beauty evident in everything from Zoe's dresses to the kitchen curtains.

Her father'd been right about her good companionship. Booker could easily see how her nature allowed others to impose upon her. She sacrificed, accommodated and obliged in such an adroit manner, doing each task competently and without complaint, that it would be easy to overload her with responsibilities.

Booker knew he would never take her for granted as her family did. And if it was within his power, he would see that no one else ever did again, either.

He wondered if she'd seen the bed, and what she thought of it. If she'd considered sharing it with him. Heat warmer than the July sun dispatched a twinge of raw desire down his belly. He'd only kissed her once. Once, but it had been enough to know he'd been right about the passion he'd sensed beneath the surface.

Lord, but she was beautiful. Sometimes when she was absorbed in a task he watched her just to enjoy her efficient movements, the delicate curve of her cheek, the way her glorious hair spiraled into tiny corkscrews around her face in the hot kitchen. He observed the symmetrical curves and lines of her hips and waist, her generous breasts, the length of the legs defined by her split riding skirt. He already appreciated her more than she'd ever know. Probably more than was wise ever to admit.

And in a few short weeks she'd be his wife.

On the bank below him, Red Horse stood ankle deep in water, prying stones from the creek bed. His bare copper back and shoulders glistened in the sun. A kerchief banded his forehead, restraining his flowing hair. He straightened and squinted up at Booker. "How much higher do you think we'll have to pile these, Major?"

"A half dozen more wagonloads ought to do it," Booker replied with a wry shrug.

"Did you know this creek was deeper than the Missouri before we started?"

Good-naturedly, Booker tossed a stone a few feet in front of his friend, splashing water across his bronze flesh.

Red Horse laughed, a wide-toothed smile splitting his ruggedly handsome face.

"You need a hat," Booker admonished. "The sun is frying your brain."

"I wondered why white men wore hats. I thought it was to hide those awful haircuts."

It was Booker's turn to laugh. He'd laughed more these past weeks than he had in all the previous years. Until lately, he hadn't had much to laugh about. The thought, of course, returned his attention to the woman responsible for his uncharacteristic good humor.

Booker threw his energy into stacking the heavy rocks on a raft to be dumped in the center of the swiftly flowing water. If he kept busy, he wouldn't have time to torture himself with lusty thoughts of Thea Coulson...soon to be Mrs. Booker Hayes....

Chapter Eight

The day of the housewarming party promised to be sunny and warm. Thea woke with the birds, packed supplies and food into the springboard and drove it to Booker's—her new home. Red Horse greeted her on his way from the barn.

"Morning, miss. I don't think the major's up yet."

"That's okay." Thea carried a basket heavy with jars of pie filling toward the back porch. "I wanted an early start. There's so much to be done today."

Red Horse intercepted the basket. "Let me unload the wagon for you."

She released her hold and met his deep-set eyes. "Thank you."

She had a fire going in the stove by the time he'd carried several more baskets into the kitchen. "I'll have some coffee ready in a minute, if you'd like a cup."

"I don't care for coffee, thanks. I wanted to speak with you."

She nodded and waited.

He stood beside the table. His flowing black hair had been gathered into a tail that hung down the back of his chambray shirt. "I wish you the best, Miss Coulson."

She smiled. "Thank you."

"I've known the major for quite a few years. We've shared many campfires. He is an honorable man. A man anyone would be proud to call friend. A man you will be proud to call husband."

"As you're a good friend, Red Horse."

The Indian didn't avoid her eyes or seem uncomfortable speaking to her. "You are good for him."

She hoped so. She prayed they'd be good for each other... and for Zoe.

Obviously not a man to waste words, Red Horse turned and left the house.

Later, four pies sat cooling on the table. Humming a soft, wordless tune, Thea sensed someone behind her. Booker stood in the doorway, boots in hand, white shirt over one long forearm. Soft-looking black curls carpeted his chest and dived into the waistband of his tapered black pants.

Thea couldn't resist running her gaze across his muscled shoulders and sleek torso. What would it be like to see this man first thing in the morning every day for the rest of her life? The thought did not distress her.

"Morning," he said, his gaze flickering over her hair and dress. His freshly shaved jaw was almost shiny in the morning light. The roomy kitchen seemed to shrink with his brawny presence.

"Morning," she replied, pulling herself into action and reaching into the cupboard for a cup. "Coffee's ready."

"You've been up awhile, I see." He perched on the chair, where he draped his shirt over the back and tugged his boots on.

The skin around his waist creased in the most fascinating manner as he bent forward to his task. She tried not to notice the tendons across his sun-kissed shoulders flex with each movement. Suddenly her mouth seemed parched, and she poured herself a cup of coffee. "Yes. I wanted to get a head start on the day."

"Don't wear yourself out. This party is supposed to be fun."

The coffee scalded her tongue, a painful distraction. She sat the cup down. "It will only take me a few minutes to put your breakfast together."

He stood and plucked the shirt from the back of the chair. Shoving one arm carelessly through a sleeve, his molded shoulder rolled in a timelessly masculine gesture. He reached behind and caught the other armhole, exposing a black thatch of hair and a marble-perfect bicep.

Thea couldn't drag her captivated attention from Booker. He glanced up and his fingers stumbled over the buttons.

Thea touched the numb spot on her tongue to her lip.

Something in the air changed and made breathing difficult. Booker held her gaze until she allowed hers to drift to his boots.

"I'll let the horses into the corral while you get breakfast," he said.

She nodded and watched him go out the back door, her heart slowing to a rate she could live with. Merciful heavens, if just being within six feet of him without his shirt on had this effect on her, what would happen the first time he touched her... the first time he...?

Footsteps running across the wood floor snagged her attention. Zoe flung herself across the room and hugged Thea's knees. Lucas appeared in the doorway.

Thea knelt and kissed Zoe. "Morning, Lucas," she said, straightening.

"Ma'am," he replied with an awkward duck of his head. "Ma'am?"

"Yes, Lucas?" She turned from reaching for a basket of eggs.

"Thanks for the shirts and dungarees." He shot through the back door without a backward glance.

Mentally tallying how many days it had taken him to muster that much courage, Thea smiled at the patch of sunlight breaking through the opening. "You're most welcome, Lucas."

* * *

"Thea?"

She turned toward Maryruth. They had most of the food prepared and covered, the tables set up and the decorations in place. In less than an hour, the neighbors would begin arriving.

"Are you all right?"

Thea took her sister's hand and led her upstairs. Ushering her into a sparsely furnished bedroom, she closed the door.

"Whose room is this?" Maryruth asked.

"Mr. Hayes offered it to me until we're married. He thinks I need to rest more often."

Maryruth's eyebrows shot up. "Are you going to stay here at night?"

"Of course not. How would that look?" She perched on the bed's edge and remembered the day they'd stood looking at Mr. Hayes's bed. Ever since, she'd wondered what Maryruth had wanted to tell her. "Can I ask you something?"

Her sister nodded and stood in front of the open window.

"Remember when we were girls, and we used to talk about what it would be like when we got married?"

"Yes."

"Is it frightening? Is it wonderful?" She slipped to her sister's side. "I feel like I'm just a naive girl again."

Maryruth gave her a sad-sweet smile and touched her hair. "It can be wonderful, Thea. It can."

The regret in her sister's voice frightened her. "What's wrong, Maryruth? Can you tell me?"

A tear formed and slid down Maryruth's pale cheek. "I'm not sure." She slumped into the armless rocker near the window. "I don't know what to do."

"Is it Denzel? Has he done something?" Anger made her voice sharper than she intended. She knelt at her sister's feet. "Has he hurt you?"

"Oh, no! No, he would never hurt me. That's the problem . . . I think."

"What's the problem?"

"Thea, you know how happy we were at first. Until . . . until David."

"What's happened?"

"I don't know!" Maryruth's voice trembled. "Ever since David was born, Denzel doesn't . . ."

"Doesn't touch you?" Thea asked.

She nodded. "He touches me . . . but he doesn't . . ."

Thea sat back on her heels and let breath whistle through her lips. "Oh, my."

Maryruth's shoulders shook softly. "I don't know what's wrong. I just know we can't go on like this."

"Have you talked to him about it?"

"He won't. He just says he doesn't want to hurt me."

"Well, you're going to have to make him talk about it. Or—" Her head snapped up. "Or you're going to have to get him to do it."

"How?" She stared at Thea through her tears.

"We'll figure that out." The rumble of a wagon in the yard below caught their attention. "Don't worry anymore." Thea stood and pulled her sister to her feet. "Here, use my things and fix your hair and face." She pushed her toward the dressing table. "We're going to have fun today, remember?"

Thea hugged Maryruth and hurried down to greet the guests. There had to be something she could do to help her sister.

The biggest share of the men showed up prepared to work. By late afternoon, a barn had been constructed and stood waiting for a roof. A few complaints grumbled among the settlers; some of them didn't like Red Horse's presence among the workers. Booker ignored their superior attitude. On the whole, he couldn't believe his good fortune. The men finished eating, and the musicians carried instruments from their wagons.

He caught sight of Thea. She stood near the corner of the back porch, a pitcher of lemonade in her grasp, talking to Odessa Woodridge. Listening to her aunt, her gaze drifted across the yard and settled on him.

Booker smiled, and she responded with a shy grin, sharing the secret. His stomach turned over. It was time to announce their wedding plans.

Jim Coulson ambled through the throng toward him. "Need some moral support, son?"

Booker smiled. "I'm not going to get cold feet."

Jim slapped him on the back. "Let's do it, then."

Booker focused his attention on Thea as Jim shouted for the gathering to come close and listen to Booker's announcement. She handed the lemonade to her aunt, smoothed her red-gold hair off her neck in a self-conscious gesture, and came to stand between Booker and her father.

Hip to hip, Jim slid his arm around Thea's waist. "Listen up, everybody! Booker has some news."

Booker cleared his throat.

Thea smiled.

"First of all, I'd like to thank the women for the meal. And thank the men for the hard work and the barn. It would have taken me weeks to finish it alone." He waited through a pattering of applause. "And I'd like to thank you men for something else, too. I'd like to thank you for leaving Thea, here, for me."

Thea glanced at her father and he kissed her cheek.

"It's my good fortune," Booker continued, "that someone as beautiful and unselfish as her waited for an old soldier like me to come along."

Silence fell over the men and women. A few children's voices carried across the yard from where they played games near the corral.

"I asked Thea to marry me." He turned a hand out and she slid from her father's embrace into his. "And she said yes."

Madeline stepped from between her girlfriends and stared in disbelief. A few surprised murmurs turned to congratulations, and the bystanders applauded. Agnes Birch and Malvina Beck put their heads together and chattered.

Thea looked up into Booker's eyes, her cheeks flushed in becoming embarrassment. He squeezed her waist.

A ruckus from the back of the throng drew the crowd's focus, and heads turned to see the source. Reluctantly, Booker turned his attention away from Thea's pink-faced pleasure and followed the sounds.

The shouting grew louder, and the settlers parted. A wiry, dirty-clothed man was dragging Lucas through the crowd by the shirt collar. "No good son of a bitch!" the man snarled into Lucas's face and shoved him to the ground. "Look it here what I found hidin' back o' the stock pens."

Lucas spun on the ground and pulled himself to a defensive crouch.

"What the—?" Booker loosened his hold on Thea and started forward. Thea grabbed his wrist and glanced around at the crowd. Her hold on his arm dragged her with him. "Who are you?" Booker asked. "What are you doing?"

"That's Ronan Bard," Jim Coulson supplied. "He indentured that boy when the orphan train came through."

Booker glanced down at Thea. "That true?"

She nodded, fear apparent in her expression. "I knew he'd run away. I didn't tell you."

"Skinny bastard ran off," Bard shouted, and started after Lucas again. Lucas tried to scrambled away with agile, crablike movements.

The fear on Lucas's face told Booker everything he needed to know. It also left him no choice. Anger such as he'd never known surged, blurring his vision. Thea must have sensed it and tightened her grip on his wrist.

Calmly, Booker pried her fingers from his arm and focused his eyes until the hateful man's face became clear. In three long strides, he stood between Bard and Lucas.

The man looked up at him, rage distorting his rheumy features. Booker leveled a stare back, seeing only the web of scars lacing Lucas's scrawny back—some faded by time to atrocious memories, others bitter-fresh evidence of this man's obvious brutality.

With shameless deliberation, Booker drew his fist back and hammered Bard's nose with a deft blow. The man howled and fell back in the dirt. "You son of a bitch!" he shouted, and rolled over, blood spurting down his lip.

Booker stood over him.

Bard pushed himself to his feet and dug in his filthy pants pocket. "Here!" he pronounced with a triumphant flourish. "I got the papers. He's mine!"

Scornfully, Booker yanked the document from his grasp and tore it into a dozen pieces. "Here's what I think of your paper," he said calmly.

Bard sputtered and swung at Booker. Another big mistake.

Booker caught his arm and glared in his face. "And here's what I think of you."

One punch and the man sprawled on the ground, his eyes rolling back in his head. Booker caught Lucas's shocked expression. He swung around to Thea. The setting sun set her marmalade hair aglow. Her face blanched, and she opened her blue-green eyes wide in apparent dismay.

What had he done? he thought. He'd ruined her day.

Thea stared down at the horrid man crumpled in the dirt. He'd ruined her day. This day that was to have been special. Thea raked her gaze over the detestable man on the ground and tried to bite back her sore disappointment.

Poor Lucas! Thea watched as he picked himself up and brushed off his new dungarees, all the while gawking at Booker as though the flashing-eyed man was a bigger-than-life hero from a dime novel. Thea started toward Lucas and noticed the mortified expression on Booker's face. He met her eyes with a mixture of dread and . . . fear?

"Booker?" she said softly, placing her hand on his arm without thought.

She didn't understand the troubled question on his face, but knew he was waiting for something, some reaction from her. Releasing his arm, she held out her hand to Lucas.

The boy came to her uncertainly, his chin dropping to the front of the shirt she'd sewn for him. She took his chin in her hand and brought his face up. "Are you all right?"

He nodded, his cloud gray eyes sliding to Booker. Thea wrapped her arm around Lucas and pulled him to her side. Surprisingly enough, he came willingly and turned his temple against her breast. His whipcord-lean body trembled within her embrace.

"Thank you, Booker," she said softly.

Booker's gaze lifted from Lucas to her, his mouth a pleasureless line, and one black brow raised in question.

Thea smiled, and the distress lines smoothed from Booker's forehead. He gave her a brief nod. She released Lucas, and Booker hooked a large hand around the boy's neck.

"Let's get this fella home," Jim Coulson suggested. "We have a dance to commence with."

Several men jostled Bard's limp body into a wagon bed. The crowd broke up, the ladies packing away food and dishes, the men setting up beer kegs near the wood-plank dance floor. Lucas disappeared into the house.

Booker pulled Thea aside. "Where's Zoe?"

"Maryruth took her and David inside earlier."

"Good. I'm glad she didn't see that." He cleared his throat. "I'm sorry you did."

"Booker." His ebony eyes softened at her use of his name. "I knew Lucas ran away from Bard. Lucas was one of the children who arrived on the train with Zoe. He seemed so much better off with you...I didn't say anything when I realized he'd run away. Perhaps I should have told you, and we could have contacted Mrs. Vaughn. I was just so afraid that Lucas would run. I still am." Unbidden tears filled her eyes, and Thea blinked them back. "He has a history of being a runaway."

A muscle jumped in Booker's jaw. "Can't say I blame him. I'd run from someone who beat me, too."

A sad-hearted ache throbbed to life in Thea's chest. "Oh, my—" her voice caught on a sob. She pressed her fingertips to her lips and composed herself. Dropping her hand, she asked, "What can we do?"

He set his chin at a determined angle. "We'll do something. I promise." He studied the darkening sky for a long minute. "I'll wire Mrs. Vaughn first thing in the morning."

Thea nodded, encouraged.

"But for tonight..." he said.

"What?"

"I think as a newly engaged couple, we should dance, don't you?" Those beguiling smile lines crept into one side of his mouth.

Her heart tripped and steadied itself. Engaged. To this man. He reached a palm toward her. She regarded the proffered hand: a long-fingered hand that had loaded rifles, pulled triggers and fought battles; a strong hand that could send a man into unconsciousness with a single blow. Her gaze flickered across his hard-angled face and back to his hand: a gentle hand that had clumsily brushed baby-fine platinum locks; a tanned hand that had built a house with love in every stone and each length of wood.

Warmth flooded Thea's insides and expectancy bubbled through her veins: a man's hand that would soon know every inch of her body as his wife.

She placed her fingers in his and turned them over to study his scraped knuckles. She lifted her chin and met his gaze. "I'd be more than pleased to dance with you, Mr. Hayes."

Lucas dallied in the roofless barn as long as he could that night. The last wagon had rumbled away from the yard an hour ago. Since then he'd checked on Gideon and brushed the horse Hayes had bought for his use until its speckled gray coat shined. He'd hate to leave this horse behind.

He'd hate to leave all of it behind. He glanced around the stalls and savored the fresh-cut wood smell. He'd never smelled anythin' like it. Never seen anythin' as fascinating as the delightful curls of wood that had fallen in a fragrant pile at Booker's feet that morning as the man had shaved lengths of wood until they were straight. Lucas had gathered the precious scraps and saved them in a tinderbox next to the new cast-iron stove.

It'd be nice to stay somewheres long enough to have the place feel like home. He wondered what home felt like, anyhow. He'd discovered people out here built cabins and houses and lived in 'em for most of their lives.

Lantern light swung across the interior walls, and Lucas spun.

"Wondered what was taking you so long," Booker said, and set the lantern on an upended nail keg. "Watered Gideon for me, did you?"

"Yes, sir."

"Think he likes it out here?"

"Dunno." Lucas followed Hayes's gaze as he dropped his head back and stared at the diamond-studded sky above.

"Ever slept under the stars, Lucas?"

"Yes, sir."

"Beautiful, isn't it?"

Lucas dropped his gaze back to the black-haired man. "Sky in New York ain't as big as here."

Hayes lowered his eyes. "No. I suppose not."

As a small boy hiding in a smelly back alley, a narrow strip of heaven was all he'd ever seen. And then the sky had only pointed out his vulnerability to rain and cold.

Hayes leaned against an empty stall and crooked a leg, the toe of his boot pointed at the dirt floor. "Lucas."

"What?"

"Remember that day I said you don't have to tell me anything you don't want to?"

Lucas nodded.

"Well, that still stands. I think I know now, anyway. I'm going to wire Mrs. Vaughn first thing in the morning."

Lucas's heart sank into his belly. He'd known it'd been too good to last. Now he'd have to run—before the agent came back and dragged him off to the next hellhole. Damn.

"I'm going to tell her what happened with Bard."

Lucas avoided Hayes's eyes, cautiously. Shame wound itself through his bones. He was street trash. Nothin' more. Nothin' better. And now everyone knew.

"I want to ask her if you can stay here. Miss Coulson and I will be married soon, so I think there's every chance the Home would agree to let you stay. But it has to be what you want."

Stunned for a long moment, Lucas could only stare back. He couldn't believe he'd heard right! Slowly, the realization hit him full force. Hayes wanted him to stay here. Here with him and the angel lady.

"I'm not a jailer, Lucas. You'll stay because you want to, or not at all. I won't be chasing after you. The decision is yours."

A breeze snaked inside the barn door. The lantern's flame guttered and spat. Beside him, the gray horse snorted and flicked a fly with his coarse tail. Lucas steadied himself against the stall gate. "M-Miss Coulson? She wants me to stay?"

"Yes, she does, Lucas."

Something had to go wrong. This was looking too good. The agent probably had a rule to keep this from happening. But he had the money. If something went wrong, he'd take it and go. "Okay," he said. "Okay."

Hayes grinned, pushed himself away from the stall and lifted his saddle down from the horizontal side. "Good. Now I have a more pleasant task ahead of me. I'm taking Miss Coulson home."

Thea waited in the spotless kitchen, the lantern backlighting her marvelous hair. She turned from the table. Booker wiped his boots on the rag rug she'd placed on the floor.

He'd seen it again today, even on her special day, the way she dedicated herself to tending to others, the way she quietly saw to it that all the work was accomplished. She possessed a subtle talent for getting things done without drawing attention to herself.

"What did he say?"

He studied her, poised and self-disciplined, qualities he'd shown an obvious lack of today. "He said okay."

She slid her fingers around one of the the spindles on the chair back. "Do you think he'll stay?"

Booker wished he knew. At least he understood now. "I told him the decision was up to him. He has to want to stay."

She averted her head and tucked a clean towel around the leftover loaves of bread.

"Are you ready to go home?" Booker asked, stepping closer.

She nodded.

"I saddled Gideon. Your father took the springboard."

She nodded again and a glistening drop fell to the back of her hand.

He reached out and touched her shoulder, gently turning her toward him. An ache pooled in his chest. Surely the heavens mourned and the earth tilted in sympathy when this woman cried. At that moment, nothing else mattered but her happiness. "Please don't do that," he whispered.

She whisked the tears away impatiently and tried to turn her head. Booker caught her chin.

"I can't bear to think of how he lived before he came here," she said in a quavering voice. "I grieve for a little boy who had no one to love him, no one to care if he buttoned his coat all the way or cleaned his teeth before bed. I can't imagine the things that he's seen and the loneliness he's lived in his short life."

Booker had to swallow and take a slow, deep breath.

"He should have had someone to love him," she said on an angry sob. "If he runs away and I don't know where he is or what's happening to him, I'll—I'll..."

He pulled her against his chest, his own heart ready to join hers in anguish. "Thea," he said against the top of her head. "We can't make up for Lucas's past. We can only take care of right here and now and try to see to his future."

His words must have comforted her somewhat, because she relaxed against him in an easy embrace. She curled a fist against his chest, and her other hand crept to his arm, just above his elbow, where her fingers curled around his bicep and sent a betraying shudder up the back of his neck.

Booker cherished her fragrant hair beneath his nose, her soft breasts against his chest, and wrapped an arm across her back, flattening his other palm in the hollow of her spine. Heat stormed in his blood. They stood like that for long minutes, Booker wishing he had no shirt on so he could feel her hair and skin against his sensitized flesh, until she slowly raised her head from his chest and lifted her nerve-shattering blue-green gaze to his face.

"Yes," she said on a sigh. "We must take care of here and now."

Her dewy lips caught and held his attention, and he struggled to remember what she spoke of. His here and now was folded against the throbbing front of his body in a delight-mustering, primevally simple embrace.

He lowered his head at the same time she raised her face, and he met her lips, closing his eyes and savoring the soft, sweet taste of her. Her palm flattened against his shirt and skimmed to his shoulder.

Thea had never known anything as good as Booker's muscle-strapped arms around her body, his insistent lips plying her mouth with his insatiable kiss. He pulled his head back and studied her face. Thea raised her thumb to touch the intriguing crease at the corner of his mouth. Booker's dark eyes smoldered, and his half-open mouth covered hers again, his firm lips and velvet tongue drawing an openmouthed kiss in return. Their tongues curled and flattened, tasted and tempted, drawing a low groan from Booker and chest-bursting excitement in Thea's heart.

His hand came up to cradle the back of her head and hold her steady for the thrust and parry of their delicious duel. Thea met each nuance with no sense of impropriety or fear. Heart pounding, she reveled in his kiss, in his touch. She was entitled. She'd waited so long.

Booker pulled his mouth from hers and trailed his lips across her jaw, tasted her ear, bit the column of her neck in a nip that sent shivers down her arm and puckered her nipples. Her clothing became hot and restrictive, and she thought of that massive tree bed upstairs.

Her pulse pounded. Booker took her hand from his shoulder and pressed a damp kiss against the backs of her knuckles. Thea turned her hand and touched him with her fingertips. She ran her index finger across his bottom lip, enjoying the silken texture and moist warmth. He took her wrist, caught her fingertip with his teeth and sucked it into his mouth. He tasted her, and bit her gently.

Thea wanted to climb inside of him and die of pleasure in his heat and strength. Her lips parted, and her breath escaped in a shallow pant. Oh, Lord, was there more? How could it get any better?

Booker nudged his thigh against her skirt, against that part of her that responded with a tiny eloquent throb, and answered her unspoken question. Oh, yes! It could get better.

She wondered how they would get past this stage. Did one of them just undress, or would he invite her upstairs? How would he say it? Would she be embarrassed? Would the lantern be lit or would they hide themselves in darkness?

He kissed her again then, his mouth working its graceful magic on her senses and his rock-hard thigh doing unspeakable things to her long-denied body. For the first time she wondered how many women he'd tempted with his kisses, how many he'd pleasured with his hands and mouth and... But any others didn't matter, she realized. He was with her now, and they must see to the future.

Booker held her shoulders and eased away. Hazily, Thea regarded his incalculable black eyes. The future with this man seemed too good to be true.

"I'd better get you home," he said.

She nodded and dropped her gaze.

He caught her chin on a knuckle and brought her face up, pressing a gentle kiss against her lips. "How much time will you need to arrange the wedding, Thea?"

Her heart smiled. Booker Hayes was anxious to marry her! "A week," she promised them both. "Only one week."

Chapter Nine

Seven days, seven nights. It was the longest week of her life.

Even though she stayed busier than usual, what with food to arrange and moving her belongings to the new house, it seemed to Thea like the days and nights would never pass.

On Thursday Trudy called her in for another fitting, and she stood for what seemed hours while Trudy pinned and hemmed and Madeline gave her sidelong glances.

She had dreaded this part of the ritual. Standing in the sewing room before Trudy and her half sister dredged up memories she'd rather forget. Memories of how they'd clucked and lamented over her size as an impressionable schoolgirl. How they'd tried to dress her like they did themselves in frills and lace, and how she'd wanted to disappear before their eyes—before they could display her and she died of shame.

"You were right about this dress, Thea," her stepmother commented. "It's understated enough not to draw attention, but it has a certain hint of sophistication that compliments you."

Thea turned and surveyed herself in the mirror. The cream-colored satin toned down her orange hair and freckled skin more than pure white would have. And the fitted bodice and waist proved she had an adequate figure.

She pictured herself in the sunny church on Saturday morning and actually felt feminine.

"Even with the slippers, Mr. Hayes is taller than you. Oh, what good fortune!" Trudy clapped her hands with glee.

Thea met Madeline's gaze. She couldn't blame them. She'd given up, too. She'd been dedicated to the needs of her family and the community until Booker Hayes had shown up. At long last she would have a few needs of her own met.

The thought warmed her heart.

Never having had any children of their own, Odessa and Adler Woodridge excitedly offered to hold the reception at their home. Since they lived in a central location, and close enough to Omaha to make last-minute trips easy, Thea accepted their generous offer. On Friday evening, before the wedding, Denzel, Booker and Red Horse stacked the planks for the dance floor in the wagon bed and hauled them to the Woodridge farm.

Booker spotted Thea and Zoe on the return trip and jumped onto their wagon seat, waving the men off.

"I can use your help," Thea said. "I wanted to have all the food and linens here at my aunt's tonight so I wouldn't have to think of anything tomorrow."

"Think you'll be nervous?"

She shrugged with a smile.

"Where's Lucas?"

"With my father."

Booker reached over and touched Zoe's hair. "How's the pumpkin?"

Zoe cast him a flirtatious smile.

Uncle Snake met them in the yard. He gave Thea a sound hug. An inch or so shorter than she, he grinned up. "Your mama would sure be happy for you. I remember how pretty she was on her wedding day."

No one could know how much she'd wished for her mother these past weeks. Thea touched her cheek to his stubbled one. "I wish she could be here."

Uncle Snake squeezed her hand. "She is."

He and Booker carried the baskets into her aunt's kitchen. Odessa poured coffee, and they visited for a brief time. Thea still had a few last-minute chores back at Booker's house, so she gathered Zoe and Booker.

Zoe fell asleep on the ride, and Booker carried her up to her room. Thea undressed her and together they tucked her into bed. Was this what being married felt like? she wondered, folding Zoe's quilt and placing it over the footboard. Was this the way husbands and wives did things?

Booker followed her down the hall to the room he'd provided for her use. She'd already moved most of her belongings, except for the things she would need tonight and tomorrow. He lit the lamp and watched her kneel and sort through a trunk. "What are you looking for?"

"I remembered a strand of pearls that were my mother's. I thought I'd wear them tomorrow. I think my jewelry case is in here. Ah." She retrieved the rough-textured, tapestry-covered box and opened it. She started to lift the necklace out, then let it fall back. "No. They're longer than I remembered."

"So? Let's see." He reached into the box.

"I don't know—" she hesitated "—I don't think they'd look right on me." Thea's cheeks grew warm.

"Look." Booker let the glossy pearls slide through his dark fingers. "If it's too long, you can double it. Stand up here and turn around."

"No, I—"

"Come on." He led her to the mirror over the washstand and wrapped the strand around her neck. She contemplated the lovely jewels against her somber brown dress. Booker adjusted the necklace, sliding the pearls along her skin until he'd wrapped it around her neck twice and fastened it. The cool pearls caressed the base of her throat.

She met his obsidian gaze in the mirror. His warm breath caressed the back of her neck.

"You're lovely," he said softly.

Her heart tripped against her breast.

"Let me see your hair," he said, his voice low and gruff.

In the mirror, her gaze skittered from his to her unruly hair. Several strands had come loose during their ride and spiraled against her neck and cheek. Might as well break him in a little at a time, she thought with wry amusement. He'd see it sooner or later. Just like he'd see her body and her freckled skin.

She reached behind and plucked the pins from her hair. Booker's hands pushed hers aside and took over the task, dropping pins on the washstand. The knot loosened and draped over her shoulder. He untwined the hank of hair and threaded his fingers through, grazing her neck and sending shudders coursing through her body.

She turned her head to see his face and he captured her mouth in a kiss. He coaxed her shoulder with a gentle hand until she turned easily. Cupping her face in both hands, he drew the kiss out, delicately nudging her nose with his, playfully darting his tongue along the crevice of her parted lips, lingering at the corners, nipping at her lower lip, driving her mad.

His kiss was too gentle, too considerate, too teasing and unsettling. Thea grasped his shirtfront and pulled herself against him, closer to his evasive mouth, closer to the hard-muscled, boundless attraction of his body.

As if sensing her need for a deeper connection, for a less tender fusion, Booker covered her mouth in an ardent, all-consuming clash of lips and teeth and tongues, and tugged her against his wildly beating heart.

Thea's fickle body gave itself over to his, pressing, fluttering, yearning, on a blast of quick-springing desire. He kissed her until her knees grew boneless and she slumped against him. He kissed her until she couldn't breathe and he had to let her up for a staggering breath. Then he kissed her again until he made her completely, perfectly, accessibly his.

He spanned her waist with his enormous hands, stroked her ribs and spine and crushed one breast beneath his palm.

He drew back and more tenderly cupped her through the fabric of her dress.

Thea ran her palms over his chest and tentatively touched the skin at the open throat of his shirt. Booker released her long enough to jerk his shirttails from his waistband and coax her hands underneath.

The instant her fingertips met his warm flesh, she was lost. His skin was fevered satin to her touch, smooth and firm—and a heady, tangible, nerve-zinging pleasure.

She stroked her palms upward from his iron-hard belly to his curl-carpeted chest, and he sucked in a spontaneous breath. He reached behind her neck, and she thought for a moment he intended to remove the necklace. Instead, he manipulated the buttons on the back of her dress free.

Thea closed her eyes and waited without breathing while he worked his way down the buttonholes to her waist. So this was how. He hadn't needed to say a word. He urged the dress forward, and she had to release him to peel the sleeves down her arms. Her bodice bunched at her waist.

She wasn't the least bit embarrassed.

Booker bent his head and touched his mouth to her collarbone. Waves of pleasure lapped at a soul too long denied hope. She relished his breath against her flesh, his hair as it touched her cheek. She savored the coarse texture of his palms against her bare arms, thrilled at the tingle as his tongue grazed her shoulder.

Covering her lips with his, he moved her away just enough to urge her toward the bed. The backs of her molten knees hit the mattress and buckled. He released her mouth and tugged his shirt up and over his head in a fluid motion, not bothering to unbutton it, and followed her down, tugging on the ribbon that held the front of her chemise closed. The white cotton parted and his dark, hooded eyes drifted to the bare skin between her breasts.

"I knew you'd have freckles here," he whispered.

Thea would have brought her hand up to cover herself, but he lowered his head. She caught her breath. He touched his tongue to the spot he'd mentioned, turned his head and nuzzled the soft, sensitive flesh of first one breast, then the other. His evening beard prickled, a titillating contrast, she discovered, and she drove her fingers through his silky hair.

He raised and kissed her, pressing her shoulders against the bed with his weight. Through the thin cotton chemise, his springy chest hair teased her nipples.

She was his tactile prisoner.

Through her haze of passion, Thea heard her name. "Thea?"

She stiffened and listened. Booker obviously heard it, too, and pulled away.

"Thea?" Lucas's voice called down the hall. "Zoe needs you."

"She'll be right there," Booker called over his shoulder.

Their gazes collided and danced away. Booker sat back, and Thea's hand fell from his shoulder. She touched her tongue to her puffy lips and frowned. She couldn't get her fingers to turn her sleeves right side out.

Booker moved and caught up her sleeves for her. "After you see to Zoe, I'll take you home."

Embarrassed now, she turned her back for him to button her dress. She tried ineffectually to gather her hair into order.

"It's okay," he said against her neck. "Just one more night."

She turned then and looked him full in the face. His eyes shone with an ardent light, his lips glossed and full from their kisses. The shadows the lantern cast defined each hill and plane of his solid shoulders and muscled torso.

"One more night," she agreed and turned, knowing in her impatient heart it would be the longest night of her life.

Lynette Rawlings, decked out in her best summer batiste dress, finished playing a hymn, and the last organ notes quavered on the morning air. Every head turned and every eye trained on Thea, where she stood in the rear doorway of the wood-frame church, a delicate bouquet of violets trembling in her grasp.

"This is it, Thea-girl," Jim Coulson said softly at her side. She thanked God for her father's size and strength as he took her elbow and led her toward the preacher and Booker. The aisle they walked seemed an interminable length, the parted onlookers an obscure sea of faces. Thea drank in the sight of Booker, tall and smart in his dark suit, shining knee-high black boots encasing his feet and calves.

Watching the play of emotion in his night-storm gaze as they neared, a ripple of excitement darted up her spine.

"Who gives this woman to be joined in holy wedlock with this man?" Preacher Newland asked.

"I do." Her father passed her hand to Booker's and, after a final watery smile, stood beside Trudy.

Preacher Newland read a passage from his dog-eared Bible. Booker squeezed her hand. She gazed into his eyes. *Holy wedlock.* He was to be her husband. Hers. She would live with him now, sleep beside him, sew his shirts, bear his children, see the first streaks of gray appear in his lustrous ebony hair. The rest of the ceremony passed in a blur.

"You may kiss the bride." The preacher gave Booker permission and closed his Bible.

Booker's gaze slid to the pearls at her throat and danced across her hair. He leaned toward her and pressed his lips against hers. Chaste. Proper.

She'd done it. She'd married Major Booker Hayes.

Applause broke out behind them. Booker straightened and took her arm. Lynette pounded out the wedding recessional, and they walked arm in arm down the aisle toward the door, everyone's eyes on them. Her friends. Neighbors. People she'd known for most of her life—her unmarried life. She'd worshiped with her father and sisters in the third row on the left since she could remember. She'd sat with them during church and gone home to put out the meal she'd started at dawn the same morning.

Booker Hayes had changed all that.

From here on for the rest of her life, she'd go home with him. Booker opened the door and led her outside. Hot midmorning sun beat down on their heads and shoulders.

Thea tugged on her white gloves. The congregation poured out around them, talking, congratulating, breaking up and heading out toward the Woodridge farm.

Thea perched beside Booker on the wagon seat, Zoe and Lucas with Maryruth and Denzel in the back. Fields waved congratulations at them as they passed.

"Most of this wheat will come through our mill," Booker said, tugging his black hat low over his eyes. He'd removed his jacket, and his white shirt hurt her eyes in the sunshine.

"Our" mill, he'd said. Not his anymore: theirs. Happiness stung at the backs of her eyes, and she blamed the sun. Booker pulled the wagon alongside the row already forming, and reached for her.

A picture of him lifting Mrs. Vaughn down from the wagon as though she were a child's doll shot from Thea's memory. "Booker," she said, her voice lifting on the last syllable.

Maryruth took Zoe's hand and walked toward the house.

"No one has helped me from a horse or a wagon since I was a child," Thea said, feeling silly.

"You deserve the same courtesy anyone does," Booker explained. "More. You're my wife."

"But..."

He tilted his hat back on his head and stared up at her, his hands bracketing his hips in exasperation. "Look, Thea. Let's get this straight. What is the problem you have every time I try to help you?"

Thea's face burned. "Well, I'm too big," she said simply.

"Too big for what?"

She glanced around and took comfort in the fact that the others had left them behind. "Too big to be carried, obviously. Now, move before we make a spectacle."

"I'm not moving," he declared stubbornly. "My mother raised me to be a gentleman, and by God, you're going to let me be one."

She regarded the determined set of his shoulders, the way he'd planted his feet firmly on the ground. He faced the sun, the side of his cheek pulled up in a squint. His squaring off amused her in a fashion she couldn't explain. Mirth bubbled up inside, and Thea laughed out loud.

His stance relaxed, and one corner of his wonderful mouth quirked up.

"Oh, very well, then," she said with a flippant wave of her gloved hand. "But don't say I didn't warn you." She placed her hands on his shoulders and leaned forward.

He caught her waist and eased her to the ground, his shoulder muscles bunching beneath her fingers. "There now, Mrs. Hayes. Was that worth all the fuss?"

She blushed and tried to turn toward the house, but he caught her wrist and hauled her back to face him. "Here's where you say, 'Thank you for not dropping me on my bottom, Mr. Hayes.'"

She grinned and swatted him playfully. "I didn't think you'd drop me on my bottom."

"What did you think?"

She inspected a tiny speck of dirt on her gloved finger. "I'm as tall or taller than most men, Booker. No one but you ever dared do that before."

"Do I look overtaxed by the task?"

She blinked up at him, then away. "No, of course not."

He took her elbow and started toward the gathering in Aunt Odessa's dooryard. "I'll be up to my husbandly duties tonight."

Thea let that comment sink in, fire licking a consuming path from her breast to her ears. Daring a glance at him, he graced her with an innocent smile.

"Here they are!" Trudy piped up from the back porch. "Come see the cake and the lovely decorations, you two!"

Booker grabbed her gloved hand and pulled her toward the crowd.

Lunch turned out to be a lavish spread of everyone's special dishes. The womenfolk provided their best canned relishes, and Lexie presented an enormous three-tiered cake draped with ribbons and bows of pastel frosting.

"Lexie, you did this?" Thea cried in astonishment.

Lexie dipped her dark head in a becoming blush. "Aunt Odessa helped me," she admitted.

"Why, it's absolutely beautiful!" Thea caught up her little sister in a hug. "You couldn't have given me a nicer gift. Thank you." She kissed Lexie's cheek.

Odessa pulled Thea and Booker to the back porch where a pile of gaily wrapped packages waited in the shade. The newlyweds took turns unwrapping linens and kitchenware. Jim Coulson gave them a heavy Seth Thomas mantel clock. Maryruth had embroidered sheets and pillowcases, and Thea's sister Elsbeth and her husband had brought them a set of china from St. Louis.

The excitement settled down. The men wandered off to play horseshoes, and the women scattered through the house and yard. Lucas found Thea sitting beside Booker on the porch swing. "I brung ya somethin', too," he said, hands behind his back.

Thea smiled and admired the haircut she'd given him the day before. "What is it?"

He handed her a thin, flat package wrapped in brown paper and tied with a string. She glanced at Booker, and he shrugged. She tugged the bow and the paper fell open, revealing the back of a picture frame. Thea turned it over.

A charcoal drawing lay captured beneath a piece of glass. Variegated shades of black, white and gray brought the picture to life. A fair-haired little girl sat on a carpet of grass, one leg jutting out beneath her skirt. A playful kitten climbed the front of her dress, its tongue lapping her cheek. The child's head tipped back in a delighted laugh. Zoe.

Thea glanced back up at Lucas and smiled through her tears. "It looks just like her."

He stuffed his hands in his pockets. "Mr. Hayes bought me the paper. Charcoal sticks and pencils, too."

"You certainly put them to good use." She glanced over at Booker. "Had you seen this before?"

He cleared his throat. "No."

"How did you have it framed?" Thea asked Lucas.

"Red Horse 'n' me went to the tradin' post at Bellevue."

"Thank you, Lucas. I have a special place for it."

"Yes, ma'am." Lucas flushed and smiled bashfully at her obvious pleasure. He backed off the edge of the porch and shot across the yard.

She studied the drawing in her lap. "He's so good, Booker. Did you know he could do this?"

He nodded. "He drew horses and landscapes on chunks of bark all the time, so I bought him paper. I saw him working on a picture of the house after the chimney was built and the walls were framed. I recognized myself hammering a doorframe."

"Where is it?"

"I don't know. This is the first I've seen him actually show anyone his picture. You're pretty special to him, you know."

Thea ran her finger across the top of the frame. "How long until Mrs. Vaughn gets here?" she asked.

"Probably another week or two. Why?"

"I've been thinking...."

"Uh-oh."

"Booker?" She raised her eyes to his. "Can we adopt him?"

He met her gaze. "I've considered the same thing myself."

"You have?" She sat forward.

"He would have to want it."

She nodded. "We'll ask him, then?"

He covered her hand with his. "We'll ask him."

Thea turned her hand and clasped his fingers. An intimate touch. A husband-and-wife touch. Underlying the rush of excitement and flurry of activity, though, she sensed a sadness about Booker this afternoon. Knowing she'd been caught up in her own happiness, she experienced a twinge of guilt. What could it be?

Thea took stock of his arresting, well-cut tanned features and wondered what could be bothering him. She'd been enjoying the day, the attention of her parents and sisters, her aunt's obvious enjoyment in preparing the—

Of course.

Thea's friends had gathered for the occasion. Her entire family had shown up, even Elsbeth all the way from St. Louis. They'd hugged her and congratulated her and brought her gifts. And Booker had no family.

Except Zoe.

Moisture sprang to Thea's eyes. How he must be missing his sister!

"Thea! What is it?" He pulled her hand to his chest and laid his palm along her jaw.

She blinked ineffectually, and a tear slid down her cheek. "I just realized how hard this must be for you. How you must miss your sister."

He frowned and wiped the droplet with his thumb. "You're crying for me?"

She gave a half smile through the tears and licked a salty drop from her lip. "How difficult it must have been for you to go through your sister's belongings and fill Zoe's room and your house with things familiar to her."

"It makes me feel closer to Julia to have some of her things around." Booker took his hand from her face and rested against the back of the swing.

She let her gaze fall to his black-clad knee. "How about your parents, Booker?"

He let their clasped hands fall to his lap. "My father died when I was young. My mother and Julia and I had some rooms over a dry goods store in Illinois. Mother died a few years after I joined the army."

"I barely remember my mother," Thea said. "We lived in a soddy back then, and she got sick. It was so cold that winter."

"I know one thing about her, for sure," Booker said.

"What?"

"She must have been beautiful."

Thea surveyed his expression to see if he was serious. "Is that important, do you think? That a woman is beautiful?"

"No," he replied immediately. "I've known a lot of beautiful women who couldn't hold a candle to you as for what's on the inside."

"You barely know me," she whispered.

"I know what I need to know."

Did he? Did he know he'd been her last chance—her only chance? Did he care? Did he know she'd agreed to marry him to stay close to Zoe, but that those reasons had shifted and changed with her sharp, escalating attraction to him?

Was he so sure of himself? Of the situation? Of her?

"Booker!" Denzel called. "How about a game of horseshoes?"

"Go ahead," she urged.

He kissed her fingers and joined her father and the other men.

He'd known a lot of beautiful women. The thought stuck with her. Thea wandered into the house to see if there was anything she could help with. She glanced around the empty kitchen, and voices drew her toward the dining room.

Madeline stood replacing bowls in their aunt's china closet, and Elsbeth sat at the table wiping spots from the silverware.

"I mean, did you see him, Elsbeth? Isn't he just the most perfect man you've ever laid eyes on?"

"He is handsome," Elsbeth replied.

Thea paused in the doorway, wondering who they were talking about.

"He could have had any girl in the county—or Lancaster county, too!"

"Do I hear a spark of jealousy in your voice, Madeline? Did you have your eye on Mr. Hayes?"

Mr. Hayes! Thea froze where she stood. Her half sisters were discussing her new husband?

Madeline closed the china closet door with a snap. "Well, we would have made a better match. Think of it, for heaven's sake, Ellie! She's so big and dresses so awful. She doesn't have the first idea of how to behave with a man... how to treat him... how to please him."

Thea's slice of wedding cake lurched in her stomach. She'd always suspected her half sister's opinion of her, but hearing it put so baldly brought new pain.

"Oh, and you do, my world-wise little sister?" Elsbeth asked.

"Better than she does. Why, you know he just married her for Papa's land. She's an old maid with a considerable inheritance."

"She and Maryruth will get this farm one day, too," Elsbeth agreed.

"You should see him with that little girl, Ellie." Madeline sat on a chair. "He would do anything for that child. He came all the way from New York to find her. He built her a house. And now he gave her the mother she wanted. He'd have done anything for Zoe."

Thea's stomach turned over. She pressed a shaky hand to her lips. Would Booker have done anything for Zoe? Even marry an old maid he had no desire for?

No. No man was that good an actor. Shocked, she dropped her hand to her side.

Madeline caught the motion in her side vision.

"Thea!" she cried and stood, the blood draining from her face.

Elsbeth turned toward Thea, but Thea spun in the doorway, ran across the kitchen and flew out the back door. She calmed herself, stepped down into the yard and deliberately walked toward the tree where Aunt Odessa sat in the shade with Agnes and the other women. Had Madeline really wanted Booker for herself? Is that why she'd sounded so mean—so spiteful?

That was ridiculous. Madeline drew all the young men to her, why would she begrudge Thea a measure of happiness? Thea had never been anything but loving to all of her sisters.

"We need to ask you something," Lynette Rawlings called to Thea from the edge of the gathering. "None of us has ever finished the hem on a mission quilt. Can you show us your special stitch?"

"Sure," Thea replied, glad to have something to take her mind off her sister's comments and the misgivings that were eating away at her heart.

"The quilt's in the house," Odessa said. "Why don't I go get it and you can show us?"

"We could probably finish it today," Thea predicted, and glanced across the yard. *He'd known a lot of beautiful women.*

Booker straightened up from another near miss and grinned at his new father-in-law.

"Don't take up gamblin', son," Jim advised, and drew on his pipe. Smoke curled around the bowl until a breeze caught it.

"Don't plan to," Booker assured him. As it had all afternoon, his attention strayed from the game of horseshoes, and he searched for Thea.

"Saw her in the house a while back," Denzel offered.

Booker crossed the yard and entered the house. The kitchen felt delightfully cool. She worked at a long table stretched down the center of the room, slicing bread and stacking it on platters.

David sat in a wooden-trayed chair beside her, mangling a crust of bread.

Booker studied her straight shoulders and flared hips in the sleek cream-colored dress. A white apron covered her skirt, and a hasty bow nestled in the small of her back. An infinite row of tiny fabric-covered buttons ran from the back of her neck to below her long waist. He imagined unbuttoning each button and hearing the satin dress rustle as it slid from her marvelous body.

What did she wear beneath it? Garters? Stockings? He shifted his weight and changed the direction of his thoughts. "What are you doing?"

"Just laying out some food for the evening meal. Everyone will need to get home to their chores after the dancing." She brushed her palms together.

"But this is your wedding day," he objected. "Surely someone else could have done this."

"They were all busy with the quilt. I don't mind." She glanced up, her eyes a more vivid aquamarine than he remembered.

The ivory dress turned her fair skin to porcelain, and in his mind's eye, he saw the freckles dappling her chest beneath the concealment of the fabric. Where else did she hide those charming sprinkles? Spangled down her long, supple legs? Spattering her knees? Angel kisses, he'd heard them called, and experienced a twang of jealousy at the thought of even angels kissing those most tempting parts of her body.

Booker's gaze slid to the pearls at her neck and the backlash of his thoughts sent a spear of unappeased desire to his groin. He remembered the cool texture of the pearls against her warm, satin skin. He could picture her glorious hair like a fiery nimbus around her head and shoulders. Booker could even taste her skin, smell her hair and—

He clenched his fists and jaw muscles tightly and forced himself to relax them, slowly. Oh, God, she was pure in mind and body, and he'd never wanted a woman with such a ravenous degree of carnal desire as he wanted her.

David slapped his hands on the tray and diverted Booker's attention. Thea wiped the baby with a cloth and plucked him out of the chair. Holding him straddled on her hip, she kissed his rosy cheek soundly.

"I suppose Maryruth needed a little time to enjoy herself," he said, annoyance lacing his tone.

Thea's bright eyes darted across his features. "Is something wrong?" she asked.

He couldn't look at the pearls. "Thea, you're so tolerant. Everyone takes advantage of you, can't you see that?"

She shook her head.

"This is your day. You shouldn't be doing this. Look at you." He reached behind her and snatched the apron away, tossing it over the back of the high chair.

She raised her face to his, worry in the depths of her gaze. "I'm sorry. I didn't mean to displease you."

He heard the concern in her voice. What was he doing? What a hypocrite he was! The idea of her family and friends using her angered him, while at the same time he stood lusting after her! Wasn't he imagining taking advantage of her, too? He wanted to satisfy his own needs, just as selfishly as they did.

On the previous night he'd seen her last-minute touches to the day's festivities: crisply pressed tablecloths, dozens of loaves of bread, along with numerous jars of beets and pickles.

Today—even today—she'd shed unabashed tears over his loss, his sadness, she'd tutored the other women sewing a quilt, and she'd thought to prepare an evening meal at the same time she took care of David so Maryruth could enjoy herself.

Everyone wanted a piece of Thea. Even him. What would she have left for herself when all of them were finished?

She deserved more. She deserved more than a life of servitude, and Booker meant to see to it that her own needs were no longer neglected.

Booker stepped close and dropped a kiss along the fragrant hairline near her temple. He took David from her arms. "The dancing's about to start. Would you like to dance?"

"I'd love to dance," she answered.

"Then you shall." He led her from the house, his mind made up.

He could give her pleasure. He knew that, but she didn't. Whatever happened in that respect would have to be what she wanted. He would not use her for his own pleasure.

Chapter Ten

Exhausted, on edge and embarrassed beyond anything she'd ever known, Thea waved to the group of young people who'd escorted them home, banging pans and singing and shouting playful encouragement to Booker.

Red Horse and Lucas had come home earlier to tend to chores, and Red Horse explained that Lucas would spend the night in the barn with him.

Denzel had carried a sleeping Zoe to his springboard, and Maryruth promised to bring her home first thing in the morning.

Booker closed the front door, and the sound echoed through the foyer and up the stairs. Outside the clamor of their neighbors disappeared into the warm summer night.

Alone. They were completely alone.

Thea placed her wilted bouquet of violets on the small table in the foyer while he lit a lamp. "Would you like some coffee?" she asked.

He shook his head and ran a hand through his midnight hair, endearingly mussing it. "I ate and drank enough today to sink a barge."

"Oh?" she said, frowning. "Do you need a spoon of extract of peppermint to settle your stomach?"

He took her wrists as though that would silence her, and his gaze danced over her hair and eyes. "No, I'm fine."

His hands were warm against her skin. She wondered if he could detect the slight tremble that coursed through her body at his touch. What now? What should she do now? Go up to his room? Wait for his lead? Oh, Lord, she hoped she wouldn't die of embarrassment or—her heart skipped a much-needed beat—or pleasure.

"Thea, we have to talk."

The lantern cast a solemn shadow across his features, leaving one side in ominous darkness. "All right."

He took her hand and the lantern and led her toward the stairs.

Thea's heartbeat sounded like an anvil ringing in her ears.

"I did a lot of thinking today," he said, reaching the staircase. "As much as it hurts me, I have to say something."

"About what, Booker?"

"About you and me. About us."

"What is it?" In confusion, she followed him upstairs and down the hallway. The shadows the lantern cast stretched and shrunk along the walls like ghosts playing hide-and-seek.

Booker stepped into the room he'd given her and lit the lamp on her wall. "I'm leaving the sleeping arrangements up to you."

Speechless, she stared at him—at her husband. He'd been thinking about the sleeping arrangements. Madeline had been right. *He could have had any girl in the county.*

"You can sleep in here, or you can come to my room."

Thea doesn't have the first idea of how to behave with a man—how to treat him—how to please him.

He'd known a lot of beautiful women...and she was just an old maid with a considerable inheritance. *You know he just married her for Papa's land.*

"I'll accept any decision you make."

You should see him with that little girl...he would do anything for that child. Booker loved Zoe enough to do anything for her—even marry Thea! Even sleep with her, if that's what she insisted on!

She backed up and steadied herself with a hand against the doorway. Yes, she'd most assuredly done a lot of unpleasant things in her twenty-nine years, but she'd be damned if she'd beg a man to let her come to his bed!

"Please understand," he said softly.

Oh, she understood. She hadn't lived her life as Too-Tall Thea not to understand that a man didn't find her attractive. "I understand," she assured him.

She edged a step toward the door.

"I can live with whatever you want," he said.

Sure, he would live. People didn't die of disgust. But she'd spare him the confirmation of that fact. She took the doorknob in her hand.

"Thea, I want you to be happy," he said, and stepped to the doorway.

Slowly, she swung the door on its hinges until he moved into the hall. "It's okay," she replied. Just before she closed the groom out in the hallway, his wide-eyed expression registered on her consciousness. Was that surprise? Relief?

Thea stared in the mirror over the washstand. Reaching up, she tugged the sprig of baby's breath from her hair and threw it on the floor. "Fool. Idiot," she said to her detestable reflection. *Did you really think he wanted you? Did you really imagine this was anything more than a convenient arrangement to give Zoe a mother?*

Outraged, she trembled with the helpless fury of having something precious and special torn from her grasp. Quick-sprung anger burned until it consumed itself. Despair washed over her in a momentous wave so grim and crushing, she sank to her knees on the hard floor. She dropped her forehead against the wood stand and flattened both palms on the cabinet doors.

She was too old. Too unattractive. The same old story returned to haunt her.

He was the man she'd dreamed of. She'd been so foolishly naive. He'd been so relentlessly convincing. She'd wanted a husband for herself. He'd wanted a mother for Zoe.

Booker's rejection stole the life from her soul. Hope withered and cracked and left her sullenly despondent. Thea cupped a sob in her hand and staggered to her feet.

The satin dress hadn't been made to get into or out of by herself. By pointing her elbows at the ceiling, she managed to undo six inches of buttons at the neck, then reaching behind, unfastened another six inches up from the waist. Thea stared over her shoulder in the mirror. The middle twelve inches of tiny buttons might as well have been twelve miles for all she could reach them. Perspiration trickled down her spine and dotted her forehead.

Reaching behind her neck once again and gathering the fitted fabric upward, she managed a few more. Panting, she sat on the bed's edge and cursed Booker. She should march right down that hall and demand he get her out of this dress.

She didn't, however. After working upward from the bottom and loosening a few more until she thought her shoulders would pop from their sockets, she yanked and sent the last buttons flying. Smoothing out the wrinkles, she hung the garment on a hanger in the wardrobe and blew out the lamp.

Dressed in her chemise and drawers, Thea peeled back the coverlet, crawled between the crisp sheets and stared at the ceiling.

Old maid. Too-Tall Thea.

She twisted to her side and pulled her knees up to her chest. Discouragement settled in her breast like the grippe. Misery hovered in the hot night air. All the self-condemnation in the world wouldn't change the fact that she'd placed her trust and expectations on the dark-eyed major. No matter how much she cursed her own folly, she'd married him.

Thea didn't know any other way than to deal with what life dealt. Make the best of it and go on.

She had Zoe, after all. Hadn't that been her primary concern? Of course it had. All these other fanciful pipe dreams had developed after the fact.

She was now Zoe's mother. No one and nothing could change that. And after all, what more did she really need?

Booker, sitting on the cowhide trunk at the foot of his bed, leaned forward and thrust his fingers into his scalp, painfully.

He'd muddled it good, this time; he knew by the look on her face. He'd wanted her to be happy. He'd wanted it to be her decision. What else could he have said?

He wanted to run back down the hall, kick the door in and take her as swiftly and shamelessly as his body demanded. She would let him, too. Oh, Lord, she'd let him.

But of course, he couldn't. He wouldn't. He tugged on his hair until the pain brought tears to his eyes. He dropped his hands and sat up, his posture slumped, dejected.

Maybe she'd come to his room. A vague spasm of hope flickered. He'd made it perfectly clear it was what he'd wanted, while trying to convince her it was all right if she didn't want a physical relationship yet. He would respect her decision—and he would live with it.

After all, using Zoe as the bait, he'd practically blackmailed her into marrying him. But he'd wanted her. Damn, he'd wanted her!

Booker stood and shrugged out of his white shirt, tossing the wrinkled garment on the trunk. A hot breeze wafted through the open window, and he stood before the opening, staring out at the land he owned and the dam he'd built. The footings for the mill, too, were there in the moonlight. His dreams were coming together, the dreams he'd planned so long and patiently to see come to life.

Booker turned back to the room. He'd ordered that bed specially built from a wood crafter near a logging camp in Virginia. The trunk at its foot he'd bought from a family traveling west on a wagon train.

He yanked off his boots and sat in the chair near the fireplace. The bearskin he curled his toes into had been a gift from Red Horse's father, given to him for saving his son's life. Explaining that Red Horse had returned the favor many times over had done little good.

Booker leaned back in the overstuffed chair and closed his eyes. He'd planned it all so well. The wife part had been vague. One didn't just choose family during his travels and store them until the time was convenient.

He'd imagined visiting Julia, Robert and Zoe. They should have had another little one by now. Zoe was something he hadn't planned for, and the responsibility of providing a good life for her gave all the rest of this meaning. He would have to cling to that thought.

He hadn't planned on Thea, either. The women of his experience were all self-seeking, conniving little balls of fluff who either wanted him because an officer was a good catch or because they were seeking mindless romps while their husbands were afield.

Thea wanted him for neither of those reasons. Booker opened his eyes and stared at the closed door. Thea didn't want him for anything, if his empty bed was any proof.

She wasn't coming. She'd made her decision.

Slowly, regret in every joint and muscle, Booker removed his trousers, peeled back the coverlet and lay on his cavernous bed. Something else had sneaked up on him, caught him unaware and left him heart-stricken. He hadn't realized an emotion could overwhelm, could plumb the depths of his soul and make him animated and joyous one moment, then leave his spirits drooping and heartstrings lacerated the next.

He hadn't planned on loving Thea.

She awoke sometime before dawn, after what seemed like only minutes of sleep. Avoiding her puffy-eyed reflection in the mirror, she slipped down to the kitchen and carried warm water back to her room and bathed. Dressed, she tidied her room, pausing reflectively over the wedding quilt.

She must focus on Zoe and Lucas, her primary concerns, and forget her foolish, girlish fantasies.

She'd gathered eggs, and the bread dough stood rising when she carried up warm water for Booker to wash and shave. She tapped lightly on the door and left the pitcher on the floor. Reaching the stairs, she heard his door open and close.

Later, Thea turned evenly browned slices of bacon over in the skillet, and sensed him behind her. She concentrated on the meat, loathe to turn and let him see her face.

"Morning," he said in a rough, sleep-tinged voice.

"Good morning."

The back door opened and closed and she heard his wash water splatter on the ground.

He poured himself coffee from the pot on the stove and a chair scraped the floor. Cracking eggs into another skillet, she thought he'd seated himself, and jumped at his touch on her arm. "Shall I go collect Lucas and Red Horse?"

"Yes. Everything's almost ready."

"Thanks for the water."

She'd always carried warm water to her parents and sisters in the morning. No one had actually thanked her before. "You're welcome."

By the time he returned with Red Horse and Lucas, she had the table set and the steaming food waiting on their plates.

"Ma'am," Lucas said and slipped into his seat.

Red Horse, too, greeted her. "We dig today?" he asked Booker.

Booker nodded.

"What're we diggin'?" Lucas asked around a bite of biscuit. He licked honey from his lower lip.

"A pit to set the turbine in," Booker answered. "The turbine'll get here next week, and we still have to dig the trench."

"What for?" Lucas cast a fascinated gaze on Booker.

"For the flume," the man replied.

"The what?" Lucas asked.

Booker grinned. He and Red Horse exchanged a look that said they were used to the boy's questions. "A long trough we'll build out of wood to carry the water from the headgate where we control the flow of water to the penstock."

Lucas chewed a strip of bacon thoughtfully. "I think I know. You changed the way the water flows so you could control it with that headgate thing. It runs down the flume and hits the turbine, and the turbine turns the—the other thing."

"Drive shaft," Red Horse supplied.

"The drive shaft, and the drive shaft turns the stone wheels inside that grind the wheat."

"You've got it." Booker reached to ruffle his hair, and Lucas ducked skittishly. The stricken look that Booker quickly hid shot right to Thea's heart.

"How deep does this pit have to be, anyhow?" Lucas asked, obviously unfazed.

"We chose the location because the land already dips in that spot. We want at least a twelve-foot head to generate the most power."

Lucas turned to Thea. "The head is how far down the water falls to hit the turbine," he said in an instructional tone.

Thea formed an O with her lips and nodded her head. Finally, she met Booker's gaze. He would be a wonderful father. Lucas already idolized him.

Obviously, he was a wonderful friend. Red Horse had chosen to follow him back to the frontier and work side by side with him on this venture.

She thought she read a twinge of wistfulness in his dark eyes. Regret, perhaps? He would probably be a wonderful husband, too. Given the right woman. A woman he could love.

Last night she'd been angry—hurt angry. Today she was exhausted. Resigned.

Thea lowered her gaze to her plate. She had her own house, now, and children to take care of. Last winter she would never have dared to dream her life could have changed this much. She refused to sit around sullen and self-punishing when she had so many things to be grateful for and glad about. She'd been too rash, too foolish. Had he really made her feel that good?

Booker Hayes had asked her to marry him. He wanted her here taking care of the house and the children. That had been the whole point, hadn't it? Her whimsical dreams had simply tricked her heart into seeing something that wasn't there. He needed her domestic skills and she intended to provide them. That was the deal.

And she never went back on her word.

"It's here!" Lucas shouted in the kitchen door. "The turbine's here!"

Thea dried her hands on her apron and left it on the table, gathering up Zoe.

"How far away?" Thea called to Lucas's back. She tied bonnets on herself and the little girl.

"They're not to the mill yet," he shouted back. "An' it'll be a while. You want I should get you a horse?"

"No, thank you, Lucas. Zoe and I will walk."

Lucas stumbled on his own feet and turned back toward them, losing his battered hat. He retrieved it and pulled the brim down over his forehead. "I'll walk with you, then. Case Zoe gets tired, an' you need help carryin' her."

Thea smiled fondly down at his tanned face. "You're becoming quite the gentleman, aren't you?"

Lucas stuffed his hands in his pockets and walked importantly beside Zoe. "The train brought the turbine all the way from Springfield, Ohio. Got here this mornin'. The men have been wrestlin' it from the flatcar ever since. Wait'll you see it! Gees!"

The going was slow because of Zoe's limp and the uneven ground. Thea could practically see impatience burst

Lucas's shirt buttons, but he restrained himself to their pace.

By the time they passed the mill site with its cavernous pit awaiting the turbine, the late July sun had Thea's bodice clinging to her chest. She tried loosening the waist for circulation. Crossing the wide bridge Booker had recently built across the creek, she watched the inviting water bubbling along its new banks.

Staying in the center, she led Zoe across. "Lucas, why doesn't this bridge have any sides?"

"So they can get wide loads across, o' course."

"Of course."

"There! There! See 'em?" Lucas couldn't wait any longer. He burst ahead, his long legs rapidly eating up the ground.

Ahead, a dozen men stripped to the waist, bodies glistening in the sun, followed the flatbed wagon carrying the unwieldy iron waterwheel. It looked more like a fat wheel lying flat. It had raised spokes, which were actually rotating vanes, with an iron axle-looking thing sticking upward from the center.

Booker and Red Horse led the team of oxen that pulled the heavy iron load, surveying the land, adjusting the direction so as not to encounter uneven spots and tip the wagon.

Thea watched the approaching party in awe. Certainly no one in these parts had seen anything like it. She'd heard her father say that wooden waterwheels were built on location. She took a silent head count, recognizing local farmers and their sons as well as Denzel and Preacher Newland, and wondered how much it was costing Booker to pay all of these men.

Wanting to look away, Thea stared transfixed, nonetheless, as men, beasts, and iron waterwheel crossed the bridge.

She and Zoe kept their distance, watching as the oxen's straining efforts took the turbine closer and closer to the dam. Just before reaching the destination, they encountered a small rise. Booker left Red Horse with the oxen and ran back with the others to push. His hat blew off, exposing his sweat-glistened black hair to the sun. His muscle-strapped back and shoulders bunched and flexed with the strain. Thea held her breath. If the iron wheel slid off the back, they'd all be crushed.

Red Horse prodded and the oxen lurched forward. Booker gave one final lunge and the wagon and turbine came to rest on the flat spot of land above the pit.

A dozen men headed for the creek. Booker stood, hands on hips, and surveyed the task ahead of them. His gaze sweeping the area, he discovered Thea and Zoe crossing the bridge and waved.

They met him halfway. "What now?" she asked.

Sweat ran in rivulets down his temples. His ebony chest hair glistened with moisture, the golden skin of his torso and shoulders glowing in the sunshine. "Now we rig it to the frame we built," he panted. "And crank it down into the hole. What do you think of it?"

"It's something," she replied with a shake of her head.

"Yeah," he said, inhaling deeply and blowing the air out through pursed lips. "It's something."

Thea smiled at the proud way he looked at the hunk of metal. "Booker, how will you pay all those men for their work?"

"The farmers will get their first crop milled at no charge. The others get paid in flour and oats."

What a clever man. He had business lined up for the mill already. "Bring everyone down to the house for the noon meal."

"Oh, I don't..." He took in her raised brow. "You sure?"

"I'm positive. You can't work men half to death in this heat and not feed them."

"All right. We'll be home for dinner."

Maryruth and Lexie showed up to help Thea with the preparations. Thea watched her sister efficiently shave carrots and plunk the chunks into the kettle of boiling water. They needed both rooms, so Lexie busied herself with setting the dining room table.

"Maryruth?" Thea asked finally.

"Hmm?"

Thea edged closer and checked over her shoulder to make certain Lexie was still in the other room. "Do you think Mr. Hayes married me for Papa's land?"

Maryruth brought her head up sharply. "Why would you ask that?"

Thea shrugged, knowing her sister would see straight through her if she tried to shrug the question off as unimportant. "I wondered, that's all."

"Who put that idea in your head?"

Thea picked up a knife and scraped a carrot.

"Thea, has Booker done anything to give you that idea?"

"No." But he hadn't done anything to make her think otherwise, either.

"Well, then, don't put worries in your head that have no business being there. You're a beautiful, wonderful woman, Thea. He could have had a million reasons for marrying you. Think about those."

"Okay. What are they?"

Maryruth laughed. She turned and took Thea's hand. "You're serious, aren't you?"

Thea nodded.

"Well." She handed Thea another carrot. "I'm not as tall as you are, but I'm taller than most every other woman in the county, and Denzel doesn't mind a bit. He used to call me..." Maryruth paused and blushed.

"What!"

"Willowy," she confessed.

Thea looked her sister over, then ran a damp palm down her midriff and over her hip. "Willowy, huh?"

Maryruth nodded. "And you know how we cursed this red hair when we were girls?"

Thea nodded.

"Denzel says it has more brilliant shades of fire than the most beautiful sunset."

Thea widened her eyes in disbelief. "Denzel said that?" She couldn't imagine her staid brother-in-law waxing poetic. Did men talk that way when they were in love?

Her sister nodded. "And besides that, you're fun to be around, you're sensitive, you have a lovely, relaxing voice. I remember when you used to read to me at night."

"You haven't said a word about me being a good cook or a good mother for Zoe."

"Were those the things you wanted to hear?"

Thea dropped the last carrot into the water and slanted Maryruth a glance. "No." She turned to pull a stack of plates from the cupboard. "I needed to hear just what you said."

Maryruth scraped the shavings into a pail and gave her a smug smile.

Lexie appeared in the doorway. "How much longer? I heard a wagon."

"By the time they wash up, we should just about be done," Thea replied.

Sure enough, the men came through the back door as Thea set the last platter of chicken on the table. "Half in here and half in the dining room," she called out over their banter.

On his way past, Thea saw Denzel touch Maryruth's waist, and her sister turned, acknowledging his presence. Thea wondered about the situation Maryruth had told her about before. The man was obviously in love with her, so why didn't he—?

"Ma'am?"

Thea turned and found Lucas waiting for her attention. She smiled. "What, dear?"

He blushed. "Where do you want me?"

She glanced around. Booker, Denzel, Preacher Newland and a number of others had settled themselves comfortably in the kitchen. Thea stepped to the doorway and discovered some empty chairs at the dining room table. She motioned to Lucas and he took a few halting steps toward her.

It hit her, then, that he'd always sat in the one specific kitchen chair she'd originally offered him. He obviously wasn't familiar with routines others accepted as ordinary. "Take any seat you'd like in here, Lucas."

The boy immediately scooted in beside Red Horse. Platters passed and the meal was on.

Sometime later Thea delivered a full bread plate to the table and noticed Lexie sitting across from Lucas. The two studied each other, only when the other wasn't looking. Thea hid a smile.

The workers finished eating and filed from the house. Booker paused beside her at the sink. She glanced over and noticed the damp shirt sticking to his broad chest. He'd wet his hair before dinner and it stood in unruly finger rows. Leaning forward, he brushed her cheek with a kiss, and she caught his scent: sun and sweat and all man.

"Thanks, Thea. You did me proud."

Her stomach gave a tremulous lurch, and she watched him saunter out the door. All right, it had been her cooking, but she had made him proud. He'd said so. She caught Maryruth's passing smile and turned back to the dishwater.

She'd made him proud.

After her sister was gone, Thea carried a blanket and took Zoe outside. They had to walk a ways from the house to find a few shade trees, and there Thea spread the blanket.

"It will be cooler out here for your afternoon rest," Thea said. Zoe pillowed her head on Thea's lap and Thea opened the book she'd brought.

Minutes later, Thea glanced down and saw Zoe playing with the acorn, rolling it in her palm, studying each side.

"Zoe, darling, what is your obsession with that acorn?" Thea asked, and placed her book on the blanket.

Zoe's innocent blue gaze rose to her face, and Thea wished for the hundredth time that Zoe could speak to her. Zoe brought her tiny palm up to Thea's face.

"Yes. It's an acorn," Thea said.

Blue eyes drifted beyond Thea's head to the green-leaved branches above. With her other hand, Zoe pointed to the branches.

Thea glanced up. The green canopy protected them from the afternoon sun. Every now and then a gentle breeze rustled the leaves in a hypnotic, sleepy summer sound. Thea leaned her head back against the rough bark and let her eyes drift shut. It was a wonderful, lazy sound, one she'd listened to as a child, one she loved to this day. A sound that reminded her of home, of summer—

Thea's eyes flew open and she took stock of Zoe's reflective expression. Zoe had been born in New York City. Thea's mind rolled back to the April day she'd first met Zoe and the little girl she'd thought of as Freckles. They'd been fascinated with the oak trees in her father's backyard because they'd never seen trees before...hadn't known where apples came from, hadn't known so many things she took for granted.

What had she told them that day? Zoe had pulled the acorn from beneath a checkered tablecloth and held it toward Thea with a question on her pert face. Thea racked her brain. How had she explained it to Zoe? *It's an acorn. If the squirrels don't eat the acorns, they turn into trees.* A nuisance, really, when one had to go out and pluck out all the little seedlings before they got out of hand.

Zoe had looked at the nut in amazement and tucked it into the limp pocket of her pinafore. Thea hadn't seen her without it since. Almost as if she were waiting for something.

Thea sat forward. "Oh, my." Zoe thought Thea's word was gospel. She was waiting for the acorn to turn into a tree. "Zoe, do you think that acorn will turn into a tree?"

Zoe sat up, excitement on her features. She nodded.

Thea leaned back. "Oh my." She took Zoe's hands in hers. "Darling, you have to plant it first. The acorn is like a seed. It has to be in the dirt and have rain and... How will I ever make you understand?"

Zoe climbed into Thea's lap and laid her head against her breast. The contact made her hotter, but Thea didn't care. She smoothed the baby-fine silken locks and kissed her damp forehead. Zoe was hers now. Thea'd already begun teaching her the alphabet on a slate she'd found in one of Julia's trunks.

She wanted to teach her so much, give her so much, open the whole world up to her. How was she going to turn that acorn into a tree? Zoe'd carried it around for so long, what if it was dried up, no good?

Zoe slept, and Thea made plans for after supper that evening. She couldn't let Zoe down. Zoe thought that acorn was going to turn into a tree, and by golly, it would.

She hoped.

Chapter Eleven

Zoe followed Thea into the barn. The gray kitten, now good-size, discovered them and brushed against Zoe's leg. Thea found the gardening tools in a corner and carried the shovel out of the building, Zoe and the kitten trailing behind.

Thea sized up the land gently sloping upward behind the house and pumped a bucket of water from the well. Zoe followed eagerly.

"This should be a good spot," she said, setting the bucket down. "A shade tree here would be just right for picnics in the backyard." She pointed the shovel into the hard-packed earth, stood on it and made a dent. She stabbed it a few times and tried again, wedging the shovel into the ground. Finally, a chunk of sod came up.

How deep did the acorn need to be? Not very, since they fell from the trees and grew on their own, she figured. She poured the water into the hole, creating a white foam on the black liquid. Slowly, the water seeped into the earth, leaving a puddle.

"Okay, Zoe. Drop the acorn in."

Zoe looked at the nut in her hand, glanced at Thea, and trustingly plopped it into the hole. Thea ladled the dirt back into the pit and smoothed the ground over the top. The gray kitten sniffed the spot.

Zoe looked from the ground to Thea.

Thea, leaning on the shovel under her arm, raised a brow. "It'll need water every day. We've done the best we can." She glanced around, helplessly. "It's awfully late in the summer. I really don't know when the best time is to plant an oak tree."

Zoe picked up the kitten.

"Come on, let's go put this stuff away."

From the corner of the house, Booker watched Thea carry the shovel to the barn, metering her pace so Zoe could keep up. What was she up to? He appreciated the fluid stride of her long legs, the late sun glinting off her hair.

Thinking of that night—their wedding night—he cursed himself for the hundredth time. He'd messed it all up somehow. He wanted to bring it up again, tell her exactly how he felt, find out how she felt and what she thought, but how could he? She'd made her decision.

She'd decided to sleep in her own room, and he'd promised to live with that decision. He couldn't get out of it now without going back on his word.

But he wanted to. Lord, how he wanted to. He wanted to throw his word out the window and storm down that hall, roll her up in that colorful quilt and carry her back to their room.

Take her prisoner.

She'd be hot. Wild. Eager.

Booker's body responded to the thought. He shifted uncomfortably. He hadn't spent so much time in this embarrassingly aroused condition since he was sixteen.

Maybe not. Maybe she'd be shocked. Maybe she would never want to advance their relationship. God help him, how would he live with that? But he'd promised her he would. And a man was only as good as his word—even if he'd given his word hastily and without thought to the days and endless nights of torture that lay ahead.

He'd take one night at a time—and live with her decision. Somehow.

* * *

Face buried in the pillow, Lucas awoke with a start. Someone was in the room. Instinctively, he threw his arm up to protect his head, but instead of the blow his sleep-clouded brain anticipated, a cool touch rested on his spine.

It had been too hot to wear his sleep shirt last night. Lying on his stomach, his back and shoulders were exposed in the morning light. He craned his neck and took stock of Zoe beside his bed.

She wore a lightweight cotton gown, and her near-white hair was tousled prettily. With one finger, she traced the scars on Lucas's back.

"Ow," he saw her lips say without a sound coming from her mouth.

"Yeah." He rolled over, keeping himself modestly covered, and sat in the center of his narrow bed.

Zoe climbed up and sat at the foot.

Lucas rubbed sleep from his eyes and squinted at the child. "You got it awful good here, Zoe, an' don't you forget it. You 'member the Home? That big, big room with a hundred tiny wood walls to sleep behind? The whole place smelled like wet beds. Nobody there at night. Nobody to hear if ya cried or hurt or got sick. Even that was good compared to places I seen."

Her wide blue eyes offered understanding.

"I ain't never seen food like here, Zoe. I ain't never gone so long without bein' hungry. At the Home we usually got milk an' sometimes fruit, but never, never all at the same time." He scratched his head and stretched. "One family I stayed with, the man used to come out to the stable an' wake me up by throwin' the milk pails at me."

Zoe cocked her head.

"I learned real fast to wake up when the door squeaked."

Her blue eyes sympathized.

"I used to save scraps from the compost pile 'cause if'n I didn't work fast enough they wouldn't feed me. I think I was ten."

Zoe crawled over to Lucas. Her plump little body radiated warmth through her nightgown into his arm. She smelled fresh and kind of flowery. She snuggled against his side, and Lucas experienced an awkward, unfamiliar surge of feeling.

Reaching out a tiny hand, she patted his arm and slid her fingers into his.

A rush of disciplined emotion broke through Lucas's learned reactions. Distrust and caution were his nature. Anyone who'd ever shown the least bit of kindness had a motive he wouldn't like. Fact. That ingrained reservation kept him from returning her touch; his hard-earned skepticism prevented him from feeling too much.

Even though his head told him Zoe didn't want anything from him, would never hurt him in any way, just allowing her touch was a major concession.

They sat like that with the morning sun filtering through the filmy curtains, a warm breeze caressing the folds.

"You got it good here, Zoe," he repeated. What would it feel like to have the angel lady for a ma? As good as it felt to eat her pie and wear the clothes she made? Yes. As good as it felt to sleep on the clean sheets she washed and hear her voice on the morning air? Better.

But as good as it all felt, he couldn't help wondering how long it could last. Nothing this good could last forever.

As if his thoughts had conjured her up, her soft hum carried down the hallway. "Zoe? Where are you, darling? Lucas, are you up?"

"In here, ma'am," he replied, and scooted away from Zoe.

"Good morning, you two," she greeted them, and her smile shined brighter than the sunshine.

"Mornin'."

Zoe jumped down and wrapped her chubby arms around Thea's legs. Thea smoothed her hair.

"Breakfast is ready. We're going into town this morning. Won't that be a grand adventure? Hurry down, now,

Lucas. Mr. Hayes and I want to talk to you about something.'' She took Zoe's hand and led her out of the room.

Lucas grabbed his dungarees and stepped into them. Sure enough. This was probably the bad news. He dropped to his knees and rooted beneath his mattress, pulling out the tobacco tin Thea's father had given him.

Methodically, he counted out his money.

He had enough to make a run for it when the time came. He hoped it wasn't today, but he stuffed the cash into his pocket just to be on the safe side.

Good thing he'd planned ahead.

Twenty minutes later, dressed in his best shirt, Lucas slid into the chair he'd grown familiar with.

''Where's the firing squad, Lucas?'' Hayes asked, pouring a cup of coffee and sipping it while he surveyed the pretty picture the morning made from the kitchen window.

Lucas gave him a baffled glance.

Hayes just chuckled.

Thea placed a platter of griddle cakes on the table. ''Where's Red Horse?''

Hayes seated himself. ''He cooked himself something outside earlier. He's getting the horses ready.''

Thea poured thick maple syrup on a griddle cake and cut it for Zoe. Hayes forked a slice of bacon onto her plate, and she ate happily.

''We're meeting Mrs. Vaughn in Omaha, Lucas.'' Hayes delivered the news like he was talking about the weather.

Lucas watched syrup drizzle from his top griddle cake, down the side of the stack, one cake at a time, and pool on the plate.

''I wired her after the housewarming. Then I wrote the Foundling Home and explained what had happened.''

This was it. That woman was coming to get him. Hayes and the angel lady—he couldn't bring himself to look at her—were ready to turn him over, to send him back to New York. His mind rolled over the things in the room he'd used upstairs: the shirts she'd made him. They'd know he planned to run if he packed them. He'd miss them. He looked down at the one he had on and ran a hand across the front.

"Booker told them about Bard, Lucas," Thea said. "About the way he treated you. That indenture agreement is no good, of course, so that means you're free again."

Sure. Free. About as free as a chicken in a stinkin' coop.

"Mrs. Hayes and I have talked it over," the big man said from the end of the table. "We want to know if you'd like to stay here with us."

Lucas's attention shot from Hayes's face to the angel lady's waiting expression. Zoe stopped eating and regarded each of them with solemn perusal.

Thea twisted her napkin. "We'd like to adopt you, Lucas. But only if it's what you want."

All three gazes locked on his heated face.

"What's the catch?" he managed to say, finally.

Thea turned an anxious look on Hayes.

The man took a bite and said around it, "No catch."

Lucas couldn't quite grasp the concept. "You mean—" he surveyed both of their faces "—I'd be your kid?"

Thea nodded. "Yes. Legally."

"An' I'd never have to go back to the Home? I'd never have to go nowhere but right here?"

Hayes nodded. "Stay as long as you like. A few more years and you'll be old enough to be on your own. Until then, we want you here."

Lucas still couldn't believe his good fortune. Was this really about to happen? "What about Mrs. Vaughn?" he asked skeptically. "What if she don't want me to stay?"

"I don't think that will happen," Hayes replied. "She wants to see you permanently settled, too. She's a fair and caring person."

Lucas nodded in agreement. Mrs. Vaughn had always treated him well. He'd wait and see if it worked out before he let himself think about it too much. "Okay," he agreed.

Thea smiled and exchanged a glance with Hayes. Zoe gave a beaming smile and went back to her breakfast. And

Lucas looked at the people around the table in a whole new light.

Family.

They stood in the shade under the mercantile's awning, avoiding the dust that blew up from the street with each passing rider or wagon. Booker drew a watch from his front pocket and checked the time. "She should have been here by now."

Red Horse sat on the long bench that fronted the building and pulled a sleepy, bonneted Zoe onto his lap.

Lucas perched on the top step and squinted down the street.

"Something must have happened," Thea said.

Booker slid the watch back. "I'll go check the telegraph office. Maybe she sent word that she'd be delayed."

Thea nodded and watched him cross the street.

Three of her friends from church, all finely dressed, approached and stopped in front of Thea. "Thea! Where have you been?" Agnes Birch asked. A huge purple brooch held a lacy handkerchief pinned to her enormous breast. "You weren't there to conduct the ladies' missionary meeting."

"No, I couldn't get away that evening," Thea explained.

Penelope Dodd stepped up beside Agnes. "Some of us went and helped Widow Barnett clean out her husband's things and get her house ready to sell."

"Oh, yes." Thea nodded, feeling a little guilty. She hadn't realized Mr. Barnett had passed on. "That was so nice of you. I'm sure she appreciated it."

"We all wondered where you were, Thea," Malvina Beck, the livery man's wife, added. "I have to wonder if you're safe out there with that—" her voice lowered to a whisper "—*Indian* on the premises."

Surprised, Thea hoped Red Horse hadn't heard that last comment.

Agnes leaned forward and her chin waddled when she spoke. "It's not wise to let that innocent little girl near an Indian, Thea."

"That's ridiculous," Thea denied. "Red Horse is Mr. Hayes's friend."

Agnes clucked and waved her pudgy hand. "Well, it seems Mr. Hayes is turning you into an Indian-lover and a recluse, my dear. If you stay away from town much more, we'll have to think you've dropped out of society."

Thea could only stare at her in shock.

Lucas looked up from his seat on the step, and she read the disapproval on his face.

The women passed by and entered the dry goods store. Thea glanced back at Red Horse and Zoe. Both seemed absorbed with a string of painted beads. If Agnes and the others pushed, they could do Thea some real damage in the eyes of the townspeople. She didn't want them talking about her behind her back, thinking ill of her, but her life had changed. Couldn't they see that? A glimmer of anger sparked within her breast. How dare they be so judgmental toward a person they didn't even know?

Booker returned with a square slip of paper. "She wired," he announced. "Mrs. Vaughn's delayed until tomorrow morning."

"Oh, my." Thea glanced at Zoe, now falling asleep on Red Horse's lap. "It's so late. We waited all afternoon." They'd done all their shopping, and their purchases waited in the wagon.

Booker stared off across the street.

Lucas's stomach rumbled.

Booker turned to her. "We'll spend the night. Lucas's horse is in the corral with hay and water. Red Horse's pony will fend for himself another day. We'll stable the others and take a couple of rooms in the hotel. We can have dinner in the dining room tonight."

Thea considered the expense.

"Don't even say it," he warned.

Too hot and tired to argue, she nodded.

"Set, then." Booker gestured with a long thumb to the store behind them. "Anybody needs anything extra to spend the night, go get it now."

"Maybe one or two things," Thea replied, and entered the store.

A short time later, they waited in the hotel lobby while Booker registered and checked their weapons. "I paid the stableman to store our purchases until morning," he said, and led the way up the stairs. "Let's all get washed up and meet in the dining room."

A young girl carried water into the room and left silently. Even though Zoe was exhausted, she good-naturedly allowed Thea to wash her and brush her hair with a new hairbrush. Thea did her own and met Red Horse in the hallway.

"You ladies look lovely," he said, and escorted them down the stairs.

A burly manager, sausaged into a too-small shirt and bow tie, stepped in front of them, preventing their entrance to the dining room. "We don't allow Injuns," he said, and leveled his hostile gaze on Red Horse.

Beyond him she saw the few patrons turn their way with interest. "Red Horse is our friend," she said softly. The man could see Red Horse appeared the genteel picture of civility in his white shirt and tie. "He's having dinner with us."

"Not in here, he ain't. Our customers don't take to eatin' with savages."

Thea stared down at the pompous man. "He's no more a savage than you are!"

"It's all right, Mrs. Hayes," Red Horse said, and touched her elbow. "You go ahead and meet the major. I don't mind."

"I'll do no such thing," she huffed.

"Is there a problem?" With relief, Thea turned at the sound of Booker's voice. Dressed in dark trousers, a crisp white shirt and string tie, Booker couldn't have arrived at a more timely moment.

Irving Jackson, the owner of the hotel, dressed in brown trousers and vest, appeared at the same time. "What's wrong, Clancy?" he asked.

Thea turned to him. Jackson's presence always threaded dread through her system.

"The lady's tryin' to bring the Injun into the dining room," the burly man said with a sneer.

"I'm sorry, sir," Jackson said to Booker, "Indians aren't allowed in the hotel."

"Do you know that a long and bloody war was fought over attitudes like that?" Booker asked calmly.

Lucas hung in the doorway as if prepared to make a quick escape.

Jackson flustered. "I hardly see what—"

"No, I'm sure you don't." Booker regarded the man. "I've booked two rooms for the night. My family and I wish to have our meal in the dining room. If my friend is not welcome, then I'll have to ask for a refund on the rooms, and we'll eat elsewhere."

So there, Thea wanted to shout in Jackson's reddening face. He thinned his lips into a tight white line, obviously torn between losing the cost of their night's lodgings and offending other guests by allowing an Indian in their midst. Thea glanced into the room beyond and observed a few of the faces. Most merely looked interested in the outcome, but a few glared in outright hatred, among them Agnes Birch.

The proprietor must have noticed Agnes, too. "I'm sorry, Mr. . . . ?"

"Hayes."

"Mr. Hayes. But I would lose business by allowing you to stay."

A muscle jumped in Booker's chiseled cheek. "Very well, give me my money back."

"I can't do that. We registered you in good faith. The fact that you choose to leave has nothing to do with the quality of our service."

"Then we're staying." Booker turned and ushered Thea and Lucas toward the tables. "And we're eating."

"Sir!" Jackson followed. "Sir, you can't do this."

Under Booker's silent direction, everyone took a seat, including Red Horse. Thea held Zoe on her lap and felt her little body trembling.

"Sir, you must leave."

"Then I guess you'll have to throw us out," Booker replied.

Jackson glanced at each of them. The man he'd called Clancy waited at his elbow.

"You so much as touch my wife or children, and you'll reckon with me," Booker added, threat evident in his tone.

Jackson seemed to size up Booker, calmly seated at the table. His gaze flickered to Thea, his hesitation obvious. The thought came to her that he'd been at the housewarming the afternoon that Booker had pounded Ronan Bard into the dirt. Apparently at a loss as how to remove the Indian from the hotel without meeting a similar fate, Jackson stiffly turned and hauled Clancy away with him.

At the next table, Agnes huffed indignantly, threw her napkin on the table and stood. "Come on, Edgar. We're leaving."

"No need to leave, Aggie," Edgar Birch replied. He reached for his coffee cup. "We haven't had our dessert yet."

"We're leaving, and that's that!" She grabbed his arm and yanked the slight man from his seat. He grabbed his bowler from the next chair.

"Booker," Edgar said with a polite nod and an apologetic shrug.

Thea realized Edgar Birch had been among the men who'd helped bring the turbine from the train to the mill.

The other husband and wife who'd been seated with the Birches, rose and followed them from the room.

"She didn't need dessert, anyway," Booker said.

Red Horse and Lucas grinned, and the tension eased.

Thea glanced at Booker's friend. How awful for him. How must he feel being treated as less than any other man? "I'm awfully sorry, Red Horse," she said, but the words were inadequate.

She'd known Agnes Birch since she was quite young and had never imagined the woman's hateful reaction to a red man. Wasn't this the same woman who helped sew quilts for the missionaries to take to foreign peoples and tell them about God's love?

"Don't be sorry, ma'am. You would be treated much the same among my former people."

"Former?" she asked, refocusing her attention.

He nodded. "I'm too white for them. I worked for the army trying to bring peace, but they didn't understand."

She nodded thoughtfully.

The waitress came and took their orders.

Even after the struggle, Thea enjoyed eating someone else's cooking. Lucas commented that the apple pie wasn't as good as hers, and blushed at her smile. Clancy and the proprietor watched from the corner of the room. Thea glanced at them every once in a while and noted that Booker kept his eye on the pair, too.

It seemed Booker had made a few more enemies.

Thea brushed out her hair and glanced around the stark room. Zoe slept peacefully in the center of the feather mattress, candlelight illuminating her angelic features.

A gentle rap sounded at the door.

"Yes?" Thea replied.

"It's me."

Wearing only her chemise and drawers, she pulled a blanket around her shoulders and opened the door. Booker strode into the room. Thea regarded him.

"They just assumed I'd be sleeping in here," he said, jerking a thumb over his shoulder toward the room next door. "The two of them took over the bed."

Her eyes must have shown her surprise.

"I'll just get another room." He started back toward the door.

"No." She stopped him with the word. It would be senseless to spend any more on rooms for just one night. After all, he was her husband! "Zoe doesn't take up much room. Sleep with us."

He nodded and hung his hat on a hook near the washstand.

Thea dropped the blanket and sprang between the sheets. She curled around Zoe and buried her face in the silky locks. Fabric rustled. Two thumps hit the floor in succession as he removed his boots. Fabric slid again.

The candle was blown out. The bed dipped and took his weight.

His fingers touched Zoe's hair and came in contact with Thea's nose.

"Sorry," he said, and withdrew his hand.

"It's all right." She turned her face toward the ceiling now that the light was out. A mistake. She could smell him. His hair. His skin. He'd used bay rum that day. Her husband lay a foot away in the darkness. Oh, Lord.

Thank goodness Zoe separated them, or she'd probably be sorely tempted to do something stupid. Like reach across and see if he had anything on.

A hundred tiny moth wings fluttered inside her belly. Like press herself full length against him and enjoy every inch of his hard frame.

One of the moths found passage to her heart and tripped it double time. Like turn her lips against his jaw and feel the late-night rasp of his beard. Inhale against his skin and his hair and matted chest—

Yes. Good thing Zoe was there.

Her eyes had adjusted to the darkness, and she could make out his profile. Without moving her head, she rolled her gaze downward over the white sheet draping his long form.

The moths took a plummeting dive and created a tingle in the most disconcerting spot. Thea pressed her knees together, hard.

Thank goodness for Zoe.

Zoe had brought them together in the first place. And now, unknowingly, innocently in her slumber, kept them safely apart.

Sounds from the street drifted up to the window, reminding her how strange this situation was. Finally, she turned onto her back. Her heels touched the edge of the mattress. How did Booker manage to fit?

Between them, Zoe sighed. Sometime later, Booker shifted his weight. Sometime, long into the night, Thea slept.

Her midnight lover came to her during the night. He found his way into her dreams, into the need she fervently denied, and stroked her aroused body with his dark, ethereal fingers. Thea moaned and rolled over.

Her dark-haired, dark-eyed, sleep-woven lover kissed the freckles on her chest, nuzzled his rough cheek against her breasts, whispered incoherent words of dark desire. He wove an erotic web of passion around the two of them, indulging, delighting, enticing....

His hand on her thigh was hot. Hot. Thea's eyelids fluttered and she resisted waking. No. She didn't want to miss this. He felt too good, his hard body pressed along the length of hers, his searing arousal pressed against her hip. Too good to wake up and—

She opened her eyes.

Lavish heat encompassed her entire back and buttocks. The hand on her thigh twitched. Zoe slept on the side of the bed where Thea'd been last night, and Thea...

Oh, Lord. She garnered enough courage to look over her shoulder. Booker lay sprawled behind her, over her, one bare, hair-roughened leg entwined with hers, his hand resting familiarly on her thinly clad thigh. The sight of his naked hip gave her a start.

She dropped her head and took a few cleansing breaths. Maybe she could slip away before he woke up, before he discovered how brazenly she'd insinuated herself against his naked body!

Slowly, she drew her foot from beneath his ankle and slid her leg away. Turning to her stomach, preparing to rise on her hands and knees and climb over Zoe, she turned to peek at him.

Wide-awake, the major stared back.

Chapter Twelve

"**M**orning," he said, greeting her.

Mortified, she managed to croak a reply.

He reached down and pulled the sheet up to his waist. Thea hadn't taken her gaze from his, didn't trust herself to. "Hand me my pants, and I'll let you get ready," he said.

She scrambled over the top of Zoe, a skein of tousled hair falling across her face. She held it back and padded around the foot of the bed. His trousers lay over the back of a chair. She grabbed them and approached him from the other side of the mattress.

Booker rolled onto his back, raising one knee beneath the sheet, and took the pants from her. He sat up and she spun away. Looking for something to do, she found the blanket on the floor and wrapped it around her shoulders.

Zoe sat up, blinked at them both in dreamy-eyed confusion, and glanced around the room.

"Mornin', pumpkin," Booker said, and reached over to ruffle her hair.

Apparently satisfied with her surroundings and companions, Zoe fell back on the pillow.

Thea sat and pulled the child's head against her breast. Booker placed his feet in the trousers and stood, tugging them up over his muscled buttocks. Thea couldn't help herself; she stared. The skin below his waist was a dozen shades paler than the rest, but no less appealing. The taut muscles flexed, and much too quickly disappeared beneath the fabric.

My, my. She released Zoe for fear she'd inadvertently choke her.

Booker turned and met her transfixed gaze. He knew she'd looked. Knowing she blushed to the roots of her hair, she looked away.

"I'll go for water," he said, and shrugged his wrinkled shirt on.

She nodded.

By the time he'd washed and finished dressing, she had Zoe's hair braided and was working on her own. She'd obviously spent a restless night dreaming unseemly dreams and hogging the bed.

"May I?" Booker asked from beside her.

Casting him a quizzical glance, she turned the brush over. He took the curved handle in his enormous palm and ran his thumb over the bristles. Thea lifted her gaze. What thoughts lurked behind those obsidian eyes? How did he feel about the way they'd awakened tangled together like two worms on a hook? She turned away.

He settled on the bed's edge behind her, and a long silence ensued. Before her, Zoe played with her rag doll. Finally, Thea turned her head.

Coming to life, Booker straightened her shoulders, forcing her head forward, and ran the brush through her hair. Once down the center. Twice more, all the way to the ends. On the side, he found a snarl and gently worked it loose with small caresses of the bristles. Stroke after mesmerizing stroke, he brushed her hair from the roots at her forehead and temples all the way to the tips.

Thea closed her eyes and sighed with pleasure.

Gathering the ends, he held them and wrapped the mass around his wrist several times, taking up all the length until he held her fast by the nape of her neck.

With her hair in his fist, he tilted the angle of her head and brushed his lips against her cheek. His unshaven skin scraped her jaw. A shiver danced across her shoulder and shimmied down her arm. Beneath the chemise, Thea's nipples tightened.

Abruptly, he released her hair and stood. "I'll check on the others and meet you out front."

She nodded, grateful he hadn't suggested breakfast in the dining room.

"We'll eat in the boardinghouse restaurant down the street," he continued, as if guessing her thoughts. "And then we'll wait for the train."

His boots sounded on the floor and stopped short of the door. "Thea?"

She glanced over her shoulder.

"You're lovely in the morning."

The moths were back, multiplying and lining up for a strategic attack on her insides. She managed a disbelieving smile.

"Could you manage a thank-you?" he asked.

She raised a startled brow.

"It's my opinion that you're a beautiful woman. I've told you that before. You treat the compliment like it's hogwash, and that insults me."

She had to back up over quite a few years and a good many opinions that differed from his in order to approach his words from another angle. He really thought she was attractive.

Maryruth had told her many times, but she'd just considered her sister was trying to make her feel better about herself. Booker's compliment was different. Way different.

"Thank you," she said.

Booker smiled, went back for his hat and disappeared through the door.

Baking beneath the blanket, Thea flung it off and bathed in the water from the basin. Cooling her skin, Thea thought of the dream. She thought of how near they'd lain all night and how close they'd awakened this morning.

He'd been with a lot of beautiful women. But now he was married to her. Men had normal, healthy urges, didn't they? Booker did, didn't he? Of course he did. The fact had been pretty evident that morning.

What would have happened if Zoe hadn't been there?

Thea pulled on her blouse and recalled the night before their wedding, the night he'd kissed her senseless. What would have happened if Lucas hadn't called out to them?

She tugged on her skirt, found her kid belt and buckled it around her waist. She retrieved her shoes from under the bed's edge and stared at the rumpled sheets.

She reviewed their wedding night in her mind. His words, her reaction.

Her conditioned response. Roll over, Thea. Play dead. She'd never expected more of herself. Even Booker had said she needed to think of herself more. Doing things for others had always filled her hands and her time. Church work gave her a sense of importance, of being needed. But it had never made her feel the way waking up next to Booker did. And she wanted more of that...more of him. Maybe she'd gone about this all wrong.

Okay, so she wasn't the catch of the county. She didn't have the tiny feet and waist and the pearl complexion men cottoned to. She wasn't coy or cute or practiced in the art of flirtation.

But she *was* right there under his...nose. And this far west, availability meant something. He'd complimented her. He was interested.

Thea sat and tugged her shoes on. She'd handled it all wrong, she could see that now. No use getting her feelings hurt; what good had that ever done? He was a man. She was a woman. Nothing could be simpler. He was her husband. She was his wife.

She stood.

He may not have fallen in love with her at first sight. He may not ever fall in love with her. But she could meet his needs. And that was for darned sure what she needed.

She dressed Zoe, all the while thinking, planning. Here she'd been trying to think of an answer for Maryruth's marital dilemma, and both solutions looked identical.

With a smile on her face, she took Zoe's hand and led her out the door. Thea Hayes was going to seduce her husband.

Two days with this tie on was more than a body could abide. Lucas ran a finger around the inside of his prickling collar, lifted his hat and shook the hair from his forehead with a toss of his head. In the distance, the mournful train whistle announced the eight-twenty's arrival.

He'd dangled his legs over the edge of the platform until his feet had fallen asleep. He turned around and sat Indian-style, adjusting his hat back on his head.

Mrs. Vaughn had best be on this one. If she wasn't he'd melt into a puddle on the wooden structure by noon. The whistle lamented again and he met the angel's sympathetic gaze. Beneath the brim of her blue cotton bonnet, her eyes were brighter than the cloudless sky...a clear color, like blue water running over mossy green pebbles. Eyes that saw things only angels could see.

Lucas smiled, and she winked in return. Was he really lucky enough to get an angel for a ma? He'd had a ma once. If he let himself remember, he could sometimes picture her: nothing like Thea. Nothing like he wanted to remember, so he didn't do it much. Only once in a while. Just to tell himself he could remember if he wanted to, which wasn't often.

She'd been dark-haired. Thin. She cried a lot. Sang sometimes when she'd had too much to drink. Cried and sang and waited for a ship to come in. Lucas figured it must have come for her, 'cause all of a sudden she'd been gone and he'd never seen her again.

He didn't remember a whole lot about the early days. He thought he must have stayed with someone for a while, but then that's where his Home memories began. So many children. Too many nights. Too many families that didn't want him. Faces and years and beatings ran together until only the worst ones were clear pictures in his mind. And those were the ones he tried to forget.

The rails hummed and Lucas's stomach lurched. He took stock of Hayes calmly watching the horizon, his black hat pulled low over his eyes. Lucas had never had a pa. Never wanted one. Never saw one that he'd of wanted to have. Mean sum-bitches most of 'em were. Hayes wasn't so bad, though. He'd never laid a hand on anybody that Lucas had ever seen. 'Cept Bard, Lucas corrected himself with a smug twist of his lips.

The engine rumbled into view, and black smoke belched into the sky. The rails vibrated, and Lucas remembered every inch of the long, arduous trip west from New York City. If he had his way, he'd never get on another train again as long as he lived.

Beneath the platform, the ground trembled. Steam hissed as the locomotive neared the station and slowed. The engine passed and Lucas held his hat on against the rush of hot, dry air. The cars rolled to a grinding stop.

A Negro porter in a hat and suit unfolded the metal stairs from the passenger car, and a man and woman descended. Mrs. Vaughn came next, smiling as Hayes took her carpetbag and offered his arm. Thea greeted her, and Lucas followed them into the dim station building.

"Congratulations," the slight woman said, looking up at Thea. "I received Mr. Hayes's telegram."

"Thank you," Thea replied. "Will you be able to stay with us?"

"No. Thank you, but I'm getting back on the train and heading east. I'm already a day behind schedule."

"Can we buy you dinner?" Hayes asked.

"Thank you, no. I have provisions in my bag." She opened her reticule and took out some folded papers. "I just need you both to sign these. While you look them over, I'd like to talk to Lucas alone."

Thea glanced over at him and pointed to her head. "Lucas," she whispered loudly.

Belatedly, he doffed his hat, crushed it to his chest and stepped nearer the agent. "Ma'am?"

Mrs. Vaughn led him to the straight-backed chairs along the front wall and sat. Uncomfortably, Lucas perched beside her and rolled his hat brim. Across the room, Thea and Booker seated themselves and watched.

"How are you, Lucas?" she asked. He noticed the way her high-necked dress bunched the loose skin at her throat.

"Fine, ma'am."

"Lucas, I'm awfully sorry about Mr. Bard. You must understand I couldn't have known anything like that would happen."

"No, ma'am."

"I feel quite responsible for the children I place. I pray every night that they'll find good homes."

"Yes, ma'am." She had some kind of oval jewelry pinned to her collar that looked like a woman's profile raised off the surface.

"Lucas, do you like the Hayeses?"

"Yes, ma'am."

"Will you be happy to have them adopt you? Once the legal procedure goes through, I'll have no more say in your welfare. The state of New York will no longer be your legal guardian."

Lucas stared in disbelief. This adoption thing was really going to happen? He'd expected something to go wrong, the agency to remember some rule against good things happening to street trash.

Mrs. Vaughn blinked her hazel eyes, which were skimpily fringed with short dark lashes. "Lucas? Do you want them to be your parents?"

Lucas tore his stare from her. The papers lay forgotten in Thea's lap. She and Hayes openly studied him from across the room.

"I'll—" he began and had to start over. "I'll belong to them? For good?"

"The court has to look over the files and sign the documents, but there's no reason why the case won't be finalized in a few months. I've handled many adoptions, Lucas. The court is eager to place you with good parents."

He wasn't so sure about that. Seemed to him all they'd ever been eager for was to pawn him off on any old person who would have him.

"Is this what you want, Lucas?"

"Yes, ma'am."

She patted his hand with her gloved fingers. "Very well, then." She stood. "Let's get those papers signed before my train leaves."

The agent produced a fountain pen from her bag and marched across the lobby. Lucas's future—he blinked in awe—*parents* signed the pages. He watched Mrs. Vaughn refold and tuck them in her reticule, and didn't let himself conjure up images of something happening to the papers on their way back to New York City.

He swallowed and barely noticed the tie constricting his throat. Maybe—just maybe—he wouldn't have to leave after all.

Their party was headed for the livery when a horse and rider came alongside them. "Hayes!"

Booker stopped. Beside him Thea paused, and the others stood still as well. Booker tilted his hat back on his head and glanced up.

"You Hayes?" the marshal asked around a fat cigar.

"I am," Booker replied.

"Heard you caused a little ruckus at the hotel last evenin'."

Thea looked up at Marshal Hardy with a feeling of unease curling through her chest. What had gone wrong with this town? Everyone she knew was becoming an enemy!

"Seems the problem was settled satisfactorily," Booker replied.

"That right?" The beefy man flipped open a pocket watch and glanced at it, taking his time. Slowly, he poked it back into his vest pocket. "Care to tell me where you spent the night last night?"

"I'm sure you already know I was registered at the hotel," Booker answered, annoyance lacing his tone.

"Where were you shortly after one o'clock this morning?"

"Room seventeen," he said.

"Anybody here can back that up?"

"I can," Thea said quickly. "He was with me all night. Why are you asking these questions, Marshal?"

Hardy rolled the cigar from one side of his wet lips to the other. "Someone gave Irving Jackson a beating last night. He left the hotel and somebody pulled him into the alley. Man's in pretty bad shape."

Knowing Jackson the way she did, it was no wonder he'd made his share of enemies. "Time or two I'd liked to have done that myself," she admitted. "But I can assure you it wasn't my husband, and I resent the fact that you suspect it was."

"Now, Thea, you know how it is when there's strangers in town. People just get suspicious." The marshal turned his attention to Red Horse. "How about you?"

Thea's heart sank, fearfully. She'd heard about cruel vigilante justice, and she was frightened for Red Horse. What if the marshal took him off to jail? What if the townspeople lynched him? Zoe clung to her skirt and she reached down with a trembling hand.

Red Horse replied without hesitation. "I was in the room next to his."

"Anyone there with you?"

Lucas stepped forward. "He was with me, an' he didn't beat nobody up. He ain't that kind."

"You don't think I'm gonna take a kid's word for it, do you?" Hardy asked.

"Did anyone see one of us leave our rooms or the hotel?" Booker asked. "Do you have anything to back up your accusations, Marshal? Both of us have spent time in the army, fighting to earn peace for this country. Red Horse has a shining record with the government. Why don't you wire Washington and ask for a character reference?"

The marshal leaned back until his saddle creaked. He contemplated them both for several seconds. "I'll just do that," he said finally. "Until then, keep your noses clean."

Thea watched his retreating back with anger festering in her chest. The whole town had gone loco.

Thea helped Zoe carry a bucket of water to the spot where they'd planted the acorn and poured it into the barren ground. Both of them watched the water soak into the dirt. Two weeks and nothing.

Thea glanced at the gray clouds gathering on the horizon. "Looks like we won't need to carry any more water today."

The jingle of harnesses alerted her to the arrival of a wagon creaking toward the house. Booker rode on horseback alongside a wagon pulled by a team of mules. The sight of him called the moths back to active duty in her belly. She hadn't managed a minute alone with him for days. How was she going to carry out her plan for seduction? She followed Zoe, who carried the bucket to the back porch. The wagon pulled to a halt.

Booker dismounted and a bandy-legged little man with a grizzled salt-and-pepper beard climbed down from the wagon seat. He hit the ground flat-footed, and Booker shook his hand. Bowlegged and stooped slightly, he came only to the middle of Booker's chest.

Booker motioned her closer. "Thea, this is Skeeter Gunderson. He's the millwright I told you would be coming. Skeeter, this is my wife, Thea."

The little man leaned backward and craned his neck to look up at her. "Oh-o-ee! Big one, ain't she?"

Thea couldn't help a smile.

Skeeter Gunderson cackled.

Booker grinned. "Now, Skeeter, you're going to have to mind your manners around my wife. She puts out a fine spread, and you wouldn't want her throwing you out on your ear before you've had supper."

"No, sirree!" Skeeter said, chuckling. He bowed comically. "I like a tall woman, I do."

Booker laughed. "Let me get the plans for the inside of the mill. We'll have time to go over them before supper. Okay?" he asked, turning to Thea.

Caught off guard, she merely nodded. Booker entered the house. Zoe sat near the corner of the porch, watching a butterfly flit over a clump of violets.

"Didn't know 'e had a woman waitin'," Skeeter commented, and moved his sunken lips in a habitual mincing pucker. Thea wondered if he had any teeth left. She hoped she had something to serve him for dinner that he could chew.

"We didn't meet until Mr. Hayes was discharged and came looking for his niece," she explained.

He pursed and unpursed his seamy lips. "That her?"

"Yes. Her name's Zoe."

"Zoe, huh. Me pappy had a goat named Zoe once. Damned awnry critter. Ate my mammy's pantaloons right off the clothesline."

Thea stifled a grin.

"Fine barn," Skeeter said, squinting at the new structure. "Me 'n' my mules'll be right comfortable."

"Oh, Mr. Gunderson, I wouldn't want you to stay in the barn. We have plenty of room in the house."

He eyed the house skeptically. "Dunno. Fancy, is it?"

"No. It suits Mr. Hayes." How true that statement was. She loved the house, the simple, basic furnishings, and the wide-open, uncluttered spaces. There wasn't a piece of needlepoint or a doily in the entire house. After living in the midst of Madeline and Trudy's handiwork, the lack of frippery was a blessing. "It's not fancy at all. Would you like to see it?"

"Show me at dinner," Skeeter consented. "I ain't cleaned up right now."

She nodded.

Booker returned with the plans.

Thunder rolled across the heavens like a lopsided boulder gaining momentum. Zoe ran and clung to Thea's skirts.

"Looks like we'd better hurry over to the mill," Booker said, squinting at the darkening sky.

Skeeter jumped back up on the wagon.

Booker mounted Gideon. "See you at dinner, Thea."

She nodded and waved them off.

The rain was still just a threat by the time she had the meal on the table. The men came through the back door with slicked-back hair and an outdoorsy smell clinging to them. Thea had set the meal out in the kitchen as usual. Even though Skeeter was company, and company called for the dining room and the good dishes, she wanted him to feel comfortable in their home.

Booker nodded his silent approval and brushed past her with an unexpected peck on her cheek. She covered her surprise by turning away for the basket of warm rolls.

Skeeter surprised Thea by helping himself to an extra-large slab of beef, and chewing with gusto. She caught the amused look Red Horse and Lucas exchanged and gave them a wink. The others spoke politely about their day, but Skeeter didn't say anything until he'd finished eating. He wiped his mouth on the back of his hand, and then, as if realizing that's what the checkered napkin was for, scrubbed his hand with the napkin.

"Fine eatin's, ma'am," he said.

"Thank you."

"Good spot you got there, Booker," he said, apparently ready for conversation. "Jest like ya said."

"I figure we can get about fifty horsepower with that headway," Booker replied.

"Sixty or I'll be go'd t' hell," Skeeter returned. "Pardon me, ma'am. You'll have them buhrstones spinnin' like a whirlin' dervish. And with the water sitiated a far piece, storage'll be dry as a bone."

Booker sat back and nodded, obviously pleased with the old man's approval.

Skeeter patted his belly and tapped his fingers on the rim of his empty coffee cup.

Thea stood and gathered plates. "I'll get dessert and more coffee."

His disheveled brows climbed his forehead. "Sweets, too?" He addressed Booker. "Damned fine woman ya found. Got her up a stump yet?"

"What does that mean?" Thea asked.

Booker's neck actually turned red. "These two are enough children for right now," he said to Skeeter.

Children? What had Skeeter asked? If Booker had her pregnant yet? Rather difficult to accomplish from separate bedrooms, she wanted to add, but bit her lip.

Finally, Booker met her eyes, and she held the gaze. *Pregnant.* The idea knocked her off balance. Going into this marriage, all she'd cared about was Zoe. Now she wanted Booker for herself. And the possibility of having a child of his was almost too overwhelming to dwell upon.

Her husband changed the subject, turning his attention back to his guest. "If it's not raining in the morning, I want you to show me how the cables should be installed."

Thea carried the dishes to the kitchen and came back with two apple pies. Lucas's face lit up with a youthful glow that brought a lump to her throat.

With deft strokes, she sliced one pie into quarters for the men. "Your favorite," she said, leaning close over Lucas's shoulder.

"Yes, ma'am." He turned, his storm gray eyes near.

"I made them for you this morning."

His eyes met hers. She set the plate in front of him and casually placed her hand on his shoulder. He allowed the touch, not shrugging away as she'd seen him do with Booker. She smiled and gave his shoulder a gentle squeeze before she moved away.

Thunder shook the house. Zoe dropped her fork onto her plate with a clatter and hopped into Red Horse's lap in a movement so fast, Red Horse had to set his coffee cup down before the steaming liquid spilled over.

Thea caught the hooded expression in Booker's eyes. Boots sounded on the back porch, and a hearty knock hammered the solid door.

Closest, Thea spun and opened it to her father. "Papa!" She hugged him soundly. "How nice. You're just in time for pie."

He gave Booker a friendly swat with his hat. Thea took it and ushered him into Zoe's unoccupied chair. She pushed a slice of pie toward him. "Rest assured I miss you for more than your cookin', Thea-girl, but I'm beginnin' to feel gaunt."

She laughed and poured him a mug of coffee. "You just missed the rain."

"I did. I heard you had company."

Booker made the introductions, and Jim Coulson stood to shake Skeeter's hand.

"Jim's spread adjoins me, on the south."

"Mmm," Skeeter acknowledged around a mouthful of pastry. "You got sons?"

"Five daughters," Jim replied "My son-in-law works the land with me."

"We're going to go over the plans this evening," Booker said to his father-in-law. "Care to join us?"

"That's what I came for." He shook his head at Thea's offer of more coffee. "Ever since Booker told me about the turbine he planned to use, I've wanted to see it work for myself."

"Damned fine piece o' machinery, 'scuse me, ma'am," Skeeter said. "This here's only the second 'un in Nebraskie. Purty soon, they's all you'll see. Weather wears out them wooden sons o' bitches too damned fast. Pardon me, ma'am."

Thea heated water on the stove for dishes.

"We'd better get the horses in and bedded down before that storm breaks loose," Booker said, rising and grabbing his hat and slicker from the pegs.

Red Horse carried Zoe to Thea.

"I'll settle my mount in your barn for a few hours, too," Jim said, rising.

"Don't get wet, Papa," Thea warned. "You had a time with that last cold you caught." She found Zoe a scrap of brown paper and a charcoal sliver to draw with.

Booker opened the back door just as a jagged streak of lightning forked across the evening sky, darker than usual this late in the summer. Fat drops of rain spattered in the dust and pelted the porch roof. Booker tossed Jim his slicker. "I'll fork some hay down into the troughs and check on Skeeter's mules. Red Horse, bring the horses in."

He darted down the steps, slapping Jim Coulson's chestnut on the rump as he passed. Red Horse followed.

Thea's father sank his cup and dessert plate into the metal pan of soapsuds she'd shaved. "Trudy's makin' you some pillow slips."

"That's thoughtful," Thea answered.

"Don't sleep on the daisy parts, though. I did that once and had flowers etched into my face for half a day."

Thea laughed. "I'll remember that."

Jim slipped out the back door.

Skeeter seemed content to sip coffee and search his gums with his tongue. Zoe sat at the opposite end of the table, drawing. She cast the grizzled old man an occasional glance. Thea carried the remaining dishes to the pan.

Amid the thunder, a sharp retort rang across the doorway. Puzzled, Thea dried her hands and opened the back door.

A hundred yards from the barn, Jim Coulson's chestnut stopped a skittish dance and reared back on hind legs. A muffled shout met her ears, and she strained to see through the rain and the ever-darkening sky. Her father's horse, standing untethered, alerted her that something was wrong.

"Papa?" she called from the top steps.

Voices reached her through the downpour.

"Booker! Papa!"

Booker and Red Horse came toward the house then, an awkward, wet slickered form slouched between them. She recognized her father's gray hair plastered to his head.

"Papa! What's wrong with him?"

"Clear off the table so we can lay him out and get a good look," Booker ordered.

Fear seized her heart, and she couldn't move. "What happened?"

Booker shoved past her, supporting her father's well-over-six-foot frame. "He's been shot."

Chapter Thirteen

Lucas tossed the last few utensils on a chair seat, and Thea pulled Zoe away from the table. "Take her upstairs and stay with her."

Obediently, Lucas took Zoe's hand and led her from the kitchen.

Red Horse produced a long knife from inside his leather vest and sliced away the rain slicker and Jim's bloodied plaid shirt.

Heart pounding, Thea grabbed a clean dish towel and dipped it in the soapy water. She handed it to Booker, her hand trembling uncontrollably.

Calmly, he took the cloth and squeezed the excess water out over the gash in Jim's side. Thea's attention shot from the bloody flesh to her father's rain-wet face, and she thanked heaven he was conscious. Even though he grimaced with pain, the wound must not be terribly serious.

Obviously concerned for her fear, Jim reached for her hand and squeezed her fingers, his grip as firm and strong as ever. A sob rose in her throat, but she fought it. She moved closer and smoothed his wet hair back from his forehead.

"Glanced off this rib. Bullet's probably in his clothes somewhere," Booker commented matter-of-factly, probing the bloody fabric.

"Hit your rib and skidded across the bone," Red Horse said to Jim.

"Hell of a mess," Skeeter agreed, "but it ain't bad. Damned lucky, if'n ya ask me. Hurts like a son of a bitch, don't it?"

Thea's father raised his head and studied the open gash on his side. Blood pooled on the table beneath him. "Well, are you gonna talk about it, or are you gonna fix it?"

Red Horse turned abruptly. "I'm going to look around. It's already too late for tracks in this rain, but I might see something."

"Heat more water, Thea," Booker ordered. "We have to clean it up and stitch him. And bring your sewing basket. Skeeter, hold it together as best you can with this cloth. I'll wash my hands and find some bandages."

Numb, Thea did as instructed. Then she stood, her stomach heaving, and threaded the needle while Booker washed the wound.

"Get him something to bite on while I stitch this," Booker said.

She thought briefly and grabbed the wooden hook she used to pull pans forward in the oven. Her father clamped it between his teeth. She and Skeeter took places on either side of him.

"Lean on his shoulder and arm to keep him still," Booker advised.

"Have you done this before?" she asked barely above a whisper.

Booker nodded. He held the flesh together and sewed. Sweat broke out on his forehead.

Jim's bicep and shoulder trembled beneath her palms. "He's almost done, Papa."

Her father swore behind the wooden stick.

"'Scuse him, ma'am," Skeeter added.

Thea closed her eyes briefly and prayed for the ordeal to end. Her thoughts tumbled in swirled confusion. Someone had shot her father!

"Okay, Jim." Booker wiped the back of his hand across his forehead. He dipped a cloth out of the pan of steaming water on the stove and cleaned his father-in-law up before placing a folded wad of cheesecloth over the wound and wrapping bandages around Jim's ribs to hold them in place. "I think you'd better stay the night. You can't ride home."

She'd already promised the extra bedroom to Skeeter. Thea spun and headed for the stairs. "I'll get a bed ready."

Lucas appeared in the upstairs hallway, concern evident in his young features.

"He's all right, Lucas. He needs to stay the night, though."

"He can have my room," the boy offered hopefully.

His eagerness to help touched Thea. She could only imagine how much Lucas's room meant to him. She understood the generosity in his suggestion. Her father's close encounter with death had frightened them all.

The enormity of the situation fell upon her, and sudden tears sprang to her eyes. "Th-thank you," she choked.

Awkwardly, like a scarecrow coming to life, Lucas stepped forward, wrapped a sinewy arm around her and rested his face against her shoulder.

Thea returned the hesitant embrace, pressing her lips against his hair and allowing herself several spontaneous sobs. She couldn't remember ever being as frightened as when she'd seen them carry her father in and Booker had exposed the bloody gash in his side. She'd lived on the frontier most of her life, but this was the closest she'd come to danger. Jim Coulson had kept his family safe and insulated.

She pulled back quickly. "Okay. I have that over, now I have to get the room ready." She kissed Lucas's forehead. He blushed and turned to help.

Once Jim had been settled down for the night, Booker sent Red Horse to let Trudy know what had happened. "Tell her one of us will be over to do his chores in the morning."

Skeeter turned in early, leaving Thea and Booker alone in the kitchen. She placed the soiled towels and cloths in caustic soda to soak. With the initial scare and excitement over, her mind plagued her with questions.

Booker glanced up from his cup on the table. "You all right?"

She wrung her hands together and stood behind her chair. "I think so." She noticed his steady hand on the cup. "How did you do that?"

"What?"

"Sew up that wound like you were mending socks. My hands were shaking so bad, I could barely thread the needles."

He shrugged. "We all did what we had to."

"Well…" She ran her fingers over the back of the chair. "You did a good job."

He nodded.

"Booker, what happened out there?"

"I don't know. I was in the barn and I heard the shot. Red Horse was in the corral. By the time he got around the side of the barn, all he saw was your father on the ground."

"Who would do such a thing?" The idea of someone trying to kill her father was inconceivable. Everyone liked Jim Coulson. As far as she knew, he'd never made an enemy in his life.

Booker shook his head.

"Why would someone try to kill my father?"

A strange look crossed his face. "Let me worry about it. You get some sleep."

His unsatisfying answer exasperated her.

Red Horse came in the back door. "Rain let up," he said.

Booker stood. "Let's go into the study. Night, Thea."

She watched their retreating backs. Obviously, Booker wanted to talk the situation over with Red Horse alone. She hung her apron on a peg and blew out the lantern. Anything that affected her father's safety certainly affected her, too. She didn't appreciate being treated like a helpless female.

Thea paused in the dark hallway and listened to the murmur of masculine voices behind the solid oak door. She could barge in there, demand that Booker include her.

But he wouldn't. He'd calm her down and evade her questions.

Or... she could allow Booker to treat her like a fragile, helpless female. Wouldn't that feed into her plan to seduce him?

She tiptoed up the stairs, checked on her sleeping father and entered Booker's bedroom, lighting the lamp so he'd find his way up later. Thea surveyed the room. She cleaned it once a week, so his few elemental possessions were familiar.

She ran her thumb across the brush on his dresser, stood his comb in the bristles. A few coins and a scarred pocketknife had been dropped carelessly at the dresser's edge. On the washstand stood a shaving mug and brush, his razor and bar of soap beside them. Thea lifted the bar to her nose and inhaled. The spicy fragrance provoked an enticing ribbon of long-denied desire to unfurl and flutter from her heart to the nether regions of her maiden body.

Booker. Oh, God, Booker. She closed her eyes and sank to the edge of his mammoth bed. She relived every moment of falling asleep in the same bed at the hotel, every heated sensation of waking beside him, his hair-rough body pressed against her smooth limbs.

Thea opened her eyes and pictured him on this bed, his dark skin against the white sheets, his midnight black hair upon the pristine pillow slips. She laid a palm against her breast and exultantly measured how alive the mere mental picture of him made her feel.

She regarded the bed appraisingly. If she actually ever shared his bed, if he touched her in it, if he kissed her the way he had the night before their wedding, she'd probably die of pleasure.

And she didn't know how much longer she could wait.

"Did you see anything?"

Red Horse dropped into one of the comfortable leather

chairs that faced the never-used fireplace. "It rained too hard to make out anything. All I could tell was that someone had a horse waiting beyond the rise to the west. Probably one person. I'd say he left his mount there for about an hour and found a spot where the barn hid him and waited for a clear shot."

Red Horse's estimable guess confirmed Booker's suspicions. "He was out there before Jim got here—*when* Jim got here."

"Yes. Could have shot him then."

"But he didn't. He waited for me."

"Or who he thought was you."

Booker paced the floor, his boots echoing on the highly varnished wood. He crossed behind Red Horse and came to a halt in front of the fireplace. He'd been shot at before. He'd been a target before. But that had always been because of the army he represented or because of the white invaders he led into Indian territory. He had land, a home and family now, and that set new words to the old music.

He stared at the gold lettering on the glass door of the Seth Thomas clock Jim had given them on their wedding day. Because of him, Jim Coulson had come within an inch of death. Why?

"Who is it?" he asked aloud.

"You've never mentioned an enemy. If someone had followed you west, we'd have seen or heard something before now. Maybe it's because of me."

Booker glanced at his friend. He couldn't deny that the possibility had crossed his mind, especially after what had transpired at the hotel in Omaha, and then that Jackson fellow getting himself beat up. "But that doesn't make sense. If it was that, they'd have tried to kill you."

Red Horse shrugged. "You're the Injun-lover. To most whites, that's a greater crime than having red skin."

Booker ran a hand down his rough jaw and scratched at his chin. "Yeah."

A door opened and closed upstairs. He pictured Thea checking on her father and going to her room, undressing and slipping into her bed where she'd sleep, trusting him to take care of her—of all of them. "We'll have to stay alert. If someone wants me, everyone here is in danger. I don't plan to sit back and wait for another incident."

"I'll sleep outside from now on," Red Horse said. "I'll hear if anyone comes near the house."

Booker agreed, knowing his friend had slept beneath the sky most of his life and found it no particular hardship. "We'll ride the property twice a day. That way we'll know if he comes back."

Red Horse stood and stepped to the door. "Night, Major."

"Good night."

Alone, Booker dropped to sit on the stone hearth. Should he tell Thea? Would she be any safer? Any more comforted? No. She'd worry more, knowing the entire household was in danger because of him.

Booker climbed the stairs and entered his room. Thea had left the lamp burning for him. Always thoughtful. Always concerned for others.

Would she think less of him if she knew he was responsible for her father's injury? Would she be angry when she did find out the truth?

Those questions didn't matter. What mattered was keeping all of them safe. And that's what he intended to do.

Catching sight of the slight indentation at the foot of his bed, disappointment zigzagged though his chest. He wished she would have stayed.

After breakfast the next morning, Maryruth and Denzel arrived. Denzel spoke with Jim and headed back to the Coulson farm, leaving Maryruth to help Thea with their father.

Maryruth stayed with him for a while, and David played quietly at the foot of the bed until both he and his grandfather grew tired. She left her father to sleep until dinner, and put David down for a nap in Zoe's room.

Last night's rain left the air muggy and the floors filthy. Thea had washed the bedding and towels, hung them on the line and tackled the muddy kitchen floor. Maryruth joined her, scrubbing dried blood from the cracks.

"He seems just fine," she commented.

Thea pushed a lock of hair back from her perspiring cheek with the back of her wet hand. "He is. But he could have been killed."

"And they don't know who it was?"

"I don't think so. If they did, Booker would have gone after them." She shuddered. "I don't even want to think about what he'd do."

Maryruth finished scrubbing and dropped her brush in the pail.

Thea dumped the water outside and together they moved the table and chairs back into place. By then it was time to start the noon meal. Maryruth peeled potatoes and dropped the chunks into a kettle.

"Maryruth," Thea said.

Her sister glanced up.

"Are things the same—between you and Denzel?"

Maryruth nodded.

"I think you need to change his mind."

"What do you mean?"

"You say he's afraid of hurting you?"

Maryruth nodded. "It scared him when I had David. He said he'd never have forgiven himself if anything had happened to me."

"I was pretty scared, too, Maryruth. We all were."

"Well, the doctor said David was hard because he came out backward. It won't be like that next time."

"You know that and I know that, but Denzel's fear is real to him. Maybe he won't get over it until you have another baby and prove it to him."

Her sister raised a brow. "That's not going to happen unless things change here."

"Tell me something," Thea said.

Maryruth peeled. Skins dropped to the table. "Okay."

Thea forged ahead. "If a woman wants a man to...make love to her, how does she go about getting him to do it?"

Maryruth's hands paused, and she stared ahead for a moment. "Well," she said, coming back to life. "She'd wear something he'd find attractive. A certain dress or—" she surveyed Thea "—an undergarment or perfume. She'd leave her hair loose." She rested her fingers on the edge of the kettle. "Are we talking about you or about me?"

"Both of us," Thea replied candidly. "I need to know how. I want to get him interested." She fanned her face with her apron.

Maryruth's surprise was evident. "Why, Thea, the man's crazy about you! He follows you with this—" she paused "—positively *aching* look in his eyes. When he speaks to you, his tone of voice is different from when he talks to Papa or Denzel. Surely you know this."

Thea let those words sink in, wanting to believe that what her sister thought she saw was truly what Thea needed so badly. "So what else?"

Maryruth thoughtfully resumed her peeling. "All right. Touch him," she directed, and gestured with the knife. "When you pour him coffee or set a plate in front of him, run your hand across his shoulder or up his arm. Say something with your lips ncxt to his ear."

Thea absorbed that idea with a slow smile.

"And," she said softly, "you could let him catch you undressed."

Thea's brain fuzzed over at that one. "I'd have no reason to be walking around the house undressed. And he's never come into my room." She caught her sister's amazed expression. "That's the problem. I have my room, and he has his. Even with Papa and Skeeter here, there's enough room in this house for everyone."

"That is a problem."

"I'll start with everything else you mentioned."

"He won't be able to resist," Maryruth predicted. She carried the full kettle to the sink and pumped water over the potatoes. "You think I should try this with Denzel, don't you?"

Thea nodded.

Maryruth lugged the kettle to the stove. "That way, his—passion will overshadow his fears. And once it's done, he'll realize he had nothing to worry about."

They cast conspiratorial grins at each other. Thea turned to slice the bread, her mind already leaping ahead to the evening meal and the time that would follow.

That afternoon, Booker and Denzel helped Jim Coulson to the back of the springboard where Thea and Maryruth had made a comfortable quilt pallet for his ride home.

"I'll come check on you tomorrow, Papa," Thea promised, and waved Denzel and Maryruth off.

Zoe held the dented bucket out to her.

Thea knelt. "Sweetheart, it rained so much last night, we don't need to carry water today."

Booker read the disappointment on both their faces. He'd finally figured out what they were up to. The absence of Zoe's ever-present acorn and their fevered watering and attention to that forlorn spot in the dooryard had tipped him off. They were waiting for a tree to grow.

He intended to plant plenty of trees. This barren Nebraska landscape needed windbreaks and lumber. He'd seen wooded areas farther north. Trees grew along most of the rivers and streams, but the prairie remained desolately bare. He planned to set cottonwood seedlings along the northern ridges of his property to act as windbreaks. He envisioned an orchard with fruit and nut trees. And he'd sighted a stand of oaks with plenty of sturdy young saplings down Hazel Creek a ways. The memory gave him an idea.

He and his hired men finished constructing the stone foundation for the mill that afternoon. By supper, his sore muscles complained as he seated himself at the kitchen table.

Tantalizing sweat-beaded jars of lemonade stood at each place setting. The tangy sweet liquid cooled his throat. The others obviously appreciated Thea's extra effort, too. Lucas gulped his down and stifled a contented burp.

Skeeter didn't bother to cover his belch, but Thea graciously ignored it.

"Where'd you get lemons?" Booker asked.

"Maryruth brought them." She refilled his jar, her cool fingers resting on his neck.

He turned his head and looked up at her.

"Is it sweet enough?" she asked, her lips near his ear. A shiver shot into his scalp and down his arm.

His gaze flicked over her marvelous hair, several springy strands fallen from the knot and touching her neck. She moistened her bottom lip with her tongue in what he knew was an innocent action, but the sight provoked a twinge of desire to tighten his groin. "Plenty sweet," he replied.

She smiled and withdrew her hand.

He watched her refill Red Horse's empty jar, both of her hands steadying the pitcher.

Skeeter stabbed himself a thick slice of roasted pork and poured dark, steaming gravy over it and his bread. "Fine woman, Hayes. Damned fine woman."

Thea met Booker's eyes and grinned—a conspiratorial, intimate grin that assured him she took no offense at Skeeter's words.

He watched her slide gracefully into the chair beside him and cut Zoe's meat into small pieces. No doubt about it; she was a damned fine woman.

Conversation centered on the progress they'd made on the mill, and she listened attentively when Booker spoke. He asked for the salt, and she passed it, her fingers lingering on his. She served peach cobbler and poured coffee, pausing to absently lay her hand on his arm while she answered one of Lucas's questions.

Booker glanced around the table. Everyone ate, Red Horse and Lucas watching Thea as she spoke. No one seemed to notice what was so painfully obvious to him—the way she touched him, the way his skin and insides and body reacted. The others went about their meal as if it were perfectly normal for her to skillfully arouse him at the dinner table.

He wanted to get up and leave the room, but he couldn't risk removing the checkered napkin from his lap and standing. He needed to put some space between them before he expanded uncontrollably and burst into a million pieces.

Finally, she withdrew her hand and moved away. He stared at his plate, desire lodged in his throat, unable to finish the cobbler.

"Booker?" she asked a minute later while the others discussed a piece they needed for the wagon hitch.

He met her vivid blue-green eyes with a raised brow.

"Are you all right? You're not eating your dessert."

"I'm tired. The heat is making me cranky, and I still have some work to do on the ledgers tonight. Will you excuse me?"

"Of course."

Abruptly, he turned in his chair, stood and left the room, not waiting to see the others' reaction to his hasty retreat. Lighting the lantern on his desk, he sat and opened the ledger. He stared at it sightlessly.

What had all that been about? He'd better get a grip on himself. He lived with her, and he'd be spending a lot of time in close proximity. Booker focused his attention on the figures in front of him.

Darkness fell around the house, and one by one he heard the others leave or go to their rooms. An hour later, he was thinking about going up when the study door opened.

Thea padded barefoot into the room, her wrapper tied carelessly at her waist, her unbound hair catching fiery highlights in the lantern light. She carried a cup to his desk. "I didn't hear you come up. I thought you might like this."

The sweet-tangy smell of the apple cider met his nostrils. He took a sip. "Thanks."

She stood at the corner of his desk and glanced across the papers in front of him.

"Why aren't you asleep?" he asked.

"Why aren't you?"

He remembered the scent and texture of her hair, the silken feel of her pale skin. He rested his gaze on the overlapped front of her thin wrapper, and dropped it automatically to the hem. What did she have on underneath? "I was just getting ready to come up," he said.

"You look so tense tonight," she observed. "Are you worried about my father?"

"No. He'll be fine."

"What, then? Anything I can help with?" She stepped beside his chair. "Want me to rub your neck?"

"No!" He stood and moved away from her.

She dropped her hands and self-consciously looked at her fingers. "Okay. Sorry."

Booker drank the cider in a final gulp and plunked the mug down. "I'm fine. Really." He made a neat stack of the book work on his desk. "Let's get some rest."

She walked ahead of him into the hall, the soft, feminine scent of her hair an erotic enticement he fought every step of the way. He followed her up the stairs, unable to keep his gaze from the sway of her hips and the shapely ankles visible beneath her wrapper.

In front of her door, she paused. She reached out and touched his upper arm, the heat of her fingers searing through the fabric to ignite his skin. "I'm afraid for my father," she whispered.

Her admission cut through his careful withdrawal. She needed his reassurance. He turned her shoulders and led her into her room. "Don't be afraid," he said, his voice still sounding too rough. "He's not in any danger."

He wrapped his arms around her shoulders and held her against his chest. Just for a minute. Just long enough to assuage her fears. He ignored the jasmine scent of her hair beneath his nose. He mentally removed himself from the seductive feel of her long, supple body against his, her unbound breasts crushed against his chest. He pretended she wasn't almost naked in his arms and that they weren't standing five feet from her bed.

"Don't worry anymore. All right?" He took her arms and held her away. "You need your rest, too."

She nodded in the darkness. "I'll sleep now."

He released her, closed the door softly and moved into the hallway. She might sleep now, but he certainly wouldn't.

Thea awakened from the agonizingly familiar dream, her body drenched with perspiration. The hint of a breeze barely stirred the lacy curtains at her window. The previous night's rain had left the air heavy, oppressive. Tunneling her fingers into her damp hair, she gripped her scalp and fought for control—for her former dignity. What was happening to her?

She kicked the tangled sheet off the end of the bed and padded in the dark to the washstand. The warm water in the basin seemed cool to her fingers. Stripping her gown off over her head, she placed a towel on the floor and stood on it. Saturating a washrag, she squeezed it over her shoulders and breasts, the water running in warm rivulets down her sensation-conscious body. She dipped the rag and squeezed it over her heavy breasts again. Water streamed down the center of her belly in an arousing trickle.

Thea closed her eyes, and her thoughts centered on the perplexingly tedious state of anticipation her body constantly tortured her with. Bitterly, she remembered thinking this would all be behind her once she and Booker were married. She knew—and the fact amazed her still—that he found her attractive, that he desired her almost as much as she needed him. Why, then? Why this constant state of denial? Was he ashamed of his desire for the undesirable Too-Tall Thea?

Was that why even tonight, when she'd done everything she could think of to encourage him, he'd pushed her away and gone to his room?

Hope had lain dormant until Booker came into her life. She'd been resigned to living her days out as an old maid, stifling girlish dreams, burying womanly fantasies. But he'd appeared and reawakened every unfulfilled longing she'd ever had—and added a few more. He'd awakened her to the needs of her heart and body. Introduced her to her sensual self.

She'd lived with the burden of hopelessness for too long. Booker Hayes must be the one to change that. Thea had to experience a slice of life, know a shred of happiness before it was too late.

She remembered the words he'd spoken to her on their wedding night: it was up to her.

She had nothing to lose but her pride. And pride wouldn't keep her warm through the cold winter nights. Wouldn't satisfy her needs. Wouldn't give her children of her own.

She opened her eyes and sponged the rest of her body, drying briskly with a rough towel, her fingers trembling. From her bureau drawer, she unfolded a thin cotton night-dress and pulled it on, then brushed her hair before padding down the sweltering hallway.

Without giving herself time to change her mind, she turned the knob and entered his room, closing the door softly behind her. The curtains were pulled back from the open windows, offering a slight humid breeze. Moonlight gilded the tall, bare-chested figure propped against the window frame. He turned at the sound of her entry.

Thea's heart pounded in her ears. She'd expected to find him sleeping. That would have given her a few minutes to compose herself and wake him. Instead, he turned to her expectantly. "Thea?"

She forced herself away from the door, closer to him, then paused and steadied herself with a hand on the enormous footboard.

"What is it? Did you hear something that frightened you?" He took a few soundless barefoot strides toward her.

"No. Nothing like that." Her voice sounded as unsteady as her heart. The rough bark dug into her palm.

"What's wrong, then?"

She faced him squarely. The moonlight clearly defined his smooth broad shoulders, muscled arms and the strikingly masculine set of his jaw.

"I want something."

"All right." He moved toward the night table. "Let me light the lanter—"

"No." She stopped him with a hand on his bare arm.

Motionless, he regarded her hand.

Beneath her fingers and his perspiring, heated skin, his muscles tensed. Reluctantly, she pulled her hand back. "Booker," she said, and it came out little more than a hoarse whisper. "I want you to..." Lord, this wasn't going to be easy! "I want us to..." She took a quavering breath. "I want to make love with you."

Chapter Fourteen

He didn't move a muscle. Silence closed in and around the sultry, hot room. Her words hung between them for an eternity, but she didn't regret saying them. Outside, Zoe's cat yowled. Finally, Booker raised a hand and raked it through his hair.

He turned his upper body enough that the moonlight caught and defined the muscular underside of his arm and a thicket of black hair. The glow revealed the obsidian blanket that matted his chest. "Say something," Thea whispered through tears of vulnerability. "You're frightening me. I thought you wanted me, too."

"Oh, Thea," he groaned. He reached a hand toward her, but caught himself, drew it back and placed both hands on his hips where his low-slung trousers rode. "I want you. Trust me, I want you."

"What, then?" she asked, and folded her arms against her trembling stomach.

"Thea." He spoke as though he'd gained courage to tell her something. "Everyone takes advantage of you. Just hear me out." He raised a palm against her silent protest. "I've watched your family, the townspeople, the church members—everyone—ignore your needs. You look after everybody else while you're neglected. It angers me how you're taken advantage of.

"I've watched you with them, and I can't understand—can't fathom how they can overlook your femininity, your sensuality, your beauty and charm."

His voice softened to a gruff whisper. "I've watched you with Zoe and with Lucas and little David. I've seen how gentle and loving you are, and I've wanted that for myself."

"That's good, isn't it?" she asked hopefully.

"But don't you see?" He gestured with one long arm. "I would be just like all the others if I took advantage of those giving qualities. I want to be...different. I want to meet *your* needs, Thea."

"Oh, Booker." Hope sprang back to life in her maiden heart. "I have needs. I have so many needs." Tears clogged her throat, and her chin quivered. "I need to feel like a woman. I need a man of my own. I need to find out what this powerful attraction is all about. I need you to show me what this agonizing want for you can turn into.

"I have dreams," she whispered. "Dreams of being kissed and touched and—" A tiny hiccuping sob broke her voice. "And my body doesn't feel like my own anymore. It's wonderful, but it's terrible, and I can't sleep at night. It's a need I don't even understand. All I know for sure is that I want you. For myself."

"Oh, God, Thea." He took a step toward her.

"I have to know," she said halting him with her outstretched hand. "I have to be sure you desire me. Because I would die if you only felt pity."

He turned both palms upward in a pleading gesture. "I can show you. Let me show you how much."

Her heartbeat thudded and her body yearned for him to do exactly that.

"Everything about you excites me," he said with devastating frankness. "Your hair, your skin. Not a day goes by that I don't see you and think of undressing you, kissing you."

"But I'm so big," she said softly.

"Look at me," he demanded. "Do I seem intimidated by your height? You're tall, Thea, but you're perfectly made. Your legs are long, your waist is narrow. Your breasts...the thought of your breasts keeps me awake at night."

Already taut with arousal, her nipples responded to his words.

"The idea of making love to you has had me lathered since the first time we met. I've thought of it a thousand times. Tonight when you stood near me and touched me, I thought I'd go crazy with wanting you."

"Show me," she pleaded.

Booker took the remaining steps to reach her, and she readied herself for whatever came next. She hoped he would kiss her once like the last time. Prayed she would know what to do, how to please him. Wonder of wonders, he touched only her face at first, reverently cupping her cheek, sliding his fingertips over her cheekbone, her brow, her lips. She'd never imagined his touch could be so gentle, so good. Tears welled in her eyes at his exquisite tenderness.

He wanted her! She let her eyelids flutter shut and focused on his callused fingers administering sharp pleasure to her jaw, her neck, her collarbone. His chin scraped her neck.

"Will you kiss me once?" she asked.

"I'm afraid not," he replied, and she opened her eyes in acute disappointment. He brushed his lips across her eyelids, closing them again. His warm mouth touched her forehead, her temple, her nose, and hovered at the corner of her mouth. "Once would never be enough."

Her heart danced in joyous anticipation. She wanted to touch him, needed to learn everything at once, but held herself in check.

He closed his hands over her shoulders and pulled her toward him, covering her mouth in an eloquent kiss, a kiss that spoke of his eagerness and his desire for her. Hesitantly, Thea touched his jaw, relished the masculine texture. He opened her lips with his tongue and she met him with slick, hot thrusts of her own. He groaned into her mouth.

Booker sucked her lower lip between his teeth, nipped the corner of her lip, kissed her chin, her cheek, her neck. Thea dropped her head back, awash with delicate nerve endings her husband probed into screaming animation.

His mouth left a cool trail across her face and throat while his hands seared a burning path around her waist, her rib cage, smoothed down across her buttocks and gathered her nightdress upward until his fingers splayed over her round, bare buttocks.

Thea's breath caught.

Bending his knees, Booker pressed his face against her nightgown, nuzzled her breast through the restricting fabric.

"Here, let me . . ." Thea untangled herself long enough to yank the gown over her head. It dropped into the shadows at their feet.

Gently, Booker pulled away from her and allowed the moonlight to wash her nakedness in its silvery glow. Trembling, Thea awaited his reaction.

He reached for her left hand and placed it over his racing heart. "Don't ever wonder again, Thea Hayes. Don't ever question whether or not you're a beautiful woman."

He brought her right hand to the front of his trousers and pressed it over his burgeoning arousal. "Don't ever wonder whether or not I desire you."

Thea learned a heart-stopping, graphic lesson about the male species. She curled the fingers of her left hand into the thick, damp mat of his chest while her right elicited a hiss from between his bared teeth.

This was no fantasy, no dream, but a reality: her reality. Her right. Her due. She deserved this happiness.

Tenderly, he circled both her wrists and drew her curled fingers to his lips, pressing damp kisses against her knuckles. She imagined those lips on other parts of her body and liquid heat sluiced through her being in a downward flow.

"Show me," she begged. "Now."

"Have patience, my love," he replied, and nipped her thumb. "We have all night."

"No." His teeth raked the tender inside of her arm from wrist to elbow and higher, and tingles radiated up her shoulder and cockled her nipples. She couldn't wait all night. She would explode into a million frantic particles. She shook her head and splayed her fingers against his matted chest. She'd been patient long enough. She'd waited far too long already. "Now."

He conceded by dropping to his knees before her, gripping her bare hips and burying his face in her belly. Inhaling sharply, he groaned. Thea delved her fingers into his damp hair and watched him press kisses around her navel. His tongue darted out and he tasted her skin, flicking a path as high as he could reach. His nose resting intolerably beneath her breast, he stroked her thighs and hips until her knees trembled and she didn't think she could support her own weight any longer.

He taunted the underside of her breast with his nose and brows until she tipped forward breathlessly and offered it to his reverent mouth. His lips sealed over the peak, his tongue manipulating her nipple with first quick, then slow and exquisite, strokes.

Thea's knees buckled and she fell forward heavily. Booker caught her against his chest, let her knees slide to the floor and covered her lips with his wet mouth. Instinctively, she doubled her forearms behind his neck and pressed against his flesh, breasts to breasts, hips to hips, thighs to thighs, and victoriously returned the kiss.

Booker spanned her ribs, affably pushed her a few inches away, and coaxed her to her feet. In one unbroken movement, he scooped her into his arms and carried her to the enormous tree bed.

From the rumpled sheets, Thea observed him with a grin. "Are you all right?"

Moonlight silhouetting broad shoulders and narrow hips, he unfastened his trousers and stepped out of them, coming to lie beside her.

"Do I feel all right?" He pressed his heated length against her hip.

She touched his handsome face, his swollen lips, his smooth shoulder. "You feel marvelous. You make me feel beautiful."

He placed his thumb alongside her temple and skimmed it over her brow. "You are beautiful. Don't ever forget."

His lips hovered a fraction of an inch from hers. "Will you remind me from time to time?" she asked.

He skimmed her belly, her thigh. "I'll remind you as often as you'll let me."

He slid his hand between her thighs and cupped her. He had to feel the ceaseless throbbing, the molten dew his lips and hands had wrought. Her eyelids fluttered shut.

"Thea," he whispered, and covered her lips with his. His tongue slid between her parted lips and matched the slippery strokes of his fingers. Her breathing stopped. Her heart stopped. The entire world stood still while he keenly, unrelentingly, awakened her to the reality of physical love.

Perspiration prickled along the length of their bodies where their skin touched. Booker pulled his mouth away, and Thea sucked the hot night air into her lungs.

"Are you frightened?" he asked.

Thea gathered the unraveled edges of her mind. What was there to be frightened of?

"It will hurt some."

"I'm not frightened."

"You might get pregnant."

"Would you care?" she asked.

"You're my wife," he replied in a sensual rasp. "I want children."

She wrapped her fingers as far around his rock-hard bicep as they reached and felt his muscles quiver. "Nothing would make me happier."

He finger combed her hair across the sheet, then brought a strand to his nose, brushing his lips with the tress. "I've been dying for this, Thea. Knowing what your hair felt like, what your skin smelled like, how you respond when I touch you.''

She tried to see his eyes in the darkness, but had to be satisfied with his sincere tone. ''And knowing all about me, you're not disappointed?''

''No,'' he whispered. ''But all my questions haven't been answered yet.''

''What else?''

He rose above her then, one rock-hard knee nudging her thighs apart. ''I want to see your face in the moonlight when I'm inside you.''

Thea's heart ricocheted against her breast. He kissed her openmouthed, their tongues and lips grappling, then lodged himself on the very edge of entry and pulled back to watch her face. Thea licked her salty lower lip and stared back at him through shuttered lids.

He kissed her again, and with a gentle lunge, sheltered himself inside her. He raised his head and studied her expression. A tremulous sigh escaped her lips. With a timid and unskilled but perfectly natural movement, Thea raised her hips and grasped him tightly against her.

The August heat was forgotten. In a mindless whirlpool of clasping bodies and straining kisses, Booker encompassed her with a never-to-be-imagined frenzy of pleasure, murmuring guttural encouragement against her neck, her chin, her mouth.

She thought of all the nights she'd dreamed of him, vague imaginings of a dark shadow lover. Now she had him in her arms, in her body, in her heart. He arched and his tongue flicked fire across her nipple.

She wanted to disappear inside him, merge and become one. She swelled around him, strained against him, nurtured him at her upstretched breasts until a cry of frustration escaped her lips.

''Raise your knees,'' he urged against her mouth.

Thea obeyed, tucking her heels against his buttocks. Her head fell back in pleasure.

He cradled and lifted her hips, their slippery, perspiring bodies emitting tiny sucking sounds. An all-encompassing satiny shudder rippled outward from the center of her being and enveloped him. He groaned and hammered every last question from her mind in a series of sublime quakes.

Booker panted raggedly against her temple, rolled himself onto his back and flung his arm out. In the silvery light, she watched the rise and fall of his matted chest subside, but he lay impassive, silent.

Thea wondered if in her overcredulous haste she'd made a fool of herself—been too eager, done some unfeminine thing that had shocked him. Perhaps in her smitten passion, she'd disgusted him.

Hoisting himself on one elbow, he studied her face, her body. Thea resisted the urge to cover herself. He drew his finger through the puddle in her navel and found the edge of a sheet to dry her with. Tossing the clammy fabric over the bed's edge, he lowered his head and kissed her nipple. It puckered and he smiled.

"Well, Mrs. Hayes," he whispered throatily. "Did we meet a few of those needs?"

"Are you disappointed?"

He pulled her hand to his mouth. "Lord, no." He kissed her palm, spread her fingers over the hollow of his stubbled cheek and nuzzled. "I need you."

She rubbed her thumb over his bottom lip.

"Not just for Zoe," he clarified. "For me."

A tear slipped through her lashes and slid into the already wet hair at her temple. An unbidden sob rose in her chest and escaped in a rush of long-pent-up emotion. She buried her forehead against his chest and her shoulders heaved. *So long.* She'd waited so long and had given up before he'd come into her life. Her extreme joy almost frightened her.

"Hey," he said, his hand hovering helplessly above her head. "Why are you crying?" Delving his fingers into her hair, he pulled her head back and forced her to meet his shadowed face. "What?"

"I love you," she confessed on a quiet sob.

His fingers curled gently against her scalp. With infinite tenderness, he pulled her face up and pressed his lips to hers. He tasted of salt, and sex, and latent strength. Never had he kissed her with such delicacy, such candid reverence.

Ignoring the sultry heat, he pulled her into his arms, draped a hair-roughened knee possessively across her smooth thigh and held her until she slept.

"I didn't mean to wake you," he whispered.

"You didn't."

"Does this feel good?"

"Mmm, yes. I never knew..."

"What?"

"That you'd be so..."

"Am I?"

"That you'd be so...everywhere."

"Does this hurt?" he asked.

"Mmm. No."

"Don't move...stay like you are...."

"Can I do something to make you feel better?"

"If it felt any better, it would be over."

"Booker..."

"Hmm?"

"Just...Booker."

"Does that hurt?"

"No."

"You're beautiful."

"It's dark."

"You feel beautiful."

"I really please you, Booker?"

"I've never..."

"What?"

"I don't have to hold back with you."

"That's good?"

"It's never been so good."

"Booker?"

"Mmm?"

"I'm going to have to move now."

"Okay...oh, Thea."

"What?"

"Just...Thea."

Morning light beamed through the open windows. Beneath the sheet, she was naked. Thea forced her gritty eyelids open and oriented herself. Wincing, she sat and blinked.

The door opened and Booker appeared with a bucket of water and towels. "Morning."

"Morning." He'd already shaved and dressed.

"I brought fresh water for you." He poured it into the ceramic basin on the washstand, then picked up her wrapper from the floor and laid it across the foot of the bed. "No one's up yet. You have time to bathe."

She held her hair back. "Thank you."

He leaned over and kissed her. Frowning, he touched a finger to her chin, tilted her head back on his thumb and ran a finger over her neck. He plucked the sheet away from her breasts and inspected her.

Embarrassed, she followed his gaze and discovered her abraded red skin. She met his eyes.

"I'll shave every night for the rest of my life," he promised.

Did that mean he intended for it to happen again?

He stood. "I'd better let you get up. I'll see you downstairs."

She nodded, and he closed the door behind himself.

She washed in the water he'd provided, using the only soap available—his. She would smell spicy—like him—all day. As she dried herself, she heard the thunder of horses approaching the house. Thea put on her wrapper and stepped to the window.

Below, half a dozen riders pulled their mounts to a halt in the dooryard. Thea recognized Marshal Hardy heading the party. Beside him rode Irving Jackson. Each man held a revolver or rifle. Something about the way they set their mounts, the way their hands remained on their weapons, send a trickle of alarm through her heart.

She flew down the hall to her room and pulled on a blouse and skirt, knotting her hair against the back of her head with tortoiseshell pins without even brushing it. By the time she ran down the stairs and out the back door, Booker stood before the marshal.

Instinctively, she ran to his side. He moved in front of her, protectively.

Red Horse approached the group from the barn, holsters strapped to his thighs, a rifle resting on his forearm. Thea's stomach clenched at the defensive sight.

"Where was your husband the night before last when your pa was shot, Mrs. Hayes?" the marshal asked.

"He was right here," she replied. Why did he ask her that?

"Standing with you?" he asked.

Lips and voice tight, Booker interrupted. "If you have something to say, Marshal, why don't you ask me?"

"I'm askin' a witness I trust," the marshal replied. "Thea's always been an upstanding citizen, and since this is her pa we're talkin' about, I don't think she'd lie to me. Now, Thea, are you sayin' Hayes was right with you when you heard the shot?"

"No. He went to the barn to throw down some hay for the horses."

"Was anyone with him?"

Perplexed, she glanced at Booker's grim face and back to the marshal. "N-no."

"Where was the Injun?" Irving Jackson asked.

Thea looked up at the hotel owner. The flesh around both of his eyes was a sickly shade of purplish green and one eyebrow protruded garishly beneath a knot. A partially healed cut swelled the right corner of his mouth. What was he doing out here with the marshal? The odd assembly looked like a posse or a...lynching party. Her heart tripped double time. "Red Horse was in the corral getting the rest of the horses."

"Did he have a rifle with 'im?"

Internal alarm clanging, she cast him a wary frown. "No."

"How about your husband?" Marshal Hardy asked. "Did he have a rifle with him?"

She knew they left one in the barn in case of emergency. It rested over Red Horse's arm right now. "I don't know."

"Did he or didn't he?"

"No. He didn't take his rifle."

Eyes narrowed, Booker stepped between her and the interrogator. "What are you getting at, Marshal?"

The beefy man gripped the pommel, leaned forward and adjusted his weight, the saddle leather creaking. "Heard Jim Coulson was shot, so we came to question you."

"You haven't asked if we know who did it."

"Do you know who did it?" Marshal Hardy asked, squinting down at Booker.

"No. The rain washed away all the tracks."

"How convenient," Jackson commented, struggling with his swollen lip.

Beside her, Thea could almost feel her husband bristle at Jackson's sarcasm.

"Are you accusing me?" Booker asked.

"Maybe," the marshal drawled. "Maybe not."

Anxiety climbed the back of Thea's neck, numbing the base of her skull.

"Do you have proof?" Booker asked. "'Cause if you don't, we have work to do."

"Just tryin' to figure out who stands to profit from Coulson's death," Hardy said, and bit off the end of a fat cigar. He took his time, looking at the frayed end, fishing a match from his pocket and striking it with a thumbnail. He puffed on the cigar until the end glowed orange. "Seems to me, you're the only one with a reason. Everybody else looks up to the man."

Booker took a stiff step forward, his fists clenched at his sides. "Get the hell off my land."

Horrified, Thea jumped to life and pushed past him. "Marshal! How dare you accuse Booker of trying to kill my father! My husband wouldn't do such a thing."

"No? Well, who would, then?"

"I don't know, but it wasn't him."

"He's the only stranger in these parts, Thea. He and the Injun."

"That doesn't make him a killer."

"It couldn't have been the major," Red Horse added.

"Red Horse," Booker said in a warning tone.

"Why not?" the marshal wanted to know.

"Because Mr. Coulson was wearing the major's rain slicker. Whoever shot him thought he was getting the major."

Hardy shifted his wet cigar between his lips and squinted at Thea. "That so?"

How could she not have noticed? Not put the facts together? She'd watched Red Horse cut Booker's slicker from her father, but she'd been too shocked to think anything of it. "Yes," she replied softly. "He was wearing Booker's slicker."

Hardy holstered his gun. "All right. You're off the hook for now, Hayes." He reined his horse around and the others followed. "But I'll be watchin' every move you make."

Jackson cast a hateful glance between Thea and her husband before turning his mount and prodding it into a run.

The retreating horses kicked dust into the air. Thea watched them go, relief washing through her body, grateful they'd left before the situation got really ugly.

"I had to tell him, Major," Red Horse said. "I don't want her to worry, either, but better you be spared from their vigilante tactics."

Booker nodded.

Red Horse walked toward the house, rifle loose in his grip.

Thea met Booker's gaze. Uncertain, she stared at his somber face, realizing for the first time that she knew very little about this stranger she'd married. He could have hidden any number of things in his past. And he obviously hadn't trusted her with the information that the shot was intended for him. "Why didn't you tell me?"

"I didn't want you to worry."

"Is someone after you?"

"Not that I know of."

The news opened up a whole new perspective. If someone had followed Booker to Nebraska intending to kill him, everyone around him was in danger. Her father had already fallen under the unknown assailant's misdirected vengeance.

She'd never been protected in such a stifling manner before. Ironically, *she* had always been the strong one, used to being in control. She was the one who provided and protected. She should have known so that she could have taken her own safety measures.

She drew herself up, the thought of losing him terrifying her. "Don't ever treat me like a child or a helpless woman again!" she lashed out.

Pivoting on her heel, she marched back to the house.

Booker ate his breakfast in stony silence, the marshal's accusations casting a pall over an otherwise sunny day. The others talked of the winches and pulleys the men would use to help Skeeter set the buhrstones in place now that the floors were laid. Booker had been an outsider his whole life, living on the edges of society, of family life, traveling from one post to another, never sending down roots, never making a place for himself.

Until now. This land, this house—he glanced across the table—this woman were what he'd dreamed of.

Thea sliced Zoe's ham and fed her a bite of syrupy flapjack, ignoring him. Zoe glanced at him and lowered her eyes to her plate.

What was it? What was it about him that kept everyone at a distance? Zoe adored Thea, clung to her, loved her. The child accepted Red Horse, as well. Hell, the kid already liked Skeeter better than she did him.

And Lucas. Booker watched the boy's Adam's apple bob as he polished off his second glass of milk. He understood the boy had been abused, understood his hesitation and mistrust. Booker had taken the same approach he'd use with a wary horse; he'd shown him he wasn't going to hurt him, building trust with actions and words and hoping to slowly win him over with a gentle taming. Thea could touch him. Lucas flinched every time Booker laid a casual hand on him, but Thea touched him, hugged him, ruffled his hair.

Booker dropped his fork on his plate with a clatter. Did he have the plague, or what? Some half-wit with a rifle was out there trying to kill him—had shot Jim instead—and the first person to be accused was himself! He stood and grabbed his hat.

"We won't be able to leave the site at noon today," he said, more gruffly than he'd intended.

"Fine. I'll bring your dinner," Thea said, her voice as sweet as the maple syrup on her lips.

"Lucas, you grab a stack of those four-by-fours in the barn and bring them after you finish your chores."

"Yes, sir," Lucas said respectfully.

Booker turned and left the kitchen.

"My belly thinks my throat's been cut," Skeeter said, catching sight of Thea laying out the noon meal on a tablecloth she'd spread on the springboard's open tailgate.

"I fried you chicken," Thea said with a smile.

Shirtless and perspiring in the noonday sun, Red Horse and Lucas appeared next. She opened jars and uncovered dishes, helped them fill their plates, and dipped cool water from a crock into jars. They turned to sit in the shade provided by the wagon, and Thea caught sight of Lucas's back.

She was obviously the only one who'd never seen the scars crisscrossing his upper body from his shoulders to the waistband of his denims, because the others went about their meal eagerly. His skin had taken on a healthy glow from the sun, not nearly as dark as Red Horse's, of course, or even tanned as deeply as Booker's, but the lines that crossed his knobby back were sunburned a bright, painful-looking pink.

Tears smarted behind her eyes, and Thea turned back to the food. Anger welled up in her, anger so strong and overpowering that she wanted to pound her fists helplessly on the wagon and scream out her frustration. What kind of person would do that to a child? She glanced at Zoe happily gathering a bouquet of clover from the grass beside the wagon.

What if she hadn't been the one to take Zoe? What if she'd been placed somewhere else and Booker hadn't found her? The possibilities were unthinkable!

"What's wrong?" Booker asked, coming up beside her.

Rapidly, she swiped the tears from her cheeks and handed him a plate. "Nothing."

He shifted the plate to his left hand and took her upper arm. "Don't tell me nothing. What's wrong?"

Her throat choked with tears. She met his midnight black eyes. "I'd never seen Lucas's back before."

Booker's expression flattened and his grip on her arm gentled. He nodded. "Oh."

"Did Bard do that to him?" she whispered.

"Bard and a lot of others before, I'd say."

Inconceivable. No wonder he'd been so wary. She shook her head. "He's had no woman in his life to mother him...only men beating him." She blinked back more tears and glanced at Zoe again. "They'll never have to be afraid with us. They will always know we love them."

He squeezed her arm gently and released it. His wife was some kind of woman. He'd watched her stifle her porcelain coloring in drab hues, recognized her ineffective efforts to diminish her splendid body with dull clothing, hide her glossy red-gold hair with simple hairstyles. In downplaying herself, she'd only painted herself more lovely and desirable. All her fire and color and passion lay within. And he wanted to be the man to unleash them.

Her strong, supple body exhilarated him beyond reason. When she'd offered it to him last night, he couldn't have denied her—or himself. She was a respectable, sensitive person. She hadn't presented herself out of self-pity, but with a down-to-earth common sense he'd come to respect.

And she'd said she loved him. He wanted to ask her if she meant it, but if it had been merely a careless utterance in her passion, he didn't want to know. She loved everybody.

That morning she'd come to his defense before the marshal and his cronies. But perhaps that was simply part of her sense of loyalty toward her entire flock.

Booker accepted the pieces of chicken she placed on his plate and helped himself to the freshly grated coleslaw. Thea wiped her hands on her apron, and his attention skittered over the crisp white fabric tied at her narrow waist, hiding her generous breasts. His thoughts jumped ahead to the night to come, and heat beyond that of the blistering sun radiated through his body.

Her vivid blue-green gaze met his, dropped to his perspiring bare chest, and back to his face, a tinge of additional color in her cheeks.

No. He would never deny either of them again.

Chapter Fifteen

She'd really put her foot in it now. Thea tucked a needle in the sunny yellow dress she was making for Zoe and glanced around the room she still had trouble calling a parlor. Skeeter and Booker had been deliberating over a checker game for the better part of an hour.

Skeeter stomped his foot and cackled. "Hah! Beatin' you's 'bout as easy as pickin' fly dung outta black pepper, but I done it!"

Booker grinned and arranged his checkers on the board. "Two out of three. It's still early."

"I see why you married this lughead now, missy. He could sell you a anvil if you was treadin' water."

Thea smiled and nodded.

Booker regarded her and she glanced away. All afternoon and evening, she'd regretted losing her temper that morning. She'd raised her voice, practically given him an order and stomped away. She'd behaved like a child after accusing him of treating her like one. But she wasn't sorry for what she'd told him; she didn't want to be kept in the dark over things concerning all of them. She had as much right to be informed as anyone else. However, she did regret the way she'd said it.

Zoe, chin propped on her fists, lay on the floor beside Lucas, watching him sketch on his tablet. She pointed to something in the drawing.

"Recognize your cat?" Lucas asked. "What's his name, anyhow?"

Zoe shrugged as if names and words were unimportant, and rested her head on the floor.

Thea stood. "Come on, sweetheart. You're ready to fall asleep on the floor."

Zoe's bottom lip curled out.

"My, my." Thea stood over her.

"I'll carry her," Lucas offered, and scrambled to his feet.

Thea watched him kneel and lift the child into his arms, and she imagined the big strong man he'd be someday. Thoughtful. Sensitive. Not soured by the dirty hand his young life had dealt him thus far. And someday he would trust, she decided.

Lucas went on to his room, and Thea helped Zoe change and tucked her into bed. She lit the lamp in her own room and removed her dress. Enjoying cooling off in only her chemise and drawers, she washed her face and neck and brushed out her hair.

In the dark, she stood before the open window and allowed the night air to seep through her thin underclothes. Her fingers trembled on the curtain. What was she supposed to do now? Last night, she'd gone to Booker, made it perfectly clear that she needed him, wanted him. Reality had been a thousandfold better than her wishful dreams. Thea crossed her arms over her breasts and hugged herself. He thought she was beautiful. And with him, she was. A beautiful, desirable woman.

How was a wife supposed to behave? She'd done it all just as she'd planned. Seduced him. Now what? Did it change anything? Footsteps sounded on the stairs and her heart hammered girlishly. The sound traveled on past her room. A door closed. Another door closed.

Knees trembling with uncertainty, Thea sank to the edge of the bed. Should she go to him? Should she wait? Oh, Lord, would every night be like this? Life was too short to waste with silly self-denial and hesitation. But she wouldn't make a fool of herself. So she waited.

* * *

Booker stood barefoot in his enormous empty room, and unbuttoned his shirt. Where was she? Hadn't he proved to her last night that he wanted her? Hadn't he shown her he could be gentle and patient?

Oh, come on, he told himself. Did he think he'd swept her off her feet and that she wouldn't be able to resist him in the future? He'd encouraged her to go after what she wanted, to take a slice of life and savor it.

He'd let her down by not telling her that the bullet was intended for him. He'd meant to spare her, instead he'd insulted her. He was sorry for that, but he'd made the decision he felt was best at the time. He'd know better in the future.

The future. He closed his eyes and released a heavy sigh. He'd had such big plans for the future. The mill was coming along as intended. But everything else was in a mess. Zoe resented him for trying to take her away from Thea in the first place. Would he ever be able to make that up to her? Win her over?

Lucas shied away from him like he was a dangerous animal. He couldn't blame the boy, though. The only treatment he'd ever received from men had been abuse. Booker would just have to be more patient. More tolerant.

And Thea. He'd left the decision up to her. He'd sacrificed and waited, and even when she'd finally come to his room, he'd given her another chance to change her mind. She hadn't. He didn't think she'd been disappointed.

Hell no! She'd told him she loved him! Then what the hell was she doing down the hall in her own room, right now? Making him pay penitence for his mistake?

Booker jerked the door open and strode silently down the hall. He resisted banging on the door and rousing the entire household. Instead, he tried the unlocked door, threw it open and stepped into the room.

Seated on the edge of the bed in her underclothes, Thea stared at him.

Booker closed the door behind him. "What are you doing in here?"

He thought her lip trembled when she answered, "I don't know."

Her marvelous hair spilled over her shoulders and across the milky skin of her arms. Moonlight caught the glimmer of tears in her eyes. She was frightened.

Her lost expression sucked the wind from his sails. She was as confused as he was. Booker plucked her wrapper from the hook and tossed it to her. "Get some clothes for tomorrow."

Stepping to her dresser, he gathered her brush and comb and hairpins. "Tomorrow you can move the rest of your things to our room, all right?" He stepped in front of her and reached a hand down. "We should have done it today."

Thea clasped his hand and pulled herself to her feet, using his grip as a support. She buried her face against his neck, and her fragrant hair caressed the bare strip of skin at his open shirtfront.

He hugged her, enjoying the arousing press of her strong body, the softness of her breasts and hair. Lord, this woman set his blood on fire! She was as strong and determined as she was sensitive and gentle. Her strength of character matched her supple body. She could handle problems and fears as easily as she could match his physical desires. He'd never known another woman like her.

"Come on," he said roughly. She gathered clothing and her toiletries, and he led her from the room and down the hall. "Look."

Booker opened a drawer and revealed the space waiting for her clothing. She placed her few items in the drawer, closed it and turned to him. He'd laid her brush and comb on the nightstand and turned back the coverlet. She met him beside the bed, and he sank his fingers deep into her hair, held her head and pressed his lips against her forehead, drinking her in—her scent, her softness, her incredible beauty.

Her hands spanned his ribs and climbed his back, drawing him closer, setting his heartbeat at an eager, staccato rhythm.

"Booker," she whispered, and her breath fanned his throat.

He pushed her back gently and looked into her flawless face.

"Are you angry with the way I spoke to you this morning?" she asked.

He thought a second. "Because you told me not to treat you like a child or a helpless female?"

"Yes."

"No. You were absolutely right."

Her reddish brows raised in surprise.

"I won't keep anything from you again," he vowed. "And I have another promise to keep." He released her.

"What's that?"

"I have to shave."

She smiled shyly.

He trailed a finger down her warm, satiny throat and caught the front of her chemise. "Why don't you undress and wait for me?"

Her eyes flickered to the bed and back, and her cheeks pinkened perceptibly. Thunder rumbled in the distance.

Booker turned away to afford her privacy and lathered his face and neck. In the corner of the mirror, he caught a provocative glimpse of her pale skin as she slid between the sheets. His mouth went dry and he swallowed, barely missing slitting his own throat with the razor. He forced himself to take his time, finish shaving and rinse his face well. Turning, he discovered her watching him, tears glistening in her eyes.

"What's wrong?" he asked. He removed his shirt and sat on the bed's edge.

She wiped the corners of her eyes with the sheet. "I'm just happy. I never watched anyone shave before."

"Do you cry about everything?"

She shrugged one bare shoulder, and the sheet slid enticingly lower. "I don't know. Do you mind?"

He leaned close, realizing he hadn't kissed her since early that morning. *An eternity.* "No."

She met his lips eagerly, hers soft and warm, drawing him to her like a thirsting man to a sparkling stream, like the moon draws the tides. He drank at her lips, savoring the pleasure of her pliant mouth, the erotic taste uniquely hers. He pulled back and beheld her, touched her hair and ran his fingers over her collarbone. Out of all the places he could have gone and all the women he could have met in this barren frontier land, he'd found her.

Beautiful and vital and full of life and love, and she'd chosen to marry him. Him. He hadn't been looking for a wife, but fate had stepped in and carried him right to her doorstep. He'd be eternally grateful.

Booker ran a finger across her jaw, her pretty lower lip. He'd treasure her, hold her close at night, perhaps plant children within her, and—he kissed her eyelids—grow old with her.

She turned her face up, obviously unsatisfied with his leisurely perusal of her face and hair, and caught his lower lip with her teeth. She released it and kissed his clean-shaven chin, his jaw.

He responded to her unspoken demand, covering her mouth with his, running his tongue across her closed lips, making his own request. She parted her lips and met his tongue, pulling him down to lie beside her on the bed.

He slid his tongue into the warm, wet cavity of her mouth, reminded of the more intimate joining to come.

Her scent enveloped him, and her skin enticed him with the age-old promise of pleasure. Her response set him on the edge of sanity. Hard and ready, he pressed himself along her length and cupped her bottom in his palms, determined to go slow. She nudged his knees and inserted one thigh between his. Thunder rumbled again, closer this time.

The sheet became an unbearable nuisance, and he tugged it away, exposing her body to the lantern light and his appreciative gaze. With his lips and tongue and hands, he explored her, kissed the freckles on her chest, taking her nipples slowly and languorously into his mouth. He discovered how sensitive the insides of her arms were, gooseflesh rippling across her skin when he lightly stroked the satiny, pale limbs.

Booker darted his tongue in and out of her navel, ran his nose along the enticing valleys at her hipbones, and admired and stroked the well-formed length of her lithesome legs.

"You even have freckles here." He chuckled, kissing her knees. In the delicate glow of the lantern, he worshiped every satinlike inch of her body, gratified in the most elemental way that he was the first to touch her, the only man to know her as a lover.

Her china white thighs trembled at his touch. Booker petted the curls, as soft and red as the hair on her head. She gasped, but yielded to his mollifying touch. He eased his fingers inside her malleable flesh, gentling, softening, coaxing. Hardy internal muscles quickened, eager to bring him pleasure. His pulse dipped and soared.

Thea whimpered and grasped at his shoulders. Tenderly, he left her to remove his trousers. Eyes swimming with passion, she watched, and he gave her time to absorb the sight of him. Her gaze moved back to his, and she smiled. A lover's smile.

For an instant, lightning illuminated the room like daylight. Thunder followed, but Booker ignored it. He lowered himself over her, kissing her face, her lips, her eyes. Thea wrapped her arms around him and held him close, their hearts hammering at each other, insistently. He closed his eyes and held his breath when her palms slid across his shoulders and arms and worked around. He pushed away so she could bury her fingers in the curls on his chest and rake his nipples with her nails.

"Thea," he said against her parted lips.

She urged him wordlessly, and he adjusted his weight so she could reach between them. She touched him, timidly at first, and then at his helpless sound of pleasure, stroked until his arms quivered and he smashed her hand between their perspiring bodies.

He kissed her hard, sucking air through his nose in a harsh intake of breath. She met the kiss, returned his passion, greedily gripped his shoulders and raised her hips in an irresistible invitation.

Booker buried himself deep within her and remained motionless, garnering control. In the past, women had seduced him in hopes of catching an officer as a husband. Delicate women mostly, women who didn't enjoy the physical act, but performed it as a means to get what they wanted. He'd held back, respecting their size and their reserve.

With Thea there was no holding back, no reticence, no sparing her anything. She wouldn't allow it. She took all of him and gave ecstasy in return. Booker indulged himself in her rapturous body, her seeking mouth and pleasured sighs. He clenched his jaw and tried to think about something besides the precious glide of his flesh inside hers.

She stiffened beneath him, her nails digging at the flesh of his pounding hips. Booker answered her sensual distress with increased fervor. She groaned and he intercepted the guttural sound with his mouth before it became a scream. She panted against his mouth, her body relaxing in satisfaction. Booker kissed her ear and throbbed out his own climax.

Exhausted, he lay without moving, without breaking their intimate bond. He knew he was heavy, but she didn't seem to mind. Beneath him, her breast quaked gently, and he eased his weight away to look at her.

Tears rolled down her temples into her already damp hair, but she smiled.

He would never understand her, but he would always want her, always need her. "Are those happy tears?" he asked.

She nodded.

He wiped them away with blunt fingers. "I have a wife who cries when I make love to her," he said in wonder.

"You make me happy," she whispered.

A lump rose in his own throat, and he rolled to the side, pulling her with him. She snuggled along the length of his body, nestling her head on his arm beneath his chin. "You're so beautiful, Thea."

He felt her smile. "I love you, Booker."

He would always want her, always need her, always... When had he begun to love her? When he'd seen her with Zoe and Lucas? When she'd responded to his first kiss? When he'd discovered the freckles between her breasts? When she'd come to him and asked him to give her a shred of happiness? When she'd stood up for him before Marshal Hardy and the others?

He had no idea. It didn't matter.

The rain had begun in earnest, pattering against the windowpanes. A rain-soaked breeze buffeted the curtains.

"I love you, Thea." A minute passed and a trickle slid down his bicep, tickling his underarm. She was crying.

The storm continued throughout the night, and the following morning no sunlight broke through the window. Pulling on her wrapper, Thea stepped to the opening and surveyed the gray, overcast sky. The thunder and lightning had let up, but rain fell in a steady downpour.

Booker tugged on a clean pair of dungarees and scratched his matted chest. The sight of him filled her with a warm, secure feeling.

"What will you do today?" she asked.

"The workers from town know not to come if it rains. We can't do any of the heavy work," he replied. "But the rest of us will find things to do."

She sensed his displeasure. "Will this set you back?"

"The farmers can't work, either, so we'll be all right. After the rain quits we'll get back on schedule. We'll be in operation by the time the wheat's in."

Thea wrapped her arms around his bare torso and hugged him soundly. He'd told her he loved her. A radiant warmth filled her heart and brought a bubble of giddy emotion to her chest. How could she be so lucky? Her! Thea Coulson.

She pulled back and studied the morning-whiskered face she'd once considered so hard and unyielding. Thea Hayes, she corrected herself. This handsome, wonderful man's wife. She still couldn't believe her good fortune. Fate had delivered a lover right out of her dreams...and children, too. She'd never been so happy in her life.

"You're not going to cry, are you?" he asked.

She laughed and pulled away to dress.

He didn't come to the house for dinner that day. Red Horse and Lucas voiced their surprise, having thought he'd stayed at the house. Red Horse showed no concern, but Thea worried the entire afternoon. Her father's close call had made Thea worry about Booker's safety, considering someone had apparently tried to kill him.

Trying not to infect Zoe with her increasingly distressed mood, Thea baked bread and pies, waxed the upstairs floors until they shone and dusted every corner of the house.

An hour before supper, the sound of boots pounding on the back porch floor caught her attention. Thea flew through the kitchen and out the back door. Booker shook out a new slicker and hung it on a nail, then removed his hat and sat on one of the wicker chairs to pull off his muddy boots.

"Where have you been?" she asked breathlessly.

"I had some errands," he replied, and stood.

She followed him into the kitchen, where he removed his damp shirt, hung it over the back of a chair and tested the coffeepot on the stove. "This hot?"

She brushed him aside. "Go get some dry clothes on. I'll make fresh."

He turned to leave.

"Booker?"

He turned back.

"I was worried."

His black eyes seemed to take stock of her serious expression. "I can take care of myself, Thea. Don't let this thing make you crazy, because it will if you let it."

He'd offered no explanation, no excuse, no apology. She didn't want to be a demanding, smothering wife, but neither did she want to spend more days like this one. "Could you just let me know ahead of time if you won't be here?"

He leaned forward and kissed her, and he smelled like rain and horses and man. She couldn't bear to lose him. Not now. Not ever. She curled her fingers into the matted damp hair on his chest, and he groaned. Comforted, she pulled back.

"I'll let you know next time," he promised.

She handed him a kettle of hot water to take upstairs, and he thanked her with a nod. She had everything she wanted. Why did she feel as though she were hanging on to it for dear life?

The following day was humid and rain sodden like the last. This time Booker told her he wouldn't be home at noon, and she didn't see him until supper. And, like the day before, he gave her no indication of where he'd been or what he'd been doing.

On the third day, the sun returned, and with it Thea's optimism. She was stepping around puddles in the yard, hanging out the laundry she hadn't been able to dry for days, when Zoe tugged on her skirt. She looked down.

The child held the dented bucket up, hopefully.

Thea had hoped she would eventually forget, but it seemed the child had a powerful determination. "We won't need to water today, darlin'. But we'll go look just to make you happy, okay?"

Zoe beamed her reply.

Thea tossed the wooden clothespins on top of the remaining laundry in the basket and followed Zoe. Before they reached the spot, Zoe grabbed her hand and pumped her arm in excitement.

"Whatever—" Thea lost track of what she'd been about to say and stared ahead.

Standing on the exact spot where they'd dug the hole and dropped in the acorn was a sturdy young sapling about four feet high. Thea stopped, fists on hips, and sized up the infant oak tree. No grass or weeds grew within two feet of where the hole had been dug. Someone had obviously tried to erase their footprints, and the rain had cooperated.

But the enormous boot prints leading away through the spongy sod told Thea everything she needed to know. The rapturous expression on Zoe's face was worth a dozen rainy days, a hundred afternoons of wondering where her husband had disappeared to. If only he could have been there to see it. Thea's heart swelled with love. He cared so much for Zoe, loved her more than she could ever know. He tried so hard to earn her acceptance.

And this. Zoe didn't know her uncle had planted that tree. She believed in miracles. And Booker had given her that belief, the same belief every child should have.

Thea smiled through her tears, knowing Booker would tease her if he were there to see them. Zoe was a lucky little girl.

For two days Skeeter chiseled grooves into the buhrstones. He would chisel, and then the men would fit one stone on top of another to check the fit. The heavy stone would come back off, and Skeeter would set to work again. The old man was obviously a perfectionist at his craft.

Finally the stones were set in place.

The time had come for the temporary dam to be dismantled so that the creek would go back to its original bed where the turbine now sat in its penstock. It was a big day. Most of the men who'd helped since the beginning came to lend a hand and see the turbine work. Even Edgar Birch showed up, and Thea wondered where Agnes thought he was.

She, Zoe and Maryruth, carrying David, watched from high on the bank—a wonderful vantage point, and well away from any potential danger.

Maryruth's cheeks held more color than Thea'd seen in weeks. She smiled and waved at Denzel below.

"Things better between you and Denzel?" Thea asked perceptively.

"Much better." She gave Thea a knowing smile. "And you?"

Thea surveyed her husband working in the creek bed. "Much better."

The sisters shared a grin.

Red Horse caught their attention. He stood among the men in the hip-high moving water, and called to Booker. "If I'd known how many times I would have had to move these rocks, I might have gone on to Colorado."

Booker steadied a raft half loaded with rocks already taken from the top of the dam. "Believe me, if I'd have been able to come up with an easier way to do this, I would have."

"How about dynamite?" Red Horse asked.

Booker grinned. "Don't think I didn't consider it."

Before an hour had passed, water poured over the considerably lower stack of stones. In minutes the men were drenched. They tied lines from one person to the next in anticipation of the final breakthrough.

The moment came in a great rush of water and a cacophony of men's shouts and shrills of excitement. The swiftly moving creek broke across the dam and rapidly ate up the dry ground, splashing against the sturdy headgate and rising. Booker, Red Horse and the townsmen splashed to shore and watched the waterway flow back into its original bed.

Thea and Zoe followed along the bank, stopping over the headgate, a wooden box shaped like a platform with a wooden gate that held the water at bay.

Booker and Skeeter climbed the ladder on its side and stood on the platform. "Ready?" Booker called to Lucas, and the crowd gathered in wait.

"We're ready!" Lucas shouted.

Booker and the millwright gripped the top of the wood gate and pulled upward. The muscles across Booker's wet back and shoulders flexed and bunched in the sun. The gate slid upward. Water rushed beneath it, pouring into the long wooden flume and rushing toward the penstock.

Booker jumped from the platform, ran down the bank and leapt up onto the wide stairs that overlooked the turbine set into the penstock. Water poured over the fifteen-foot drop and hit the iron turbine below. Slowly, the iron wheel began to turn.

He glanced up at the main cog gear that turned the drive shaft and saw it rotate. Elated, he threw his head back and let out a whoop more Indianlike than anything he'd ever heard from Red Horse.

"Thea!" Where was she? She had to see this!

"Here!"

He turned and found her watching from the bank above him. "Did you see it?"

She nodded, a wide grin spread across her face.

He jumped down and motioned to her. She met him, and he scooped Zoe up and led Thea toward the mill at a run. She followed him up the red-painted stairs, through the sliding double doors, across the milling room and down the stairs into the basement.

Booker watched in awe as the drive shaft rotated, picking up speed and turning the cog gear beneath the buhr-stone upstairs. The building trembled and overhead came the sound of the stones turning. "We did it, Thea."

He turned and saw pride shining in her eyes.

"You did it, Booker. You accomplished your dream."

Zoe still on one arm, he crushed his wife against his side. "No. This is just the beginning."

* * *

With the mill in operation, Skeeter announced his plans to leave that night.

"You're welcome to stay as long as you'd like," Thea offered, and settled on the sofa beside Booker. The family had gathered in the parlor after dinner.

"No sense in lollygaggin' around on my backside. I lurnt a long time ago not to let grass grow under my feet. I got a heap o' jobs waitin' fur me."

Booker laid his arm along the back of the sofa and absently fingered a lock of Thea's hair. "It's been a pleasure to have you here, Skeeter. Your approval of the site and the mill means a lot to me."

"Next time I'm here-'bouts I'll stop and let your missus take care o' my hankerin' for good hoecakes and 'tater soup. She can make ennythang taste plumb scrumptious!"

Booker smiled and squeezed her shoulder. "Yeah. I think I'll keep her."

Lucas's charcoal scratched across his paper as he busily sketched before the fire.

"You done real good, Hayes." Skeeter chewed his gums a moment. "Her tongue ain't loose at both ends, and she don't get her bowels in an uproar over ever' little thing. She didn't know me from Adam's off ox, an' she made me right welcum."

Used to his talking about her instead of to her, Thea smiled. "Stop by any time you like, Skeeter."

The old man pursed and unpursed his pruny lips and gave her a toothless grin. "Freckled as a turkey egg, but purty as a horse built for speed."

Booker cast her a sidelong grin, and she burst into laughter. Crossing to the chair Skeeter sat in, she bent over and kissed his grizzled cheek. "I'll take that as a compliment, Mr. Gunderson."

Skeeter scratched his nose self-consciously, and watched her gather Zoe's playthings and lead her toward the door.

Thea knelt beside the little girl. "Would you like your uncle to tuck you in tonight?"

Zoe glanced between the two of them. Just when Thea thought she would refuse to answer and hurt Booker's feelings, Zoe nodded bashfully.

"Good girl." She kissed her forehead. "Give us a few minutes and then come tuck Zoe in," she said in parting.

Booker watched them leave the room. Lord, he loved that woman. He glanced at Lucas and saw some emotion flicker across the boy's face.

Across from him, Skeeter closed his eyes and snored.

"I'm headin' up, too," Lucas announced.

"What did you draw?"

Lucas carried the paper to him. Booker took the sheet and stared at the charcoal-drawn portrait of his wife. Lucas had captured Thea that evening—relaxed, content, humor shining in her eyes. "Lucas, I can't begin to tell you how talented you are," he said.

Lucas glanced down at the picture and back at him, eagerness flushing his youthful face. "Really?"

"Really." Booker studied the drawing minutes longer, thinking. Finally, he spoke again. "Lucas, if you had the opportunity, would you like to go to school somewhere?"

Lucas's features flattened. He swallowed, and a defensive glaze shuttered his expression. "Somewhere away from here?"

Booker realized what he'd said. What Lucas must think. "I'm not trying to send you away if that's what you're thinking. I like having you here."

Lucas didn't meet his eyes.

"How much school have you had?"

"Some."

"Well, that's something we'll have to work on. I want you here as long as you want to be here, understand that. But when you're a few years older, if you don't want to be a farmer or a rancher or a millwright, that's okay, too. We could find you a good school where you could study."

Slowly, Lucas's hesitant gray gaze rose to meet Booker's.

Booker waited patiently, hoping the boy understood.

Finally, Lucas said, "I'll think on it."

Booker nodded. He admired the incredible likeness of his wife a minute longer, then handed it back.

"You—you want it?" Lucas asked.

"Your picture?"

Lucas nodded.

"I'd like that."

Lucas handed it back to him. He stood for a moment looking decidedly uncertain, and finally thrust his charcoal-stained fingers toward Booker. "G'night."

Booker shifted the drawing to his left hand and shook the hand Lucas offered him. "Good night, Lucas. Thank you."

Lucas nodded and almost ran toward the stairs.

Booker regarded the picture. One day at a time. Every day things got a little better. His mill was in operation in time for the harvest. Thea had accepted him as her husband. Soon Lucas and Zoe would accept him and love him, too. Soon. Everything was going as he'd planned.

Chapter Sixteen

Even though the weather was fine, Booker mysteriously spent another afternoon away from the mill. This time Thea didn't concern herself. He was probably off on another mission of love concerning his niece.

Several days later, what did strike her as curious was his announcement that he had business in St. Louis and that he'd be gone for a few days. In the past he'd made an issue of trying to get her to go shopping or to visit her half sister, and this time she wondered why he didn't ask her to go along. But she had assured him time and again that the city held no interest for her, so why should she feel slighted that he hadn't offered?

Leaving Red Horse with instructions for the mill and Lucas in charge of the horses, Booker kissed her goodbye and rode off.

She busied herself canning her early peas, unpacking the remaining trunks of Julia's belongings and deciding what to do with the items. Booker's sister's dresses were made from lovely colorful fabrics, but useless to Thea. Her own sisters already had more clothing than they needed, and it would be years before Zoe would wear them, so Thea decided to take the garments apart and use the material to make clothing for Zoe and blouses for herself, saving the scraps for quilts and doll clothes.

On the second day, needing thread and trim, she asked Lucas to saddle her mare and another for Zoe, and escort them to the mercantile in Omaha. Lucas was thrilled at the responsibility and rode beside them proudly.

"I'll give the horses water and find some shade for them," he offered when they arrived, squinting up at Thea on the boardwalk.

"Thank you, Lucas. Zoe and I will be busy for a couple of hours. Why don't you meet us at the hotel dining room for lunch?"

"Okay!" He turned and led the animals away.

Thea admired the hats displayed in the front window before leading Zoe into the shady interior. She'd never owned anything other than a bonnet, and the hat display intrigued her, especially a lovely wide-brimmed hat with a sprig of artificial violets nestled against the band. Two wide purple ribbons streamed off the back.

Impulsively, she tried it on and peered at herself in the glass on a nearby display shelf. She could wear anything she liked when she was with Booker. He didn't think she was too tall. Only a week ago when she'd mentioned it, he'd said, "Too tall for what? Not too tall for me. Too tall is like too brave or too beautiful. There is no such thing."

"Good morning, Thea," Natalie McKee called from her post near the back. "Need any help?"

"I'll take this hat," she decided. "Zoe and I are going to look around."

Natalie came forward and took the hat back to wrap it.

Zoe stayed close, occasionally releasing Thea's skirt long enough to touch a glass counter or finger a particularly pretty strip of lace. She showed Thea cards of buttons, and Thea knelt to admire them with her.

Absorbed with Zoe, she barely noticed other patrons entering the store. She discovered a row of velvet ribbon on the bottom shelf of the cabinet, and examined the colors.

"Did you notice the orphan boy down by the livery?" a female voice asked.

"I did," another replied. "The Hayes tribe must be in town."

The other woman snickered.

"Morning, ladies!" Natalie called, apparently still in the rear of the store. "Need any help?"

"Can you find me a nice bag of pecans?" This time Thea recognized the speaker as Penelope Dodd.

"Sure thing," Natalie called.

"I wasn't in town much while Abner was ill," the voice on the other side of the counter said, identifying herself as the Widow Barnett. "I heard about the housewarming, and all Agnes talks about is the Indian."

Thea's legs grew tired from crouching behind the fabrics. Mortified at overhearing the women's conversation, she was tempted to stand and identify herself.

"I don't think Thea knew what she was getting into when she hooked up with that Hayes fellow. A wild one, he is," Penelope intoned. "A real skirt chaser, that one."

"Yes," the widow said with a sigh.

Anger suffused Thea's neck and face with heat. How dare they talk about her husband like that! They didn't even know him!

"Ben and Ellie Wallace were in Lincoln last night and saw him with a woman."

"No!" Widow Barnett clucked her disapproval.

Thea forgot her aching thigh muscles and clutched a skein of ribbon to her breast. *No!* her mind echoed. She wanted to jump up and shut them up but she remained frozen to the spot.

Zoe glanced at her curiously.

"Yes. Ellie said it was an attractive little dark-haired woman, best she could tell. Well-dressed. They were in the hotel lobby."

The widow clucked again. "Poor Thea. Who do you think it was?"

"My best guess is that tramp, Lorraine Edwards. Calls herself a seamstress. Harumph!"

Lorraine Edwards. Thea remembered seeing her at church, and recalled the attention she earned with her tiny waist and petite figure. Hurt as swift and piercing as a razor sliced her soul.

"She's a beautiful woman," the widow admitted. Her careless words burned like salt heaped into the fresh wound.

Booker had known a lot of beautiful women.

The destructive thought stung so badly that Thea grimaced and caught her lower lip between her teeth. No. There was some mistake. Not Booker. Not with Lorraine Edwards. Thea closed her eyes and the image of their dark heads together taunted her. She saw his strong, chiseled body against the seamstress's perfect, delicate curves.

She couldn't think that about him or she'd go crazy. She forced her eyes open. Not Booker. Not with that woman. And if he *was* with her, there was a good reason.

But what?

"Hayes is a good-looking scoundrel himself," Penelope added, her voice moving away with her footsteps. "Maybe Thea will just have to look the other way if she wants to keep him."

She couldn't hear Widow Barnett's reply. They'd moved to the rear and Natalie took their money. Thea's legs gave way and she fell to her bottom on the hard, dusty floor. The bell over the front door tinkled.

Zoe plopped down beside her and played with a spool of red thread she'd found under the shelves.

Thea stared at Zoe's hands without seeing. Booker with Lorraine Edwards? Impossible! Not after everything they'd shared. Not after the things he'd said to her, the way he made her feel. He'd told her he loved her. There must be some mistake.

She told herself that and pushed to her feet. "Come on, Zoe. Let's pay for these and go."

At lunch, instead of enjoying the meal, Thea picked at her roast beef and potatoes.

"Ma'am?"

She glanced up at Lucas.

"You gonna eat that?"

Thea laid her fork down. "No. Help yourself."

Lucas shared her glazed carrots with Zoe and ate the rest himself. Thea paid and Lucas led them to the horses. Zoe, used to an afternoon nap, nearly fell asleep riding her mare. Too distracted, Thea didn't notice until Lucas stopped, took Zoe from her horse and held her before him on his mount. Thea's numb mind turned thoughts and images over during the entire ride.

Lucas had to have noticed her mood, but said nothing.

Unbidden, she recalled the recent afternoons Booker had stayed away from the house and mill with no explanation. She swallowed her panic and blamed the ride for her tight-in-the-neck physical discomfort. There had to be some mistake. Booker had told her he was going to St. Louis, not Lincoln. And he had no reason to meet Lorraine Edwards. The Wallaces must have seen someone who *looked* like Booker. Sure, someone else well over six feet tall with black hair, a face and mouth that weren't as hard as they looked, and whose appearance commanded attention. There were probably a million men like that.

Confused and somewhat horror-stricken, she prayed he'd be home that afternoon. Maybe he'd be at the house when they arrived, and he'd have a perfectly reasonable explanation. She had everything she wanted. Nothing was going to spoil that. Nothing.

He didn't come home that night. And the next day brought a worse implication than the last. After a sleepless night, she rose to prepare breakfast for Red Horse and the children. They'd just finished eating when the pounding hoofbeats and the jingle of harnesses alerted them to riders.

Thea's heart leapt to her breast. Booker?

She dried her hands and moved to the back door. With dust swirling around their horses' hoovcs, Marshal Hardy and Irving Jackson led a dozen riders. Apprehension clambered in Thea's chest. She moved one foot ahead of the other, stepping out the back door and down the stairs.

Thea disguised her alarm behind a bright smile and greeted the marshal. "Morning, Marshal. What brings you out so early?"

"Is your husband here?" the marshal asked, ignoring the pleasantry.

Red Horse came to stand beside Thea.

"No, he's not," she replied.

"Do you know where he is?"

"He went to St. Louis on business."

"I suppose you know where we can reach him, then, if we wire St. Louis."

She didn't know. Should she? "N-no," she answered. "I expect him back any time."

"Is he on horseback?"

Thea exchanged an uneasy glance with Red Horse. The Indian spoke up. "He took the train."

Marshal Hardy bit the end from a fat cigar and wet the other end between his rubbery lips. "Guess we have no way of reachin' him, do we?"

"What do you want him for?" Thea asked.

The marshal took his time inspecting his cigar and scratching his protruding belly with a thumb. Finally, he drew a match from his pocket, struck it on the pommel of his saddle and puffed on the cigar until a wreath formed around his head and the odious smell reached Thea. "It's serious this time," he said ominously.

"What is? What are you talking about?" Thea took a few steps closer to the men.

Irving Jackson had begun to squirm like he couldn't wait to be the one to tell her. Finally, he spoke up. "Clancy's been killed."

Thea rolled the name over in her mind. Clancy? The manager at the hotel with his belly sausaged into his shirt? The man who'd tried to keep her and Red Horse from the dining room? "What does that have to do with my husband?"

"Everything," Jackson stated. "Other times we couldn't prove it. This time we got him."

"Got him where? Got him for what?" She insisted on knowing.

"Clancy was stabbed last night. Cook found 'im in the alley this morning," the marshal informed her. He rolled the smoking cigar from one side of his mouth to the other. "Hayes's pocket watch was lying beneath the body."

Thea tried to remember Booker with a pocket watch. Nothing came to mind. "I've never seen my husband with a pocket watch. How do you know it's his?"

"Inscription right inside the cover. Someone named Julia gave it to him."

Thea glanced at Red Horse. He confirmed the information with a nod. A weight settled on her heart. "There must be some mistake?"

Was that the best she could do? Hadn't she already been telling herself that for two days?

"Dodd, Victor, check the house." The marshal gestured to two other riders. "You take the barn."

The riders dismounted and Thea bristled. "Here, now! What do you think you're doing?" She hurried to stand on the porch steps above the two men. "You can't go in my house! I've told you my husband's not here. You'll frighten the children!"

She beseeched the marshal. "Tell them not to go in there."

"Don't get in their way or I'll have to stop you."

Thea straightened, and Red Horse caught her attention. "Let them look," he said softly.

She rushed in ahead of them. "Lucas! Zoe!"

Both of them stood, wide-eyed, at the kitchen window. She moved beside Lucas and knelt to take Zoe in her arms. Zoe must have felt her body trembling, because she patted Thea's face comfortingly with a chubby hand. Thea buried her face in the little girl's neck and waited an eternity for the men to search each room and return, exiting through the kitchen door.

Through the glass, Thea watched the other men return from the barn. All of them mounted their horses and the posse rode away. Posse. Thea rolled the word over in her brain. What in heaven's name was going on?

She set the children about their normal tasks and stacked the dirty dishes with a clatter. Anger insinuated itself between the confusion and fear constricting her chest. He should be here! Where was he, anyway? Didn't he care how she felt? Didn't he know she'd be worried?

He still wasn't there by dinner. They ate sullenly. The afternoon crept by while she listened for his horse, his step, on the back porch. Finally, a rider approached the house. Thea flew out the back door and down the stairs.

It was Victor Penn, one of the men who had been there with the marshal that morning. Thea shaded her eyes with a hand.

"Your husband's in jail, Mizz Hayes. Marshal sent me to tell ya." He spun his mount around and galloped back in the direction he'd come.

Thea stared after him. Jail. How could this be happening?

Red Horse ran to her side.

She met his dark eyes. "He's in jail."

Red Horse guarded his expression. He placed his hand on her sleeve. "I'm responsible."

Thea frowned in confusion. "What do you mean? You didn't kill that man, did you?"

"No. But none of these incidents would have been blamed on the major if I hadn't been here. It's me they don't like and they hate him for bringing me here."

"Red Horse..." What could she say? How could she make up for other peoples' cruelty and hatred? She'd grown up with many of these people as neighbors, had attended school and church with them. Some she would have expected to behave this way, but others... like Agnes and Penclope...

"I understand," he stated.

"How could you? I've been treated like an outsider most of my life, and I still don't understand."

"What do you want to do?" Red Horse asked.

She glanced back up at the house. "I want to go see him."

He nodded. "I'll get the wagon."

The ride into Omaha took forever. Zoe got hot and cranky, and finally napped. Lucas remained quiet and withdrawn, and Red Horse stared ahead. The wagon bounced in and out of ruts and the sun glared until Thea's head throbbed. Finally, they pulled up alongside the building that served as the marshal's home and the jail.

Thea debated leaving the children in the wagon, but the sun was too hot and they would want to see Booker. All of them trooped into the office.

Marshal Hardy glanced up from a battered desk where he sat eating an enormous plate of beef and noodles, mopping the liquid with a slice of thickly buttered bread. He looked up and wiped his mouth with the back of his hand.

"Marshal. I'd like to see my husband."

He stood and plucked a set of keys from a nail on the wall behind him. "One at a time."

Thea followed him through a door. The back of the building was stone, and the temperature a few degrees cooler. Hardy unholstered his revolver, unlocked another door and gestured her down. Glancing between the gun and the doorway, she stepped through. A narrow set of warped stairs led to the dim underground recesses. She held her skirts and descended.

At the bottom, she stopped and beheld the narrow, cavelike hallway with two doors flanking each side. The dank, cool, musty smell sent a shiver along her spine. A single smoke-blackened lantern lit the area.

Good God, he was down here?

The marshal moved behind her and she stepped out of his way. He lit another lantern, handed it to her and unlocked the first door on the right. The thick wooden door, a tiny square window its only feature, opened.

Marshal Hardy gestured her in. Her heart hammered, and she stepped through the opening.

The door closed and locked behind her.

"Thea."

She jumped and turned.

He unfolded himself from the cot he'd been sitting on and came to her, blinking against the light. "Are you all right?"

She lost herself in his black, black eyes. A hundred questions bubbled to the surface of her mind. Only one came to her tongue. "Where have you been?"

"I told you I had business," he replied.

"Where?"

He frowned. "Thea, what is it?"

"Someone said they saw you in Lincoln."

He nodded. "I was there."

Thea's heart plummeted. He'd been there. "At the hotel?"

"Yes."

"Did you go there to meet a woman?"

"Yes." He reached to take her upper arms in his hands.

She pulled away. *Was it Lorraine Edwards? Was it that beautiful seamstress with the raven hair and the hourglass waist?* The questions screamed through her mind, but he'd answered them all. He'd told her the truth, and this was the one truth she couldn't bear to hear. "Why couldn't you have been honest with me?"

He drew his hands back and uncomfortably hooked his thumbs at his waist. "I didn't want you to know until—"

"What else don't I know?" Heat nipped at her face and cold ate away her heart. He'd kept the knowledge of her father's shooting from her. He'd met a woman in Lincoln when he'd said he was going to St. Louis. What else had he not told her? What else had he lied about? "Was that your watch they found under Clancy's body?"

He nodded.

"Were you there?"

Something dark and pained moved behind his eyes. He guarded the emotion quickly and raised his black-stubbled chin an inch. "You mean did I kill him?"

"No-no, I mean how did your watch get there?"

He backed away from her. "I don't know."

"What do you mean you don't know?"

"I mean I don't know. I don't use that watch. I haven't seen it since I unpacked my things in my room. I think it was in one of the drawers."

She stared at him, not knowing what to say or do. God, everything was in such a mess!

"Are Zoe and Lucas all right?" he asked dully.

"They're waiting up there. They'll want to see you."

He shifted his weight and leaned against the stone wall. "I don't think I want them to see me here, not like this."

"They love you."

His obsidian gaze flickered to hers, then away.

I love you, she wanted to say, but she'd made a big-enough fool of herself. All the while she'd been basking in the glory of his lovemaking, feeling loved and attractive and buying whimsical hats, he'd been seeing another woman.

Despondent tears stung her eyes. He'd fooled her. He'd said and done all the right things to manipulate her lonely heartstrings. For a brief time he'd made a discouraged spinster feel like a beautiful wife.

She blinked back tears. She couldn't even hate him for it.

"Thea," he said.

She met his stare.

"Take care of Zoe for me. Whatever happens."

Something in the depths of her soul shattered into a million ragged pieces. Zoe. All along it had been Zoe. Everything had been for Zoe.

"You didn't even have to ask." Her voice sounded like dry leaves skittering in the dirt.

He turned his face away.

"Shall I send Red Horse down?"

He nodded.

Thea knocked on the door.

Immediately, the marshal unlocked it and gestured her out with his revolver. Heart and legs and feet numb, she followed him out of the room and up the smooth, worn stairs. "He wants to see you," she said to Red Horse.

She dropped onto a dusty, scarred bench. Lucas and Zoe knelt in front of her and took her hands. She looked down into their youthful faces.

"Is he all right?" Lucas asked at last, worry storming in his cloud gray eyes.

Thea nodded.

"What's gonna happen?"

She shook her head. "I don't know."

Lucas had never seen her frightened, and her grief-stricken expression shook him to the core of his being. Thea always knew what to do, always took control and handled things. Damn. Just when his life seemed to have taken a turn for the better. Just when he'd begun to feel settled in with them. Just when they'd begun to feel like . . . parents.

That pig-faced marshal led Red Horse from the back room at the tip of his revolver. Lucas wanted to yank the gun from his greasy hands and ram it down his throat. "Wait!" The marshal started to return the keys to their peg. Lucas stepped forward. "I have to see him."

Hardy looked from Lucas to Thea. She nodded. "Let him."

Lucas followed Hardy into the stairwell. He'd been in some pretty awful situations in his life, but this was one of the worst places he'd ever seen. Lucas stared hard at the tiny window on the massive door and imagined how little light must get into the cell. His heart leapt up into his throat when the man unlocked the door and poked him with the gun barrel. He handed him a lantern.

"Knock when you're ready."

Lucas stumbled into the tiny stone-walled room. Booker pushed away from the wall and faced him. Lucas avoided his eyes. He took a step forward and looked at the floor, then at the rumpled gray sheet on the narrow cot.

"Hello, Lucas."

Finally he brought his face up and looked at Booker. "Hi."

"Did you take care of the horses like I asked?"

"Yes, sir!"

One side of Booker's mouth tugged up in a grin. "I knew you would."

Several silent minutes passed. Finally Booker asked, "Do you want to know if I killed him?"

Lucas shook his head and placed the lantern on the floor. "I know ya didn't."

Booker seemed to absorb that.

"I want to..."

"Want to what?" Booker prompted.

He wanted to do something. He felt so helpless. What could he say to make anything better? "You said if I ever felt like you was my friend, I should tell this."

"All right."

Lucas looked at his thumbnail and picked it with his other hand. "Them scars you asked about?"

"Yes." He barely made out Lucas's voice.

"Well, this man in the city took me to his shop. I had to chop wood and keep the steam engines fired up."

"How old were you?"

"I don't remember. But if I didn't keep up, he'd hit me with his cane."

Booker remained silent.

"The next one I remember had a whole passel o' kids. I slept in a building outside. The father'd get drunk and whup me with a razor strap."

A muscle in Booker's jaw twitched.

"Worst time I ever got beat was one o' the times I ran away. A state man found me on the wharf. He took me into an alley and beat me until I didn't remember nothin' for a week. That's when I got put in the Foundling Home."

"And Bard? You ran away from him because he beat you, didn't you?"

Lucas nodded.

Booker took a few steps closer. "Lucas, those things that happened to you, they aren't fair. Nobody should treat another person like that. You didn't do anything to deserve that. I wish—"

Booker stopped and gave a rueful shake of his head.

"What?" Lucas asked.

"I'm sorry. I wish I could do something to take all that away, to change it all."

Lucas regarded him with surprise. "That's what I wish, too." He gestured with a lanky arm. "About this."

Booker stepped directly in front of him and Lucas swallowed and looked up. "I'll be okay, Lucas. You just see after Thea and Zoe for me, all right?"

Lucas knew Thea and Zoe meant more to him than anything. Trusting them to his care proved he thought a lot of him, too. Nobody'd ever trusted him before. Nobody'd ever cared enough to see that he had a warm bed and enough food to eat. Nobody'd ever been sorry before. Booker Hayes was the finest man he'd ever met. Staring up into eyes as black as midnight, Lucas realized something important. He'd changed.

He wasn't scared for himself any longer. This man had shown him there was hope. Good people existed and there was work to be done. Food was available any time he needed it. Life didn't have to be about pain and loneliness. Life didn't have to be about running.

With a step as shaky as a newborn colt, he breached the space between them and pressed his face against Booker's rock-hard shirtfront. Muscled arms banded his back, and an enormous hand closed over his shoulder. Lucas squeezed his eyes shut tight and willed himself not to cry like a baby.

"I'll take care of 'em," he managed to say.

No, he wasn't scared for himself anymore. He was terrified as all hell for Booker.

Chapter Seventeen

"He'll be arraigned before the justice Monday morning," the marshal told Thea later that afternoon.

She'd heard tales of the justice that was dealt in the frontier court. The *Omaha Republican* reported fines and imprisonment and hangings every day.

"Got a wire," the marshal said, directing the information at Red Horse. "Band of Crow attacked a wagon train north and west of here. News has it there were no survivors. All those whites—men, women, children—all dead and scalped. Wagons were looted."

"I'm sorry to hear that," Red Horse said.

"Thought I'd tell ya, case someone saw you and started shooting."

"Thanks for thinking of me. I guess you know people don't care that I'm not Crow."

The marshal ignored that.

"This is all because of me, isn't it?" Red Horse asked.

Marshal Hardy eyed him. "How's that?"

"Major Hayes is being singled out because he brought me here."

"White folks just don't trust Injuns," the marshal said. "We get news like this every week. Hell, last winter a couple of drunked-up Injuns killed one o' the sportin' women with a tomahawk."

"White men kill people in saloon brawls and gunfights every day, too," Thea spoke up.

"That particular Injun got hisself killed with his own tomahawk," the marshal added, sounding almost pleased to deliver the news.

"I think people would be less likely to accuse him if I weren't here," Red Horse thought out loud.

Thea looked at him in surprise.

"Everybody'd sleep a lot easier if you weren't here." The marshal sat back in his chair and the overtaxed springs screeched.

Exasperated with his narrow-minded idiocy, Thea grabbed Red Horse's hand and led him from the building. "I'll be at the Woodridge farm," she said over her shoulder.

Red Horse lifted Zoe, assisted Thea and waited for Lucas to scramble into the back of the wagon. They didn't speak much on the ride.

They pulled into the dooryard and Uncle Snake appeared on the porch. Thea helped Zoe down and led her up the stairs.

Aunt Odessa let the screen door slam behind her, took one look at Thea's face and held her hand out to Zoe. "Come here, child. Have you and Lucas eaten?"

Zoe shook her head.

"You, too, Mr. Horse," she called. "Put your team up and come eat supper."

Red Horse smiled and waved, leading the animals toward the barn.

Uncle Snake took Thea's hand and led her to the wicker chairs on the end of the porch. "Sit, Thea."

Stiffly, she turned and lowered herself onto a wooden swing. Snake sat beside her and kept her hand engulfed in his.

"What's happening?" he asked.

She raised her eyes to his kind, familiar face, and noticed the thick white shocks of gray in his red hair. "They have him in that awful jail. Have you seen it?"

"Yeah," he said, sighing.

"They say he killed Clancy, that man who worked for Irving Jackson."

"The cook found him," Uncle Snake intoned, "and when he brought the marshal they found Booker's watch under the body."

"Yes."

"Is it his watch?"

She nodded. "He didn't carry it. He thinks it was in a drawer in his room."

"How many people could have gone into Booker's room and taken it?" her uncle asked.

She thought about it. "Just the family. Zoe, Lucas, me, Maryruth. Maybe Papa. And of course . . ." She shook her head.

Snake nodded.

"Red Horse," she said. "But he was with me."

"Not all night."

"He slept outdoors."

"Then he could have left and gone into town and you wouldn't have known."

She squeezed his hand. "Not you, too."

He squeezed back. "No. I don't think he did it, but when they go to figuring out the possibilities, he's gonna be among 'em."

Thea gave her head a mental shake and tried to clear her thoughts. "Booker admitted he went to Lincoln to meet . . . someone," she faltered. "When they question him to prove where he was, everyone will know he was with . . ." Her voice broke.

"With who?"

She shook her head and fought tears.

"Ah, Thea," he said, and pulled her close.

She collapsed against her uncle and sobbed. "I've been such a fool." She accepted the bandanna he pulled from his hip pocket. "I was so blind." She pressed the cloth against her eyes. "So *stupid!* Oh!" Disappointment and shame quickly turned to anger. She clenched the now-damp fabric in her fists. She'd been duped! "How could he?"

She sat up and stared ahead. "And how could he so uncaringly admit it?"

"Exactly what did he admit?"

"He went to Lincoln rather than St. Louis like he said. He went to the hotel, and he met a woman."

"Who did he say she was?"

"He didn't say. I already knew."

"You did, did you?"

She leaned against the back of the swing, exhausted, and gazed across the yard.

Red Horse returned from the barn.

"Go on in," Snake directed. "Ma'll have something hot for you." He'd always called her ma even though they'd had no children of their own. "You, too," he said to his niece. "Come in and eat."

Resignedly, she followed him into the kitchen.

Later, she helped her aunt with the dishes, and Red Horse entertained Zoe and Lucas in the parlor.

Snake sat at the kitchen table with a cup of coffee. Odessa had waited so patiently, caring for the children and preparing the meal. Thea hugged her and explained the situation.

The three of them sat at the table, sipping coffee from their cups.

"Well, at least he has a witness," her uncle said a few minutes later.

"What?"

"If he was in Lincoln with a woman, she can prove he wasn't here murdering Clancy."

Thea stared at him. She stared at the cup in her hand and the chipped bowl of cookies in the center of the table. She hadn't even thought of that. Here Booker had a perfect alibi for his whereabouts, and she hadn't stopped feeling sorry for herself long enough to put the facts together. "What time is it?"

Uncle Snake pulled a watch from his overall pocket. "A little after eight."

"I'm going back into town."

"What for?"

"To talk to her."

"I'll take you."

She agreed and stood.

Her aunt took her hand. "Don't worry about the children. They'll be just fine here with me and Mr. Horse."

Half an hour later, Thea stood before a tiny, well-tended house at the edge of town. Even in the dark she could tell the yard was neat, the fence and the shutters in good repair. The woman obviously had the means to care for her home. The sewing business must be successful. Or, if what the other women all said was true, entertaining men was profitable.

What would she do if there was a man in there? Worse yet, one she knew? Thea raised her knuckles to the wood and hoped Lorraine Edwards would have enough sense to hide him when someone came to the door. She rapped and waited, her heart hammering.

Steps sounded inside, and the door opened. The petite woman peered around the edge of the door. "Hello?"

"Miss Edwards?"

"Yes." Seeing Thea was alone, she opened the door wider.

"I'm Thea Hayes."

"Yes, I know. Won't you come in?"

Thea took a tentative step forward. "Thank you."

"I was just going to have a cup of tea. I'd love to have you join me."

Surprised, Thea agreed. She hadn't known how she would be received, but she hadn't expected such cordiality. She followed the much smaller woman into a room decorated with obvious feminine taste. White lace doilies were tacked to the backs and arms of flowered chairs, others, starched to attentive ruffles, topped the spindly legged tables. Several half-completed sewing projects were strewn across a drop-leaf table before the window. An enormous fern sat atop a slender oak column in the corner.

Thea watched her return with another cup and saucer and pour tea from a matching painted china pot. Her hands were tiny and soft looking, her skin clear and obviously protected from the sun. She sat on a love seat at Thea's left. She had a waist so tiny, Booker could nearly have spanned it with one hand. Thea's gaze drifted from the woman's gentle curves to her angelic face. *Had he?*

"It's so nice to have a caller," the woman said, interrupting Thea's thoughts. "I don't know many people in town yet. Most seem pretty standoffish."

"Do you know my husband?" Thea asked, blurting out the first words that tripped off her tongue.

"Yes, I do." She handed Thea a cup and saucer and took one herself. She sipped tea and gazed at Thea.

"Miss Edwards—"

"Oh, do call me Lorraine. It's so much friendlier. And I'll call you Thea. By the way, did you like the fabrics?"

Thea held the cup to her lips. "Excuse me?"

"The fabrics." She tilted her head and cast an apologetic glance. "Oh dear, I haven't spoiled a surprise, have I?"

"I—I'm afraid I don't know what you mean."

"Your husband ordered some lovely chintz, a black sateen and the most beautiful German linen. After I saw it, I ordered some for myself."

"When was this?"

"A couple of weeks ago. I thought he'd have given it to you by now." She placed her cup on the low table. "I'm sorry to spoil the surprise."

"Not at all." Thea sat her cup down, too. "Lorraine." If she was seeing Booker, she certainly didn't behave like the "other woman." More confused than ever, Thea bolstered her courage. "Did you see my husband last night or the night before?"

Lorraine shook her dark head, slowly. "No."

"Were you in Lincoln during the past few days?"

"No. This is the farthest west I've been. Sometimes I wonder why I came this far."

Was she lying? Thea regarded the woman's black-lashed, kind eyes and her earnest expression. She didn't think so. She glanced around and couldn't for the life of her imagine Lorraine hiding someone's husband behind the curtains. What had she been thinking of?

She stayed long enough to drink a second cup of tea and listen to Lorraine chatter about a wedding dress she'd made and another she had taken an order for.

"I'm so glad you came by," she said to Thea with a sincere smile. "It's nice to have someone to girl chat with. I hope you'll come again."

"Thank you, Lorraine. I will."

Thea stepped through the gate and stared back at the little house. What a nice person. How could she have suspected her? She was as bad as Agnes and all the other busybodies, listening to gossip and jumping to conclusions. She had more character than that, didn't she?

But Booker had admitted he'd met a woman. In her heart, she didn't believe Lorraine Edwards had lied. Booker hadn't been with her in Lincoln. But he had purchased fabrics for her. Where were they?

Perhaps another little dark-haired woman had received the gift. If the woman at the hotel wasn't Lorraine, who was she? Thea walked to the end of the block where her uncle waited with the buggy. She climbed up and seated herself beside him. "It wasn't her."

He lifted the reins and urged the team forward. "Who was it, then?"

"I haven't the faintest idea."

"Why don't you ask him?"

Thea stared at the fireflies flickering in a corner lot as they passed. Her uncle headed the horses toward his farm. Why didn't she ask him? Why hadn't she asked him? Because she'd been so sure it was Lorraine.

"I'm gonna send one of the hands for your pa in the mornin'."

"Good," she replied. Hopefully, her father would have some insight into this situation. Maybe he wouldn't shake his head and say, "I wondered if you knew what you were doin' when you married him." Maybe the new day would bring some sense to this whole mess.

Maybe she'd wake up and it would all have been a dream—a bad, bad dream.

Booker stared into the blackness overhead. The wick on the lantern outside the door had burned out hours ago. Before that the marshal had hauled a drunk down the stairs and shoved him into one of the other cells. Booker was grateful for the resonant snore that tied him to humanity with its crude thread.

He could have been forgotten down here, for all he knew. The town overhead could have been swept away in a monstrous storm and he wouldn't know. The isolation was complete.

He'd wired his commanding officer at Fort Scott, who wired right back that he would try to be here by Monday. Booker'd wired Lincoln, too, but he'd had no luck reaching his alibi to testify that he hadn't been in Omaha the night of the murder. He doubted Marshal Hardy would deliver his return messages.

Still, Booker wasn't afraid.

He was mad. He stacked his hands beneath his head and tried to find a comfortable position on the lumpy cot. He couldn't forget Thea's reaction—her behavior...her words. Her voice had been accusing, her eyes filled with mistrust and doubt. She'd pulled away from his touch. Nothing had ever left him so cold. So empty. So hurt. He'd never needed to hold her so badly, never wanted to see love shining from her eyes as much as he'd wanted to see it that day. When she turned to leave he'd wanted to stop her, pull her into his arms and find the strength and love he needed to survive this ordeal.

Of course Red Horse knew him as well as any man could, and knew the truth instinctively. Even Lucas hadn't had a doubt in his mind. But Thea. Thea.

Lord, how it hurt to have her think he was capable of cold-blooded murder.

From far away, a metallic sound roused him from his thoughts. He strained his ears and listened. Footsteps sounded on the stairs, and a deep voice murmured. A square of light bobbed on the ceiling. Who would come this late at night? A lynching party? Booker's heart hammered up into his throat. On the other side of the door, the marshal must have been relighting the lantern. The key rattled in the lock, and the door swung open.

He sat up and blinked against the painful light.

"Knock when you're ready," the marshal said. Through squinted eyes, Booker made out Marshal Hardy with trousers on over his union suit. The tall woman beside him couldn't be anyone but Thea. Booker pushed to his feet.

"What are you doing here?" Booker asked after the door closed and locked.

She placed a napkin-wrapped bundle on the end of the cot. "I brought you something to eat."

"In the middle of the night?" he asked.

"It's morning," she replied. She held the lantern up and studied his face. "I should have thought to bring a razor."

"They wouldn't have let you," he told her.

"Oh." She glanced away, and then back at his face. "You're angry with me, aren't you?"

"Yes."

Her brows rose at his reply. "Have you reached someone who can be here on Monday?"

"My commanding officer said he'd try to be here."

"How about the woman you were with in Lincoln?"

"I tried."

"And?"

"And I didn't reach her."

Apparently, that information riled her. She straightened her spine and lifted her chin. "Why did you bother to pretend with me? I would have helped you with Zoe, you knew that. You used me. You used my needs and my feelings.

You took everything I had to give. You only married me for Zoe.''

Booker absorbed those words and they blended with the hurt already in his own soul. He knew his own motives, and he knew why he'd married her. "Okay," he admitted. "I manipulated you."

She turned her face sharply toward the door.

"But who used who?" he asked. "You wanted Zoe," he reminded her. "That's why it was so easy. I knew how badly you wanted her, how much you wanted to have her as your own child."

"You admit you took advantage of me?" she asked.

"Hell, yes."

She turned her face back, and the lantern light revealed her anguish.

"I wanted you," he said simply. "I married you because I wanted you. Were your motives that noble? Who should be feeling used here? You wanted Zoe. I wanted you. That's why I married you."

She took stock of his expression, and let her gaze wander his face. "What kind of man are you?" she asked.

"Just a man," he replied.

"And the woman? Where does she fit into all of this?"

"If you had trusted me, you would have seen. If you had trusted me, you wouldn't have doubted."

"Everything you've done, you've done for Zoe," she said, denying he'd ever thought of her. "The tree," she said, as though just remembering. "I know you planted that tree for her."

"I planted that tree for you." He let the words sink in. "I knew how helpless you felt. And I didn't want you to feel like you'd let Zoe down."

They stood like that for what seemed an eternity. Booker wished he could turn the clock back, rearrange events and say things he should have. He prayed it wasn't too late. But, her doubt pierced him like nothing ever had, and no words could heal the gaping hole in his chest where his heart should have been.

He wanted to tell her again that he loved her. Wanted to pull her close and feel her heartbeat, gather comfort and reassurance from her warm touch. But he couldn't. His feet and hands wouldn't move. His voice stuck in his throat.

She turned, and her skirts swished in the silence of the dank room. She knocked on the door. A minute later, the marshal unlocked the door, and she stepped out. The key clicked in the lock. The marshal's voice dissipated. Booker sank to the edge of the smelly cot and, his elbows resting on his knees, clutched his head in both hands. It almost didn't matter anymore. If they hung him, he'd be dead and wouldn't know the difference. If they set him free, he had nothing to live for. Except Zoe. And Lucas. Was that enough to keep a man going? It would have to be.

Thea lay in the darkness of the Woodridges' spare room, staring up at the night sky through the open window. Beside her, Zoe slept fitfully, occasionally whimpering. She'd gone back to the house for clothes that afternoon, and had walked the airy silent rooms of their home. The entire house reflected Booker, his simple tastes, his strong masculine appeal. The house itself was nothing but wood and stone, but he'd breathed character into each room, sealed each crack and crevice with love and polished it off with care and concern.

It was more than a house. It was a symbol of his love, a testimony to his faith and his hope for the future. She'd let him down.

How could any man do all this—work his fingers to the bone building the house and the mill, spend time with Zoe and Lucas, plan their future, make all-consuming passionate love to her—and still have time or energy left for another woman?

He couldn't. Her own insecurities, her self-doubt and low opinion of herself had conjured up that other woman. Was it true? Had he planted that tree for her, so that she wouldn't feel inadequate? He had told her that he loved her.

She, Too-Tall Thea Coulson, the child who'd been ridiculed, the woman who'd never received a flirtatious glance or a kiss, and hadn't seen herself as someone a man could love. She hadn't felt beautiful or admired or worthy of attention and praise.

She truly hadn't believed Booker could love her. Hadn't seen herself as a woman who could hold a man's attention. She might as well have called him a liar, for all the doubts she'd voiced and the accusations she'd made. She'd actually done what she'd accused him of doing—married him for Zoe. Hadn't she? Good old self-sacrificing Thea had used Booker Hayes. She scoffed at herself in the darkness.

You've really done it this time, Thea. How could she make it up to him? What if it was too late? She closed her eyes tightly and squeezed back tears. She'd been behaving so selfishly.

Sounds registered, interrupting her thoughts. Riders approached the house. Thea climbed over Zoe and looked out the open window. "Who is it?" she called down to the two riders below. At the same time, her uncle's voice carried across the yard. "What's going on?"

"Came to warn you!" Thea recognized Edgar Birch's voice. "Irving Jackson's got the men all...riled up! They're goin' to bust Hayes from the jail!" he panted.

"Oh, my—" Thea spun back to the room and yanked her dress from a hook. She stepped into it and struggled with the buttons.

The door slammed open, outlining Lucas in a golden halo of lamplight. Zoe sat up and blinked in confusion.

"Don't bother with the wagon," Thea said to the boy. "We'll ride, Lucas." She stepped in front of him and took his shoulders. "I want you to go get my father. Do you think you can find the farm on your own from here?"

"Yes, ma'am," he replied, and shot back out the door. Thea lit a lantern and quickly dressed Zoe. Snake and Red Horse waited with the horses. Red Horse helped her mount and took Zoe into his own lap.

The ride took forever. Thea was afraid one of the horses would stumble in the dark, but Red Horse led the way without mishap.

Thea could hear the crowd before they saw them. The throng gathered in front of the marshal's quarters, lanterns bobbing, rifles raised. Two men restrained Marshal Hardy. He wore his one-piece underwear. A trickle of blood ran down his chin from the corner of his mouth.

"You can't do this," the marshal shouted. "The justice is going to hear his case in the morning."

"You know old man Henney will let him off," Irving Jackson shouted. "And we won't stand for it. The man's been nothing but trouble since he came here."

Snake Woodridge helped his niece dismount, and spoke to Red Horse. "Stay back. Y'hear?"

Red Horse nodded.

Thea clutched Zoe in her arms and followed her uncle toward the front of the crowd.

"I say we hang 'im now and get it over with!" Shouts of agreement went up around the mob. Grateful for once that she was tall enough to see above most heads, Thea found the man who'd received the reaction from the crowd.

Ronan Bard, swaying on his feet, led a cluster of men toward the boardwalk. She realized the men leading the offense had been drinking. Irving Jackson stepped onto the boardwalk. "Are we gonna let outsiders come in and start killing off our townspeople? First he tried to kill Jim Coulson. Next he cornered me in the alley and damned near killed me. And now this! Who's gonna be next? Are we safe?"

Shouts merged and the crowd surged forward.

"Wait a minute!" Ezra Hill worked his way from the edge of the milling crowd to the boardwalk. "Just hold on. Hayes hired me to work for him, and I spent a lot of time at his place. He's not the kind of man who would kill someone in cold blood."

"He's got you fooled," Irving Jackson shouted.

"What about the watch?" Bard joined in. "His watch was under Clancy, wasn't it? Couldn't've been no one but Hayes."

The marshal struggled ineffectually against the men holding him. Irving and several others strode into the building through the office door.

Panic filled Thea's chest. Clutching Zoe, she pushed against the bodies in front of her, progressing only an inch or so at a time. My God, they couldn't do this! "Stop this!" she shouted. "Stop!" but her words were lost in the mingled shouts and curses.

Jackson and another man came through the door with Booker struggling between them. He got one arm loose and gave Jackson a bone-crunching fist in the jaw. Stunned, Irving staggered and drew his pistol. Another man took his place holding Booker's arm, and Jackson held the gun to Booker's temple.

In his other hand, Jackson held up a gold pocket watch on a long chain. The lantern light reflected off the precious metal. "This yours?"

Booker glanced from the watch to the crowd. "It's mine, but I didn't kill that man."

"He did. That proves it!" Bard shouted.

Jackson tied Booker's hands behind his back. The crush of bodies parted to absorb Booker, and the pack moved into the street. Thea lost sight of her husband. Her heart hammered in horror-stricken fear.

At the edge of town, lights came on in the last few houses. Lorraine Edwards appeared on her stoop in a housecoat and observed the crowd. Catching sight of Thea, she fought her way through the throng to her side.

Two enormous oak trees grew at the edge of town. Someone produced a rope and threw the end up over a sturdy branch. Thea fought her way toward the front with Zoe on her hip and Lorraine tugging at her elbow. A bearded man, reeking of whiskey, grabbed her arm and tried to push her back.

In that cumulative moment of complete chaos and terror, her eyes met Booker's across the bobbing sea of heads separating them.

"Get your hands off her!" her husband shouted, rage contorting the hard lines of his face. With a burst of formidable energy, Booker threw himself against one of the men holding him, knocking him down and throwing Jackson off balance. Shouts went up from the crowd. Jackson cursed and reached for Booker. Booker twisted and sent another body toppling into the crowd. From the crush of bodies, a rifle butt rose, and the attacker struck Booker on the side of the head. He staggered.

Smothering panic rose in Thea's throat, restricting her breathing. For an instant her vision blurred, then cleared.

Numb, Thea saw Booker lifted onto a horse. The animal pranced restlessly, nostrils flaring. Booker sat stiffly, the noose tight around his neck, blood trickling to his ear from a cut on his scalp. With a burst of strength, Thea shoved her way forward, Zoe clinging to her neck. She lost Lorraine in the crowd.

Nothing had ever been as imperative as getting to that horse. Thea broke through the last human barrier and grabbed the bridle. Ronan Bard growled a curse and smacked Thea away. She held fast to the leather bridle, Zoe clutched on one hip. If this horse ran, she went with it.

A shot came from the back of the crowd, and the animal pranced squeamishly. Thea held on with every ounce of strength she possessed.

Someone bobbed beneath the horse's neck and a slender arm grabbed the reins. She glanced down at Lucas, his youthful face indicating both fear and determination.

"Let him down." Heads turned and Jim Coulson made his way through the parting crowd. Thea wanted to feel relieved at her father's intervention. She needed to think he could make a difference, but knew the bloodthirstiness running through these drunken men wouldn't be reasoned with. "This isn't justice," Thea's father warned the group of men. "You've all had too much to drink, or you wouldn't be doin' this."

"Too late!" Bard shouted.

"This is our justice," Irving Jackson added. He raised his hand to slap the horse's rump. Bard tried to peel Zoe from Thea's grasp. Her heart stopped.

"No-o-o-o-o!" A shrill scream pierced a sharp pain in Thea's ear. Thea turned her head and stared at the child in her arm.

Chapter Eighteen

Even the crowd quieted.

"No-o-o!" Zoe screamed again.

Frantic tears rose in Thea's throat. She swallowed hard and held fast to the bridle. The frightened horse bobbed his massive head, nearly ripping her arm from its socket. Pain shot across her shoulders. Lucas, too, strained to keep the horse in place.

"No! Not him!" Zoe screamed. "The bad man had the watch! I saw the bad man take it!"

Jim Coulson strode to Thea and took Zoe from her trembling arm. Thea used the freed hand to clamp onto the leather strap across the animal's nose. "What bad man, darlin'? Tell Grandpa what bad man."

Zoe pointed a finger. "Him. He took the watch the day he hurt Lucas at the warm house."

Shocked to the core, Thea met her father's eyes. "The housewarming," she clarified.

All eyes turned to the man Zoe indicated.

Ronan took a step backward. Hate glittered in his dark eyes. "You gonna believe a kid for godsakes? A stupid kid, who never even talked b'fore?"

"I think she didn't have anything important to say until now. That right, Zoe?" Thea's father asked.

The little girl nodded.

"You're as stupid as she is, then," Bard yelled, and staggered. "I shoulda killed ya when I had the chance."

A murmur ran through the crowd at his admission. Jackson gaped at Bard. He helped Lucas and Thea steady the horse, keeping Bard under his scrutiny. The horror creeping across his expression was clearly visible. "You shot Jim—and killed Clancy."

Bard turned and ducked between two men. One of them reached out and grabbed his shirt, and the other restrained him. Bard kicked and fought against the hold.

"I guess we have a different man for the arraignment tomorrow," Marshal Hardy said. "Take that son of a bitch to the jail," he said with a jerk of his thumb. "And let Hayes down."

Relief swelled in Thea's chest, but she couldn't move. Irving had to peel her lifeless hands from the bridle. He avoided Thea's eyes and stood her away from the horse. Edgar Birch appeared with a knife and cut the binding holding Booker's hands. Booker reached for the rope at his neck and tugged it off over his head. He raised one long leg over the horse's back and slid to the ground.

Immediately, Thea moved into his embrace, wrapped her arms around his solid torso and clung to him. He cupped the back of her head and pressed his lips against her temple. Oh, God, he was safe. He was alive. He was in her arms. She pulled back and looked at him. Blood glistened in the hair above his ear. She'd come so close to losing him.

If he'd died, she would never have had the chance to tell him she believed in him. Never again would she let a minute pass that he wasn't assured of her love and trust.

Lucas moved to her side. Both she and Booker loosened an arm to include the boy in their embrace.

"I want Booker now." The childish voice interrupted Thea's desperate reunion, a voice she was unaccustomed to hearing, a voice that brought such sad-sweet joy to her heart, she wanted to weep. She stepped back and let Booker take Zoe from her father. Lucas took Thea's hand.

Her platinum hair streaming in tangled disarray, Zoe clung to Booker's neck. "The bad man won't hurt us now," Zoe said.

"No, darlin'," Booker replied, his voice choked with emotion. "He won't hurt any of us anymore."

"I love you."

The child's words brought glistening tears to Booker's eyes. He met Thea's gaze, and her vision blurred through her own haze of tears. "I love you, too, Zoe," he said softly.

Behind them, the crowd had dispersed and moved toward town. A few persons waited for Jim Coulson and the Hayeses, among them Red Horse, Lorraine Edwards, Ezra Hill and Marshal Hardy.

The marshal wore an embarrassed expression. The blood on his mouth and chin had dried to dark, long-fingered stains. "Not much I can say to make it up to ya, Hayes."

Booker graciously offered his hand. "You tried your best to protect me and get me a fair hearing."

The marshal shook his hand.

"You did your job, even if you don't have the best manners for accommodating overnight guests."

"Come get your things from my office." They watched him walk away in his one-piece drawers, occasionally limping over a pebble.

Lucas walked close beside Booker. Booker looked each of them over, and something akin to pride softened his features. He didn't say a word, and Thea knew he couldn't. Right now there was nothing to say. He was obviously as tired and emotionally drained as she.

She thanked Lorraine with a hug, and Red Horse walked the woman to her door.

Walking back to them, Red Horse stopped in front of Booker. "I've made a decision."

Booker studied his friend.

"I'm going to move on to Colorado."

"No!" Thea stepped beside the Indian. "This is all settled now. You don't have to leave."

Red Horse contemplated her words. "You're a kind woman. Booker is an honorable friend. But I should go on. Start a life of my own."

Thea watched the two men shake hands and clasp each other's shoulders in a masculine embrace.

"I understand," Booker said, honesty lacing his tone. "I wish you happiness."

Thea embraced Red Horse. "You're welcome in our home anytime."

"I know that," Red Horse replied.

She took her father's hand and turned to Lucas and her husband, still holding Zoe. "Let's go home."

Thea heated water and filled a tub in the kitchen for Booker to bathe. No bath had ever felt as good. Booker scrubbed the filth from his hair and body, trying at the same time to wash away the hurt and disappointment that had seeped into his pores the past two days, and lodged in the marrow of his bones during the endless black nights.

He stepped from the tub and briskly dried his body with the toweling she'd left on a chair. Wrapping the length around his waist, he climbed the stairs with effort. Lord, he was tired.

In their bedroom, the lamp burned a welcome from its spot atop the washstand. He observed the familiar room as a weary traveler coming home after a long journey.

"Booker."

He turned to her.

"Your head?"

"It's a fair-size knot. It's sore, but I'll be all right." The lamplight cast a sensual glow across her features. Ronan Bard was in a cell. They'd seen Jim Coulson home. Red Horse had resumed his occupancy in the barn, and the exhausted children were sound asleep.

"Booker, I—"

"Let's not talk about it now." He hoped his voice hadn't sounded as pleading as he knew it must. "Not tonight."

"There are things I need to say," she whispered.

He stepped in front of her and appreciated her delicate features, the soft wisp of red-gold hair that fell from its mooring at her neck, and the fragrant woman scent that drove a shaft of desire to his groin. "Do you love me?" he asked, because he needed to hear it so badly.

"Yes."

Tiredness forgotten, he rubbed the silken skein of hair between thumb and forefinger. "Do you plan to be my wife forever?"

"Yes."

"Then that's all I want to hear now. We'll have time to talk about all those other things." He ran his finger across her cheekbone, outlined the arch of her brow and brought the fingertip to her lips. He traced the delicate bow of her upper lip, then curled his fingers in and dragged the pad of his thumb across her full bottom lip, watching the pliable softness flatten and resume its shape.

He waited, torturing himself with the promise of covering her lips with his. Her expressive eyes grew soft and sultry, and her gaze fastened on his mouth.

"I love you," she said, her breath feathering against his thumb.

"Take your hair down."

She obeyed, reaching behind her head and deftly plucking pins. He opened his palm and she dropped the hairpins in. He placed them on the washstand and turned back. "Now your dress."

She turned for his assistance with the buttons, and let the fabric fall, puddling at her ankles.

"Sit down."

She sat on the bed's edge, and he knelt in front of her and unbuttoned her soft leather high-top shoes. With long fingers, she brushed away beads of water that had dropped from his wet hair to his shoulders. Booker felt her touch all the way to his soul. How he needed this woman. How he loved her!

Impatiently, she rolled her stockings down the unending length of her marvelous legs and kicked them off. Booker kissed her freckled knees and ran his calloused fingers up her calves. He looked up and saw untamable desire transform her usually gentle expression into one of consuming hunger.

She didn't need any prompting to unlace her chemise. She crossed her arms, elbows pointing at him, reached for the hem and raised the garment up over her head, wincing.

"What is it?" he asked, seeing her pained expression.

Placing one hand on her right shoulder, she rolled her arm in the socket and bit her lip. "My shoulder," she explained. "It got jerked a good one holding that horse."

"Here, let me." He moved, letting the loosened towel drop from his waist to the floor. He knelt behind her on the bed and brushed her hair aside. "Here?"

A responding groan of pleasure served as a reply. He massaged her arm and shoulder, kneading her supple flesh and working the tightness from the muscles. He skimmed his hands down her sides, spanned her ribs and moved around to the front, coming up to cup her breasts in his palms. A thigh on either side of her hips, he pressed his body along her back, enjoying the contrast of her silky smooth skin against his hair-dusted body.

Her head fell back against his shoulder and she turned her face into his neck. Her breath sent shivers across his shoulders and down his spine. Her nipples hardened beneath his gaze and his touch. She arched back against him, and he watched the pink tips point upward and outward in a manner that flashed yearning through his veins in a wild surge.

Booker rose on his knees, urged her to the center of the bed and slid her drawers down her legs. She kicked them off and met him eagerly, reaching for his shoulders, pulling him close, whispering a harsh, urgent demand against his mouth.

Delicious heat spread through his body like the afterglow of good bourbon. At last, he covered her impatient lips with his, molded his body against hers and fed her craving with a deep, soul-reaching kiss he filled with enough love and longing to prove his sincerity, his desire for her. Only her.

She curled her fingers into the hair on his chest and tightened them painfully. Immediately, restlessly, moving on, she ran her palms eagerly down his rib cage. Booker rolled to his back. Thea gripped his hips, pulled her face from his and placed openmouthed kisses along his collarbone, the swell of his bicep, the sensitive spot he hadn't known was at the concave of his hip.

Desire blasted through his blood, pumping rock-hard into that part of him her hair draped across in a silken sensation so erotic he feared he'd embarrass himself.

He urged her back, ran his hands over her skin, returning the sweet, extravagant pleasure, giving himself much-needed time. Her breath sucked in through slackly parted lips. An all-over shudder encompassed her. Booker took the cockled tip of one nipple into his mouth and she made a tiny noise of pleasure. With his fingertips, he breached her pleated flesh and quickened her with steady, slippery strokes. A sand-washed sigh of pleasure escaped her lips.

Booker caught it with a breath-stealing kiss and pulled her beneath him.

"I love you," she whispered through a silken sigh. She reached for him, guided him.

He buried himself deep and pressed his face against her hair. "You know you're the only one," he said, the need to hear her say it overpowering everything else.

"I know," she whispered and tilted her hips in a way that she knew would send him over the edge.

"Say it," he insisted, holding himself still.

Thea caught her breath on a small sob. "I know there's no one else," she said. "I'm sorry, Booker...." He moved within her. "Sorry I said it...." He let himself enjoy the staggering sensations. "Sorry I thought it," she somehow managed to say.

He bracketed her face in his hands and stared down at her. "How could you think it?"

"It wasn't you." She gasped. "Never you. It was me. I didn't believe in me."

"You will now," he stated. Her internal muscles rippled, impelled, urged.

She smiled because she knew the effect she had on him. "I will now," she replied.

Senses sharpened to singular intensity, Booker raised himself to watch the play of physical and emotional joy cross her features. He'd promised himself when he'd married her that he wouldn't use her for his own pleasure, but he knew now that her pleasure was his. One in the same. With deliberate and intense strokes he brought her to swift fulfillment, finding his own gratification in her keen sounds of delight and her wholehearted participation, finally submitting and allowing his own satisfaction to seize him.

She wrapped her arms and legs around him tightly and ran her palms across his cool, perspiring back. Booker loosened her hold, held her head and soundly kissed her eyes, her nose, her chin and jaw.

"Booker." His name fell from her lips on a ragged whisper. She touched the bump on his scalp, tenderly.

He kissed her mouth and rolled to his side, pulling her with him. He closed his eyes and let bone-weary tiredness wash over him. God, it was good to be home. Home. With his family...his wife...his love...

Something rough scraped her cheek. The sensation came again. Thea opened her eyes and stared at the gray cat lying on her chest.

Zoe giggled.

Thea shooed the cat away and sat up. Sun beamed through the open window, indicating most of the morning was gone. Zoe sat cross-legged on the other side of the bed.

"Where's Booker?" Thea asked, still half-groggy and not expecting an answer.

"He got a message. He said get you up 'cause he's bringin' a surprise."

Thea stared at the child, still not believing her ears. "Zoe, I'm so happy you can talk!"

Zoe smiled, and a contagious giggle escaped her pink lips. "Yup."

Thea laughed with her and hugged the child to her breast. "Oh, Zoe. You make me so happy. Do you know that? And you made your Uncle Booker awfully happy last night, too."

"Yes. And he makes me happy, too. And you make me happy, too. And Lucas makes me happy, too."

Thea studied her, fascinated with the childish voice. She wondered if she'd ever get tired of hearing Zoe speak.

"Get up, get up, get up," Zoe directed with a series of playful bounces on the mattress.

"Okay." Thea tugged the sheet from its final mooring and wrapped it around herself. "Is there hot water on the stove?"

Zoe leapt from the bed and opened the door. She pointed to a bucket in the hallway. "Nope. Lucas brung it up here."

Thea rolled her eyes at Zoe's grammar and carried the pail to the basin on the washstand. "You scoot and let me get ready. I'll be down in a minute."

"Is that a regular minute, or a just-a-minute?" Zoe asked, tilting her head coquettishly.

"That's a Thea-minute, and not a second sooner. Scat." She closed the door with a smile and went about her toilette. Her sore shoulder didn't want to cooperate when she fastened the buttons down the back of her dress. Thea remembered Booker's considerate massage and his passionate lovemaking. Love warmed her insides like a crackling fire on a crisp winter day.

An hour later, she was kneading a double batch of bread dough when Lucas and Zoe clambered across the back porch and flung open the screen door.

"He's back!" Lucas shouted.

"Come on, come on, come on!" Zoe said, in a singsong voice, jumping up and down.

Thea wiped her hands on her apron and removed it, laying it on the kitchen table. She followed the children down the stairs, and they shot ahead of her.

The springboard pulled up to the dooryard. Immediately, Thea recognized the woman sitting next to Booker on the high seat. She waved and smiled. "Mrs. Vaughn!"

Booker assisted the petite woman to the ground, and Thea couldn't help but remember the dread with which she'd watched him perform that same courtesy the day he'd come to the Coulson farm to take Zoe away.

Mrs. Vaughn adjusted her prim little feathered hat on her head, gathered her skirts and approached Thea.

"How nice to see you," Thea said, and took her gloved hand.

"Your husband has offered me the use of your spare room for a few nights while I check on the children I placed here. He assured me you wouldn't mind."

"Of course I don't mind. It will be lovely having you."

"Good," Mrs. Vaughn said with a smile. "We have some business to take care of while I'm here, too."

Thea studied her face attentively. Mrs. Vaughn turned her gaze on Lucas. "We have final adoption papers to review."

Thea's heart soared. Lucas gave her a bashful smile.

"And of course, another matter to work out."

Thea turned back to Mrs. Vaughn. Whatever could that be? "There's no problem, is there? The court approved us as Lucas's parents?"

"Yes, yes. No problem."

"Thea." Booker's voice broke into her concentration. "There's someone I'd like you to meet."

Thea turned and realized Booker had been helping someone else from the back of the wagon. Her gaze slid across her husband's enthusiastic expression, and encountered the girl at his side.

She couldn't have been any older than thirteen, although her lack of weight may have made her appear younger. Straight, lackluster brown hair had been sheared across her wide forehead and beneath her ears in a clumsy, almost boyish fashion. Straight brows winged above enor-

Land of Dreams 293

mous wide brown eyes, eyes that gave her face a haunting, older-than-time wisdom.

Her rumpled calico dress hung on a lanky frame, disguising budding breasts. Beneath a downhill hem, slender legs barely held up a pair of dark stockings. Scuffed brown shoes completed the pitiful ensemble.

She gave Thea the same all-over scrutiny. Her gaze fell to Zoe and then landed on Lucas. Recognition flitted across her lifeless expression.

Thea's chest ached, and she wasn't sure why. Something about the girl made her so sad...filled her with sympathetic loneliness.

"Thea, I'd like you to meet Claudia. Claudia, this is my wife, Mrs. Hayes." Booker watched them both with an expression of anticipation.

The girl looked like she wanted to move closer to Booker, but on second thought she remained rooted where she stood. She seemed to find her voice. "How do you do, Mrs. Hayes."

"Thea," she said, stepping closer. "Call me Thea. I'm happy to meet you."

Booker must have decided an explanation was due. "Lucas, could you take our guests in and get them something to drink?"

Lucas led Mrs. Vaughn toward the house.

"Go on, Claudia," Booker said gently. "We'll be right in."

Thea watched the girl hesitate, then follow the agent. Zoe skipped along behind them, humming.

Booker took Thea's hand and looked into her eyes. "I met Claudia last spring while I was in New York looking for Zoe. When I asked about her, Mrs. Vaughn found out she'd been returned from a foster home just a few weeks ago. I didn't tell you because I didn't want you to be disappointed if it didn't work out, Thea."

"This is why you were in Lincoln. You went to meet Mrs. Vaughn."

He nodded.

"Booker, your life depended on her testifying that she was with you! Why didn't you wire her?"

"I tried. She said she's been visiting homes where she placed children. She never got my message."

"Did you tell the marshal about her?"

He nodded. "Maybe that helped him stick up for me. He was almost convinced to wait for her."

Thea lowered her lashes. "But you didn't tell me."

"You immediately thought the worst of me."

"I didn't," she denied. But she had. He'd been making arrangements to bring a child home, and she'd jumped to the conclusion that he'd spent time with another woman. She should have been ashamed rather than astonished. She should have looked at him like he was out of his mind. But she wasn't. She didn't. She took stock of the sincere love and caring flowing from his entire being.

"I want us to adopt her, Thea." His obsidian gaze pleaded for her understanding. "I know it'll be hard taking in a girl her age, and she has a lot of problems that we'll have to deal with, but if you could see where she came from ... how she lived. Thea," he whispered. "No matter what the weather, they're herded like cattle into a little courtyard where they stand packed together inside an iron fence.

"None of them receive or even expect love or affection or tender care. Their parents either died or didn't want them, and the orphanage workers consider them part of the job—here today, gone tomorrow. They're just a bunch of hard, untrusting, fearful kids fighting for survival and—"

"Stop." Thea placed her fingers over his mouth. "I don't want to hear any more." She dropped her hand to his chest and measured the steady beat of his heart beneath her palm. A heart as big as the Nebraska sky. "I want her."

The supplicating expression vanished, replaced by a smile of pure elation. He ran to the springboard and pulled a paper-wrapped bundle from beneath the seat. He handed it to her. "Material for you to make her some clothes. Enough for you and Zoe, too, of course."

Of course. "Don't tell me. Black sateen and German linen, right?"

He tilted his head. "Right."

Thea laughed aloud.

Booker swept her up in a ferocious bear hug and twirled her around in a circle until her head spun.

"Ah, Thea!" He held her head and planted a sound kiss on her mouth. "We're going to fill this house with children."

A smug smile tugged at the corners of her mouth. "Yes, we are, my dream lover. Yes, we are."

Epilogue

Thea spread a colorful cloth on the makeshift outdoor table and glanced up at the towering branches of the oak tree overhead. The screen door slammed and she turned to Zoe carrying another bowl across the backyard. Her beautiful Zoe.

A lump formed in Thea's throat as it always did when she saw the beautiful woman her Zoe had blossomed into. Her platinum hair still reflected the sunlight like spun silver, though she wore it in an elegant, upswept love knot. Her figure was curved in all the right places. All those years ago Booker had taken her to a special doctor in St. Louis. With exercises and corrective shoes, her limp had all but disappeared. A person who didn't know would never guess she'd once had a problem walking.

"Remember when we planted this tree, Zoe?"

"Yes, Mama."

Thea touched the rough bark and remembered the faraway day like it was yesterday.

"I remember Daddy sticking this tree in the same spot where we'd buried the acorn, too."

Thea's gaze flew to Zoe's wide blue eyes. "Zoe! You knew?"

Zoe laughed, a sound that always brought a responding smile to Thea's lips. "I knew."

Around the corner of the house, Ben and Alex came flying.

"Boys! You're supposed to be cleaned up when your daddy comes home from the train station with Lucas," Thea scolded.

"Ah, Ma, we'll just get dirty again." Ben, at fourteen, was an uncontrollable ball of mischief. With hair and eyes as black as his father's, his good-natured, relentless teasing was difficult to find fault with.

Alex, two years Ben's junior, but already as tall, had been dubbed "Little Jim" because of his striking resemblance to his grandfather. "If we clean up can we eat?" Alex asked.

Their cousin, David, shot around the house and slammed into Ben's back. The three of them tumbled to the ground and convulsed with laughter.

"David, your mother will skin me alive if you ruin another pair of pants at my house," Thea called to her nephew. David, the spitting image of Denzel with his fair hair and green eyes, jumped up and brushed off his dusty knees.

A springboard approached the house.

"Go in and clean up," Thea said, with a wave at the boys. "I think this is Claudia, now."

Claudia and her husband, Selby Hill, pulled up near the barn. Selby unhitched the team, and Claudia herded her two children toward the house.

Maggie threw herself against Thea's skirts. Thea knelt and hugged the five-year-old.

"Got new kittens, Nana?"

"There's a litter under the porch, Maggie."

The child squealed and darted away.

Nine-year-old Jesse approached the table. "When do we eat?"

"When Grandpa gets here with Lucas," Claudia told him and hugged Thea.

Zoe touched Thea's arm. "I hear them! I hear the buggy!"

Thea ran out from beneath the oak tree's shade, smoothing the skirt of her bright green dress, and waited expectantly, the sun warming her hair and back. Booker's team drew the black buggy into the dooryard.

Booker, his black hat shading his eyes, climbed down, and Thea's heart tripped at the sight of him as it always did. Behind him, Lucas stepped down from the back seat and turned to assist a young woman.

Thea let her gaze roam over Lucas. Tall and solidly built, wide-shouldered and lean-hipped, he'd grown to manhood under her loving gaze. He turned and wrapped her in a warm hug. Her heart, filled to bursting, couldn't believe it had been an entire year since she'd last seen him. He kissed her cheek and pulled away.

"I have someone I want you to meet."

Thea focused on the young woman. "Claire, this is my mother," he said, pride lacing his man's voice.

"Pleased to meet you, Mrs. Hayes." Thea took in the young woman's wide blue eyes and the blond ringlets escaping her bonnet, and liked her immediately.

"Thea," she corrected her. "Where are you from?"

"Indiana, originally. My family moved east. I went to school, and now I've been teaching at the same academy where Lucas instructs his art classes."

"I was born in Indiana, too," Thea told her.

"Claire speaks four languages, Mama," Lucas bragged.

"Goodness!" Thea turned a warm smile on the young woman.

Lucas's eyes lit up and his attention was drawn away. "Zoe! Claudia!"

Zoe slipped into his embrace for a long, tearful hug. She pulled back and let Claudia step into his embrace. The two stepped apart and took Zoe's hands. The three of them formed a circle and stood that way for a long moment in the warm sun. They reminded one another of another time, another life. And remembering gave them a deeper appreciation for today.

The screen door banged and the air was filled with the commotion of youth as Ben, Alex and David tromped down the wooden stairs and ran toward the gathering.

"Now you get to meet my brothers," Lucas said around a half grin. He pulled away from his adopted sisters and took Claire's hand. "Hold on to your bonnet."

Thea slid her arm around Booker's waist and peered up into obsidian eyes shaded by his hat brim. He removed the hat and plopped it on her head. "You're going to freckle," he warned in a low tone for her ears only.

"Oh, my." She placed a hand over her heart. "We can't have that."

Their family moved toward the food spread on the tables beneath the oak tree.

Booker hugged her, and she glanced up beneath his hat brim and admired the sprinkling of silver enhancing the ebony hair at his temples. Arm in arm they studied the family they had raised in this frontier land. A love so enormous her heart couldn't hold it all, pushed tears into Thea's eyes. They spilled over and Booker caught one on his finger.

"I wonder what their children will look like," she said aloud, studying Lucas with his head bent near Claire.

Booker chuckled, a rumble that started in his chest and carried across the Nebraska prairie. Thea drank in his laughter, the sunlight and the dappled shade of the oak tree. Her deepest longings, her most impossible fantasies, her every wish and yearning, had been fulfilled in an astonishing manner—a manner that even her wildest dreams couldn't have predicted.

"Got any apple pie, Mama?" Lucas called.

"All the apple pie you can hold, Lucas," she called back.

* * * * *

Harlequin® Historical

What do A.E. Maxwell, Miranda Jarrett, Merline Lovelace and Cassandra Austin have in common?

They are all part of Harlequin Historical's efforts to bring you longer books by some of your favorite authors. Pick up one of these upcoming titles today and see what a difference an historical from Harlequin can make!

REDWOOD EMPIRE—**A.E. Maxwell** Don't miss the reissue of this exciting saga from award-winning authors Ann and Evan Maxwell, coming in May 1995.

SPARHAWK'S LADY—**Miranda Jarrett** From this popular author comes another sweeping Sparhawk adventure full of passion and emotion in June 1995.

HIS LADY'S RANSOM—**Merline Lovelace** A gripping Medieval tale from the talented author of the Destiny's Women series that is sure to delight, coming in July 1995.

TRUSTING SARAH—**Cassandra Austin** And in August 1995, the long-awaited new Western by the author whose *Wait for the Sunrise* touched readers' hearts.

Watch for them this spring and summer wherever Harlequin Historicals are sold.

◈ HARLEQUIN®

PRESENTS
RELUCTANT BRIDEGROOMS

Two beautiful brides, two unforgettable romances...
two men running for their lives....

My Lady Love, by Paula Marshall, introduces
Charles, Viscount Halstead, who lost his memory
and found himself employed as a stableboy by the
untouchable Nell Tallboys, Countess Malplaquet.
But Nell didn't consider Charles untouchable—
not at all!

Darling Amazon, by Sylvia Andrew, is the story of
a spurious engagement between Julia Marchant
and Hugo, marquess of Rostherne—an engagement
that gets out of hand and just may lead Hugo to
the altar after all!

Enjoy two madcap Regency weddings this May,
wherever Harlequin books are sold.

Harlequin® Historical

WOMEN OF THE WEST

Exciting stories of the old West and the women whose dreams
and passions shaped a new land!

Join Harlequin Historicals every month as we bring you
these unforgettable tales.

Don't miss any of our **Women of the West!**

Harlequin invites you to the most romantic
wedding of the season...with

MARRY ME, COWBOY!

And you could WIN A DREAM VACATION of a lifetime!

from HARLEQUIN BOOKS and SANDALS—
THE CARIBBEAN'S #1 **ULTRA INCLUSIVE**℠ LUXURY RESORTS
FOR COUPLES ONLY.

Harlequin Books and Sandals Resorts are offering you a
vacation of a lifetime—a vacation of your choice at any of
the Sandals Caribbean resorts—FREE!

LOOK FOR FURTHER DETAILS in the Harlequin Books
title MARRY ME, COWBOY!, an exciting collection
of four brand-new short stories by popular romance
authors, including *New York Times* bestselling author
JANET DAILEY!

**AVAILABLE IN APRIL WHEREVER
HARLEQUIN BOOKS ARE SOLD.**

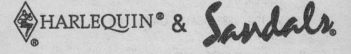

HARLEQUIN® & *Sandals*

MMC-SANDT